MW01129457

Buttermilk Bottom

Buttermilk Bottom

H. Victoria Hargro Atkerson

Copyright © 2011 by H. Victoria Hargro Atkerson.

Library of Congress Control Number:		2011903757
ISBN:	Hardcover	978-1-4568-8439-0
	Softcover	978-1-4568-8438-3
	Ebook	978-1-4568-8440-6

All rights reserved. No part of this book may be reproduced or transmitted in any form or by any means, electronic or mechanical, including photocopying, recording, or by any information storage and retrieval system, without permission in writing from the copyright owner.

This is a work of fiction. Names, characters, places and incidents either are the product of the author's imagination or are used fictitiously, and any resemblance to any actual persons, living or dead, events, or locales is entirely coincidental.

This book was printed in the United States of America.

To order additional copies of this book, contact:
Xlibris Corporation
1-888-795-4274
www.Xlibris.com
Orders@Xlibris.com
79298

Other Novels by H. Victoria Hargro Atkerson

Stones Along The Path
Stones Along The Path, Part II
Walking Among The Kudzu

About the Author

H. Victoria Hargro Atkerson is an imaginative writer who uses the history of her people and their struggle for equal rights as the foundation of her storytelling techniques. The process of writing is a personal journey, which she takes with every character that she develops. In Buttermilk Bottom, Victoria employs colorful and strong personalities in this story to bring historical events to life for the reader, allowing them to revisit the past and feel a part of the attitudes, customs, and policies that affected so many people during the 50's & 60's. Born in Atlanta, Georgia and raised in the environment she writes about, Victoria now enjoys a full and rewarding life with her husband and family in Philadelphia.

Dedicated to my best friend,
S. Lawrence Wright, who insisted that I write this story.

Acknowledgements

To God Almighty who makes all things possible.

To my family, I thank you for your support and encouragement and my sincere thanks to Joseph W. Atkerson, S. Lawrence Wright, Odessa Hargro Huff, Frank Gaines, Brandi Huff Reed, Ellen Young, Claudette Thornton Johnson, Paul Chick, and Shirley Phillips for their insights and reflections. I am grateful to Felicia Jones for researching the topic of blues singers, which proved insightful. Special thanks must go to Debra Mack of the Atlanta Public Library and Mike Brubaker of the Atlanta History Center. During the writing of this story, I spent valuable hours at the center, researching information, studying old photographs, reading books, magazines, and newspaper articles about Buttermilk Bottom.

To the following people who knew Buttermilk Bottom first-hand, I give my heartfelt thanks for their reflections about the spirit of a community that will live in our hearts and memories forever. I give my deepest appreciation. To my cousins, Dorothy and Pete Weaver, who for a short time once lived in Buttermilk Bottom, my brother, Bartlett H. Hargro, my nephew, Larry D. Anthony, and to my dear friend, Mr. N. A. Davis, who worked in Buttermilk Bottom as an Atlanta police officer, and to the memory of my brother in law, Frank Anthony, Sr., who knew how to tell great stories, I honor you all in these pages.

Introduction

April 21, 1956, WERD Radio Report: "The residents of Buttermilk Bottom are flooded this week with college students from the Atlanta University Center. Buttermilk Bottom is the focal point of a new citywide voter registration drive along with the entire Negro community. Many socially active groups have, in the past, ignored and neglected Buttermilk Bottom. Starting today, people, the residents are joining the struggle to get equal rights for all people, as promised under the constitution. No need to holler and scream about what they won't let you do anymore because you will have the power to set your own destinies by registering to vote and going to the polls on election day. Let's welcome these young people to our neighborhood. They trained under the National Urban League, and the NAACP. Come on, Fourth Ward, let's all make our presence known and register today."

Headline Story: "You are listening to WERD in Atlanta, Georgia, and here is the news for this morning, July 5, 1956. The top story of today is the mysterious disappearance of two Atlanta police officers. The last place they called in was from Fourth Ward near Buttermilk Bottom. Anyone having any knowledge of the whereabouts of Officer Nathan Buford and Officer James Elber should contact your local police district."

"Sept 24, 1956, this is the radio station, WAOK 1080 on your dial in lovely Atlanta, Georgia. We are calling on all the folks in Buttermilk Bottom to register to vote. There will be groups of college students knocking on your door this week to get you registered for the next upcoming election. They have all the forms and all the information you need to sign up. This is your chance to get involved in our government.

Voting is the most powerful weapon we have against racism and oppression. So, take a giant step and register to vote."

"Here's a bulletin just in. . . two Atlanta Police Officers are still missing along with their vehicle, last seen near Buttermilk Bottom. Anyone with any knowledge of the police officers' whereabouts should contact the Atlanta Police Department."

Headline: "Two Atlanta Police Officers Missing"—*The Atlanta Constitution*

Headline: "Police Officers, Missing, Last Seen Near Buttermilk Bottom"—*The Atlanta Daily World*

Chapter 1

Atlanta, Georgia 1966

Big obnoxious bulldozers stood menacingly at the top of the steep hill, waiting for the workers who would rev their powerful engines and descend upon the fragile remains of a once vibrant community. It was six o'clock in the morning, when Cameron Fielding stood, gazing upon his past, a past that was full of warm memories, in spite of all the dark shadows it held. His work crew would start arriving soon to plow down all the dilapidated houses and the essence of a neighborhood that existed for more than a hundred years. Its people were not famous. No one built a monument in honor of the bravery it took to survive for many years in substandard conditions. No one sang their praises, but many would remember their fortitude, and their struggle to survive in the climate of prejudice and hatred that gripped the South and all of its inhabitants for generations.

Hauntingly, threateningly, the silent machines stood ready to demolish all the physical evidence of a once impoverished yet lively and colorful community. The memory of the people who lived there will hang in the air for an eternity, long after the dark dust has settled, removing all evidence of the strong, determined people who once occupied a small yet a significant portion of our planet. Buttermilk Bottom did exist. Its people portrayed a spirit of determination and a strong will to survive in spite of fear, harassment, extreme poverty, and torment. They gave each other energy, humor, and courage, which pierced, then awakened their minds and souls, allowing them to endure under the constant pressures and attacks that stemmed from outside their borders and that caused The Bottom to exist in the first place. Simultaneously, those who lived in 'The

Bottom' enjoyed a natural geological isolation from the rest of the city, sunken several feet below the normal elevation of the city's landscape, a capricious and isolated world because of its chaotic reputation.

Seizing the time to be alone with his memories, Cameron walked down the dirt road to his old neighborhood; a place that once occupied an important part of his life for a span of ten years. Smelling poignant odors of poverty and despair, he quickly discovered upon arrival in Buttermilk Bottom that the indigent thriving community also gave off distinct scents of hope and optimism. . . Cautious optimism, but it was optimism just the same. As he walked down the always wet, black dirt road of Buttermilk Bottom, he calculated that it was about seven thousand two hundred and fifty days ago that he first laid eyes on the infamous neighborhood. The empty rustic wooden framed apartment buildings, the abandoned dirt roads, and the chilling cold silence were epitaphs of a time carved out of segregation, racism, and a system of Jim Crow laws that inhibited and paralyzed blacks in the South socially, educationally, and economically for many generations.

The large, empty, single home across from where he stood once served as a 'juke-joint' and the Mecca from which all the neighborhood's activities and gossip emerged. Even with the windows and doors nailed shut, Cameron swore he could hear the sounds of Billy Holiday, Muddy Waters, and sensuous, cool notes of the blues, easing out to him in sobering mellow sounds. He could hear the happy sounds of children playing wildly on the mud-covered roads, singing and rhyming out playfully as they sang tunes derived from Africa, slavery, and years of suffering. No matter what the circumstances were in the community, Buttermilk Bottom's resilient children always found a place and a time to be joyful and carefree. It was hard to visualize or remember Buttermilk Bottom as it was at the height of its life span without thinking about the sounds and sights of children running, playing, and singing in its often muddy, unpaved, and rough roads. With toys and playthings at a minimum, the children used ropes, sticks, and rocks as well as their bodies, hands, and feet as playthings and instruments to tap out rhymes for their many games and songs.

"There was an old lady from Brewster,
She had two hens and a rooster.
The rooster died the hens all cried
Ya can't lay eggs, like I use to."

Ole ma, you look so,
Ole pop, you look so,
Who been here since I been gone,
Two lil' boys with the red hat on,
Hang 'em boys on a hickory stick,
Papa's gonna punish 'em soon."

Nothing fascinated Cameron more than watching the children play, using their well coordinated bodies as they clapped their hands, stamped their feet, and danced to play songs of fun, hardships, and hope; songs and riddles that were handed down from generation to generation.

"Pain in my head, ranky tanky,
Pain in my neck, ranky tanky,
Pain in my shoulder, ranky-tanky,
Pain in my leg, ranky tanky,
Pain in my feet, ranky tanky,
Pain all ov'er me, ranky tanky.
Pain all ov'er me, ranky tanky."

Slivers of the past filtered through the air, and no written record existed to reflect the lifestyle and traditions of this abandoned neighborhood. No one knew how many people managed to live and survive during the life span of the once notorious Buttermilk Bottom and there were no accurate maps of its dirt roads and alleys to show its structure or layout. The entire community sat in a gigantic ditch, surrounded by acres of long-needle pine trees, covered with thick, uncontrollable, unrelenting kudzu vines.

It was ironic that Cameron and his work crew won the bid from the city to knock down the dilapidated houses that they once occupied. The death of Buttermilk Bottom was depressing and joyous. It gave him a rush of excitement, knowing that his people would never again have to live in deplorable, substandard housing. The sadness in his heart came from knowing that he was about to erase all physical evidence of his people's struggle for respect, equality, and their own humanity. There should have been a monument erected in their honor to remind the world of man's innate ability to endure hardship, prejudice, and abuse because the residents of Buttermilk Bottom were experts in survival and tolerance; tolerance in the face of intolerant people, and tolerance of conditions that were intolerable.

Without the urban renewal project, Cameron knew that Buttermilk Bottom would still exist because the people who lived there would cling to its dilapidated dwellings and shabby dirt roads, as if "The Bottom' was the air that they needed to survive. The predictability of behaviors, traditions, and the comfort of familiar faces gave residents a feeling of assurance and security in a place that outsiders avoided and even feared.

Cameron looked up at his old front porch where he saw his beautiful wife for the first time; he felt remorse because in a matter of minutes it would all be gone forever. She was a vision of grace and exquisiteness, and he wished with all his heart that he could climb the steps of the apartment building he once owned and look down on the old neighborhood just once more, but the steps were too weak and too rundown. No one would ever climb those steps again. He celebrated this day because his people would no longer be isolated and condemned to live in unfit, unhealthy, and unattractive housing on the fringe of society where they had to scrape and fight for every morsel of food, clothing, shelter, and self-respect they could glean from their pitiful surroundings and from a society that did not want them.

Big husky men in their coveralls with their wrecking balls, earthmovers, and tractors were on their way to push down all traces of the once notorious neighborhood to make way for modern construction. A new civic center would take its place on the land previously occupied by Atlanta's most invisible population. What no wrecking ball could ever destroy were the memories, reflecting more than a hundred years of occupation, a place where proud black families struggled and lived life as zestfully as they could under the legally enforced poverty that locked them out of normal society. It was a neighborhood with its own set of values, beliefs, and practices that its people often distorted and mutilated, originating out of hate, prejudice, and racism, but those same conditions served as the glue that held its people together. People referred to Buttermilk Bottom as 'the pit of human depravity,' 'the home for social rejects'. . . . They called it, 'The Bottom' because, in reality, it was.

In addition to being a unique and dangerous place, Buttermilk Bottom was one of the closest-knit communities, which ever existed on our planet. Everybody knew everybody and everybody knew everybody's business. If someone farted on one side of the street, someone on the other side of the street held their nose. One could do little to keep people out of their private affairs; in fact, the concept of privacy was an alien concept to its inhabitants.

Every neighborhood produces a busybody, a comedian, a gossip, a blabbermouth, a storyteller, and a historian. Buttermilk Bottom was no exception because all those personality traits subsisted in one neat human package. From its loins was born a legend in his own right, a sharp witted, clever, handsome, and elegantly dressed young man who stood tall on his custom-made wooden crutches, whom everyone called Cripple Jake. He was the heartbeat of Buttermilk Bottom. His paralysis was the result of an early infection of infantile paralysis, commonly called polio, which resulted in years of hospitalization and personal care at home. During his childhood, people knew very little about polio and how it affected the human body, but his mother read everything she could find about the disease and followed all the instructions to the letter. Polio was a disease of monumental proportions during the forties and fifties, striking fear into all parents with young children. Cripple Jake's legs, malformed, twisted, and lifeless, hung sandwiched between two wooden crutches with hard rubber tips at the base to keep him from slipping or sliding off balance.

Equipped with acute intelligence and a strong sense of self-worth, he took great pride in his appearance, always dressing in the most stylish clothes, keeping his wavy hair and mustache cut and trimmed to perfection. Ignoring his obvious disabilities, one would readily acknowledge that he was a very handsome man of twenty-seven years who used his crutches as a platform to pose and dramatize his astounding verbal theatrics. The amazing thing about Cripple Jake was that the people of Buttermilk Bottom did not see him as disabled because he handled himself on his crutches better than most people did with two healthy legs and feet.

The residents of The Bottom nicknamed him Cripple Jake not as an indication of his disabled status; it served as a description of the person. 'Black Jeff,' who was so-named because of his jet-black skin, and they named 'Raggedy Raymond' to mirror the normal state of his clothes. 'Yellow Emma' had what they called 'high yellow' skin, and to distinguish her from 'Black Emma' who lived in the apartment several doors away. 'Flat Foot George' had bare, duck-like feet. 'Big Ester's' name was given because she possessed the biggest breasts and the largest ass in 'The Bottom.' In Buttermilk Bottom, a person's nickname coincided accurately with his or her physical appearance.

Everybody, in and around 'The Bottom,' loved Cripple Jake because he could guarantee them several hours of total hysteria and sidesplitting laughter that were always at someone else's expense. He entertained his followers by telling hilarious tales of real life experiences that occur in the sunken community where he spent his entire life. No one was exempt from his whimsical verbal attacks, criticisms, or dramatizations. He mastered the art of observing human behavior as he professed and defended one ridiculous hypothesis after another, such as, *All big niggers are stupid.*

With that introductory statement to his attentive listeners, he said, "Watch Jonesy over there. You just watch him. I'll bet you a dollar that he'll do something stupid before the night is over."

It was a fact that if you watched anyone long enough, you are bound to see something you could interpret as dumb. Cripple Jake had his audience convinced before he proved his point while he relished in all the attention he was getting. Then miraculously as he predicted, the object of his character assassination would do something that would confirm his ridiculous assertion. Once Cripple Jake identified the offense to his entourage, they would respond with uproarious laughter that fed his ego and filled him with delight. He was fascinated and amused by human behavior and Cripple Jake made it his business to know everything that was going on in Buttermilk Bottom. He remembered every detail involved in the lives of his neighbors using his remarkable memory to recall and recant incidents and local legends accurately upon demand. Everyone marveled at his ability to remember events dating back to his early childhood. His astounding memory allowed him to recall everyone who ever lived in the neighborhood along with all the personal history detailed in chronological order. If anyone had a dispute about something or someone, people would call on him as the final authority.

Cripple Jake lived with his mother but there were no maternal apron strings attached to him. His mother encouraged and insisted that he function independently from a very early age. She gave him no opportunities to feel sorry for himself or his physical disability.

She said, "One disability is all you're allowed and being born a Negro in America is enough."

His independence was her success, and she was proud of the man he became. Cripple Jake was outspoken, funny, and they enjoyed their mutually respectful relationship. He was an adult living in her house, and she was careful to respect his privacy long before he knew he needed it. The fact that he had polio never stopped Cripple Jake from believing that he was a man about town because chasing women was his passion. He proudly alleged that he was the best lover around if given the chance to untwist his legs. Given the opportunity, he swore that he could be any woman's dream. Over the years, he developed several long-term relationships, and the word came back from the whores he frequented that he was a kind and an accomplished lover.

All kinds of odd relationships formed in 'The Bottom'. The most bizarre was the one between Cripple Jake and Cameron Fielding, the number writer, better known in Buttermilk Bottom as the 'Bug Man', after the illegal lottery on the streets coded by those who played the game as 'The Bug'. The two men were best friends, co-conspirators, and respected leaders in the community, especially to those who benefited from their escapades and antics. The odd appearance of the two very different men raised eyebrows as they walked side by side down the black muddy roads of 'The Bottom'. Cripple Jake's height reached five feet ten inches on his crutches while Cameron was a cool six feet two. Both men had noticeably muscular frames, but they differed considerably when one looked at their legs. Another noticeable characteristic about their appearance was their skin color. Jake had a very light complexion, 'damn near white' was the description the officers at the local precinct gave him while 'the bug man' had rich, dark-brown skin.

The dissimilar lifestyles of the two men added to the mystery. Jake was extremely talkative with a colorful personality and a very public life, while the quiet and reclusive number man treasured and craved his invisibility and his privacy, taking full advantage of the isolation that Buttermilk Bottom guaranteed its inhabitants. People, who did not live there, generally did not want to go to the impoverished neighborhood, out of fear of being robbed, caught-up in a shooting, or a knifing incident.

Both Cameron and Cripple Jake treasured the time they spent at the local juke joint owned by a beautiful and well-endowed woman whom everyone called 'Queenie'. Cripple Jake fell immediately in love with Queenie when he first spotted her generously built body, noting the excellent way she maintained her appearance. Because of her sense of style, her perfect hair, and her impeccable dress, she was his favorite person to admire. Jake would have done anything to have her, but she chose to give her love to Cameron. She made that fact known to everyone within hours of Cameron's arrival in Buttermilk Bottom. Queenie approached Cameron boldly every time she saw him; sometimes she was successful in luring him to her bed and other times she went hopelessly lacking. Everyone in the neighborhood could see that Queenie's feelings for 'The Bug Man' was one-sided by the casual, consistently insensitive way that Cameron responded to her constant flirtations.

Watching Queenie move seductively around the large parlor at the juke joint made Jake's heart swell with mounting desire, as she circulated around the elaborately decorated room, checking on her customers and simultaneously making certain that her staff was performing up to her high standards. To bring in extra money, she rented rooms to prostitutes who paid her monthly for room and board, plus taking a commission off every 'Joe',' they took up the stairs. It was an excellent arrangement, and Jake took full advantage of the convenient services that the prostitutes provided every chance he could.

"How is everything over here, gentlemen?" Queenie asked, leaning seductively over the shoulders of one of her customers at the poker table.

"Much better now that you're here," Jake responded longingly.

Then to Cameron, she whispered into his ear, "I'll be free by ten, if you want to join me."

"Maybe some other time," he said, engrossed in the poker games that he discovered was a handsome and profitable second career for him. That entire evening, he had a continuous stream of unbelievable hands and proudly raked in his winnings. Obviously disappointed, Queenie went to the bar, sulking where her oldest friend, ex-lover, and partner, Luther, poured her a stiff glass of scotch. Seeing her disappointment, Jake picked up his crutches and joined her. Filled with hope, he sat quietly next to her, admiring her until she turned to acknowledge his presence.

"Your friend is so moody. I can never tell when he's in a good mood," she said sadly.

"Why do you keep trying?"

"Because I happen to love the guy, Jake," she said, wanting attention from her infrequent lover.

"Maybe it's time for you to love somebody else."

"I love him."

"I know. What a waste," he said, scanning her generous attributes. "If you'd like to spend some time with me. . . I'm free all night."

"No thanks, he's worth waiting for," she said, sliding off the barstool, noticing a group of people coming in the door. "I'll talk to you later."

Pensively, Jake admired Queenie as she swayed her round shapely hips while Luther, observed Jake's interaction to Queenie.

"Man, you look like you need a stiff drink."

"A double," Jake said, knowing he needed it to calm his longings for the beautiful woman.

"It hurts dat much?" Luther asked.

"Does it show?"

"Sho' do. I don't know who I feel saddest for. . . You, Queenie, or me," Luther said, drinking a small glass of whiskey to soothe his own feelings before serving Jake's double. "We both love, her and she loves 'pretty boy' ov'r there."

"I'm prettier than he is."

"She don't know that."

"She's a lot of woman," Jake said.

"I know," Luther said, remembering when he had her all to himself.

"Hey! Gimme a damn drink over here," yelled the juke joint's most frequent customer, Lucille. Slurring her words, she said, "You love-sick mutherfuckers' always sittin' 'round here watchin' dat fat-ass Queenie."

"Here, drink yo liquor and shut d' fuck up, Lucille," Luther said, annoyed with his best customer.

"What's wrong wit you? Shamed 'cause I caught you two sickies' gittin' a hard-on fo' Queenie."

"Lucille, shut up and mind yo' damn bizness," Luther said.

"You ain't foolin' nobody. Everybody in d' Bottom know you two niggers git hard every time she swings dem fat-ass hips o' hers."

"You's drunk. Why don't you shut d' hell up or go d' fuck home?"

"'Cause I don't wants to. . . Damnit. I wanna know why ya'll always gittin' yo' tongues 'n dicks hard fo' her. . . When there's plenty women 'round here. . . Wantin' a man?"

"I sho' hope d' hell you ain't talkin' 'bout yo'self." Luther said, laughing.

"What's the matter (hiccup) wit me?" she asked getting off the barstool, turning around, and popping her fingers to her favorite tune that was playing on the jukebox, *Ain't Nobody's Business, If I Do.* Lucille loved Billie Holiday because she claimed that Billie's singing voice sounded like her own speaking voice, and her songs echoed her personal feelings about life. She got dizzy from turning around in circles as she danced to the music. Her dizziness was the result of the large amount of corn liquor that she consumed. "Look . . ." she yelled out while laughing too loudly and shaking her fanny at Luther, who picked up the evening edition of *The Atlanta Journal*, trying desperately to ignore her. "Babe, I still got it. Look at me, Luther. I still got it, but don't nobody want it," she said, laughing along with Jake and a few other listening customers.

"Lucille, you drunk," someone called out.

"Hell, I know that. I cain't even give it away," Lucille said, laughing at herself and leaning unsteadily on a barstool. "Fuck it. I'm old. . . Too fuckin' old. Gimme a quarter fo' d' jukebox, nigger," she said.

Both Jake and Luther gave her a quarter. Lucille stumbled crookedly over to the jukebox to play more music.

"Now, look at dis mess," Luther said to Jake, referring to an article in the evening paper. "White people don't know what to do wit demselves. Here's some fool dat spent time figurin' dat he kin stop a damn tornado by blowin' it up."

"What?"

"He wants to fly ov' it and drop a bomb in it t' blow it up."

"The only thing he's going to do is blow up his own stupid ass," Jake said. "Did you hear about, Yellow Emma? She got herself a job at the Atlanta Life Insurance Company on Auburn Avenue."

"She and her mama's real decent people and smart too. I don't know why they still live down here," Luther said.

"They live here because they never lived anywhere else. Maybe with this new job, they'll move away. I was sitting in Yates and Milton Drug Store having a cup of coffee when she walked in with some of her co-workers. Those girls sure looked good, all dressed up, piling in that drug store for lunch. That's the place to be at noon. I love to see those brown women, marching in there looking like new money."

"I needs t' go down there and do some lookin' myself."

"Auburn Avenue is the colored man's Wall Street. More money's being made by black people on that street than any colored street in America," Jake said proudly.

"You's right about dat and it shows, too."

"On Auburn Avenue, women look like they stepped out of a magazine. . . Pretty. . . And fine as wine. The Avenue is the place to be. On Sunday mornings, you can dress-up and go to church, in the afternoon you can sit in Yates and Milton and get yourself a big ice cream soda with your best girl, and at night you can put on your finest and hit the nightclubs," Jake said, smiling. "You can live a life-time on Auburn Avenue."

After failing to entice the beautiful voluptuous owner, Jake decided to choose one of the whores for what he called his 'treatment.' Dellah, who had worked at the juke joint since it opened, sat across the room from Jake and the card players, watching and waiting for someone to ask for her services. For reasons of her own, she preferred Jake because he was knowledgeable, fun, and he tipped well. When Jake gave her a signal, she sauntered over to the steps and waited for him with a big smile on her face.

Just before he went upstairs, he said, "Queenie, I'm giving you a second chance to say yes. You can put an end to my misery, once and for all."

"No thanks, Jake, you may give me a heart attack," she said, responding in her usual witty manner.

"Too bad, I could have set your world on fire." Jake said teasingly.

"You're too hot for me, Jake." she said, laughing.

"Hell, I'm too hot for most women," Jake said. Everyone laughed including Jake, but deep down, he was hurting inside because he knew that he could love her for an eternity if given the opportunity. To his public, he said, "People think a cripple man can't screw. . . But that's a big mistake. Not only do I have the biggest dick in the world. . . I know what to do with it. Don't I, babe?" he asked, pinching Dellah's rear end. She laughed and ran up the steps.

Although he said it in humor and needing a jovial response, Cripple Jake was dead serious. His heart crashed because he could not have the woman he loved and wanted most in the world, but Jake had learned how to live with disappointment years before. With a quick adjustment in his attitude, he became excited about having sex whenever the opportunity became available. With his crutches under his arms, he skillfully climbed the stairs behind the young beautiful twenty-two year-old woman whom he developed an on-going, special relationship with over the years.

Chapter 2

All his life, Cameron Fielding thirsted for fairness and justice, not only for himself but also for anyone who was downtrodden and underprivileged. Raised on the streets of Atlanta with no visible family, he went from one sympathetic family member to another until he finally landed at age eleven with his aunt, who learned of his existence and stepped in to care for him. The match was good for both of them because she was unmarried with no children, and he never had a permanent home. They were the answer to each other's prayers. With her encouragement, he excelled in all subjects in school. For her sake, he brought home excellent grades because they kept a smile on her face. She died the year he entered college, but she left enough insurance money to pay for his college tuition. He had to work at odd jobs to pay for food, clothing, and any extras he needed. Many things he learned to live without, but he never regretted his circumstances.

Having material things did not matter to Cameron, what did matter was football. His love of the sport kept him focused and willing to do whatever it took to stay in school. He found a family among his teammates and found a good friend in his coach, who supported and encouraged him. Grateful for all his coach's help and influence, Cameron wanted to do for others, what his kind and sensitive coach had done for him, guiding him through many days of uncertainty. Coach Ben Ross was the father he never had.

A month following his college graduation, he married his college sweetheart, Eva Weston, the socialite daughter of Southern Life Insurance Company's owner and president, Malcolm R. Weston. With him being the captain of the football team and with Eva being the homecoming queen, they drew attention from their classmates and their faculty. Against her father's wishes, Eva moved into Cameron's house that he once shared with his aunt, during their senior year in college and began a relentless campaign to persuade Cameron to marry her. Being determined to have Cameron as her husband, Eva arranged every aspect of the wedding and their future. Despite his lack of enthusiasm, she was constantly at his side, planning their wedding that turned out to be the most beautiful and lavish affair of the season. Cameron's college coach was his best man, and his teammates were his ushers. For almost three months, the wedding was the talk of Atlanta's black elite because of the Weston family's prominence.

As fate unfolded its ugly obtuse head, the happy couple soon found living as husband and wife was frustrating after only six months but managed to cope with one another for almost two years. Although Cameron did not love her, he went along with the marriage because he never expected to love anyone, and he knew she loved him. The descriptions that his friends gave him about being in love was an enigma to him, and he often wondered why he did not feel what other people felt. Being deeply passionate about another person was foreign to him. He knew that he loved having sex with women, but he could not generate any emotional attachment with anyone, and he began to depend on his detachment, which he interpreted as objectivity, and he depended on it because he felt in control of his life and his emotions.

With Eva, he felt comfortable because she was more fun than any woman he had been with plus the fact that they were good friends and great sexual partners. Eva was the ambitious type, very goal oriented, and she knew what kind of life she wanted for herself and for him. They had many conversations about their future, but she failed to reveal her true intentions until after they were married. Although, he explained many times that he intended to be a high school football coach, she never took him seriously. She was disappointed when she discovered that he accepted a job coaching. When she married Cameron, her plans were to persuade him to become an executive in her father's insurance company. She envisioned taking the spotlight next to her parents at gala events, political functions, and on the society pages of newspapers and magazines. When he refused repeatedly to accept her father's offer, her interest in their marriage began to dwindle. By the end of their second year together, they had a quiet, friendly divorce.

Before moving to Buttermilk Bottom, Cameron worked faithfully as a physical education teacher and football coach. He was living his dream, and his social life was one any man would envy. An unforeseen incident occurred that he could not control or avoid that interrupted and derailed his career forever. While taking a beautiful friend out for an evening of dancing, he saw a white couple on the sidewalk at the corner of Ripley and Currier Streets, fighting. The man, twice the size of the woman, was beating her with his fist. Outraged, Cameron stopped his car and pulled over to the side.

His date, Grace Talbert, who was an elementary schoolteacher at the time, pleaded with him not to interfere, pulling his arm to prevent him from getting involved.

"What are you doing?"

"Don't worry. I'll be back in a moment," Cameron said.

"Please, don't go," she said, hanging onto his arm. "They're white and you shouldn't interfere."

"I have to go. . . Or I won't sleep tonight," he said, kissing her softly on the lips.

"Please, stay out of it," Grace pleaded. "Look, there's another white man over there. . . Let him help her."

Cameron saw a white man standing nearby with a dog, watching the conflict, but he did nothing to help the woman. The man was practically beating the woman to death.

"He's not doing anything. Don't worry. This won't take long."

Kissing her on the forehead, he got out of his car, went to where the man had the woman pinned against a brick wall and pulled the white man off the badly beaten woman.

The irate man turned around, seeing Cameron's dark skin and yelled, "You fuckin' nigger!" He was about to punch Cameron in the face, but instead, Cameron grabbed the man's fist and pushed him away.

The man fell backwards against the brick wall hitting his head, killing him instantly. Consequently, Cameron spent over a year in jail, waiting for his trial. When the case finally went to court, his lawyer proved him innocent with the help of the woman he rescued, Grace, and the white man with the dog. They all testified that the dead man was beating the woman, and that Cameron intervened to save the woman's life. They also stated that the man's death was an accident. Many people from his school showed up to testify on his behalf, but the woman whom he rescued testified convincingly in court and proved Cameron's innocence.

During his incarceration, Cameron's relationship with Grace was the only steady and reliable force in his life. To his surprise, she was smiling and waiting for him at the gate on the day he got out of prison. Without consulting him, she purchased clothing and personal supplies for his return to society. There was ice-cold beer, wine, and a hot dinner waiting for him to sit down and enjoy. For the first few hours, he walked around her house and touched everything he missed seeing, like curtains, the record player, fancy drinking glasses, china, and colorful soft towels, which he picked up and smelled. As he stood in the window appreciating the trees and the normalcy of being in a community again, she walked up behind him, hugging him around the waist.

"Welcome home."

"I will never forget what you've done for me. As soon as I get back to work, I'm going to pay you back."

"Please, don't worry about any of that now. Everything will work out. You'll see."

Cameron took Grace into his arms, kissing her generously on the lips, remembering the most precious thing he had missed while behind bars, making him hold her tighter. The taste, feel, and smell of the female body overwhelmed him. It was a pleasure he chose not to think about while in prison. Instead, he spent his time reading. Cameron read so many books in the prison library that the other inmates called him 'The Professor'.

With Grace in his arms, his heart began to beat strongly as he lavished her with warm sensuous kisses. Unable to stop himself or contain his emotions, he pulled her to the floor, tearing her dress from her body.

When he realized that he may have hurt her, he stopped himself and held her close to him, saying, "I'm sorry. . . It's just that it's been a long time. I didn't mean to . . ."

"Darling, no harm done. It's just a dress."

"I hope I didn't hurt you."

"No, darling, you feel so good to me."

With those words, he eased her slip over her head, exposing her body and for several minutes, he appreciated seeing her in her bra and panties. Admiring all her feminine assets, he rubbed his hands all over her body, making his hardness more pronounced, filling him with an urgent desire.

"It's been a real, long time, Grace. Do you mind if I skip all the preliminaries, just this once?"

"No, darling, I don't mind. I want you."

Without any further conversation, he slipped out of his pants and nervously placed a condom over his hardened shaft then carefully removed her remaining garments. The condom, he picked up at the drug store on their way to Gracie's house, which bothered her much more than she wanted to admit. As he eased his manhood into the warmth of her body, he began to whimper softly in her ear. Slowly, he began to move inside her, feeling the rush of erotic spasms that took his mind and body to sweet gentle places where prisons did not exist. He could only think about and feel the warm moistness that her love provided him as it sent torrents of pleasure throughout his entire body in increasing waves of passion. Even when he dared to remember how good it felt to be with a woman, his memories and dreams were never as vivid or intense as the actual act of loving a woman as he did at that moment. After several minutes of his slow yet methodical stokes, he began to ejaculate away all of his pent-up emotions, hurts, and frustrations from the past year. A surprising primal moan of satisfaction emitted loud and long from his mouth in blissful ecstasy along with a warm flood of passion. Grace held him tightly, nurturing his body in a strong loving embrace, trying to ease the pain he must have felt deep inside his tortured mind.

He lay with her for several minutes, when she tried to move, he whispered, "Please don't." They slept on the floor for hours with his love still inside her and with his arms wrapped tightly around her warm body.

In the middle of the afternoon, they shared a hot bath together and a bottle of his favorite wine. To Grace's delight, Cameron insisted on bathing her, but when he started to massage and wash her breasts, he began to fill-up with longing. Rejoicing in his recent freedom and most especially in his ability to touch a woman, he found her warm succulent lips and kissed her with all the passion that overflowed from his physically and emotionally deprived body. After rinsing her off, he sat her on the edge of the tub, he began to feel her center with his fingers, she responded with sweet amorous sounds that made him want to possess her quickly and completely. Forcing himself to maintain control over his own body, he tasted her womanliness and enjoyed the sweetness of loving her, layer by beautiful soft layer. With all his heart, he wanted to instill a state of ultimate pleasure within Grace because she supported him during the most difficult time of his life. Her climax was his triumph as she held on to him. Feeling as if he would explode, he took her to bed where they spent the entire evening making love to each other.

After spending a week with Grace, Cameron went back to his aunt's house and prepared it for sale to pay for all the legal fees and unpaid bills that accumulated because of the year he spent in jail. It was time for him to get a job and find a place to live. Although, Grace encouraged him to stay with her, he knew he needed a place of his own. As grateful as he was to her, he did not love her. Wishing with all his heart that he loved her, he knew there was nothing there despite her faithfulness and her uninhibited display of affection. He felt nothing more for her than sexual attraction, and when it was over, he wanted only to get away from her as quickly as possible. With one bad marriage based on friendship, he did not intend to marry anyone again for the wrong reason, friendship.

Due to his incarceration, he soon discovered that he lost his job, and his teacher's certification was lost to him forever. When he applied for reinstatement, they bombarded him with the old southern waltz, commonly known as avoidance and postponements. He soon became so frustrated that he gave up. Although proven innocent, they purported that he was still a convict; therefore, he was unfit to teach children. After several months of frustration and anger, he went from one menial job to another until finally he stopped what he referred to as 'playing the white man's game.'

With the help of one of his childhood friends, Rufus Taylor, who was a major gangster in Atlanta's Fourth Ward, Cameron started a completely new life in the number writing business. Rufus was living-proof that a black man could survive and be successful without depending on the white establishment. He dressed sharply, drove a brand new car, and lived in a beautiful home.

"Look, man," Rufus said. "I have the perfect setup for you. I own an old building in Buttermilk Bottom that I'll sell you. You'll be able to afford it with all the cash you're going to have rolling in. In Buttermilk Bottom, it won't take long for you to earn all the money you think you'll need."

"Buttermilk Bottom? That place is the pits," Cameron said.

"True. It's the pit of human depravity, but. . . It's heaven on earth for the number writing business in the city of Atlanta, and you'll make a fortune. The beauty of it is. . . The cops can't touch you. They're too damn scared to go into 'The Bottom,' man. If they do, they go in a hundred strong because they need that many to protect their pitiful asses. You wouldn't have a thing to worry about."

"I would like to have a little anonymity."

"Man, everybody who lives in Buttermilk Bottom is anonymous. Ain't nobody looking for anybody down there. Believe me. . . Once you move in. . . You can call yourself the fucking invisible man. Plus, in a few years, you'll be rich."

Realizing that there was very little in the way of jobs for a black man in the south except those that catered to serving whites, he decided to look into Rufus' offer to be a number writer and to purchase the old four-unit apartment building with the money he had left from the sale of his aunt's house. The next day, Rufus drove Cameron to Buttermilk Bottom where his friend would introduce him to his prospective tenants. Cameron was not surprised at the substandard condition of the roads and houses because he grew up a few blocks away when he lived with his aunt. As Rufus' brand new 1954 Buick came to a stop in front of the two-story building, a group of children played a funny looking game.

Did you go to the hen house? (Yes, M'am!)
Did you get any eggs? (Yes, M'am!)
Did you put 'em in the bread? (Yes, M'am!)
Did you bake it brown? (Yes, M'am!)
Did you hand it over? (Yes, M'am!)
Good old egg bread, (Shake 'em, shake 'em)
Good old egg bread, (Shake 'em, shake 'em)

Cameron was enjoying their rhymes and slowed down long enough to watch and listen to the children keep rhythm, using words with a series of complicated hand and foot movements. Hearing the remainder of the verse, he felt shocked and sad by the ending phrases.

Did you go to the lynching? (Yes, M'am!)
Did they lynch that man? (Yes, M'am!)
Did that man cry? (Yes, M'am!)
How did he cry? (Baa, baa.)
How did he cry? (Baa, baa.)

Looking around the dilapidated community, no one appeared concerned or bothered about the words that the children chanted. Observing the parents of the children sitting on the front porches and steps chatting away made his heart sad. A few people noticed the two well-dressed men approaching. Cameron looked around for someone to intervene in what he considered was inappropriate play, but no one did. Instead, they smiled and waved hello.

"Rufus, did you hear what they were singing?"

"Yeah, man. . . They have a million of those songs. You'll hear that all day long and half the night," he said, climbing the steps to the first floor porch.

The three families who lived in the building had been there for years and from all indications, they were not planning to move. The most colorful of the three families was a set of elderly twins who lived on the first floor; their warm reception made Cameron feel right at home. Reminding him of two aged teachers, he smiled when he saw them pull out a dozen big, moist, delicious cookies and a hot pot of coffee.

"Our cookies are man-size," one of the twins said.

"We always made these for our father," the other one said, completing her twin's thought. "He was the only minister down here for many years."

"He was very fond of our giant-size cookies," her sister said.

"Thank you, it's very nice of you to share them," Cameron said, biting into one of the delicious, moist cookies.

"We miss having you come for Sunday breakfast, Rufus," Gussie, the oldest of the twins, said.

"We enjoy company and we love cooking even more," Essie said with a brilliant smile.

"I miss being here," Rufus replied. "But. . . Now you can fatten up my friend. He's the new owner and you can invite him for Sunday breakfast. I'm sure he'd like that."

"Would you like to have Sunday breakfast with us?" Gussie asked with a sparkle in her eyes.

"We would love to have you," Essie said eagerly.

"Sure, I love to eat. Sunday breakfast sounds great," Cameron said, smiling.

"Good," Essie said.

"Are you married?" Gussie asked.

"No."

"Will you be living here alone?" Essie asked.

"Yes."

"Just like Rufus," Essie said to her twin.

"Will you take the numbers for us?" Gussie asked in a whispered tone.

Surprised at her request, Cameron stopped eating to laugh and said, "Yes, I will, but not for a few weeks. I want to get settled first."

"It sounds like we have a deal," Rufus said, shaking his friend's hand.

With the sales agreement for the building in his hand, Cameron made plans to move into the second floor apartment that following week.

It was March and all the dogwood trees were blossoming. It only took a few hours to complete his move to the sunken community. Cameron's possessions had dwindled to his clothing, his jazz collection, and two items that belonged to his aunt; a book of family photographs and a large blue and white pitcher and bowl set. They were special to his aunt, and therefore, they were precious to him. All the other furniture, except for the items he needed for his new apartment, he sold in order to pay off his legal fees. The remaining money, he placed in the bank, but he used some of it to help him get on his feet in his new home and to repay Grace for the purchases she made on his behalf. Although she told him it was too much money, he insisted that she take it for all the trouble she went through while preparing his homecoming and readjustment to society. After preparing a romantic dinner for Grace, he mentioned that he was moving to Buttermilk Bottom while Grace sat at the table studying for her master's in education. She was completely engrossed in her books when he made the shocking announcement.

"Of all the places on the face of this earth to move to. . . You chose Buttermilk Bottom? Man, you must have lost your mind," she said, putting her books down.

"No. . . I thought it through carefully, and I decided it would be the best thing for me right now," he said, clearing the table.

"How could you live there with those. . . Those. . . Crazy people? Have you read the papers in the last twenty-five years? There are murderers, thieves, and prostitutes living there," she yelled, unable to keep quiet or to control her emotions.

"It's the best place for me right now," Cameron said calmly.

"You can't be serious," she said as he placed the leftovers in the refrigerator.

"I'm moving in tomorrow."

"Cameron, people get stabbed, shot, and killed down there every weekend. That place is full of rats, and God only knows what else," she said, raising her voice for the first time, since he met her.

"I've heard the stories, and I've read all the newspaper accounts, and I'm still moving in. . . Tomorrow," he said, sipping the remainder of the wine in his glass.

"Why? Why are you doing this?"

"Because. . . I want this for myself."

"What about teaching and coaching? You always wanted to coach."

"That was another life. I have to look for something different now."

"You can make another appeal to the board. They are bound to revise their decision."

"I have appealed it twice and that was one time too many."

"What about a job? How are you going to make a living?"

"Don't worry, I'll be fine."

"Please, don't tell me you're going to do something illegal?" He said nothing. "You are, aren't you? Have you lost your mind? Do you want to end up back in jail? I can't believe this."

"If this move means that we can't see each other. . . I'll understand."

"What?" she said, startled. "I never said that. Cameron, why don't you move in here with me? There's plenty of space and we could get married. . . Have a family," she said, throwing her arms around him as he sat at the table.

"That's not the life I want, Grace, but it's a life you should have. . . But not with me," he said, looking directly into her eyes.

"Marriage isn't that bad. At least, our's won't be."

"I can't marry you. But you, beautiful lady, should be someone's wife and mother," he said, touching her soft brown face.

"I don't want to be with anyone but you," she said, sitting in his lap, kissing him.

"Marriage isn't an option for me. I have other things in mind for my future."

"I don't want to break-up over this."

"It may be for the best," he said, kissing her lips gently.

"No, it can't be. We can work this out," she said, clinging to him.

"You think about it, and we can talk about it on the weekend," he said, picking her up and taking her into the bedroom.

Cameron Fielding's arrival in Buttermilk Bottom caused quite a stir. All the available women in Buttermilk Bottom stood watching from their front porches, waiting for an opportunity to meet the tall, dark, and extremely handsome stranger. They whispered softly among themselves. The twins bragged to everyone about the new property owner. They did not fail to mention that he was unmarried and extremely good-looking. To the delight of all the single women, he had no visible wife or girl friend moving in with him. Among the many women, who observed Cameron, was the owner of the speakeasy across the street from his new home, and she made it her business to let him know that she was on the planet. Cameron had been in his apartment building for only an hour when the cook from the juke joint knocked on his door.

"Good afternoon, sir," she said, smiling from her large round face.

"Hello, come in," he said, smiling at his first guest.

"My name's Cora Lee Jones. Miss Queenie, at d' juke joint across d' road, axed me t' bring this over t' you." She handed him a hot, aromatic platter of home-cooked food.

"Thank you. My name is Cameron Fielding. I really do appreciate this," he said sincerely.

"We knew you wouldn't have time t' do no cookin,' bein' dat you jes' moved in and all."

"It was nice of you to be so thoughtful. Would you like to have a seat?"

"No, thank you. I better git back. . . Got's plenty of cookin' t' do. Friday night's our busiest night. I got a mess o' greens t' clean and cook. Colored folks loves theyselves some greens no matter what else ya give 'em."

"What's on your menu for tonight?"

"Ribs, greens, tato salad, cornbread and for dessert, we's havin' banana puddin'."

"That sounds delicious. You must save a plate for me."

"It's gonna be my pleasure. Anytime you wants a good, home-cooked meal, jes' come and see Cora Lee. I'll take good care o' you."

"I really would appreciate you looking out for me. I can pay you by the week. I can't cook, but I love to eat."

"Shoot. . . It ain't nothin'. If you git hungry and don't feel like messin' wit people in d' joint, jes' come 'round d' back way and eat wit' us in d' kitchen, or you can take yo platter home if you like."

"Cora Lee. . . I think you and I are going to be best friends," he said, smiling at her beautiful round jovial face.

"You looks like a fine boy. I's gonna love fattin' you up," she said, giggling as she backed out the door.

"Thanks again." He watched her as she sprinted across the road. She had a lot of energy for a woman her size. She looked back, waved at him and he waved back. For the first time, he felt certain that his decision to move to Buttermilk Bottom was going to be a good one.

When Cora Lee returned to the juke joint, her employer was standing at the door, waiting impatiently for her to come inside. Cora Lee knew that she wanted to know every detail, but she felt her boss was too pushy when it came to men.

"The gent'man say thank you, Queenie. Seems like a nice, young fellow," she said, heading for the kitchen.

"Cora Lee, come back here and tell me. . . What did he look like up close?"

"He look mighty fine, and he's nice as he kin be," Cora Lee said, trying to dart off to her kitchen where Queenie never entered.

"Cora Lee, come back here."

"Now, what you want?"

"Did you tell him I sent the food over to him?"

"I sho did, and he thought it wuz right nice of you t' think o' him, wit him moving' in 'n all."

"Was there a woman with him?"

"Seems t' me like you should've gone over there yo'self if you wanted t' know all that."

"I don't want him to think I'm desperate."

"Too late fo' that. 'Specially when ya done sent him dat food 'fore he could even put his first bag down. If you axe me, dat's as desperate as you kin git."

"Thank you, Cora Lee," Queenie said, irritated with her cooks frank words.

"You's welcome, Queenie. You sho is welcome."

After Cora Lee reached the kitchen, she went straight to the stove, poured herself a cup of hot coffee then said to her helper and lifetime partner, Addie Mae Long, "That Queenie's gots her eyes peeled fo' dat new man 'cross d' road already."

"What he like?" Addie Mae asked.

"He's d' nicest man we ever had 'round these parts, I'll tell ya dat. He got good manners and everythang. Axed me t' sit down, but I had t' git back here and git d' greens on d' stove." With her cup of coffee in her hand, she sat down at the table, grabbed the wooden crate of fresh collard greens, and removed the lid. She checked each leaf, removing all the yellow and brown spots. She was also careful to remove any worms that may be lingering on the rich, dark, green leaves.

"Addie Mae, you mark my words, Queenie's gonna break her neck tryin' t' land dis one. She ain't even seen him good, and she's already waterin' at d' mouth."

"Po' thang, she ain't never gonna find what she wants."

"She may find what she wants all right, but she ain't gonna git nothin' but what d' good Lord wants her t' have," Cora Lee said, certain of her prophecy.

"Ain't dat's d' truth," Addie Mae said.

"I told him t' come t' d' back if he wants. I think he might from time t' time," Cora Lee whispered.

"Well, you better not let Queenie hear 'bout dat. She'll have herself a fit."

"I ain't thinkin' 'bout Queenie when it comes t' my kitchen. She might owns dis whole place, but I runs dis kitchen," Cora Lee said emphatically.

"I heard dat," Addie Mae said, laughing as she walked over to Cora Lee and kissed her on the lips. She then sat down at the table across from her lover to help clean the greens.

"You put d' fatback in d' pot t' boil?"

"I sho did. It's 'bout ready fo' d' greens, soon as we clean 'em."

"I told you a million times dat I cleans my own greens," Cora Lee said.

"I know, but I kin do it jes as good as you kin."

"Maybe so but I feels better when I do 'em myself."

"You told me a million times how t' clean d' greens. Believe me, I kin do it wit my eyes closed."

"What do you do?"

"Wash 'em three, four times in soap and salt, then wash 'em three times mo' in clear cold plain water."

"See. . . Dat's why I washes my own greens. Nobody kin clean 'em like I do. You have t' wash 'em in Tide and no other soap. Den you puts in salt and vinegar in d' water and lets 'em soak fo'. . . Least fifteen minutes. Den you cleans 'em in clear water three times and put 'em in d' pot wit d' fat back or ham hocks."

"Don't matter what kind of soap you use as long as ya use some," Addie Mae said.

"See, you don't know a thang 'bout cleanin' greens. Nuthin' cleans greens better than Tide. Plus. . . It gives 'em a good taste. You ought t' know dat. You love my greens."

"I loves you and dat ain't got nuthin' t' do wit no greens."

"You's a mess, girl," Cora Lee said, laughing and blushing all at once.

"I know."

"Lord, who in dis world would've known dat you 'n me would be t'gether all these years? Not me," Cora Lee said, shaking her head.

"We had our ups and downs, but we's still got each other. Nuthin' kin change dat," Addie Mae said.

"Dat's mighty comfortin' fo' a old lady t' hear."

"You ain't old," Addie Mae said, getting up to embrace her lover.

"I's old 'n you is old, too. Dat's a fact. Ain't no use in lying 'bout it t' ourselves," Cora Lee said.

"Well, I don't feels old and neither do you," Addie Mae said, placing her hand down the front of Cora Lee's blouse to fondle her generous breasts. "I loves you," she said as she bent down to kiss her sensuously on her generous lips. "You ain't feelin' old t' me."

"You jes' stop dat nasty stuff in my kitchen. You knows I ain't havin' no carryin' on in my kitchen. Git t' work and wash yo' nasty hands 'fore you touch any food in my kitchen," Cora Lee said firmly but a huge smile was on her face. "I gotta feelin' we's gonna need a lot o' greens t'night."

"You wants me t' start planting' yo greens in d' yard. You should start 'em early so we kin git a good crop dis year."

"Now, you knows dat I don't start no plantin' til d' dogwoods finish bloomin'."

"D' ground's all ready fo' plantin'," Addie May said.

"Not one seed goes in d' ground 'til d' dogwood finish bloomin' and dat's dat. Where's dat old man, Luther? I ain't seen his behind all day."

"He went fishin'."

"Dis time o' day? No fool in his right mind go fishing in d' middle of d' day. He jes wants t' go sit by d' creek, dat's all. And he ain't gon' catch nothin' less it jumps in his lap," Cora Lee said, laughing.

"Why not? D' fish's in d' water. They ain't goin' nowhere til somebody catch um."

"Chile, you still gots a lot t' learn. Any fool knows dat d' only time a fish eats is right after d' sun rises and a hour or so b'fore it sets. Dat's d' Lord's doing. . . Always' been and always' gonna be."

As Cameron was finishing his lunch of fried chicken, string beans, and macaroni salad that Cora Lee brought over, he heard another knock on the door. When he reached the door, he saw a man on crutches.

"Hey, I'm Jake. I live across the road in that green house over there." Jake pointed to his house.

"Hello, I'm Cameron Fielding."

"Come on out on the porch. Let's sit a while. Got any beer?" Jake said, taking his crutches off and sitting down on the faded dark green glider that sat in front of the window.

"Sure, wait here. I'll be right back," Cameron said, happy to meet another neighbor.

Taking two beers from the refrigerator, he could not help but laugh at himself for thinking it would take two or three weeks to get to know the people of his new neighborhood. He smiled as he walked back toward the front porch because he remembered his own hesitation about moving to Buttermilk Bottom. He also wondered how long it would take him to find a friend. The way the day was starting, it did not seem as if he was going to have any problems at all.

"Here you go," he said, handing Jake a cold bottle of beer.

"Thanks, man. It's hot as hell out here. Looks like we're getting an early Summer."

Cameron sat on the banister with his back resting on the support post, looking where he had a great view of the whole neighborhood. Rufus said that he chose this particular building because of the advantage it gave him in surveying the whole community. From his front porch, he could see everyone and everything coming and going in Buttermilk Bottom. Cameron smiled at his friend's cleverness.

"Rufus told me you were coming. He said I should look out for you," Cripple Jake said.

"Great."

"Everybody's been expecting you so all you have to do is show up. It's been almost a month, since we had someone here to run the numbers, and you know how colored folks get when they can't play their numbers."

"I can imagine," Cameron said, but he had no idea about the number business much less how people felt about it.

"By the way, you thought of how you want to collect the numbers?"

"Word of mouth."

Jake frowned and looked at him strangely, saying, "Word of mouth? How do you expect to keep track of everything with all the business you're gonna get?"

"I'll remember."

"That's a hell of a lot of remembering, pal," Jake said with a touch of concern in his voice as he evaluated their new neighbor.

Without a care or concern, Cameron said, "I can handle it."

"You mean to tell me you don't write anything down?" Jake asked.

"No need. . . I'm pretty good with numbers," Cameron said.

"Pretty good? Shit, you must be fucking brilliant." Cameron laughed. "All you need to do is show up at the juke-joint, and your customers will take care of the rest."

"Before I start doing business, I have to learn who's who. It'll take me a week before I'll be prepared to start."

"That's where I can help you. I know everybody, and I can tell you anything you want to know about anybody."

Cameron smiled. "How about taking me around tomorrow night?"

"Why not tonight?"

"I want to look the place over first."

"Good idea. . . That makes sense. I think you're going fit in real good around here, Cameron Fielding, the way you like to take things slow and easy. Yep, you'll do just fine," Jake said, smiling.

Wanting complete anonymity, Cameron slipped into an invisible lifestyle where he could live with his head up and not bow down to the racism that permeated the south. In the Bottom, no one would judge or accuse him of anything. The only reason for his exile was being born the wrong color, a fact that locked him out of his chosen career field and most of the respectable jobs in the Atlanta area.

On Cameron's second night in the Bottom, Jake met him on the front steps of his apartment building. They walked across the street together and immediately, Jake began telling him who lived where. Cripple Jake wanted to introduce him around first, but Cameron wanted to go to the juke joint for a drink of whiskey.

When the two men of opposite looks and traits walked into the smoke-filled room, everyone turned around. There was an unusual number of women in the juke joint smiling and checking out the new man in the neighborhood, while the men in the room looked on and wondered. No one was happy hearing that the number man would not do business for a whole week. When Jake explained to his friends, that Cameron did all of his transactions from memory, they began to moan and groan about him messing up their money, doubting his ability to do the job properly. As people whispered quietly about the newcomer, Luther, the bartender came over to welcome Cameron to the juke joint and to give him a drink on the house.

"What's yo' pleasure?" the old man asked.

"Whiskey, neat."

"Good drink. I think I'll join ya. How 'bout you, Jake?"

"My regular poison." The old man poured whiskey for Cameron and vodka for Jake. "The place sure is crowded tonight," Jake said as Dellah eased over and stood next to him. Dellah was a young, attractive prostitute who worked and lived there. Jake automatically placed his arms around her waist.

"Yep, everybody wants t' git a close-look at our friend here, 'specially d' ladies. They all came last night, hopin' you'd come in," Luther said, grinning. Cameron looked around the room and saw that all eyes were on him. "We never had this many women in here at one time. Thanks fo' d' business," he said, toasting Cameron.

"Whatever I can do to help out," Cameron said, raising his glass.

"Cameron, this is Dellah. If you need anything special, call on her. She's the best," Jake said, smiling.

"Hello. Nice to meet you," Cameron said.

"Hey," Dellah said then she whispered something in Jake's ear, giggling. Jake smiled and gave her a light kiss on the lips.

"How's yo' poker hand?" Luther asked with a glimmer in his eye.

"Not as good as I want it to be."

"Wanna sit in? We start in a few minutes," Luther said.

"Why not?"

"I gotta go in d' cellar t' git some mo' liquor. Be right back." Luther said, heading down the basement steps as Cameron looked around the room at the many faces watching him. He smiled at those who smiled at him. Jake laughed and shook his head. Then suddenly Luther yelled, "Damn-it. Gotdamn, son-of-a-bitch," he yelled loudly. Everyone ran to see why Luther was yelling. Dellah was the first one to reach the basement door and Luther almost knocked Dellah down because right behind him was a huge sewer rat that chased him back up the steps with its teeth bared, growling. He reached the top step just as his friend

Moses slammed the door shut, blocking the rat from entering the room. The women began to scream. "Oh shit," Luther said angrily. "Here we go agin. Where's my fuckin' shotgun?"

"I'll git it," Azalene, the nineteen-year-old prostitute said, running behind the counter. She picked up the gun and quickly tossed it to Luther.

"Be back in a minute," Luther said to Cameron. "Dat mutherfucker ain't stayin' in here," he said while pulling his socks up over his pants-leg. Someone gave him a piece of string, which he tied around the bottom of each leg. He threw open the door and ran down the steps, shooting. Five minutes later, he came back upstairs with a big, bloody, dead rat, holding it up by the tail, enjoying the screaming reaction from the women in the room. He walked through the kitchen and through the back door then threw it outside beyond the limits of their backyard into the kudzu vines. As soon as he came back inside, Cora Lee gave him a jar of Clorox and a bar of brown Octogon soap that he took into the bathroom to wash his hands.

When he came out, smelling of bleach, he sat down at the poker table and said to Cameron, "Welcome t' Buttermilk Bottom." In the next breath, he asked, "Who dealt dis shit?" He spread his poker hand out to discover that he had no matching cards. "Dat wuz d' biggest gotdamn rat I seen all year."

"Shit, dat wuzn't big," Moses said. "Man, dat ain't hardly big. I use t' nail metal covers ov'r d' holes in my floor to keep d' son-of-a-bitches from comin' into d' house, but it didn't do no good. The next mornin', dem suckers would bite right through d' metal and walk all over me." Moses was a very tall, broadly built man with a dark complexion and a big generous smile on his face. He was as gentle as a lamb if left alone. Only a few people challenged him, and once they did, they never tried it a second time.

"Man, you lying'," someone said.

"Lying, my ass. One night, I came home late and wanted t' heat up my dinner. . . I opened d' damn oven dor and all I seen wuz two, great-big eyes, lookin' back at me."

"They do git in d' stove," another person testified. "I seen dat myself."

"One day. . . I came home from work and found my whole damn family, standin' in d' middle o' my damn bed. . . My wife and my four boys. I yelled, 'What d' hell ya'll doin' standin' on my damn bed?' I yelled, mad as hell. They all stood there hugging each other, yelling back, at me. . . 'R-A-T', pointin' behind me. I turned 'round and saw a rat d' size of a big ole' dog. I jumped up on d' fuckin' bed wit 'em," Moses said, laughing with his friends and enjoying his own plight. "Dat wuz d' biggest mutherfucker I ever seen."

"What did you do?" someone asked.

"What d' hell ya think I did? I jumped on the bed wit my family then I waited fo' dat bitch t' leave. . . Then I took my family and moved d' fuck out," Moses said with a serious tone to his voice, which made everyone laugh harder.

"Man, dat ain't nuthin'," Smoke said with his ever present cigarette, hanging from his mouth. "We got so use t' rats dat my kids named dem all. One day dey found a old rat dead in d' kitchen and came running t' me crying. . . Saying, 'Daddy, Daddy. . . Poppy died.' I thought them lil' niggers wuz talkin 'bout my daddy, but they wuz talkin 'bout a ol' ass rat. Those lil' fuckers wanted me t' bury him, so they could have a fuckin' funeral." The room filled with laughter.

"Shit, we had so many rats when we lived in d' back dat we had t' ask permission t' sleep in our own beds," Moses said, wanting to keep the laughter going.

"They get in your bed?" Cameron asked, making everybody laugh at his innocence.

"Shit. . . B'fore we moved, I found out dat d' rats had made a hole in my mattress and made a nest in it. I wuz sleepin' on one side of d' damn mattress and they wuz sleepin' on d' other side." Everybody made sounds of disgust.

"That's too many fucking rats," Jake said, dealing the cards.

"Dat's Buttermilk Bottom," Luther said, laughing with his friends.

For over an hour, twelve men stood around the card table, watching the poker game as it progressed while the new number man pulled in his winning from almost every game they played. During his year of imprisonment, he had the privilege of playing poker with some of the sharpest card players in the world. They not only taught him the rules of the game, they also taught him the psychological dynamics of the game, and he was a good student. Suddenly, the men stopped talking, looked up, and let out a collective moan of approval because Queenie was making her appearance at the top of the stairs in her usual weekend finery that always dominated the attention of her customers for at least ten minutes.

"Hot damn," Jake said as she floated down the steps. "Baby, you look good."

"Thanks, Jake. How's everybody tonight?" Queenie asked, walking over to their table. "Who's your new friend?" she asked, knowing the answer.

"Dis is d' new 'Bug Man'," someone said.

The number man stood up and introduced himself: "Hello, I'm Cameron Fielding. Thank you for the platter of delicious food that you sent over yesterday. It really hit the spot."

"I was happy to do it. Where are you from?"

"Right here in Atlanta."

"You don't sound like an Atlanta man. I could have sworn you were from up North somewhere," she said, standing close to him and lowering her voice to make it sound sexy.

"No, I'm from a street not too far from here in fact." He smiled, wanting to get back to the game. "It's a pleasure to meet you."

"The pleasure's all mine," she said, loving everything she saw because he was much better looking up close. "Can I get you a drink?"

"No, thank you. Luther took care of me." He sat down and resumed his card playing.

"Let me know if there is anything at all I can do for you," she said, batting her eyelashes as she walked away, but Cameron was too engrossed with the cards to notice.

Luther watched Queenie and all her theatrics for the rest of the evening as she tried to charm the new number man. Even he had to admit that the younger man was good looking. He understood her need to have someone closer to her age, but his heart broke as she continued to bat her eyes and swing her big hips for another man's attention. Luther and Queenie came together as lovers then after a few years they became business partners. Over the years, Queenie's interest in him faded. If it were up to Luther, they would still be together as lovers and would remain so for a long time to come. What they shared was special, and he appreciated that, but he had a wife and children at home. There was only so much complaining that he could do, and he accepted his loss gracefully, but in his heart, he was a gambler, and he bet that in the end, when all the cards were dealt and played out that Queenie would once more belong to him.

Chapter 3

The first time that Queenie and Cameron were intimate, happened five months after he arrived in Buttermilk Bottom. To everybody's amazement, Queenie took much longer than anyone expected her to entice Cameron to her bed. It took so long that people were placing bets on when and if it would ever happen, including Luther.

"Queenie's done lost her touch," Dellah said.

"Maybe dat man jes don't like no big ass women," Lucille said, gulping down another shot of corn liquor. "Maybe she oughta t' go see dat voodoo bitch, down d' road, and git some hoodoo t' help her out."

"How come every time a woman wanna git a man, she gotta use roots?" Luther asked.

"'Cause she can. . . Dat's why?" Lucille said, laughing too loudly.

"Dat's a crock o' shit. You know what dat ol' song say 'bout dat. 'Don't go spreadin' goober dust 'round my bed. When ya wake up. . . Ya gonna find yo own self dead,'" he sang. "Ya'll better be careful wit dat shit," Luther said, pointing his finger at the women in the room.

"Yeah. . . But sometimes dat shit work and work good," Lucille said, stumbling over to the jukebox. "And, Queenie gonna need some o' dat shit if she wanna git dat man."

"I know Queenie. She ain't gon be satisfied 'til she gits in his pants. He might as well pull dem pants down ret now 'n give it up," Azalene said, laughing.

"I feel sorry fo' her myself," Luther said, happy that she had not succeeded.

"The only person you feel sorry fo' is yo'self, old fool. You been lickin' her fat ass fo' years," Lucille blurted out, reaching for her glass and drinking the contents.

"You shut d' fuck up. Ain't nobody talkin' t' you," Luther said, fighting back.

"Dat's alright, nigger. Ya'll know dat I'm tellin' d' truth. Ya got a wife 'n ya ought t' be ov'r there sniffin' her pussy 'stead o' Queenie's."

"Lucille, what I do wit my wife is my fuckin' bizness," Luther said, refilling her glass.

"How's it gonna be yo bizness when yo wife ain't seen yo' ass in months."

"I pay all d' bills in my house, and she ain't got shit t' say 'bout nuthin'," Luther said. "I gamble t' make money, and I takes care o' home."

"Don't ya think ya oughta take yo' old ass home, too. . . . Least once a week, t' see yo' family," Lucille said, swallowing the shot of corn liquor all at once.

"I make sho' dey got food and a roof over their heads, dat's my job. When I git home, I takes care o' everything, and my wife knows it."

"Ain't nuthin' worse than a black, nigger-daddy. All ya'll mutherfuckers do is fuck people up wit a million kids den sit on yo' asses. Ev'ry now and then ya throw a lil' money in d' house and think somebody's s'ppose t' wash yo' nasty-ass clothes, fix yo' dinner, 'n be ready t' fuck ya all night long."

"Ya need t' stay out o' my bizness, woman, and take care o' yo own old, drunken ass. Dat's why you ain't gots no man now. Ya talk too fuckin' much."

"I know one thang. . . You ain't gon git no pussy 'round here, unless ya pay fo' it. So ya might as well take yo molely, old ass home."

"I ain't thinkin' 'bout you, Lucille," Luther said, walking away.

"Queenie don't want ya no mo', fool. She got her eyes on dat young, good-lookin 'Bug Man,' and I sho' don't blame her," Lucille said, laughing.

"She sho' love herself some 'Bug Man.' I ain't never seen her dis messed up ov'r nobody b'fore," Dellah said. "Cain't say I blame her 'cause he's damn good lookin' wit a body t' match. I'd like t' have some o' dat myself."

"If I wuz a few years younger. . . I would've raped his lil' narrow ass long time ago," Lucille said, laughing.

"Well, listen at you," Dellah said, laughing.

"Yeah, me. Jes 'cause I ain't twenty-one no mo, don't mean I don't want a man. I still got a pussy, don't I?"

"You sho' do, girl," Azalene said, laughing. "You sho do."

Whenever Cameron walked into the juke joint, Queenie rushed to him, flirting shamelessly, trying desperately to get his attention. She exploited every opportunity to get close to Buttermilk Bottom's newest resident. She even started playing the numbers in order to have regular interactions with the tall, dark, muscular man. Before Cameron arrived, Queenie refused to participate in gambling of any kind and playing numbers never made any sense to her, but if it got her closer to the man she wanted to love for the rest of her life, then she was going to play the numbers.

On several occasions, she asked Cora Lee to prepare a special meal for two, in hopes of luring the new number writer to her quarters, only to end up sharing it with her son or one of the whores who worked for her. He turned down all her invitations to have dinner, but his refusals were always polite and kind, which made her angry and more frustrated.

"Maybe some other time," he said as his eyes settled on her breasts, which always seemed to protrude slightly from whatever clothing she was wearing.

"Anytime. . . If you can get away from that other woman," she said teasingly.

"Don't worry, she won't mind," he said pointedly. He was still seeing Grace almost every weekend because he genuinely cared for her. As long as she allowed him, he would continue to see her because he enjoyed making love to her. "We have an understanding."

"Well, I'll be here. You know where to find me."

"If you want me to . . ." he said.

"I do, anytime."

Hearing that he had a girl friend derailed her for a moment then she realized that he was still looking at her with lustful eyes, but for some reason, he never acted upon it. She was at her wits-ends, trying to figure out how to get him in her bed. With Cora Lee's help, she remembered that she was a seasoned professional. After the joint closed for the night, Cora Lee sat in Queenie's quarters, making plans for the upcoming weekend.

"Cora Lee, maybe you could buy two of those big steaks. They may come in handy, just in case, I have company for the weekend," Queenie said with a sparkle in her eyes.

"You still tryin' t' git dat man in yo' bed?" Cora Lee asked. "I been buyin' steaks fo' months now, and he ain't took one bite yet. It's jes a waste of good money."

"I've tried everything I know, but he won't give me the-time-of-day. All he does is smile that beautiful smile of his and run out the damn door. You'd think I wanted to kill him instead of love him. Do you think he knows how crazy I am about him?"

"Everybody 'n Buttermilk Bottom knows dat chile' and he's a real smart man. He knows. D' thang is he ain't lookin' fo' no wife; love either fo' dat matter. He's one o' dem playboys. He likes all d' women."

"How you know so much about what he likes and dislikes?" Queenie asked with a touch of animosity.

"I hear thangs, but any fool kin see dat. . . If they ain't in love wit 'em. I hear some o' everythang in my kitchen," Cora Lee said, not telling Queenie that Cameron eats in her kitchen at least three times a week.

"I guess I'm the fool."

"Fo' him. . . You is."

"Everybody knows?" Queenie asked.

"Sho' do," Cora Lee said, rubbing her knees.

"Well, I don't give a damn. That's one fine ass man, and I want him. . . More than I've wanted any man in my whole life," she said more to herself than to Cora Lee. Tears were beginning to form in her eyes, but she refused to give in to them. "Cora Lee?"

"Yes, baby."

"I really do love him."

"I know."

"Do you think I'm scaring him off?"

"I sho' do."

"What can I do?"

"Ya kin go see Miss Cigam and git yo'self a magic potion."

"I don't believe in that mess."

"Well, didn't ya tell me ya started hookin' on d' streets when you wuz thirteen?"

"I did that because I had to make a living for me and my son. . . Not because I wanted to," Queenie said, annoyed and frustrated that she brought it up. "No matter what I do to improve myself, studying and reading everything I can get my hands on. . . Learning the business. . . . My past always haunts me."

"Baby, I know why ya did it, and I ain't judgin ya fo' it. I's jes sayin'. . . Ya oughta know how t' git a man in yo' bed. . . If ya wants him there."

"Cameron's different."

"D' only difference I kin see is dat you's crazy in love wit 'em. I ain't so old I cain't understand dat. . . But it seems t' me dat ya oughta know mo' than most women 'bout makin' a man do what he don't wanna do."

"I do. I know I do," Queenie said thoughtfully.

"Den you oughta start usin' what ya know, 'cause right now, ya ain't no closer t' gittin' dat man in yo bed than I is."

"You're right, Cora Lee. You're so right. I got to stop acting like a lovesick kid and be the woman he needs. I have to make him come to me," she said, thinking aloud. "I have to make him want me."

"Ya thinks you kin do dat?"

"I know I can do that. All I have to do is find out what he likes and then don't give it to him. I need to start paying close attention to my handsome friend," she said, walking around her room, forming a smile in the corner of her mouth while creating a plan of action.

"And. . . Fo' God's sake. . . Please, stop followin' him 'round like a love-sick dog."

"I don't follow him around."

"Sho' you do. D' minute he hits d' door. . . You's all ov'r dat man."

"Damn. . . Cora Lee, I've been acting like a lovesick fool. Haven't I?"

"Ya sho have. . . Like a love-sick dog, if ya axe me."

"Thanks, Cora Lee," she said, hugging her friend.

"Wuzn't nuthing, chile'. I's gonna keep my fingers crossed fo' ya, Baby. I's gonna pray ya git what ya wants, if dat's D' Lord's will," Cora Lee said, getting up to leave. It was four o'clock in the morning, when the two women parted.

The next morning, Queenie began to take control of the situation, and her emotions by relying on her past experiences and instincts. She made an art form of manipulating men to her will when she worked on the streets. Realizing that she made her biggest mistake when she allowed Cameron to control each of their interactions, although she initiated each of them, she would make certain that the situations between them would change from that point on. She was a seasoned professional, and it was time she started acting like it.

Days later when Cameron appeared in the juke joint, it was still early in the day. The weather was hot but Queenie felt calm and in control. She did not rush to him as she normally did, instead she kept herself busy at the bar, writing up a list of supplies that they needed for the coming weekend. Luther was calling out the items that he wanted her to purchase as she wrote them down.

"Queenie, don't forgit t' call the man 'bout mo' corn liquor. Dat damned Lucille drank every damn drop in d' house last night."

"Good morning," Cameron said, joining them.

"Good morning," Queenie said, refusing to look up.

"Mornin'," Luther said. "What's yo' pleasure?"

"Got any coffee?"

"Sho do." He poured Cameron a cup. "Ya wants one, Queenie?"

"No thanks. Would you check to see if we need any gin? I think we ran out." Luther noticed the lack of sparkle in Queenie's voice and the change in her behavior when the handsome number man arrived. In addition, she failed to jump off the barstool as she normally did when he came around. Cameron noticed it too, but he said nothing.

"It's a fresh pot. Addie Mae jes' brought it out," Luther said.

"No thanks. I have to finish this order and do my shopping before the stores are too crowded." Queenie climbed slowly off the barstool, smiling. "I have a feeling every woman in Atlanta will be at the Curb Market today," she said, noticing Cameron's eyes falling again on her breasts. "I'll see you both later." She left the room, knowing he was watching her, and she made no effort to exaggerate her walk, remembering that she was trying the soft approach. *So, he's a breast man,* she said to herself, remembering all the times his eyes fell on her breasts and knowing she now had a weapon to lure him in. From that moment on, she felt she was in a seat of power.

The next Friday night, the joint was busy and extremely crowded. To Queenie's dismay, Cameron did not arrive until almost midnight. She applauded herself for not running to him and putting her hands all over his strong, muscular body as she had done in the past. She wanted to because his strong physical presence always excited her. Armed with a different approach, she refused to look at him because the mere sight of him aroused her. Recommitting to her new role, she vowed to play the game of enticement consistently and perfectly and thereby win his affection in the end. She made herself relax and look away quickly to keep him from seeing the relief on her face. An hour passed before she allowed herself to greet him.

"Cameron, everything all right?" she asked, nonchalantly.

"Things are great," he said, letting his eyes appreciate her new outfit. He loved how well her clothes fit her well-endowed body and that night was no exception. The soft blue dress clung perfectly around her large hips and her breasts. He noticed that they were standing taller than usual.

"Good, Cora Lee made your favorite . . . Fried chicken, macaroni, and cheese. Excuse me, looks like Luther needs some help with Lucille." She was confident that she looked great as she walked away. She hoped that he would come to her sometime during the evening, but he did not, leaving her second-guessing her new strategy.

In the following weeks, Queenie invested in a new wardrobe, choosing outfits to enhance and display her best features, her large firm breasts, her curvy hips, and her beautifully shaped legs. She even took a suggestion from Cora Lee and lightened up on the makeup.

Several more weeks passed without any change in Cameron's attitude toward her. She was beginning to get depressed when she accidentally noticed his eyes on her. She caught a glimpse of him staring at her in the large mirror behind the bar. Luther had insisted that she buy the mirror a few days before. When she saw Cameron watching her, she could have kissed Luther for his wonderful idea then took steps to place mirrors all over the room. Secure in her knowledge that she now had his attention, she pressed harder with him unaware that he was under a full and carefully planned attack. Instead of cutting her hair short, as was her habit every Thursday morning on her weekly visits to the beauty parlor, she allowed it to grow and her beautician was delighted.

"I finally got something to style," she said, giving her soft loose curls that framed her face. "Ain't too many black folks can grow hair like you, Queenie. I'm so glad you finally decided to stop chopping it off."

Even she had to admit that the longer hair made her look more feminine, softer, and less severe. Before the month was over, she got the response she wanted. As she was placing drinks on the table for Cameron and his friends, he reached up and touched her hair.

"I like your new look," he said.

"Thanks. I just wanted to try something new."

She carefully abstained from moving her head in any dramatic way, not wanting him to know that even her new hairstyle was a plot to conquer him. Moving away from the electric charge, she received when his hand came so close to her face, she resisted the impulse to kiss his hand or to touch him in some small way. Feeling certain that she had his interest, she felt it was only a matter of time. In order to draw him out, all she needed was a spark. The next day, she found that catalyst at Lane Bryant's. It was a simply made purple dress, which hung gracefully over her hips while accentuating her voluptuous breasts. It also had a side split that showed off her shapely legs. With only a light touch of make-up and perfectly manicured nails, she knew that the stylish dress would work magically. For the first time since she met Cameron, she became the sensuous creature who started charming men at age twelve and one who knew how to use her body as a fully loaded, dangerous weapon.

When Queenie descended the steps wearing the awesomely perfect new purple dress, she immediately got the responses she wanted. All the men let out their various collective wolf calls, including Jake, whom she knew had great affection for her. Every man responded verbally except for Cameron. He watched her closely from the time she descended the steps, and as she made her rounds among her customers. Although he did not open his mouth, she knew she had won her enticing game and his complete attention. Using all her sensuality, she wore no bra because she knew her breasts were firm enough to function erectly in that dress and in his mind.

"What ya up to in dat bad-ass dress?" Lucille asked.

"I'm just minding my own business, Lucille."

"I stopped havin' bizness ten years ago," Lucille said, swallowing her drink in one gulp. "What ya doin' in dat sexy-ass dress, hussy?"

"No more than usual. Now please. . . Just close your mouth," she whispered.

"Dat's a crock o' shit. . . And you know it. You got every man in here ready t' wear diapers. If you wants attention. . . You sho' got it."

"I do love attention," Queenie admitted, smiling victoriously.

"You better watch out, gal. 'Cause somebody's gonna grab one o' dem big-ass tits o' yo's and start suckin' on it," Lucille said in her usual slurry, drunken manner.

"I bet ya anythang, Jake gonna be d' first one in line," Azalene said, laughing and knowing that Lucille's observations were true.

"There's only one man I want suckling here, sweetie," Queenie said, touching her breasts discreetly in front of the women, making them laugh.

"Who? D' Bug Man?" Dellah asked too loudly.

"Sho' it is. Dat horny-ass helfer's been after him since d' day he got here," Lucille said.

"Keep quiet, you old fool," Queenie whispered.

"Well, looks t' me like ya gots what you wanted. . . 'Cause here he comes," Azalene whispered, walking away.

"I'd better go, too," Dellah said.

"No stay. Don't move," Queenie whispered.

"Queenie, you look wonderful. I think purple is your color," Cameron said, leaning on the bar next to her.

"Thanks, Cameron," she said, smoothing the dress slowly over her hips.

"That is a beautiful dress," he said slowly, admiring it.

"You really like it? The sales woman convinced me that I should buy it. I wasn't so sure."

"That was a good sales woman, and it looks like all your fans agree," he said, indicating her many admirers.

"Well, you can't always go by them," she said, turning away. "Dellah, would you help me in the storage room?"

"Sure."

When she got up to leave, Cameron stood in front of her, preventing her departure. She looked up at him and asked, "What is it? Can I get you, a drink or something?"

"Yes, you can. Something to drink would be very nice," he said, looking into her eyes, stripping her of the hard shell she had manufactured over the past months. He did not miss the deep breathing coming from her substantial breasts as he walked closer and took her hand. Queenie tried to act coy, but he broke through her fragile façade instantly. "You have my attention, now what?"

"What on earth are you talking about?"

He looked at her guilty lips and through all her pretending, saying, "Are you that fond of playing games?"

"Games? What games?"

"Maybe I misunderstood your behavior over the past few months, but I had the distinct impression that you were trying to seduce me."

"Seduce you?"

"I'm sorry. . . I must have made a mistake," he said quickly and turned to leave.

"Wait, don't go," she heard herself say. He stopped then turned around and waited for her to make the next move. "I don't play games . . ." She started to say until his look told her that he knew she was lying. She laughed, "Well. . . At least I finally got your attention."

"You sure did. Now what do you plan to do with it," he said, looking from her eyes to her pointed breasts and back to her eyes again.

She took a deep breath and asked, "How about dinner. . . Just the two of us, upstairs?"

"And, after dinner?"

"Whatever you want," she said, feeling herself relinquishing her control to him again. This time she did not care as long as he promised to share the evening with her. When he did not respond, she said, "I'll ask Cora Lee to fix something special for us." She disappeared into the dining room where Cora Lee was taking her break over a cup of coffee and a bowl of bread pudding that she covered with a rich vanilla sauce.

"This little purple number worked like a charm," she said cheerfully with a grin plastered all over her face.

"I's glad fo' ya baby," Cora Lee said. "Ya looks beautiful. Any fool kin see dat."

"I thought he'd never come around."

"Well, thank God, he did. Now, you kin finally settle down, and we kin all git back t' work 'round here."

"Thanks, Cora Lee," she said, hugging her.

"Be happy chile'. . . Jes be happy," the cook said, going back into the kitchen.

"Cora Lee, could you send up a special meal for two?"

"Sho' chil', I sho' kin. . . My pleasure," Cora Lee said, grinning broadly.

Queenie rushed to her quarters to get ready for her big evening, but first she stopped and checked on her son, Tony, who was sleeping peacefully in his bed, down the hallway from her room. She put his arms and legs back under the covers, kissed him on the cheek, and hurried off to her room. Putting away all the clothes that she left on the bed and chairs, she wanted to make sure everything was perfect. When she left her bedroom suite earlier in the evening, she did not expect that Cameron would finally say yes to her. If she had known, she would have had the whole room cleaned and polished.

Dellah came to her room with a bottle of wine. "Here's a lil' somethin' t' git ya going," she said, smiling and happy for her boss.

"Thanks but I have a feeling, I won't need a drop of that once I get him in this room."

"Girl, you's lucky. Dat man's damn good lookin'. If ya find ya needs any help wit dat fine body o' his, call me."

"Get your horny ass out of here and don't let me catch you near him," Queenie admonished, laughing openly at her own jealousy.

"Don't worry, sweetie, I cain't make no money wit a black eye," Dellah said, closing the door behind her.

While arranging the glasses, napkins, and ice, someone knocked on the door. "One moment please," she sang out. It was Addie Mae with the food. "Oh, it's you. . . Just put it on the table by the window."

"Congratulations. Hopes ya'll like ya dinner."

"The last thing on my mind is food, Addie Mae."

"We can always eat later," Cameron said, standing in the doorway. Her heart stopped beating.

"I better go. Cora Lee may need me downstairs wit all d' people comin' in lookin' fo' food t' eat," Addie Mae said, backing out the door.

"Thanks, Addie Mae," Queenie said. "And thank Cora Lee for me." Cameron closed the door. "Your dinner's getting cold," she said, not wanting to pressure him.

"I thought we just decided to eat later," he said.

"Whatever you want," she said, losing her voice.

Walking over to where she stood, Cameron held his hand out, she quickly grabbed it because she was feeling dizzy just thinking about him being in her private quarters. Twirling her around, he admired her again in the purple dress. She felt silly, but she could not help but follow his lead. Touching her hair and face, he walked completely around her. She shivered, trying to control her need to reach out and hold him. He touched her breasts and found them much firmer than he imagined. He smiled and played with her nipples through the fabric of her dress, then kissed her lightly on the lips. All she could do was freeze to keep from pulling him to her, but out of fear of making a mistake, she stood silently wanting more. In one swift move, he reached around her and unzipped her dress. With his free hand, he pulled the top of the dress down to her waist, exposing her large firm breasts. He touched them lightly, and then he stopped suddenly.

"What's wrong?" she asked.

"We need to talk."

"Now. . . Right now?"

"Yes."

"You're sure it can't wait?"

"I'm sure. You know that I'm very attracted to you, don't you?"

"If you are. . . Then, why are we talking?"

"I want to make sure we understand each other."

"What's there to understand? We want to be together, right?"

"I want to make love to you, but I have to make sure we both understand the boundaries."

"Boundaries? What boundaries?"

"You are a beautiful woman, Queenie, and there is nothing I want more than to explore ways to make you feel amazing."

"Just being with you is enough, Cameron," she said, trying to kiss him, but to her disappointment, he pulled back.

"You must understand that I am not looking for any heavy entanglements." She stood there listening to the man she loved tell her that he only wanted to fool around, which she had already surmised, but it was difficult hearing it. "I want to make love to you, Queenie, but I am not in love with you," he said, waiting for a response. When she said nothing, he continued, "If you are looking for something permanent, then I am not the one for you." She still did not respond. "I would love to make you feel special but not if you want more from me than I can give you." She continued her puzzling silence. "Queenie, talk to me."

There was a long pause before she could speak. She did not expect him to be so candid.

"I know you don't love me now, but maybe one day you will."

"That's not in the cards for us, Queenie. I don't want you looking forward to something that will never happen."

"You want to make love to me right now, don't you?"

"More than anything," he said, looking at her full, shapely breasts.

"That's good enough for now."

"Are you sure about this?" he asked, looking into her eyes for understanding.

"Yes, man, I'm sure. It's more than good enough." When she tried to kiss him again, he kissed her back, and then he began exploring her perfectly formed breasts.

"I have been wanting to do this, since the day I met you," he said, placing his lips on her breasts then, drawing them into his moist mouth, sending chills throughout her quivering body.

When he heard pleasurable murmurs coming from her, he took the other breast and explored its hardness, which made him feel a rush of passion he did not expect. The hardness in his pants began to protrude, attracting her attention. In one easy movement, she released his powerful tool and began to artfully stimulate and elicit the passion she needed from him as her lips covered his hard pulsating shaft. Nothing made her happier than a large, well-formed, hard shaft, which promised complete satisfaction. She could tell by the feel and the enormous size that it was more than enough to satisfy her. It gave her great pleasure taking all of him in and expelling him in long irregular movements, which appeared to give him more pleasure. When she placed extra suction on the cap of his joint, he moaned sweetly and pulled her head closer to him, establishing regular smooth movements that gave him complete satisfaction.

He reached down and pulled her up to him, kissed her gently on the lips, while slipping her purple dress over her hips and onto the floor. He was pleased to discover that she had on a beautiful lace garter belt and stockings but no panties. He smiled and kissed her fully on the lips. It was a magnificent moment, one that she could dwell in for the rest of her life. Observing Queenie's generous body, Cameron noticed that all her muscles were tight. She was firm all over, no flab anywhere. Placing his hand on her center, he ignited fires deep within her. Encouraged by her display of passion, he picked her up and carried her to the sofa. That was the first time that anyone ever picked her up in all her memories, including those of her early childhood and mother. Pulling her legs close to him as he crouched down on the floor in front of her, he began exploring the secrets of her womanhood, only to find the largest clitoris he had seen in his life. When he touched it, it moved and vibrated under his touch. Fascinated, he continued to stroke it with his fingertips.

"You like that?" she asked.

"Who wouldn't?" he said, pulling her closer.

With an amazingly gentle touch, he stroked her enlarged sensory gland, moving back to see it pulsate as it reacted to his stimulation. This series of movements captivated him for sometime then suddenly he wanted more, as he placed his lips over her entire pleasure center, he felt it move in response to his presence. This was a new sensation for him, and he was in no hurry to explore, enjoy, and understand. Queenie was more than pleased as she surrendered to the amazing feeling that controlled and dominated her mind and body. Her body began undulating in reaction to his moist lips on her most receptive area. Feeling the muscles in her body tighten and relax in cooperation with his sweet tender movements, she was clearly in expert hands as her body shivered, releasing months, and months of pent-up emotions. Happy and satisfied, she pulled away from him, but he grabbed her and continued the carnal lashing he felt she deserved.

"Stop," she called out after several peak orgasms that overwhelmed her. "Please stop."

"Why don't you like it?"

"Yes. . . But I need a break. Please," she said, breathing hard.

"In a minute," he said, kissing her velvety center once more before allowing her to pull away. Her body heaved and rolled until she finally screamed out in blissful completion. His arousal intensified, making him crave shelter and comfort deep within her, where he hoped to achieve the peak erotic pleasure he wanted so desperately for himself.

"You are so sexy," he said as he quickly slip on a condom and plunged rapidly into her warm vivacious body, seeking everything she had to give.

Thrusting his hardness deeply into her velvety warm center, he began to feel what he was seeking, erotic rhythms. Stimulated and completely aroused, his whole body sought the ultimate penetrating stoke, which made him sprint lustfully out of control. Still holding on to each other, satisfied and depleted, they began to laugh spontaneously. Collapsing on Queenie's high soft bed, Cameron slept while Queenie filled her old-fashioned bathtub full of suds and fragrances then she woke him up for a leisurely bath.

"Cameron, I am so glad you finally noticed me. I was beginning to think that I would have to get completely butt naked to get your attention."

Kissing her delicious lips, he said, "You had my attention the first day we met."

"You didn't act like it."

"I wanted to make sure you knew what you were getting into."

"And what is that?"

"Friendship."

His words made her heart sink. She got out of the tub and after a moment, she was able to respond.

"As long as we spend time together like this," she said, sitting on the bed. "I don't mind."

"When the timing is right, we can get together and be intimate," he said, sitting next to her maintaining eye contact to make certain that she understood the conditions of any future contacts.

"Timing?" she asked, frowning.

"Sure. We both have to want it in order for it to be right."

"I know, but we are a couple, right?"

"No, Queenie. We are friends, very close friends," he said, placing his hands between her legs, feeling the soft fleshy tissue that made her coo with pleasure. "Is that going to be okay with you?"

"You really. . . Don't want me to. . . Answer that now . . . Do you?" she said, giving into the pleasure that she felt as her body responded to his gentle touch. "You want more?" she asked.

"All you've got to give me. Remember that you asked for it and this time, I'm not stopping. . . No matter how much you beg." She laughed, but he was already under the covers, seeking the sensuous knob that fascinated and delighted him. It only took moments for her to rage out of control. He greedily ravished her, wanting to feel and smell her femininity as long as he could. It gave him a heightened sense of pleasure to know that she appreciated and enjoyed the pleasure he wanted to share with her. He especially loved it when she tightened her big, beautiful thighs around his head, making him want to consume her completely. He loved how pliable her body was in his hands, especially when she became orgasmic. His reward was complete, but he wanted to entice her into a higher level of pleasure by continuing his clitoral exploration. Only when her body resonated in full shuddering movements did he relent and allow her to withdraw.

Nibbling his way to her breasts, he took long sweeping moist strokes around her nipples, eliciting strong jolting movements from the muscles of her already overly stimulated body.

"Are you ready for some real fun?" he asked, putting on a condom and pushing her legs over her head to ensure full penetration.

With his immense, glistening shaft, he whittled away all her frustrations. Fully inserted in her sweet mansion of pleasure, he began an artful display of well-placed, penetrating strokes that made her moan and beg. Together their feelings ebbed into a state of sheer ecstasy, rejoicing in the beauty, pleasure, and sensuous feel of their bodies. They retreated from their exhaustion with a sudden need for sleep, wrapped in each other's arms. Sometime during the night, Cameron woke up, dressed, and left the building. When Queenie awakened, she was immediately sad. She missed his presence. On her pillow was a note, *Next time, I'll want more.* She read it and laughed loudly for several seconds.

"That man is crazy," she said, aloud before falling back into a deep relaxing sleep.

The next day, Queenie woke up with her body singing his praises and craving his sensuous touch, making her moist as she remembered the exploits of the night before. Everyone noticed the song in her voice as the day grew old, but when there was no sign of Cameron, and she began to worry, remembering his too harsh words. *'I don't love you.'* and *'We can only be close friends.' How could he make love to me so completely and not feel true love?* she thought. The later it got. . . The sadder Queenie became.

It was midnight when Cameron finally arrived at the juke joint with Jake. They were both laughing as they came through the door. When the two lovers' eyes met, they exchanged a silent greeting, which brought smiles to both their faces. Cameron said something to his best friend then walked over to greet Queenie, kissing her fully on the lips, surprising everyone, including Jake.

"You feel up to a repeat performance?" he asked.

"Only if I go first," she said, making him laugh aloud.

"It will be my pleasure," he said, nibbling on her ear.

"Tonight?"

"I'm afraid not, but I'll see you in a couple of days."

Kissing her on the cheek, he walked away before she could scream out her objections. He spoke with Jake for only a moment, turned, and waved at her then left the building. Extremely frustrated and in sexual pain, she went up to her room and masturbated until she no longer saw the color red.

Chapter 4

For many years before Cameron moved to Buttermilk Bottom, gangs of white men would come into the community late at night in trucks, drunk, and fired up with hatred. They would kidnap and beat any black person who got in their way. Motivated by prejudice and pure meanness, they attacked innocent people, and it did not matter to them whether that person was male or female, young or old.

What frustrated Cameron most was the fact that white men could come into their neighborhood unchallenged and uninhibited then abuse the resident without punishment or reprimand. After years of harassment, the people of the Bottom seemed lethargic rather than angry, displaying total apathy for their sad predicament. No matter how severe the abuse, they did nothing to prevent or change what was happening to them because the gangs had firearms, ready to shoot. The residents simply complained to each other and suffered whatever misfortune came from each dreaded late night invasion. *How can they sit back and do nothing?* Cameron wondered.

During the first six months that Cameron lived in Buttermilk Bottom, he heard of two incidents that sickened his stomach. The first was the torching of an apartment building, which resulted in two families being without a home. Depending on the generosity of their neighbors and friends, the families had to separate, living in different households for the three months that it took to gather furniture, clothing, and to locate another apartment in The Bottom.

During another raid by the white invaders, he witnessed the true nature and tragedy of unbridled hatred. Yelling to the top of their voices, the rebels roared into the neighborhood on the back of an old pick-up, armed with a hundred years of authority granted to them by generations of assumed superiority. Those inhumane, white, southern traditions only existed to obliterate and demean those of the black race. They quickly descended on an old man who was trying desperately to get out of their way. Without the slightest bit of empathy, they jumped off the truck and started to beat him while howling loud enough to instill fear in everyone within their hearing range. Not knowing what else to do, Cameron stood on his front porch and fired his gun into the air. The men jumped on their truck and left The Bottom with the old man stretched-out with his body bleeding on the dirt road. As the truckload of abusive, hate mongers sped out of the area, several people rushed out to help the old man. Cameron hoped and prayed that his neighbor was not dead while he made a promise to make certain no one would be a victim in a third incident. The invaders would not go unchallenged again while he lived in Buttermilk Bottom.

The sun was rising on the stunned community as Cameron sat pensively on his front porch still wide-awake visualizing the horrors he witnessed the night before. His sleeplessness fed his determination and ever-increasing need for justice. Jake was just coming out of the juke joint heading for home. There were no other visible signs of life on the dirt roads of the frightened community.

"Jake?" Cameron called out.

"What the hell are you doing up this time of morning?" It was a Saturday morning, not a minute pass seven.

"We need to talk."

Cripple Jake walked over to Cameron's apartment, climbing the steps with ease and sat down on the glider next to his friend, placing his crutches on the floor at his feet.

"If you're going to keep me from getting my beauty rest, the least you could do is get me a cup of coffee."

"It's brewing on the stove."

"Great."

"Jake, can you get some of the men together for a meeting tonight at my apartment?"

"Sure. What's up?"

"We need to organize and find a way to keep anyone from coming into our neighborhood abusing our people. What happened last night will not happen again. I can't stand by, waiting for another tragedy to occur and not do anything about it."

"I've been feeling the same way, but I never knew what we could do to stop it. They come in here in gangs with shotguns. They wouldn't dare to show their faces down in Buttermilk Bottom if they had less than ten crackers with them carrying guns, because we'd kill every one of them. Man, this shit has been going' on for years and the police won't do a damn thing about it," Jake said.

"That doesn't mean it should continue, or that we should allow it. If we put our minds together, we could come up with something. Anything's better than nothing."

"Man. . . That would be something. The most important thing we have to do is to choose men who can be trusted," Jake said.

"I'll leave that part up to you, since you know everybody. We have to devise a strategy to catch the invaders and give them a taste of their own medicine."

"That would be something to see."

"Set the meeting up for late tonight. We have some white asses to kick."

"Ragman," Gus Roberts uttered in his barely audible vendors cry as he walked lazily behind the wobbly aged, wooden cart filled with his life's work. Gus was a short very dark man about forty years old who made his living collecting then selling rags, paper, bottles, and metal. He lived in a lone clapboard shack that sat in an open field on the fringe of the Buttermilk Bottom community. He had no running water or electricity. During the week, you hardly knew he existed because he moved so quietly in and out of the neighborhood. Occasionally, he would call out his chosen profession to solicit business as he uttered in a muffled tone, "Ragman. . . Ragman," as he pushed his rickety, wooden cart through the uneven, unpaved roads that suffered from poor drainage, debris, and neglect.

During the week, Gus, worked hard all week, but on weekends, he was another person. As certain as five o'clock approached on any Friday, he would be stumbling drunk, wandering aimlessly through the streets cursing, yelling out illogical statements, and laughing at jokes only he could hear and understood. Queenie was staring out the window, looking for Cameron to appear when she spotted the ragman as he stumbled in front of the juke joint. She shook her head in sympathy for his pitiful state of intoxication.

"I pay for my own motherfucking liquor," Queenie heard him say as he stumbled on his way.

"There goes the ragman and he's drunk again," Queenie said to Luther, who was in a habit of watching every move Queenie made, longing for what used to be.

"It's Friday, ain't it? He'll stay dat way 'til he falls asleep on Sunday night," Luther said.

"I'm sho' glad ya don't allow his stankin' ass in here," Dellah said, drinking a shot of whiskey at the bar. "'Cause dat man stank."

"It's too bad he drinks so much 'cause, he's really a nice guy," Luther said. "And, one o' d' smartest men ya ever wanna know. Did ya know that he used t' be a teacher at C. W. Hill?"

"No and I don't wanna know nuthin' 'bout dat stankin' ass man," Dellah said.

"What happened to him?" Queenie asked.

"People say that his wife died and a few months later. . . His son died, and d' next thang anybody knew. . . He wuz collecting rags. He got a brain on 'em though. . . Use to teach science. I'm tellin' ya that's a real smart man."

"If he's so damn smart. . . How come he can't find some water 'n wash his nasty, fuckin' ass?" Dellah asked.

"Well, he's not allowed in here because he always starts a fight, and we don't allow that foolishness in here. Besides, who needs Gus and Lucille in the same room?" Queenie said seriously.

"You kin say dat agin," Dellah said, laughing.

"Maybe you oughta try it. Knowin' dem', they'd kill each other and make us all happy," Luther suggested, laughing with his closest friends.

The ragman continued down the road and passed a group of people, standing in front of their shotgun shell shack, who were laughing and talking among themselves.

Gus stopped in front of the group, unable to keep his balance, saying, "I pay for my own. . . Motherfucking liquor," he said, slurring his words.

"Man, go on 'bout yo business. Nobody care 'bout you or yo liquor," one of the men said. "Why don't you take yo drunk-ass home and go t' bed? All you doin' is uglyin' up d' neighborhood." Just then, Gus leaned on the rickety fence and regurgitated in the man's yard. After jumping out of his way, people standing by laughed as Gus wiped his mouth with the sleeves of his tattered jacket.

"Mutherfucker, you puked in my yard," the man yelled in outrage.

"I'm sorry. I'm. . . A little out of sorts. . . Today," the ragman said apologetically.

"Why don't you go home wit yo nasty-ass self and puke in yo' own yard? You's puking all over d' place."

"So fucking what," Gus said calmly, bobbing and weaving as he tried to maintain his balance, trying to make an important point. "It's just puke. What are you getting so. . . Excited about? It'll wash away when. . . It rains. It's no fucking big thing."

"You nasty muther-fucker," the irate man yelled.

"It's just puke a biological. . . Necessity. It could have happened to anybody."

"Look at dis mess," the man yelled.

Gus became angry that the man would not let the matter drop. "So I puked in your yard. . . Big fucking deal. Can everybody hear. . . This shit? I puked in his yard. Fucking puked," Gus yelled, attracting more attention. "I'm a man. . . And I had to puke. What is. . . The fucking. . . Big deal? That's what I. . . Want to know. I didn't commit a. . . crime. It's just vomit. You want to challenge me or. . . Something?"

The man dared not push Gus too far because the short ragman had a reputation of fighting skillfully drunk or sober. Most people simply left him alone rather than risk a confrontation. When the man did not respond, Gus went on mumbling to whoever would listen as he wandered down the road to his one room shack. The man was relieved that Gus moved on and the watchful neighbors guardedly laughed as the incident unfolded before their eyes. A typical weekend occurrence seemed normal and comforting in contrast to the invasion by the white raiding party the night before. The weekend was just beginning as they posed on their front porches, knowing that another drama would normally be moments away, but the tragic beating of a fellow neighbor marred everyone's spirits.

All movements and interactions within the neighborhood were slow to non-existent as the day moved into the night. People whispered about the tragedy and quietly speculated if the old man would recover from the beating as he recuperated at Grady Hospital. The hordes of children who usually galloped through the streets were understandably absent, making the area seem more like a ghost town. The sounds coming out of the speakeasy that evening were oddly muted and sobering. The word went out to the most responsible men of The Bottom, regarding a meeting at Cameron's apartment. At eleven o'clock that night, filled with anticipation, twenty men of varying ages congregated in his front room. Most were apprehensive about the agenda, but they showed up to listen and to find out what was on the number writer's mind.

"I know all of you heard what happened to old Ed Johnson last night," Cameron said, looking at each of them in the eye. Many of the men in the room lowered their eyes to the floor as if to disassociate and to distance themselves from the incident. "I can't speak for any of you, but I can't allow another person in The Bottom to be victimized by those white mother-fuckers while I'm living here."

"Ya might as well git use t' it, 'cause dem crackers gonna come in here and beat any one o' us when dey gits good 'n ready. D' police ain't gonna do a damned thang t' stop 'em, and we all know it," a man said, voicing the opinion held by most of the residents in Buttermilk Bottom.

"I refuse to get use to that. We have to stop them. . . You and I."

"What kin we do?" another man said.

"D' police won't do nuthin'," another man said.

"We have the power, the ability, and the right to defend our friends and families. We are not helpless." The men sat around looking at him, as if he were speaking a foreign language. Their lack of response did not deter him; it only made his rage more pronounced. "How angry are you that they come here to rape, beat, and kill your family and friends? How does it make you feel? Cowardly? Helpless? Angry? I felt all of those things last night. No one is going to make me feel that way again." He waited to control his mounting anger and to allow time for the men to hear and process what he had said. "We have to be our own police force. We have to monitor and control everything that goes on in our neighborhood," Cameron said quietly.

"Dey ain't gonna let you do dat," a man said.

"We no longer have to ask permission to be citizens of this country because men like you and I stood up. . . And took a stand. In the early 1900's, men like W. E. B. Du Bois fought for our rights to be called an American. Ten years ago, the NAACP fought to make lynching illegal. They took our argument to the White House and spoke directly with the president because it was a just cause. Here in Buttermilk Bottom, we have a just cause. We have a right to protect our friends and families, and we are not asking anyone's fucking permission," Cameron said, staring the man down and looking at each of them in the eye.

"Is ya tryin' t' git us all killed," someone said.

"You are going to be killed anyway. . . If you continue to allow those white bastards to come into our community where you are raising your children and let them single out anyone who happens to be in their way and beat them within an inch of their lives. One at a time, we will all be affected," he said, maintaining his quiet voice and eye contact with each of the men in the room with steely and deliberate determination. When there was total silence, he said, "We can take control of our community. We can decide who comes in and who leaves. We can protect our children. . . Our wives, our friends. . . And ourselves. . . . Or. . . . We can remain helpless victims of the white man's hatred. If you allow them to continue at this rate, all the people in this room will be crippled or dead within the next five years. So, you choose. If we don't control our neighborhood, they will continue to harass and victimize us whenever the mood suits them."

"Sounds like you's tryin' t' git us all killed," someone said.

"We can die with honor, or we can die as cowards, ashamed, and humiliated. Either way, we are marked for abuse or death, whether we fight back or not," Jake said, speaking up for the first time.

"We are strong men. We are able to provide for our families, and we have the God-given right to protect them against anyone or anything that threatens them. What's it gonna be?" Cameron asked the group of silent men assembled in his living room.

"I plans t' die fightin'," said Moses, an unemployed carpenter, who was six feet four, two hundred and thirty-five pounds.

"Thanks, Moses," Jake said. "What about the rest of you?"

The group remained silent. No one spoke and neither Jake nor Cameron wanted to speak, knowing that the decision had to come from the group of men sitting in that room. Finally, the oldest man in the room stood up.

"If we don't take care o' dis problem, dis problem gonna take care o' us. I say. . . We take care o' d' problem."

The room was completely quiet then as if that declaration finally penetrated their brains; a small murmur grew into a loud rippling sound of approval that went around the entire room.

"If we do dis, we can't tell nobody 'bout what we's doin', not even our wives," another man said. "If d' word gits out, d' police gonna hunt us all down."

"Everyone has to agree to keep our activities a secret," Cameron said. "That means everybody. If we can't agree on that there is no need in us going any further." The room was silent.

"Well, what's it gonna be?" Jake asked.

"We gotta keep it secret and dat means every mutherfucker in dis room," Moses said. "If anyone talks, dey's gonna have t' answer t' me," he said, looking around the room to make sure he was understood. The men mumbled among themselves. "Speak d' fuck up. We gon' do dis shit or not?" Moses asked, yelling.

The men rushed to affirm their decision to rid themselves of the white invaders, spontaneously rising to their feet, shaking each other's hands, and patting themselves on the back.

After a few moments of celebration for their brave stand, Cameron said, "Now, let's get down to business," he said, waiting for them to quiet down. "In order to do this the right way, we are going to need lookouts and monitoring stations; places where we can see every damn thing that goes on in our neighborhood. We must know who comes in and out of here at all times."

"I kin do dat," Moses said.

"We need a twenty-four hour schedule with everybody taking a turn," Cameron said.

"I kin take care o' it," another man said.

"Good," Cameron said as he smiled at Moses. "We need to know what's going on at the precinct. Jake, you already know everything that's going on there. We need a quick way to communicate all your information and instructions to the entire neighborhood, but make sure nothing is ever written down."

"Sounds good to me," Jake said. "I'll take care of it."

"Now, it's time to decide what we're going to do to stop those fucking crackers from invading this neighborhood again and beating someone else."

After hours of heated discussions and arguments, the newly organized group came up with a plan and made several major decisions, which would bind them to a new fraternal order, committing them to each other.

"We needs t' wear black clothes 'n put black stuff on our faces so no one kin recognize us," someone suggested.

"Good idea," Cameron said.

"What 'bout guns? Kin we carry guns?"

"How many of you have guns?" Cameron asked. Almost everyone raised their hands.

"Then the next question should be. . . Do you know how to use them?" Jake asked. The same amount of hands went into the air.

"My advice is. . . Not to use guns, unless it's absolutely necessary. The police can trace bullets. Therefore, they should be our last line of defense," the 'Bug Man' suggested. For the rest of the meeting, they focused on a plan to deal with the invaders.

Before the meeting ended, everyone was in complete agreement, promising that everything said and done by the group would be a secret. The men who they did not invite to participate in the meeting were too drunk, too dumb, or too scared to get involved, according to Jake. Although Cameron encouraged the men to fight back, he did not want them to do so in an overt manner. In assigning schedules and tasks, Cameron realized that most of the men in the group had families that depended on them, and he would do everything he could to respect their roles as fathers and husbands by protecting their relationships and their identity no matter what.

For weeks, the men of Buttermilk Bottom waited for the intruders to return. Everyone talked and speculated about the new attitude of the men of their community. It was apparent that something dangerous and wonderful was about to happen, but nobody knew what. The men were careful not to discuss any of the details with wives, children, and friends, speaking only of the group's activities when they were alone. By going over the details and plans hundreds of times, they made certain nothing would go wrong. The men knew their duties and their stations, whenever the intruders returned; the group would be ready to act. Waiting was all that remained for the group to do.

It was late in the evening when Cameron came into the juke joint looking for Jake. He was not surprised to find Jake with the two prostitutes who worked there. There was a third woman with him that he did not know.

"Cameron, this is Pearl. She works here now. Queenie hired her today, nice huh?" Jake said, grinning. "It's getting real busy around here, and she's making herself right at home."

"Jake, can we talk?" Cameron said, beckoning his friend to a quiet corner.

"Sure. What can I do for you, pal?" Jake asked, standing tall on his crutches while smiling handsomely at Pearl.

"I've been wondering if we should have another meeting. It's been almost a month since our last one. It might help to keep everyone on their toes," Cameron suggested.

"That might be a good idea. Tell me. . . Do you think we're ready?"

"No reason why we shouldn't be since everything was covered and reviewed two or three times. I'm hoping the meeting will help take the edge off, easing some of the tension that people are beginning to notice. Plus, it will keep us all focused."

"That sounds great to me."

Queenie heard Cameron's voice and rushed out to greet him. Jake noted the huge change in her demeanor, earlier she seemed withdrawn and depressed. Although he was happy that she was pleasant and cheerful again, he wished her smiles and change of attitude had been for him instead of his best friend. Earlier in the week, she appeared so upset that he went to Cameron and asked that he please, pay the woman more attention.

"I would do it myself if she would let me, but she wants you."

"I told you before, I don't want any complications because she may get the wrong idea," Cameron said.

"She had the wrong idea the first day you moved in. . . Nothing's changed. You have yourself to blame for that," Jake said.

"I only did what you or any other man would do under the same circumstances."

"I know that but the difference is. . . She's in love with you."

"That's why I'm trying to cool it with her. I told you before that I'm not in love with her."

"Did you tell her that?" Jake asked.

"Several times."

"To hear her talk, you would think the two of you were ready to march down the aisle."

"Believe me. . . That will never happen. It's only in her mind."

"Maybe you're being too nice about it. You need to tell her how things really are and stop avoiding the problem. Put it to her straight."

"I've done that. She won't listen," Cameron said.

"Try harder."

"I will. Jake, I know you have a thing for her. . . So, why are you encouraging me to see her?"

"Because that's what she wants."

"Have you told her how you feel?"

"No, she's not ready to hear anything from me. She's too gone on you to see anybody else."

"How long do you plan to wait?"

"As long as it takes," Jake said seriously.

"Are you sure you want to do that?"

"I don't have a choice. . . I'm in love with her."

"I really feel bad knowing that."

"Hey, don't. I'm a big boy and I can take it. Besides, I would never want to force myself on her or have you, force the idea of me on her. I could have gone to Miss Cigam for a brew, but I don't want that either. She has to want me, if it is going to work at all. Hell, it may take years for her to come around. No sense in you not taking advantage of all that loving. If it were me, I wouldn't hesitate. Besides, I'm getting all the pussy I want."

"Are you sure about this? The last thing I want to do is hurt you."

"You can't do that because it's not up to you. . . It's the situation and we both know that. What's needed here is a change in attitude and that will take time."

"You're talking about your legs?" Cameron asked, appreciating his friend's insight.

"Sure. She can't see herself loving a cripple man."

"You really aren't cripple, Jake. You do more than men with two good legs."

"Hell, I know that. The problem is convincing her that I am just as much a man as anyone else and that includes your lucky ass."

After his talk with Jake, Cameron made up his mind to get everything straight with Queenie, for the last time. They had the same talk many times, but it seemed that he always had to repeat it. He enjoyed being with her, but he also knew there would be no future for them. In fact, he had no desire to marry or be in love with anyone.

"I have that bottle of wine you like so much," Queenie offered.

"Is it chilled?"

"Chilled and waiting."

"Good, I'm a bit thirsty," he said.

"So am I," she said, leading him up the steps to her quarters. Once inside her beautifully decorated quarters, Cameron attempted to set the record straight. "Queenie, we need to talk."

"You're sounding mighty serious," she said.

"That's because I am."

"Please, let's not get into anything too heavy tonight. I've been waiting a long time to be with you."

"We need to be clear about a few things. This will only take a few minutes." She knew he would be scampering out the door, as soon as he could manage an exit.

"I love being with you because you are a very sexy and attractive woman. I enjoy making love to you, but I don't want a full-time, serious relationship with anyone, no entanglements, remember?"

She had heard all of this before and it was never easy to hear it. She just wanted the conversation to end. "We really don't need to get into this tonight," she said.

"I think we do. You keep telling people that you love me. . . I'm flattered, but I can't return your feelings and the last thing I want to do is to hurt you. You are a wonderful woman and a lot of fun to be with, but I don't love you."

"I can't help the way I feel about you," she said.

"And. . . I can't make myself love you because it's what you want. I told you from the beginning that I am only offering friendship. You have to understand that."

"I understand that, and to be honest with you. . . I'm sick of hearing it."

He waited for her anger to subside. "I don't want to lie to you, Queenie. I love having sex with you, but that is as far as it goes."

"Do you think you could grow to love me?"

"I wouldn't count on it."

"Then, I'll just have to wait and see. I can wait," she said.

"I don't want you to wait. I want you to understand. We can be friends and nothing more."

"Can we continue to be close, loving friends?" she asked, feeling an urgent need to be near him.

"We can be close friends who make love occasionally."

"Tonight?" she said as she started unbuttoning her blouse, displaying her plump breasts.

"I don't see why not."

"Then pour me a glass of that wine. . . So I can get started being your good, loving friend."

"As long as we understand each other."

"I won't lie to you, Cameron. I don't like it, but I'll accept it."

"Friends?"

"Loving friends," she said, kissing him finally and completely on the lips.

During the next few months, Cameron was spending less time with Queenie. She knew it and everyone else in the Bottom knew it, too. Despite that fact, she continued to fictionalize their relationship, making it more than it was. The night he finally showed up to make love to her was no exception. He only spent two hours with her, leaving her wanting him so much she almost broke down in front of him, but her pride sustained her, allowing her to appear strong and in control as he dressed, kissed her, and left her quarters.

Frustrated, Queenie found that she could not sleep, so she went downstairs to socialize. She found Dellah and Pearl with Luther, cleaning up from the night's activities. When she was completely down the steps, she saw Lucille, laying on three bar stools, sound asleep, snoring, as if she was home in her own bed.

"Will someone please wake her drunk-ass up, so she can take her ass home?" Queenie asked.

"I ain't touchin' her. D' last time I tried t' wake her ass up. . . I got punched in d' face," Luther said.

"Yeah, dat woman's dangerous," Dellah said.

"Why did you let her sit there until she got drunk?" Queenie blasted Luther.

"Let her? I didn't pour d' shit down her damn throat, Queenie," he said angry that she was blaming him for Lucille's bad judgment. "She sit here all day ev'ryday, drinkin' dat hooch, and eatin' them damn pickled pig feet 'til she pass out. She pays cash money, so why would I stop her?"

"Now, she's passed out and smellin' like a drunken pig," Pearl said, laughing.

"She ate a whole gallon jar o' pig feet last week and didn't even git sick," Dellah volunteered. Just then, Lucille farted loud and long. The smell immediately filled the room, sending everyone scrambling for space and fresh air.

"Oh. . . Shit," Luther said, trying to get away from Lucille's foul smell.

"My God. . . Somebody open the damn door," Queenie yelled.

"I'll open it because I'm stayin' out there til' the smell dies down," Pearl said, running for the door with her nose covered.

"Damn. . . She smell like she been eatin' old black-eyed peas or somethin'," Dellah said, waving her hand across her nose. Just then, Lucille farted again and made everyone gasp for air. "Dat bitch stank."

"Luther, did you send for her daughter?" Queenie asked.

"Sho did. She tried t' wake her ass up, but Lucille kept right on shorin' jes like she's doin' ret now."

Defeated, Queenie said, "At least get those damn bones off the bar, it looks awful."

Dellah started to laugh hysterically, saying. "He done tried dat fifty times, but she kept on cursing his ass out and chasing him away," Dellah said, defending Luther. "Dat woman's got a mouth on her."

"I wuz tryin' t' wait t' make sure she wuz sound asleep 'fore touchin' them bones." After a few minutes, Luther quietly cleaned the bones off the bar in front of Lucille.

"Looks like she's gonna be here all fucking night, close up and throw a blanket over her drunken ass. I'd sure like to know how she manages to sleep on three bar stools?" Queenie said, shaking her head.

"'Cause she's a drunk. Drunks kin sleep any damn where," Dellah said.

"All we can do is. . . Turn the lights out. Looks like we have an unwanted guest for breakfast," Queenie said, climbing the steps.

"That's just what we need. . . T' see Lucille's ugly ass face first thang in d' damn mornin' wit our bacon and eggs," Dellah complained.

Queenie went into her son's room to tuck him in bed. It was one of the simple things that she loved that had no complications or hidden agendas. Her love for him was the only thing in her life that she knew she could depend on. Everything else in her life came with a struggle and ended up with her fighting for her own survival. In her son's room, she could be certain of his love and faith in her. Sleeping soundly with the covers hanging off the bed, she wondered where his dreams took him to create so much activity in his sleep. She smiled as she placed the covers on him. Suddenly, she became depressed, wondering if she would ever have the life she wanted with Cameron. Tears began falling down her face, as she acknowledged to herself for the first time that he was slipping away from her. Her heart seemed to turn over inside her, making her grieve for the life she wanted with him. She sat on Tony's bed, picked him up, and held him in her arms. He was getting bigger every minute. He felt good as she cuddled him to her breasts, a place he no longer needed or wanted to be. Time had taken him away from her because he was an independent spirit with a life and friends of his own. Buttermilk Bottom had been a great place for him to grow up because there were so many children to play with and everybody looked out for the children. They could play safely in the streets under the watchful eye of the whole community.

Tony woke up and smiled at his mother.

"Mom, is the Bug Man still here?"

"No, baby."

"You gonna marry him?" he asked, wiping the sleep out of his eyes.

Her first impulse was to tell him yes because that was what she wanted most in the world, but she could not lie to her son, so she took a deep breath and said, "We'll see."

"I like d' Bug Man, Mommy. He kin beat anybody in d' whole wide world."

"You may be right, sweetie. Now, get under the covers and go back to sleep."

"I love you, Mommy."

"I love you, too," she said, kissing his already sleeping eyes.

On the West Side of town, Grace was busy socializing with her professional friends, dressed in formal attire attending a yearly extravaganza given by her sorority.

"It was a marvelous evening," Grace said to one of her sorority sisters as she descended the steps of the Municipal Auditorium, following the Fashionatta, an annual fundraising event featuring students from the local colleges. She asked Cameron to escort her, but he declined because the year before he felt out of place as Grace's friend quizzed him regarding his occupation. It was apparent that their inquiries embarrassed Grace because she immediately changed the subject out of fear that he might respond truthfully.

"Yes, it was. I hope you and Horace will join us for an after-hours social at my house," Rebecca Livingston, one of Black Atlanta's richest socialites said. She openly flirted with Horace Singleton, Grace's escort and co-worker, while standing next to her jealous and aging husband.

"I'm sorry, we won't be able to attend but thank you for the invitation," Grace said, smiling and knowing that she was preventing Rebecca from spending the evening, trying to charm her handsome date.

"We are hosting a kick-off reception for the voter registration drive at our house next Saturday evening. I hope you and Horace will be able to attend. We need all the support we can get," Rebecca said, smiling at Horace, who did not appear to notice or hear their conversation.

"I'm sorry but we already have a commitment for that date but thank you so much for the invitation," Grace said. "It's a wonderful thing that you and your husband are doing. The Voter's League needs your support, and we all need to get as many of our people registered for the up-coming election. Starting next week, my civic committee will be coordinating a drive for the West Side."

"It was a miracle that the Supreme Court ruled in our favor. It only took twenty years to convince them that we were right," Rebecca's husband injected.

"It's time for things to change. . . Thanks to the NAACP," Grace said.

"If you change your minds about Saturday, please do not hesitate to attend," Rebecca said, looking candidly at Horace.

"Good night, we really had a wonderful time," Grace said, taking Horace's arm, as he escorted her to his car.

Once they were in the car, Horace said, "Thank you for getting me out of that situation. I don't think Rebecca's husband would have appreciated my presence."

"Just remember, you owe me one. I thought she was going to pluck you right off my arm," Grace said, laughing.

"Would you have been disappointed if she had?" Horace asked with a serious tone to his voice as he drove down Edgewood Avenue.

"No woman likes to be abandoned in the middle of the street," Grace responded, trying to make light of the situation.

"If it were left up to me, I would never leave your side for any reason," Horace said, holding her hand.

"And give up your status as the most eligible bachelor in Atlanta?" she teased.

"In a heartbeat," he said, kissing her fingertips.

"I could never live with myself if I took you away from your public. I know a few women by name, who would cut my throat if they even suspected that I was out with you."

"I could be happy with just you at my side," he said, squeezing her hand. "And. . . I could make you very happy. . . If you would only give me a chance to prove it."

"I'm sorry, Horace. I told you. I'm already involved with someone."

"You're speaking of Cameron Fielding that ex-football coach?"

"We've been seeing each other for some time now."

"Why didn't you ask him to escort you tonight?"

"We had a scheduling conflict."

"Another one of those. . . I see." The remainder of the ride was quiet. When they arrived at Grace's house, Horace escorted her to the door. "Are you going to invite me in for a night cap?"

"It's late, maybe some other time. . . But thank you for taking me."

"It was my pleasure," Horace said, taking a deep breath. The moment he attempted to kiss her on the lips, she turned her head. "What? No good night kiss?"

"I'm in love with someone else, Horace."

The pain in his heart began to tighten as he looked into Grace's blind eyes. He shook his head. "Good night, Grace," he said, kissing her on the cheek before turning to leave.

As Grace watched him drive away, she thought, how wonderful it would have been if Cameron could escort her on special occasions. His lifestyle no longer fit her circle of professional friends and colleagues because he stubbornly refused to seek re-instatement in the public school system. Knowing that he would be over the next day, she planned to broach the subject once more.

As Horace drove away, he could not help but be disappointed because his vision for his evening with Grace did not materialize as he expected it to. When she first asked him to escort her, he was thrilled because he attempted on several occasions to ask her out on a date, but she always refused. The day she asked him to accompany her to her social, she explained, very clearly, that she was dating someone else. This was a fact he knew because everyone on staff knew of her love affair with Cameron Fielding. Everyone knew his history as a football coach and everyone knew he spent a year in jail and lost his teaching license because of it. What Horace could not understand was Grace's continued support and infatuation with him. It was obvious that they were living in two different worlds and that it embarrassed her to be with him in public. No matter how many times Horace told himself to forget Grace, he found himself accepting her invitations to escort her, whenever she needed him. He also found himself wanting and needing to love her, which started the day she walked into his school as the new principal. For him, it was love at first sight.

From the first moment that he accepted Grace's invitation, Horace instinctively knew that her relationship with Cameron Fielding was one-sided because there was no ring and no plans for a wedding. He believed that it was just a matter of time before he could convince Grace that he was more worthy. Knowing that his feelings would not go away, he took every opportunity to be around Grace at work where he spent just as much time in her office as he did his own. When he knew she was working through lunch, he would bring her a tray from the cafeteria. It frustrated him that she relegated him as her formal escort and expected him to leave her at the door with a handshake, but he could never say no to her. He refused her several times but gave in when she pleaded with him, saying she had no one else to ask so he took out his tuxedo, picked her up and escorted her to the fashionatta.

Carrie, Grace's best friend, transferred to her school as soon as Grace got the appointment as principal. The first time Carrie saw Horace, she tried to date him herself but found out quickly that he was only interested in Grace. Carrie pleaded with Grace to go out with Horace.

"I'm still seeing Cameron."

"You hardly see the man. You know he sees other women. . . So why are you so loyal to him?"

"Because I love him," she said plainly.

"You are a fool. You always were when it came to him. Not that I blame you, the man is gorgeous, but Horace is good looking too. He's well dressed, plus he has plenty of money. His family has money, and he has that big, beautiful home out on Mosley Drive."

"I'm not interested in what he has. . . The fact is. . . I only care about Cameron. He'll have all those things one of these days."

"After his next trip to jail? You know that's where he's going if he doesn't stop hanging around Buttermilk Bottom."

"Don't say that."

"Why not? It's the truth. He was looking for trouble the day he moved down there, and you know it." Grace did not respond because she agreed with her best friend. "Why don't you at least give Horace a chance?"

"Because for the last time. . . I'm in love with Cameron."

"I give up. How long are you going to wait for him?"

"As long as it takes."

A month later, on a Friday night, about ten o'clock in the evening, the truckload of white men came rumbling into The Bottom, loud and drunk, firing guns in the air. The dust from the truck's speeding wheels floated high into the balmy summer air. As they sped through the mucky streets, their rebel yell reached everyone's ear in the community. Most people turned their house lights out to avoid attracting attention. It was well-known that if the men could not find anyone on the streets, they would raid someone's home and drag them out into the streets, sometimes using ropes, other times using their bare hands. Either way, when they came thundering in, someone was going to get hurt.

The white rebels yelled their familiar blood-chilling cry used by their ancestors a century earlier to raise fear and dread throughout the Black community. Blasting their guns off in the air, the rebels had no knowledge of the trap the men of The Bottom had waiting for them. Their plan was to give the white invaders a first and last warning that the people of Buttermilk Bottom was off limits. As soon as the truck drove onto the dark dirt road, a group of men quietly laid multiple lines of barbed wire on the ground. Behind the curtain of wire, they placed several barrels filled with dirt and rocks to block the entrance and to prevent anyone from leaving. As the white rebels drove into the community, the tires of their truck rode over more lines of barbwire, causing their tires to blow out. The truck swayed out of control propelled by the high speed and flattened tires. The group of rebels became quiet.

With faces, darkened with soot and dressed in dark clothing, the men of Buttermilk Bottom appeared out of the black starless night. There were no streetlights in Buttermilk Bottom except for one at the entrance, at the top of the hill. The word went out to all the residents, that once the rebels returned, they were to cooperate by darkening their apartments and without knowing why, they cooperated, adding to the invaders' dilemma.

The white invaders clinched their teeth as they tried to avoid colliding into the massive barricade they discovered in front of them. Their truck screeched to a halt, but found that their attempt to maneuver away from danger only led them into more barrels stacked up in the middle of the road completely restricting their movement. As the truck screeched to a halt, after sliding into the first obstruction, the men of the community quickly moved in, grabbing the men from the truck. Once they had the shocked invaders on the ground, they began beating them with axe handles that someone had confiscated from a local lumberyard. The rebel yells had quickly turned into cowardly whimpers and calls for help as the axe-handles came plummeting down on their heads, backs, and backsides. When the men of the committee were satisfied that the invaders had learned their lessons, they stopped the beatings.

"If you want to live, don't you ever come here again," Cameron said, kicking one of the men in the stomach. "We won't be this nice the next time. Now, get the fuck out of here and stay out."

The defeated rebels tried to climb back onto their truck, but the men of the committee beat them down, not allowing them access to their truck. They made them crawl out on their hands and knees as the men continued to beat them until they were certain that the radicals were out of their community. Their truck and guns remained in Buttermilk Bottom. They also left behind a new sense of pride and ownership, which made the men stand taller as they meandered back down the dirt roads.

For several hours following the incident, the men waited impatiently, watching the newspapers, the television, and listening to the radio for a report regarding the beating of the white rebels. They heard nothing and the police never came to ask questions. Morning came but nothing happened and the rebels did not return.

The smell of bacon and coffee awakened all the residents of the juke joint, including Tony, Queenie's son, who always managed to get to the table before anyone else. He dressed himself and ran downstairs where he received warm affectionate hugs from Cora Lee and Addie Mae. The two women took charge of him whenever Queenie was busy working or sleeping late.

The dining room was the central meeting room for all the residents in the house. Tony was one of the privileged few that Cora Lee allowed in her kitchen. He learned how to play games, how to count money, and how to read and write at her big preparation table. He drew pictures and sang songs with Cora Lee and Addie Mae, who stood over him like two mother hens, cheering him on. Whenever Cora Lee baked bread or cookies, she would allow Little Tony to help and never seemed to mind the big mess he made.

No matter what Cora Lee prepared for breakfast, she always made his favorite, pancakes, which she prepared that morning along with bacon, eggs, sausage, biscuits, and grits. Once she cooked it, she set it on the table in the dining room, where everyone gathered for meals. After making him say his blessing, she allowed him to start without the others, who usually drifted in slowly, one after the other.

"I swear dat boy kin eat flapjacks ev'ry day," she said, watching and enjoying him as he stuffed the light fluffy pancakes into his mouth.

"He sho' is growin' up fast," Addie Mae said.

"Looks like he's d' only child dat we's gonna git so we might as well enjoy him."

"I's gonna keep spoilin' him as long as Queenie allow us to. By d' way, there's a carnival on Highland Avenue. We kin take him Sunday after church," Addie Mae said.

"A carnival? I ain't been t' one o' dem in years. Tony, ya wanna go t' a carnival?" Cora Lee asked.

"What we gonna do at a carnival?" he asked, pouring more syrup on to his pancakes.

"We's gonna ride a big old' wheel dat goes 'round in d' sky, eat cotton candy, 'n see lots o' clowns," Addie Mae explained.

"Dat sounds like fun," he said as his mother came into the dining room looking for coffee. "Mom, can I go to the' carnival with Aunt Cora Lee and Aunt Addie Mae?"

"Sure."

"I want to see the clowns."

"That's nice," she said, distracted.

"What wrong wit you dis mornin'?" Cora Lee asked Queenie.

"I'm fine."

"You sho' don't sound fine."

"I'm fine, really."

Dellah and Azalene came in following the scent of food. Dellah asked, "Did ya'll hear 'bout d' ass whippin that Cameron and Cripple Jake put on dem white boys last night?"

"What happened?" Everyone asked at once.

"It wuz all a big secret. They been waitin' fo'dem white boys t' show up agin. . . 'Cause they had somethin' special waitin' fo' 'em," Azalene said, jumping up and down.

"What?" Queenie asked. She perked up as soon as she heard Cameron's name.

"We heard dat Cripple Jake and Cameron been plannin' dis fo' a long time. Last night when dem white boys showed up. . . Dey beat d' shit out o' 'em and sent dem runnin' d' fuck outta here," Dellah related.

"Watch yo' language in front o' d' boy," Cora Lee said.

"Sorry, I forgot, but dey said that our men beat 'em so bad dey ain't never gonna come here agin."

"They even took them white boys' truck," Azalene added.

"What?" Queenie asked.

"They been plannin' dis fo' months from what I hear," Dellah said.

"And. . . They been waitin' fo 'em t' come back. Then, Wham! They beat d' shit out o' dem white mutherfuckers wit axe handles," Azalene said, getting up out of her chair to role-play their actions. "Sorry, Cora Lee, but it's 'bout time somebody did somethin' t' dem fuckin' bastards."

"Amen t' dat," Cora Lee said, sitting down at the table, laughing at Azalene. "It's strange dat d' police didn't come down here lookin' fo' somebody t' put in jail."

"Yeah. . . Real strange," Dellah agreed.

"Maybe not," Addie Mae said. "Dem white boys don't want nobody t' know dey got their asses whipped by a bunch o' niggers."

"Addie Mae," Cora Lee admonished.

"Sorry, but it's 'bout time somebody did somethin' t' dem fuckin' crackers."

"You may be right," Queenie said, thinking that maybe that was the reason Cameron was not coming around more because he was busy planning a complicated plot against the white rebels. It must have taken a lot of planning to pull that off. She began to feel better, knowing there was a reasonable explanation for his absence from her bed, and she was very proud of what he did.

That incident began one of many tales that circulated among the residents of Buttermilk Bottom regarding the heroism of Cameron, Cripple Jack, and their team of enforcers.

Chapter 5

During the spring, the city of Atlanta was overwhelmingly green and beautiful. The fragrant blossoms of the dogwood trees lingered with the scent of tall pine trees that were ever-present in the cool, relaxed southern air. The people of the sunken community enjoyed a welcomed sense of relaxation because they no longer feared walking on the dirt roads late at night that led to the shotgun shell shacks that they called home.

For the next several years, the word spread about the men of Buttermilk Bottom standing up to the gang of white men who terrorized their community for many years. Several residents remembered the night that they watched the incident with the white rebels while peeping from their porches or living room windows in fear that the forces would turn, causing injury to their friends, but that did not happen. Instead, the men of their community were triumphant. It was the first time in anyone's memory that the men fought back against the white night-time invaders. People began to smile broadly whenever they saw Cameron or Jake on the streets as freshly baked pies and cakes appeared on their doorsteps, tokens of gratitude from those who benefited from their leadership, a role they did not want. Cameron's solution to this unwanted and unsolicited attention was to stay in his apartment and wallow in the anonymous life style he craved, which was short lived.

During Cameron's residency in the sunken community, he enjoyed a fair amount of peace and quiet, barring a few fights that neighbors called upon him to stop. Most people stopped their inappropriate behavior whenever hearing Cameron's name. He was enjoying a relatively peaceful existence after all the gossip died down about his involvement in the ousting of the white invaders from the neighborhood. A year later, a major incident occurred that hurled his reputation even higher. The incident affected all residents of Buttermilk Bottom and sparked more tales of bravery and leadership about Cripple Jake and Cameron. A man called Blackie became a target of the committee's attention because he was terrorizing his own people. Blackie and his gang of young thieves ranged in ages from sixteen to thirty. They robbed and beat people in order to take what little possessions their neighbors had.

It first came to Cameron's attention when the twin sisters who lived in one of his two downstairs apartments had their radio stolen for the second time that year. It was only the month of March, which meant the thieves were hitting people frequently. As Cameron was collecting the rent, he could see that the old women were visibly upset.

"What's wrong?" he asked.

"They stole our radio again," Essie said.

"It had to be Blackie and his gang; that's the second time this year. In the past two years, they stole two radios, silver, jewelry, and what little money we had in the house," Gussie said tearfully.

"Did you report it to the police?" he asked.

They both looked at him in disbelief. "When have the police ever come down here?" Essie said.

"They only come down here if someone gits killed or stabbed," Gussie said.

"There must be something you can do?" Cameron said.

"We's got to go buy us a new radio. We like listenin' at the Guiding Light every day, and we don't want to miss that, do we, Gussie?"

"Thank God, they didn't find our rent money this time," Essie said.

"Thank God, indeed," Gussie agreed.

"Don't buy a radio just yet. I'll get back to you by tonight. In the meantime, you can use my radio."

"Oh, we couldn't do that," they said together.

"Sure, you can. I rarely listen to it anyway."

"Thank you, Cameron. You're the best landlord we ever had," Essie said.

"Don't worry. I'll look into it for you. I'll be right back with my radio."

"Thank you, Cameron," they said together.

When Cameron's home-boy arranged for him to purchase the four-unit apartment building from him, Cameron never knew what to expect, or what owning a building involved. He had to collect the rent, which went to help pay for repairs, along with other bills pertaining to the building's maintenance. What he did not realize was that he had to do all the repairs on the building and there were many. Most of his time, he spent repairing toilets, sinks, and electrical wiring for the three tenants who occupied the building. He had never changed a washer in a faucet before moving to The Bottom. On many occasions, he called on Moses to help him make necessary repairs and to assist him in putting a new roof on the building. Moses gave Cameron a number of books on property maintenance, which he greatly appreciated. Even with his number business growing rapidly, he had to make time to manage his property. Cameron found that he loved working on the house and looked forward to spending time with Moses on one project or another to improve the appearance of the building. What he enjoyed most was seeing the final product of their labor.

After Cameron gave the twins his radio, he went to look for Jake. He had to find out about Blackie and his gang. It angered him that black men would steal from their own people, especially the adorable elderly twins. The angrier he got the more determined his steps became as he crossed the street to the juke joint. He opened the door of the once beautiful house, in such a way that it attracted everyone's attention. Jake was sitting with his two prostitute friends, who were laughing hysterically at his jokes.

When Jake saw the expression on Cameron's face, he said, "What the fuck is wrong with you?"

"We need to talk."

"Sit down and take a load off."

"This is private," Cameron said, walking out the door as vibrantly as he entered it.

"I'll be back in a minute," Jake said quickly to the women, grabbing his crutches and following his best friend out the door.

Outside on the porch, Cameron looked around to see if anyone was around to over-hear them. Certain that they were alone he asked, "Who the fuck is Blackie?"

"That creep? What do you want with him?"

"I want to know who he is and where I can find him."

"Sure, as soon as you tell me why you're so pissed."

"I want to know because he just stole a radio from the twins. It's the second time this year, plus they tell me that he's been ripping them off for years, as well as everybody else around here."

"That's true but nobody can prove anything. They wait until everybody goes out, then they sneak in the back and take what they want. In a flash, they disappear with the goods. We've complained to the police, but those fuckers aren't gonna do anything to stop them. It is a nigger problem. They're just not interested."

"I'm interested."

"What the fuck does that mean?"

"Jake, get the men together in one hour. They have stolen their last radio around here. I'm getting kind of sick of the helpless attitudes in this neighborhood," Cameron said, annoyed and angry. "Jake, people can't give up without attempting to work on a solution to the problem. As I see it, you have to keep digging until you find a way out of the situation or die trying." He crossed the street and headed back to his apartment.

The men finally gathered in Cameron's apartment and sat around mumbling about Blackie and his gang. Everybody had a complaint and everybody had been his victim in one-way or another. Blackie's gang had not only robbed their houses; they robbed them personally with a gun or with a knife pointed at their heads or backs. Usually, they worked in teams of three or four. Blackie, they said, rarely did anything except to fence the stolen items.

"We are going to put them out of business," Cameron said.

"How we gonna do dat? D' police said we need proof," someone said.

"We are the fucking police down here. You know who's stealing from you, and you know where they live. As far as I'm concerned, it's a done deal. You have just sat here and told me all the horrors these men have created for you and your families. You even know the motherfuckers' first and last names. All that remains is to decide how we're going to put them out of business. When is already taken care of because we are hitting them tonight. We can't sit by and let our own people fall prey to thieves in our own race. We are not animals. We are men and we will fight like men to protect what's ours."

"Blackie got guns," someone said.

"We have guns. . . And we have something he doesn't have, the element of surprise," Cameron reminded them.

For over two hours, the men sat and plotted what they were going to do. At eleven o'clock, they left Cameron's apartment quietly dressed in black with faces covered again in black soot, and they all wore some kind of hat.

Blackie lived in a neglected building, on a rarely used road behind the juke joint. There was nothing much back there except old abandoned garages and some broken down unoccupied buildings that sat directly across from Blackie's place. The men waited as Moses and Cameron went to check the place out. Moses said, on his return to the group, "They's all there 'cept fo' Lil' Man. They's sittin' watchin' TV and guzzlin' down beer."

"The first thing we need to do is to cut off the electricity. The darker. . . The better," Cameron said.

"I kin do dat," said a young man that everyone called 'Smoke' because he always had a cigarette in his mouth.

"They have a rear entrance so half of you go around the back. The other half, come with me," Cameron directed. "As soon as the lights are out, we'll make our move. Everybody knows what to do?" They all nodded and went to their stations.

There were sixteen men with Cameron and Jake, who stood ready to launch an attack on the eight thieves inside the shabby shack. With Jake standing right behind his best friend, they waited for the lights to go out. Listening to the noise the thieves made inside the run-down dirty shack, the two groups of men waited for the signal. Their own shallow breathing complimented the smell of adrenaline pumping through their veins. The wait was longer than they expected because when Smoke went to cut off the electricity he found that Blackie had an illegal connection. He was stealing electricity from the house in the back of him. Instead of cutting the electric off, Smoke went to the owners' house and asked the occupant if he could cut their electric off. They protested until Smoke showed them Blackie and his gang's illegal hookup that allowed them to steal electricity. The couple gladly consented after that.

When the lights finally went out, the men inside started to curse. "What happened t' d' fuckin' lights?" one man asked.

"How d' fuck I know?" Blackie responded.

Just then, Cameron and his men burst into the shack hurling their axe handles. They swung at everything that moved. They maintained a circle around the men to guarantee that none of them got hurt in the mayhem while standing shoulder to shoulder. They delivered their brutal punishment on the thieves. The thieves cursing changed to pleas for mercy, which the men ignored as they continued their attack. After everyone was down on the floor, hurting and crying, the men pulled all the thieves out of the building into the moonlight.

"You have been tried and found guilty of stealing, beating, and assaulting the people of this community. We are giving you ten minutes to get the fuck out of Buttermilk Bottom and never come back. If, even one of you, ever come back. . . We will hunt every one of you down wherever you are and kill your sorry asses, no questions asked."

"Why ya'll beatin'. . . ." Wham! Went the sound as an axe handle cracked over Blackie's head.

"Shut the fuck up. I am not your friend, and we are not having a discussion. Your crimes against your own people have ended. We are here to execute your sentence, which is to throw you the fuck out of Buttermilk Bottom. Now, get the fuck out," Cameron yelled.

Some of the beaten and badly bruised thieves struggled to their feet, while others crawled away from the crazed men. The civic group walked right behind them, not speaking a word, as the broken criminals inched and struggled to get out of 'The Bottom'. When they were well out of the area, the men stood watching as the gang of thieves crept up the hill to get away from their attackers. Cameron left double the usual amount of sentries to stand guard for almost two weeks to make sure the thieves did not return. The day after the thieves' exile from the Bottom, the men took all the stolen merchandise from Blackie's old homestead and placed it in the center of the street. Knocking on every door, they asked people to come out and claim their possessions. At the same time, Cameron instructed the men to burn down all the unoccupied buildings to the ground, including the one that Blackie used with his gang.

The people celebrated Blackie's demise and started an impromptu party, which lasted the whole day. Children were in the streets playing games while their parents sat on their porches with BBQ and anything they had to share with their neighbors. It looked like a family picnic. It was a grand day. Jake sat on Cameron's porch watching the people as they celebrated while the smoke hurled in the air from the dilapidated, burning shacks behind the juke joint. No fire truck came and no police officer came to investigate.

"See, it's a nigger problem. Atlanta has a fatal disease, and it's called chronic segregation. If we don't find a cure for it, the whole city is going to crumble, and it won't be pretty," Jake said, opening the evening Journal.

"Something is bound to clash because we are getting angrier, and they are getting more afraid. The reality is. . . . We are tired of being scared; therefore, we can and will risk everything," said Cameron.

"The evidence of our crisis is in front of us every day."

"Evidence?" Cameron asked.

"Look right here in the Journal. The white man has decided finally that we are human enough to have our death notices publicized in their newspaper. But. . . . See how they insult us. The obituaries got our names at the bottom of the page under the listing of dead white folks separated by a thick black line with the label 'colored' typed over each column. It's bad enough having to drink out of separate fountains labeled 'colored' but this is the epitome of discrimination. Those fools think that there's segregation in heaven," Jake said in disgust.

"Hatred doesn't get any thicker than that."

"It's a slap in the face, man, but they want to call this progress. Look at this shit. They even have the nerve to print a 'Weekly Roundup' for the 'po colored people'. Can you round up all our news in one tiny weekly article? Hell no."

"That's why we need our own newspapers and reporters. We have to value ourselves and not wait for someone else to tell us how important and valuable we are," Cameron said, calmly.

"It's a disease. I'm telling you, racism is a disease."

"We all know that. The problem is taking the cure."

The two best friends sat watching their neighbors celebrate in the midst of substandard conditions characterized by poor city services and unhealthy living conditions, yet they found reasons to rejoice.

A group of Grace's friends purchased a block of tickets to see Hazel Scott in concert at the Wheat Street Baptist Church and planned to go out to dinner following the event. As much as, she wanted to ask Cameron to go, she knew better than to ask him because of the many arguments, she and Cameron had over the subject of her including him in her social engagements with her friends and co-workers. Cameron preferred only spending time alone with Grace, either at her house or a quiet dinner out, followed by an evening of jazz.

Having no choice, Grace called Horace into her office and asked him to attend the affair with her. Knowing that she was still seeing the man from Buttermilk Bottom, Horace hesitated about accepting her invitation, but he still longed to get to know Grace more intimately, outside the work environment, so he consented. During the show, he held her hand, but she always managed to remove it after a few moments. Horace knew all the rumors about the ex-football coach being a racketeer. He heard all the gossip and speculations that he would probably end up back in jail. Following the show, the group went to Frazier's Café Society and had dinner in their private dining room. Acknowledging his deep desire, Horace sat with Grace close to him feeling more convinced than ever that they belonged together. All he needed to do was to convince her of that fact and the two of them could live forever in a state of bliss because he loved her, and he knew he would make her a good husband and an excellent lover.

At dinner, Grace and her friends expressed their joy over the fact that President Truman appointed the first black person as the representative to the United Nations. One of her dinner companions said that they knew Edith Simpson from their college days at New York College, where she was educated and began to show her leadership abilities and intelligence, later becoming a lawyer and a judge. They had a heated discussion about the progress of blacks integrating the city of Atlanta, especially in the Mosley Park area where Horace lived as one of the first blacks in the area.

He said, "When I moved in the 'for sale' signs started going up the next day."

"One sure sign that a neighborhood will be integrated is when black churches start moving into an area. Did you hear? West Hunter Street Baptist Church is moving on Gordon Street."

"If that is the case, the whole neighborhood will be black in a matter of months," one of her colleagues said, laughing.

"You know how whites hate to live on the same street as Negroes," another person said.

For Grace, the evening was all she hoped it would be, but it could have been wonderful if Cameron had been able to escort her. Horace was feeling frustrated but took solace in the fact that he was with the woman he loved. The evening ended rather early with Grace feeling grateful for Horace's presence, so she invited him in for coffee and a slice of chocolate pound cake that she made for Cameron, but he telephoned that he would not be able to see her for another week.

"This is the best cake I've had in years," Horace said, sitting in the living room of Grace's family home on Atlanta's West Side, an area where the majority of upper-middle class blacks resided.

"Thank you, I'm glad you like it. I enjoy baking from time to time," she said, pouring him another cup of coffee.

Horace watched her with mounting interest and passion. It took her years to invite him inside her home, making him feel grateful for the opportunity and optimistic about the possibility of loving her. Not wanting to act too quickly, he asked for a second slice of cake and talked about the evening's activities in hopes of prolonging his visit. He prayed that her invitation meant that she was ready to move forward with a relationship with him instead of her gangster boyfriend whom he heard so much about.

"I have ice cream. Would you like some to go with your cake?" Grace asked.

"What I would like is for you to come over here and sit next to me," he said, patting the sofa cushion next to him.

"Horace, you are a good friend. I don't want to give you the wrong idea."

"Are you still stuck on that gangster?"

"He's not a gangster."

"What does he do for a living?" She was quiet. "Can you honestly tell me that what he does isn't against the law?"

"I can only tell you that I trust him."

"Then you are a fool, Grace. Why are you wasting your life on the likes of him?"

"I love him. I have loved him for a long time."

"But does he love you, Grace?" Horace got up from the sofa and went over to the chair where Grace was sitting, pulled her to a standing position, and held her hand. "Is he willing to marry you?. . . . Have a family with you or dedicate the rest of his life to loving you?" When she did not speak, he continued, "I love you, and I want to marry you. We have known each other for a long time. Grace, you know how I feel about you. I'm willing to wait for you to love me, but you have to wake up. . . . That man can't be in love with you if he's not willing to commit to you."

"Our relationship is difficult to explain to anyone. . . . But the fact remains. . . . I love him."

"Okay. I realize that you are hung up on him, but I also know that I am the best man for you," he said, kissing her hand.

When he tried to pull her to him, she said, "Please don't. I love Cameron."

"Well,. . . I've tried,. . . But I won't give up on you because I know that I am the one who truly loves you. It's a pity you can't see that," he said, taking in a deep breath while trying to control his cravings and emotions. "I love you, Grace." Kissing her lovingly on the lips, he explored the full extent of his feelings for her, but she pushed him away.

"I'm sorry. I can't do this. I wouldn't be truthful if I allowed you to continue. I can't pretend something I don't feel."

"Well, thank you for that. . . But I'm not giving up. I love you." Horace picked up his coat and walked to the door. His eyes caressed her as he admired her small well-formed body.

She began to feel warm inside and said, "Good night, Horace." He kissed her lightly on the lips and left.

Big Moses was bringing Jake and Cameron up to date regarding their surveillance of Buttermilk Bottom. "I placed two men at each station, and they change shifts every two hours instead of four. Nothing's going to happen anywhere without us knowing about it first."

"Sounds great, Moses. Thank you, man," Cameron said.

"The shorter hours will work better because no one wants this to feel like a job, even if it is one," Jake said.

"Got-damn-it. I's so sick o' dem white mutherfuckers. . . I don't know what to do," Moses uttered, becoming suddenly angry.

"What?" The two best friends said at the same time wondering what could be bothering Moses as he quickly stormed away from them. The only white man they saw was the one driving the garbage truck down the road with four black men trailing behind, emptying the garbage from both sides of the road.

"That shit right there," Moses yelled, walking toward the front of the truck.

"What's wrong?" Cameron and Jake asked together.

The sight of the burly six-foot-four man, stomping down the dirt road quickly drew the attention of his neighbors. His big feet transported him to where the moving garbage truck was standing with the white driver sitting comfortably behind the wheel until Moses yelled.

"Git d' fuck out." The stunned driver looked perplexed but Moses did not change his request or his tone of voice the second time he made his demand. On the third time, Moses took out his pistol and pointed his gun at the driver's head. "Git d' fuck out, white man!" The terrified truck driver jumped out of the truck and stood, trembling, and waiting to find out what the angry black man wanted along with everyone else who watched, including Jake and Cameron.

"Git yo' sorry ass back there," Moses yelled, directing the man with his gun to the rear of the truck. The man stumbled several times as he walked backwards, trying to keep his eyes on the gun. "Move, mutherfucker," Moses yelled. The confused man kept moving backwards until Moses seemed satisfied. "Go ahead. . . Pick-up that fuckin' garbage." The man stumbled over a can of smelly garbage and hesitated. "Pick it d' fuck up and throw it in d' truck, bitch." More people gathered and laughed at the spectacle. "I'm sick and tired of seein' you white mutherfuckers sittin' on yo' lazy, white asses while black folks do all d' fuckin' work." The whole community was in an uproar, watching Moses deliver his own sense of justice to an intolerable situation. Moses looked around and asked one of the black garbage-men while still waving his gun, "Do you know how to drive dis mutherfucker?" The man nodded his head yes. "Then git yo' ass up there and drive because dis mutherfucker's gonna do some real work t'day. I'm sick o' dis shit. Move, mutherfucker, you's pickin' up all d' fuckin' garbage t'day and ev'ry day you come here," he said, kicking the man in the behind as he went from one house to another emptying the garbage. As the odd sight proceeded down the dirt road, children and adults followed, laughing hysterically.

"That motherfucker is crazy," Jake said as tears fell from his eyes from laughing so hard.

"Crazy is just another word for tired," Cameron said seriously. The two friends exchanged looks and walked over to the juke joint together.

Chapter 6

At the height of the civil rights movement black civic groups, black churches, and black educational institutions in all the southern states intensified their efforts to organize around the issue of voter registration. States enacted laws to prevent the Negro from exercising their right to vote. In some states, a poll tax prevented many blacks from voting while other states required a literacy test before blacks could exercise their right to vote, which the constitution guaranteed every citizen. According to the census bureau, the state of Georgia had less than 24 percent of its black population registered to vote in comparison with Mississippi at four percent, and Alabama had five percent of its black population exercising their right to vote. In Atlanta, black leaders were more aggressive in the pursuit of civil rights than most southern cities, and they appealed to the colleges and universities to help solve this problem. The response was overwhelming. Students on college campuses organized and began canvassing neighborhoods to rectify that wrong. It was their contagious enthusiasm, which spread rapidly through the black community. People appreciated their determination, courage, and leadership. Those not informed about the privileges of citizenship denied to them were especially grateful for the student's help.

Nine years after Cameron move to The Bottom, the college and university students entered Buttermilk Bottom with their youthful enthusiasm and their deep desire to make changes for the Negro in America. They sat on porches and steps of the neglected neighborhood and discussed personal freedom and civil rights to people who had no conception of the problem and complexities of attaining their rights as citizens. Very few of the residents could respond in any meaningful way, but they listened and smiled a lot because they were proud of the students.

The students were having no success in getting anyone to sign the voter registration forms until someone directed them to 'the Sheriff'.

"If he say it's okay then people will sign yo' paper," one woman told them.

The students descended on Cameron's apartment and found a person that they quickly interpreted as a very dangerous man. When the spokesperson for the students began to speak, he found out how dangerous. As soon as he started by telling Cameron what his responsibilities were to the community, he silenced him with a steady cold gaze that made the boy forget what he wanted to say. Cameron's gaze was so paralyzing that the boy backed all the way behind the group he was supposed to be leading. The boy meant no harm. It was the canned speech he normally gave when trying to convince community leaders of their duties to their neighbors. Cameron, who still had not spoken, looked at each of the students in the same threatening manner. The room was completely quiet because no one dared to utter a word. The group waited nervously for Cameron to speak.

"Some of the people here are uninformed and uneducated, but they are not stupid. Give them respect and speak to them as you would your own parents." He looked directly at the boy who retreated to the back of the group. "Explain to them what you want from them in very simple terms, and they will respond."

"But they won't sign the paper, unless you say it's alright," another student said.

"They don't need anyone's permission to do anything. That is the reason you came here, isn't it?" The students nodded their heads. "Then tell them that."

"What if they don't sign the forms?"

"It may take you a few more minutes, but if you talk to them long enough you may find that they can't read or write." The students looked stunned. "So, you may need to give them a little homework before they will be able to sign their names."

The students left Cameron's apartment with a new perspective and a plan to spend more time in Buttermilk Bottom. In the following weeks, the residents welcomed students and children followed the students everywhere they went. All was going well until late one night the police stopped the group of students. It was unfortunate for the students because the police officers that stopped them had bad reputations and long records of abusive behaviors toward blacks. The police officers using their spotlight made the students stand against the wall with their arms, and legs stretched out. When one of the young men questioned the police about why they stopped them, the shortest officer hit him with his Billy club. The boy fell to the ground, and when his friends attempted to help him, they threatened them with a promise of abuse. The students stood against the wall, posed with their hands up and their legs stretched out, while one of the police officers accused them of inciting a riot and various other offenses as he walked back and forth, looking over the group. Suddenly, he began to laugh with his partner, but the students had no idea why they were laughing. The short, fat officer walked over to one of the girls, and placed his hands under her dress. When one of the boys tried to intervene, the other officer hit him on the head with his billy club, causing him to fall helplessly to the ground next to his classmate.

The fat officer touched the remainder of the girls in the same way then his partner grinned and said, "Alright now, it's my turn."

Standing up, the fat officer laughed and said, "Black women sho' have some fat pussies."

Suddenly, there was the sound of a loud gunshot. Cameron with his men posed behind him, appeared out of the darkness. One of the sentries ran to organize the men as soon as the officers stopped the students. The officers froze when they turned around and saw the group of black men behind him with shotguns and axe handles. Backing away from the students, they attempted to intimidate the men, but quickly fell silent when they saw the strength and anger in the men's eyes. The next, moment, someone knocked the spot light out. The police officers felt the pains of the axe handles crushing down on the heads and fell to the ground, losing consciousness.

Cameron gave the students a steely look then told them to go home and forget everything that they heard and saw. "Nothing happened here. Go home and when you come back let us know when you are in the area, so that we can look out for you. In the future, leave here before darkness comes."

"Thank you," the student cried out.

The boys shook everyone's hands and the girls cried and hugged each of them. When one of the girls attempted to put her arms around Cameron's neck, he pushed her away, saying, "Get out of here now, and don't look back." They thanked them again, but he said in a serious tone that made them tremble, "None of this ever happened."

Because of the strained relationship between Buttermilk Bottom and the local police station, Cripple Jake made it his business to know every police officer that worked in their precinct, and they knew him. His relationship with the officers was critical since the disappearance of two police officers. Cripple Jake along with the men of Buttermilk Bottom happily disposed of the two bodies and the police officers' vehicle where it would stay for an eternity, covered in kudzu vines.

Cripple Jake made it easy for the police to talk to him, because he needed something from them, information. They loved his humor and the twisted way he viewed local dramas that unfolded every weekend on the unpaved streets of Buttermilk Bottom. The police relied on him, whenever they needed information or when they needed a safe escort in and out of 'The Bottom'. One thing that the police did not know was that Jake only gave partial information, half-truths, and lies. Jake's purpose for his frequent appearances in the police station was to gather information not to give any, and he always came away with much more than he gave, but he always left the policeman laughing hysterically.

"Did I ever tell ya'll 'bout d' fat alligator and d' skinny alligator?" Jake said, noticing the presence of a new police detective he heard about.

The desk sergeant said, speaking in a deep southern accent and sharing information with Jake a few weeks before Detective Bailey Lee arrived, "They say that d' new guy is tough as nails and a black person's nightmare, so watch out fo' him. He ain't nuthing t' play wit. The rumors say that he plans t' target Buttermilk Bottom and make it so white cops can go down there anytime they wants. 'Tween you and me, most of the officers here are afraid to go down there. . . Been that way for years. This tough lookin' red neck is hell bent on cleaning up the place single handedly."

The desk sergeant told Jake all of this because he considered Jake to be a friend, even though he would never admit it to anyone because blacks and white did not mix much less consider themselves as friends.

"No, Jake, we never heard that one," the desk sergeant said, laughing as other officers gathered to hear Jake's latest story. Some of the men were laughing as they gathered around Jake, knowing that he had a good one for them. The new detective, Bailey Lee, was hanging around the fringes of the crowd but not too close to appear interested. Jake kept his eyes and ears peeled for any new information or strategies directed toward The Bottom by the new detective.

"Two alligators wuz layin' on d' banks o' d' Okeefanokee Swamp. One alligator wuz shiny, fat, and pretty. D' other alligator wuz skinny wit ashy, flakin' skin. The skiny alligator looked at d' big fat pretty alligator and axed, 'How did ya git so big, fat, and pretty?' The big pretty alligator stuck his chest out and said proudly, 'I eat niggers.' D' lil' skinny alligator was shocked and amazed. He say, 'I eat niggers, too. How come I ain't fat 'n pretty like you?' The fat alligator said, 'You must be doin' somethin' wrong. How do ya eat yo' niggers?' The skinny alligator said, 'I sneak up on 'em, bite 'em, shake d' shit outta 'em, den I swallow 'em whole.' The fat alligator leaned back and laughed loudly fo' a few minutes. 'Well, boy, dat's what you's doin' wrong. Once ya shake d' shit out o' a nigger, ain't nuthin' left.'"

All the police officers, including the new, bad detective laughed until tears rolled down their eyes. Afterwards, Jake continued to observe the latest addition to the precinct while talking casually with the other officers. Detective Bailey Lee came over and asked the sergeant to introduce him to Jake.

"Jake, this is Detective Bailey Lee. He'll be working here and may need your help to git around in the Bottom," the desk sergeant said.

"Sure, I'd be happy t' show ya 'round, sir," Jake said, grinning more than usual.

"I got plans to clean that place up, and I'll need someone I can rely on."

"Yes, sir. Whatever I kin do. Jes let me know. I's glad to help. We sho' do need dat place cleaned up," Jake said in a serious tone.

"Can we meet here tomorrow, around noon?"

"Whatever time ya say. Whatever time ya say."

"Good. Thanks, Jake. You're gonna be a big help. I can see dat now." The detective walked away, laughing and remembering the joke.

"I sho' hope so, detective. I sho' hope so."

"Dat's right, boy, swing dat fuckin' bat," his father said. "Go 'head, Bailey, swing it as hard as you kin. Look at 'em. Dat's my boy," he yelled to his friends. "He gonna be jes like his daddy."

"He sho' got a arm on him," Mr. Charles, the owner of the corner grocery store, said, laughing.

"Hit 'em hard," his uncle Danny said. "Hit 'em agin."

The boy was tired and his arms hurt as he hit the black man who was hanging upside down from an old hickory tree. The bat was too heavy for the seven-year-old and his arms were tired, but he did not want to disappoint his father. His father had dressed him up in the same white clansmen robe he wore with the white hood. He did not realize it would be so hot under the robe, but he was proud because it looked just like his father's, his uncles', and his cousins'. At times, he could not see through the small holes his father had so carefully cut out for him, but he swung the bat with all his might.

"Hit that mutherfucker," Mr. John yelled. Bailey recognized his voice clearly because Mr. John was his first grade teacher.

He knew everybody's voices, although he did not see their faces. His father's friends came to their house almost every day to drink beer and to discuss their group's activities. Little Bailey was happy to hear Mr. Charles ask for the bat. He wanted his son to have a chance to swing the bat at the nigger whose face was already so bloody that no one could recognize his nose or mouth. That was the first time that Bailey Lee went to a clan meeting with his father, uncles, and cousins.

When he returned home to a wooden four-room shack that sat back in the woods near Unadilla Georgia, he was a hero. His father hugged him for the first time in his memory, announcing to the family that he, at age seven, was the newly inducted member of the KKK. Sitting at the shabby white wooden table with the broken leg that moved every time someone sat down or got up, his father finally heralded him to be his proud son.

"Mama," his father yelled, "You should've seen yo boy here. . . Would've made ya real proud. He's gonna be jes like his got-damn daddy." His mother patted him on the head and gave him a glass of lemonade. "Dis boy jes killed hisself his first nigger t'night. Give 'em one o' dem beers. Dis here's a man sittin' at yo table, a full, honest t' goodness man."

"He's only seven, Jim," his mother protested.

"So fuckin' what? I drank my first beer when I wuz five, and it didn't hurt me none. Dis here's special. Give 'em a fuckin' beer," his father yelled menacingly at his mother.

Without uttering another word, the boy's mother gave him a beer and left the room while the boy and his inebriated father sat, drinking beer from the bottle.

"You's one o' us now, a Klan. You's got d' right t' kick any nigger's ass you see. You proved dat t'night. I's proud o' you, boy. . . Real proud."

That was Bailey Lee's indoctrination to the world of the KKK. From age seven, his father encouraged him to be a police officer. Once on the force, he aspired to be a detective while continuing to be one of the most active members of the Klan along with his father and family members.

His father had encouraged his career on the police force, saying, "You kin kill niggers all day long and git away wit it."

Detective Bailey Lee gave his father and his Klan family a thrill when he announced that he aspired to become the police commissioner of the Atlanta Police Department. His father died of lung cancer the year he made detective, but Bailey made a promise at his father's grave to kill as many niggers as he could, thereby making it possible for his father to rest in peace.

As was his custom, Cripple Jake was upstairs having his 'treatment' with three women at once that Friday night as the tension grew in the minds of the men's committee of Buttermilk Bottom. Three members of the committee came into the juke joint to report their activities after completing their duties of monitoring the community. Moses knew everything about building and construction. Sylvester was a young twenty-year-old, newly-married, short-order cook, who worked at a downtown restaurant. His wife gave birth to their first child, a boy, which motivated the new father to make changes in the way he lived. The third man was Marvin, whom everybody nicknamed 'Wolf' because of his lean muscular frame with hair covering every visible inch of his body.

Wolf spent fifteen of his thirty-five years behind bars and said, "I wuz d' only guilty man in prison," he said, laughing like a hyena. At age sixteen, Wolf killed a man who pulled a knife on him after he discovered that the man was cheating him at cards.

The threesome spotted Cameron sitting alone in his favorite corner and pulled up chairs to join him. When they killed the two police officers, they assisted in hiding the two dead, abusive police officers deep in the kudzu vines.

Sylvester asked, "Did ya hear d' news?"

"I sure did, the first thing this morning," Cameron said.

"They questioned d' storekeeper. Dey said he wuz d' last person t' see 'em last night," Moses said quietly.

"Is that right?" Cameron said, looking around to make sure no one heard the conversation whispered among the co-conspirators.

"Yeah," Moses said.

"I heard Jake say dat they's gonna do a house-to-house search startin' t'morrow," Wolf said.

"Really? Does everyone know?" Cameron asked, looking around the room.

"Yeah, we spread d' news soon as we got d' word from Cripple Jake."

"I sho' like to know how he finds out every thang goin' on at dat police station," Sylvester said.

"He sits 'round tellin' dem crackers his old-ass nigger jokes, grinnin' like a damn fool t' put 'em at ease, then he soaks up all d' information we need t' defend ourselves. He reads all dey papers too. Crackers love it when dey see d' white teeth o' a nigger. . . It cools 'em right out. Jake wuz able t' git his hands on d' weekly report dat showed a search o' Buttermilk Bottom. D' report said dat d' killers might be hidin' out down here in someone's house," Moses said.

"Someone said dat dat bad ass detective's gonna t' clean-up dis neighborhood," Wolf said.

"I wonder how Jake got his hands on that report," Cameron said, thinking aloud.

"I told ya, by grinnin' in dey faces and actin' like d' sorry ass nigger dey want him t' be. Dat way he kin go anywhere in dat station house he wants and nobody stops 'em."

"Where's he anyway?" Moses asked.

"Upstairs," Cameron said, moving his head in the direction of the steps.

"I should've known," Sylvester said. They all smiled.

"Dat man's like a fuckin' rabbit, always fuckin' somethin'," Wolf said, laughing.

"We gotta git goin'. You take care, man," Moses said.

"You, too," Cameron said.

Noticing the three men departing, Queenie strolled leisurely over to the number man and asked while stroking his muscular arms, "Please tell me you're free tonight?"

"I am but I am a bit tired. I plan to turn in early," he said, avoiding eye contact.

"My bed will hold you," she said affectionately into his ear.

"So will mine. Thanks, but not tonight," he said, standing up and kissing her on the cheek then he walked out the door.

The juke joint was a huge house that the owners transformed 'for the pleasures of mankind,' Queenie told anyone who would listen. It would have been a stately mansion if it were in good repair, and located anywhere but Buttermilk Bottom.

Sad and distraught, she watched Cameron leave the house. He was the only man she ever ached for despite his many rejections because he knew how to satisfy her and how to give her body the attention it demanded. Magically, he physically overpowered her every time she managed to convince him to make love to her. She felt his love when she was with him, but the instant they separated, it was over. Every time they separated, she had to start over, always seeking him out because he never came to her voluntarily. No matter what she did to entice him, she could never get him to talk to her about the passion they shared. He just did it, always leaving her breathless, and as soon as he could find a convenient moment, he would disappear. As she stood in the window watching him climb the steps to his apartment, she grieved watching him until he closed his front door. While she observed him, someone filled with passion in his heart was watching her, craving her attention.

Chapter 7

The juke joint had a life of its own. People came and went all day long, but in between the quiet moments and critical incidents, they lived dramatic, funny, and sometimes, pitiful lives. One of the most popular and attractive couples to frequent this 'house of pleasure' was Harlan and Alberta. They provided many hours of amusing entertainment for Jake and his friends. Harlan and Alberta lived together, off and on, for over ten years, had several children together and mastered the art of getting on each other's nerves. When they walked in the joint, the place perked up because they brought an entourage of fun seeking people with them who were ready to party. They loved to dance, gamble, eat, and drink, all the things that Queenie's place offered. The party-seeking couple always started dancing the moment that they entered the room. It did not matter if anyone else was dancing or if the mood was good or bad. They were on their own mission, to fill their evening with laughter and unabashed fun until the doors closed. Many times, they were the last people to leave. No matter how many places they visited during the evening, they always ended up in the speakeasy in Buttermilk Bottom.

Harlan, a tall rather good-looking man, who towered over Alberta by more than a foot. Alberta was short and very well built, wearing clothes that showed off her shapely body.

"Watch Harlan, he's heading for trouble," Jake said, selecting his victim for his favorite activity, monitoring human behavior. "Every time his woman turns her back for one minute, he tries to hug up with Dellah. The only problem is he's not bright, and he's not good at sneaking around."

"Why's a man wit a good lookin' woman and pretty kids always have t' go sneakin' around?" Smoke asked.

"'Cause they's stupid, dat's why," Pearl said.

"He'll get caught because every time he tries something, she catches him. You would think the fool would wise up. Look, she's going to the bathroom, watch," Jake said, smiling. "I bet you a dollar he gets caught."

"You're on," Smoke said, slapping a dollar on the table, along with other observers who wanted a piece of the action. "Nobody kin be dat stupid." The table full of observers watched attentively until they saw Harlan make his move.

"Dellah, baby, you's d' finest thang dis side o' heaven. Gimme some sugar, baby," Harlan said.

"How come ya don't come over here 'til yo wife leave d' room, Harlan?"

"'Cause I ain't crazy, dat's why."

"Well, don't be comin' over here tryin' t' git a free squeeze when she turns her back. If ya wants me, ya need t' come on wit dat horny thang of yo's and pay me, so we kin fuck 'n git it over wit."

"I's comin', baby, soon as I kin git away. Dat woman watches me like a hawk."

"I kin see why," Dellah said, looking at his crotch. "You lookin' mighty good and healthy t' me, sweetie."

"Lemme buy you a drink. Luther, give dis beautiful thang whatever, she wants t' drink," he said, blushing as he placed money on the bar.

"Thank you, baby. Ya sho knows how t' treat a lady," Dellah said.

"Say dat after we finish doin' bizness. I cain't wait t' git some o' dis," he said, licking his tongue over his top lip.

"When ya comin' t' see me, Harlan? I got some real sweet shit fo' yo sexy-ass," she said slowly.

"I gots t' come durin' d' daytime, when she thinks I's workin'."

"Don't keep me waitin'. It might cool off 'fore ya git here."

"If it's cooled off,. . . I jes' have t' heat it up agin, now don't I?"

"Ya better git goin', yo wife is standin' in d' door watchin' yo' horny-ass, and she looks pissed," Dellah said.

"Oh, shit," Harlan said, trying to figure out what to do next.

Jake and his friends began to laugh out-loud as Jake took the money off the table. They watched as Harlan leaned over the bar, as if he were talking to Luther. Alberta walked up behind him and tapped him on the shoulder.

"What ya doin' all d' way over here, Harlan?"

"Buying ya ass a drink. Hurry up, Luther. I ain't got all damn night."

Luther gave Harlan two drinks and watched them walk away. Alberta looked menacingly at Dellah with her hands on her hips, making Dellah laugh.

"Dat fool's playin' wit a' ass whippin' if ya ask me," Luther said.

"Well, it's his ass," Dellah responded.

"It's gonna be his ass when he gits caught," Luther replied.

"Who's dat?" Dellah asked, spotting a tall dark man with chiseled facial features stepping in the door with a guitar case and a satchel in his hand. "Mmmm uh, he sho' is a pretty thang," she said, checking him out from head to toe.

"Never seen him 'round here b'fore," Luther said, checking the stranger, who walked over to him. "What ya havin'?" Luther asked after the stranger settled himself on the stool in the corner at the end of the bar.

"Whiskey."

"Ya play dat thang?" Luther asked, nodding at the guitar.

"It's my life. I'm a blues man," the stranger said, drinking his whiskey straight down. "I'll have another one."

"Sho'," Luther said, pouring another whiskey in his glass. "How long ya been playin' d' blues?"

"Since I could walk and talk," the man said, drinking the whiskey straight down.

"I'm Luther. I helps run dis place," Luther said, offering his hand.

"My name is Bernard Davis, but most people call me 'Blue'."

"Well, Blue, you lookin' fo' some work?"

"I'm always looking, and I'm always traveling."

"We could use some good music 'round here. Why don't you stick 'round 'n play fo' Queenie? If she likes ya, maybe we kin strike up a deal. Have another drink on me."

"Thanks," Blue said, sitting in the corner alone quietly drinking his whiskey. Dellah smiled at him, but he simply nodded without saying a word or giving a smile.

Cora Lee came out of the kitchen with her hands loaded down with platters of food. It was like watching a juggler as she balanced the plates in her small fat hands without dropping one or spilling anything. Everyone in Harlan's and Alberta's party ordered dinners. The smell of fried catfish filled the air. Every plate had two large portions of fish, greens cooked with ham hocks, and a large portion of macaroni and cheese. Some of the men started rubbing their hands together and licking their lips as the short round cook approached their table.

"Cora Lee, ya did it agin," Harlan said. "Friday night wouldn't be d' same witout yo' good ol' cookin'. I dream o' it all week long." He paid her and gave her a generous tip.

"Why thank ya, Harlan. Ya'll enjoy it, now. There's plenty mo' if ya wanna take a platter home." She sat their plates in front of them and collected the money, which she placed in her apron pocket. As she entered the kitchen, she saw Cameron sitting at the kitchen table. Her eyes lit up. Addie Mae had given him a hot cup of coffee, because she knew Cora Lee enjoyed serving him herself.

"Well, well, look who came t' visit," she said, smiling broadly. Cameron remained one of her favorite people in the neighborhood, and he continued to make it his business to stop in and eat his dinner with Cora Lee and Addie Mae at least twice a week. They never knew when he was coming, he just showed up at the back door.

"I hope you're not too busy."

"I ain't never too busy fo' you. Wait 'til ya taste my catfish 'n greens. You's gonna love 'em. D' vegetable man gave me a few beautiful sweet potatoes, so I made ya a pie t' take home."

"Cora Lee, you are the best." He got up and gave her a big kiss on the cheek. "Thank you."

"Ya makes a old woman feel mighty good. I ain't never had no children o' my own, but God's blessed me wit people like you who come in my life from nowhere at all. God sho's good t' me." She placed a glass of lemonade on the table in front of him. "You ain't goin' out front t'night?"

"No. I think I'll turn in early."

"Somebody gonna be mighty disappointed," she said, watching his reaction.

"We all have to live with disappointments."

"Dat woman's in love, if ya axe me," Addie Mae said.

"It has nothing to do with love I can tell you that," he said quietly.

"Ya know, Cameron, Queenie's been stuck on ya since ya moved t' d' Bottom," Cora Lee said.

"That's why I need to cool it awhile. I wouldn't want her to get the wrong idea."

"I thank it's already too late fo' dat. It wuz too late d' first day she laid eyes on ya, pretty boy," Cora Lee teased. "I's glad you don't hold it against us. We sho' love havin' yo company 'n our kitchen. I cain't believe how time flies witout ya even noticin' it. Ya know, it seems like yesterday when you first moved here, 'stead o' ten years," Cora Lee said.

"The best part has been coming to your kitchen to eat. It's not much fun eating alone. This is the only place on earth that a human being can eat delicious food like this," he said as Cora Lee sat his plate down in front of him.

"Addie Mae, ya mind carin' fo' d' customers while I keep Cameron company? I jes enjoy watchin' dis boy eat."

"Ya might wanna eat somethin' yo'self," Addie Mae said, kissing Cora Lee lightly on the lips.

Cora Lee and Cameron had become instant friends the day she showed up with the platter of food on his first day in The Bottom. She reminded him of his aunt who had doted on him until her death. He found it easy to talk to her. He loved everything she cooked, and he enjoyed watching her light up like a Christmas tree, whenever he came to visit her kitchen.

"You told me when we first met that you ran this kitchen, but I never knew what that meant until I started visiting," he said, taking a bite of macaroni and cheese. Smacking his lips, he said, "This is great."

"Thank ya. Enjoy, there's plenty where dat came from. When I first came here t' live 'n work fo' Queenie, I gots everythang straight from d' beginnin' so dat there wouldn't be no mistake. When I worked fo' dat rich white lady up 'n Buckhead, I told her d' same thang. 'If ya come 'n my kitchen, I quit.' I runs my own kitchen. It's d' only way I knows how t' work. I keep it clean as a whistle and I know how t' save a penny 'n stretch it 'til it squeaks. When Addie Mae 'n I came here, dis place wuz a mess. We cleaned it and got it lookin' like dis," she said, looking around and admiring the work that turned the large kitchen into the ideal workspace. "I told Queenie t' come in and inspect it. She liked it and I promised her I'd keep it dat way. There's only one boss in my kitchen and dat's me. Queenie pays me, and I pays all d' kitchen help. Dat way, they's clear dat I's their boss not Queenie,. . . And dat includes Addie Mae. We been workin' t'gether fo' years, and it's goin' smooth as silk."

"How long have you and Addie Mae been together?"

"Lordie, we's been t'gether so long I forgit 'bout when we wuzn't. It's hard fo' people like us t' find a place dat's understandin'. We worked t'gether fo' years, side by side 'fore we found out dat we loved each other. It wuz after a big fancy party at Miss Miller's house up on Peachtree Street. We fed dem white people fo' hours, and it seemed like they'd never stop eatin' our food. Miss Miller wuz havin' one o' dem big sit-down dinners. She loved sit-down dinners. . . Wit twenty or thirty people crowdin' in 'round one table.''

"Thirty people at one table? The place must have been huge,'' Cameron said.

"It wuz a big ol' mansion, d' biggest one up on Peachtree Street. D' kitchen wuz almost as big as dis here house. Dey had enough room t' put dis whole neighborhood in dat house and have plenty o' room t' spare. Anyway, we finally finished feedin' and cleanin' up after dem white folks and sat down on d' back porch, drinkin' up d' leftover wine. Neither one o' us knew how t' drink, but dem white folks kept sayin' how good d' wine wuz so we wanted t' find out what dey's talkin' 'bout. We got good 'n drunk, den. . .," she stopped and looked at Cameron.

"What happened?" he asked.

"Ya sho' ya wanna hear a love story 'tween two old women?''

"If it's about you and Addie Mae, I sure do. You and the twins are my family, the only family I have.''

"I know ya love us, boy, but knowin' 'bout certain thangs change people," she said, looking at him cautiously.

"Not if they love you." They enjoyed the silence between them. He took her hand and kissed it. "Now, tell me the rest."

With a warm smiled on her face, she continued her story. "Well, we wuz drunk as we could be and tired. We wuz so tired our bodies ached from head t' toe. All we wanted t' do wuz t' sit on dat back porch and swing in dat old swing in d' cool air. We wuz laughin' and talkin' 'bout dem white people and d' funny thangs dey wuz sayin'. One o' Miss Miller's friends tried t' come in my kitchen and axed me if we wanted t' work fo' her. We didn't talk t' her 'cause, we didn't allow nobody in our kitchen, but she kept axin' me t' come out, and I kept tellin' her t' go 'way. We laughed at dat fool fo' hours. We wuz laughin 'and hittin' on each other,. . . . Jes playin. Jes' playin', den we jes started ticklin' each other, laughin' like two fools. D' ticklin' turned into rubbin' and d' rubbin' turned into kissin'. Neither one o' us ever touched a woman b'fore and neither one o' us ever been wit no man, either. We thought we wuz gonna be two old maids fo' d' rest o' our lives. We never thought 'bout lovin' each other, no. . . . Not in a million years. Neither one o' us knew what we wuz doin' but we figured thangs out all right. We figured thangs out a-plenty, and we couldn't stop ourselves. It wuz d' sweetest thang I ever felt 'n my whole life, it still is. I won't give her up fo' nuthin' 'n d' world. We started sleepin' t'gether dat night and from den on, we ain't never parted. We couldn't keep our hands off each other. I couldn't breathe witout her, and she felt d' same as I did. So, dat wuz dat."

"Miss Miller allowed you to stay in the same room together?"

"She didn't know nuthing. She never came back t' our quarters, and she ain't never come into my kitchen after I got there. So, how'd she know we wuz sleepin' t'gether? We worked there almost ten years b'fore Miss Miller figured out there wuz somethin' b'tween Addie Mae and me. She didn't fire me, but she lets me know, we wuzn't welcomed no mo'. She didn't see nothin' we did t'gether, but she saw it in our eyes. It's hard t' hide it when you's in love, and we wuz in love. I ain't never thought 'bout it 'fore in my life. . . . Lovin' a woman, but I did, and I still do. Dat wuz almost thirty-five years ago and we's still t'gether."

"I'm happy that you're happy. I can see it in your eyes how much you love each other."

"You gon find love one day. I knows it."

"I don't think so. Some people are just meant to be alone."

"Nonsense, boy. Ya gonna find someone who'll make ya feel like you's their whole world, and you ain't gonna be able t' say no t' her. I knows it 'cause I's praying fo' ya, boy. Ya gonna find somethin' special, somebody God made jes fo' you."

"I know one thing that God intended me to have. . . . More macaroni and cheese."

"He sho' did," she said, laughing and getting up from the table with his empty plate in her hand. "There's plenty fo' you t' take home. I always makes extra."

"One thing that I can say about you, Cora Lee. You really know your business. This. . . . Is the best macaroni and cheese that I ever had in my life," he said, smiling down on his second helping of the cheesy casserole.

"It jes' oughta be, I puts seven kinds o' cheeses in there 'long wit eggs, heavy cream, and fresh butter."

"Stop. I'm getting fat just listening to you."

"You cain't git full eatin' skinny food."

That night Cameron lay in his bed and thought about how lucky Cora Lee and Addie Mae were because they knew true love. When he looked at his life, all he saw was a menagerie of sexual encounters that he could easily ignore. Although he was very fond of Grace, he did not love her. She was the one person he had strong feelings for, and he was grateful to her for standing by him. He cherished their friendship, but that was growing thin because she continually bombarded him with requests for a stronger commitment, even marriage. As much as he liked Grace, he did not intend to marry her or anyone. He married once without loving the person, and he would never repeat that mistake. In the dark, when he was alone, he craved what he never had, true love. He wanted to know what it felt like to be in love. It was only in his dreams that he could find what his heart was seeking, an elusive image of a sensuous woman, who touched the deep recesses of his heart, and filled his dreams but true love was as fleeting as the night.

After all the customers departed, the juke joint was subdued with only the staff sitting around chatting about the day's events. Blue continued to sit patiently and quietly at the end of the bar, occasionally talking to Luther. Dellah and the other two women who worked there had their eyes peeled on the masculine, tall, dark man with beautiful brilliant eyes. They whispered and flirted with him, but he did not encourage them.

"Man, you sho' attract a lot o' attention," Luther said, laughing. "Ya kin have anyone ya wants. . . . Dey all works here, turnin' tricks."

"No thanks, man. I never mess with professionals."

"Professionals? Hey, I ain't never heard nobody call 'em dat b'fore, but I see right now dat you gonna walk in here breakin' hearts from d' git." Blue did not say a word. He was busy looking around, observing everything and everybody.

Cora Lee came out and spoke to him, saying, "You looks mighty thin. I have some leftovers n' d' back,. . . . If you's interested? No charge."

"Yes, Ma'am, I could use a bite to eat. Could I get it after I sing for Miss Queenie?"

"Ya sho' kin. Jes come on out t' d' kitchen, and I'll start fattenin' ya up." Blue smiled for the first time.

When Queenie came downstairs, Luther introduced her to the blues man. "Well, let's see what you can do. If you're any good, we can talk about you singing here."

"Thank you, Ma'am," Blue said, carefully taking his beautiful guitar out of it's worn case then placed its decorative strap over his shoulder and walked over to the center of the floor, pulling a chair with him. He took a few seconds to tune his instrument as if he was playing for a room full of people. His fingers began expertly stroking the strings, filling the room with the low-down, gut-stirring, funky sounds of the blues. The whores began to holler and clap their hands as the sultry music drew them in. Blue played in his own unique style as he rocked and swayed his long thin muscular body to the tempo of the music, moving his shoulders, head, and his hips while stretching his neck and patting his feet in sync with the sizzling, hot music. As he hit a strong nerve-jolting note that seemed to last an eternity, he leaned back, making his pants fit tight around his legs. Dellah was the first to notice that he did not have on any underwear because his long stout member appeared predominantly on his left leg almost reaching his knees, making her scream and hit her companions calling attention to Blue's unbelievable assets. The women began to scream as the music took them where their imaginations wanted to go. They were so loud and the music so magnetic that Cora Lee and Addie Mae came out of the kitchen to hear the man lay down his folksy, funky tune. Suddenly, he stopped playing and looked around the room, after his eyes touched everyone there; he began to rock out a tune that had everyone clapping, including Cora Lee.

"Dat boy is good," someone yelled.

He opened his mouth and began to sing in a profoundly sexual voice that was so soulful and sultry it had everyone on their feet dancing and clapping their hands as his deep sensuous voice told the story of a torturous love gone bad. His tormented face reflected every nuance of sadness and grief that he sang about while bending and moving his long flexible body in reaction to every note he played. When he finished his tune, everyone, including Luther and Queenie, were standing up cheering.

"Man, that was the best singing I ever heard around here," Queenie said.

"Ya really knows how t' play dat damn guitar," Luther said, shaking his hand. "Man, dat wuz great," he said, patting the blues singer on the back while the whores surrounded him, touching and kissing him, trying to make their presence known.

"And about that job?. . . . You can sing here whenever, and however, you want," Queenie said, laughing. "You play like that every night?"

"Yes, Ma'am," he said in a quiet manner with his masterfully crafted guitar still hanging around his neck.

"You can start singing here tomorrow night if you want. . . . As long as you sing," Queenie said. "Do you have a place to stay?"

"No, not yet."

"Well, don't worry. I've got a room for you as long as you want it."

"And, ya meals' on d' house," Cora Lee said, patting him on the shoulder. "Dat kinda singin' comes from God. . . . 'Cause, I kin see it in yo' eyes and hear it in yo' voice. You's been touched by a' angel, boy, and dat's d' God's truth."

Chapter 8

It was amazing to observe how the residents of Buttermilk Bottom co-operated with each other and stuck together in a crisis or around issues that affected the whole community. Sometimes, they came together for the wrong reasons, but the time they rallied around the students was wonderful. It was amazing to see the men as they worked together to protect the students, but there were times when Cameron's hope diminished as he sat in the juke joint, listening to customers make fun of one of the neighbors. He began to doubt whether things would ever change for the better because some people never went out of their way to help those who were down on their luck. He wanted to do something about changing their attitudes, but he had no idea how to accomplish it, realizing that his goal was very illusive.

Cameron's thoughts turned to the students. They were so hopeful for the progress of civil rights in the South, filled with a tangible energy that touched his heart. People of Buttermilk Bottom were slowly registering to vote, and others wanted to watch to see what happened when their neighbors showed up at the polls to exercise their right to vote. Would they be beaten, jailed, or killed? They wanted to wait and see.

"There's too many goin' at one time. Dem white folks ain't gonna let that many colored people vote. It's jes a waste of time, dat all," one neighbor told Cameron when he asked him why he did not register.

Things were definitely getting better at least the stage was set for improvement even though no evidence of that could be seen on the streets of Buttermilk Bottom. The year before, the NAACP won its case before the Supreme Court in a long and hard fought decision, which called for the end of segregation in all public areas and deemed segregation unconstitutional. For a short time, everyone was jubilant until, part two of the legislation passed, calling for the gradual elimination of segregation, which whites held as their victory. It was a big set-back for the movement. Since the arrival of the students in the neighborhood, even Cameron felt hopeful again. Luther interrupted his thoughts, calling him over to the end of the bar and introduced him to Blue.

"What are you drinking?"

"Whiskey," Blue said.

"Give him one on me," Cameron said. "The words out that you can really belt out a tune."

"I do okay." Cameron liked his quiet demeanor.

"Where are you from?"

"Chicago and around."

"How long have you been in Georgia?"

"This time?. . . . About a week."

"This is a great place. They'll treat you well and feed you like a king."

"I know. I met Cora Lee and Addie Mae last night," Blue said in one of his rare beautiful smiles. "I was so stuffed when I left them that I don't need to eat for a couple of days."

"Good luck with trying to get away with that around those two." Blue laughed. "How long are you planning to stay?"

"Until my shoes start walking away,. . . Then I'll get up and follow them. I never stay anywhere too long."

"Got any family," Cameron asked.

"Sure do, right over there in that guitar case." They both laughed.

Listening to a group of Queenie's frequent customers as they sat laughing and talking with a few of the whores that worked there, Cameron listened again as they laughed and made fun of a man who came in for a quiet drink. Not bothering a soul, he ordered a drink and drank it slowly, paid his money, and left. Once he was clearly out the door, the group laughed hysterically.

"Dat fool wuz out there all mornin', tryin' t' shoot pigeons," one man said.

"What d' hell wuz he doin' dat fo'?" Pearl asked. There was more laughter.

"He wuz catchin' 'em fo' Easter dinner," someone else said.

"Easter? Who'd wanna eat pigeons when they kin have turkey or ham?" Pearl asked.

"Well, you ought t' be happy you ain't married t' him 'cause he don't have enough money t' buy no turkey. Dat's why he's shootin' pigeons," another man said as the group laughed.

"Wit all dem damn kids he got, he gotta shoot all day and night t' git enough meat t' feed dat bunch."

"How many he got?" someone asked.

"I think nine or ten," Dellah said.

"Damn, he oughta started shootin' pigeons a month ago. Dat's no family, dat's a fuckin' tribe," Pearl said, making everyone laugh in agreement.

After hearing the story, Cameron turned to the blues man and said, "Welcome to the Bottom. I live across the street if you want a place to hang out. Luther, give the man a double. See you around. I'll try to stop back to see your show," Cameron said as he placed money on the bar.

"Great, it's always good to see a friendly face in the crowd. Thanks for the drinks," Blue said, raising his glass to Cameron as he hurried outside.

Cameron went out the door to look for the man whom the customers were making fun of and found the man at the corner, talking to a few friends. After several minutes, he headed down the dirt road for home not knowing that Cameron was following him. When the man walked in the door of his second floor apartment, Cameron could hear the children saying, 'Daddy's home.' He smiled and went home himself. Early the next morning, Cameron was at the grocery store when it opened and purchased all the things he thought the unfortunate family would need for an Easter dinner.

When the family woke up that morning, they found two large boxes in front of their door. Besides the greens, yams, rice, flour, sugar, potatoes, eggs, candy, corn meal, salt and the biggest turkey and ham he could find, Cameron placed an envelope with two hundred dollars in it. Thinking that he may have forgotten something, he placed the money there in case the man could use it to complete the meal, or if he needed it for any other reason. The man looked out his front door and down the dirt road, trying to find the person who had been so generous to his family, but Cameron was home making coffee about to sit on his front porch.

The man was so grateful for the help he received that he started asking people if they knew who gave his family the generous gifts of food and money, but no one knew anything about it. After thinking about it, Jake figured out that it was his friend and told him so.

"I know it was you. You're the only person who is generous enough and have the money to do something like that."

"Keep it to yourself, okay?"

"Sure. Do you mind telling me why you did it?"

With a big sigh, Cameron said, "We are all related. We have to help each other . . . It's the natural law. You see someone in need; you do what you can to help. Besides, I don't have nine kids looking at me, hoping for a turkey on Easter. The least I could do was to help the man."

"That was real nice, man. . . Real nice."

"He needed help. What was I supposed to do, eat turkey on Easter knowing that they would be eating pigeons? I couldn't have eaten just thinking about those poor kids. The food would stick in my throat. This way, we're all happy."

"You made them happy, man. You're a real, good guy, Cameron."

When Cameron returned to the juke joint that evening, he found it crowded with women. The standing-room space was almost non-existent. Blue was in the center of the floor, wearing a pair of tight black pants and a skinny, black shirt that only had one button just above his belt fastened, displaying an extremely well-developed muscular chest that delighted the women who gathered all around the room. The outfit though simple, appealed to the female customers who were there to enjoy his erotic musical experience and to see all his physical assets that all in Buttermilk Bottom talked about since the day he arrived. When the room was completely quiet, the blues man pulled strikingly haunting, honky-tonk sounds out of his guitar, mesmerizing his female audience. They stood up, screaming to the top of their voices, as the blues man sang a vivid tune about his 'low-down, dirty woman'. While the crowd was still screaming, he pulled out a sparkling white handkerchief and wiped the sweat off his face then sang a second tune with the guitar hanging on his back. With no musical support, the tune proclaimed, "I need a funky black woman to keep me satisfied." Other than his voice, the only other sound in the room was the stumping of his feet and the clapping of hands by his audience to the rhythm he set in motion. At the end of the song, everyone stood up and cheered, but the blues man quieted them down with his mastery of his sensuous guitar. He screamed out his deep hurtful heart through a haunting song that brought him to his knees as he cried out in pain in an emotional song about his broken heart. The next tune everybody knew and joined

him in singing about needing someone to love and understand him.
Surprising everyone, he pulled a woman out of the audience, sat her in
the chair that was always present when he performed and sang to her,
making all the other women in the room jealous. The woman, he chose
sat in the chair in the middle of the room, and cried as he 'begged her
forgiveness because he knew he did her wrong'. The woman began to
scream every time he came near her and almost fainted when he stood
her up, moving his hips against her in erotically arousing movements
then to everyone's shock, he kissed her on the lips then completed the
song on his knees. For his last and the most memorable song of the
evening, he sang, 'Hoochie Choochie Man', which had the crowd on
their feet, cheering and screaming.

During the heated performance, Jake walked in and found his way
over to Cameron, who was standing in the corner, watching the blues
man lay down his songs of despair.

"Man, there must be a hundred women in here."

"The word got out rather quickly."

"Anytime you mention anything about a big dick in Buttermilk
Bottom, everybody takes notice. Damned, there are some horny-ass
women living all around here." Jake said, noticing who was in the
crowded room.

"Yeah and most of them are right here in this room," Cameron said,
laughing. "You have to admit it. . . The man has talent."

"And. . . A big dick. Shit, Dellah wasn't lying about that."

Cameron laughed, "It's show business. He knows what works and
he's making his pay day, pay off." They watched the women get up two
and three at a time to put money in a bucket for the sexually stimulating
singer, who brought excitement and bedlam to women whose future was
ordinarily bleak, while living out their repressed lives in a physically
deprived community.

In all the years that Cameron lived in Buttermilk Bottom, he gained
a reputation for being fair and understanding, and yet. . . Everyone knew
he did not tolerate any kind of foolishness. Because of his low-key style
and quiet demeanor, few people challenged him. He still had an eye for
justice and fair play as he quickly stepped in when he found someone
mistreated or hurt. People always called on him whenever a crisis was
brewing. The children nicknamed Cameron, 'The Sheriff,' and looked

to him as their protector. Over the years, his popularity and reputation grew and everyone respected him.

Cripple Jake and Blue sat with Cameron on his second floor, front porch, enjoying each other's company. Blue was strumming out a new tune on his guitar as Jake and Cameron played checkers on a homemade double board that Jake made, when they suddenly heard screaming.

"What was that?" Blue asked.

"Sounds like it might be Paul, down the alley, beating the shit out of one of his kids again," Jake said. "He does it all the time. If he's not beating his wife, he's beating one of his children."

"That sounds pretty bad," Blue said as he stopped playing his guitar.

The child's screams tormented Cameron's ears. He could not sit and listen to anyone abusing a child. With a strange look in his eyes, he looked at Jake then at Blue.

"Oh shit, now what?" Jake said, looking at his best friend's expression.

"I'll be right back." Cameron got up, ran down the steps, moving in the direction of the screaming. He walked swiftly around the corner followed by Blue, who was still holding his guitar and Cripple Jake, on his crutches.

"What is he going to do?" Blue asked.

"I'll be damned if I know. It's no telling what that fool might do," Jake said, walking expertly on his crutches, next to their new friend.

"Well, I guess we'd better watch his back," Blue said.

Cameron arrived at Paul Jeter's first floor apartment in time to see him raising a belt to hit his small son. The boy was trying to stay out of his father's reach by crouching down in the corner of their front porch behind a broken down wooden swing that hung from the porch ceiling. A small child, who was barely five years old, had no defense against his intoxicated father who stood towering over him. Running up the steps, taking two at a time, Cameron reached the porch where the man stood with the belt, swinging in the air about to hit his son again.

Cameron grabbed the belt from Paul and began to beat him with his own belt, saying, "Let's see how you like it." After that, the children, who were standing around watching the incident, jumped up and down, cheering.

"Git 'em, Sheriff. Git 'em," one of the teenagers yelled. That was not the first time he heard the nickname given to him by the children of Buttermilk Bottom.

"Stop, please," Paul yelled, trying to dodge the belt that was coming down on top his head in rapid succession. The children laughed as their hero rescued one of their smallest friends. They knew they could always count on 'The Sheriff' to come to their aid. Seeing him as their ultimate protector and godfather, they nicknamed him, Sheriff, after the first few years of his residency in Buttermilk Bottom.

Completely unaware of what and who was around him, Cameron was being watched not only by the people of The Bottom but by an outsider, who stood in the crowd, watching him and felt his pain as he lashed out in defense of the small child. Jazmine Cigam was touched when the child ran to Cameron and hugged him around his legs, still crying from the beating he had received from his father. Cameron picked the child up in his arms, and the child placed his little arms tightly around the number writer's neck, crying with relief. Jazmine's heart fluttered. The child's father sat slouched on the porch, trying to recover from his alcoholic stupor, the embarrassment, and the whipping he had just received while the crowd stared and jeered at him for his abusive behavior.

They yelled out, "You got what you deserved."

Dropping the leather belt on the ground, Cameron walked down the street still holding the crying child lovingly in his arms, speaking to him quietly, and calming him down.

"When he sobers up. . . Tell him to come to my apartment to get his son . . . But make damn sure his ass is sober," Cameron said to Moses with a deep frown on his face.

"Don't worry. I got him," Moses said, making his way through the crowd.

"Thanks, man," Cameron said, heading for his apartment with the child bound to him, passing Jake and Blue, who followed him back to his apartment.

Jazmine, his silent admirer, stood watching the tall beautifully built man while the tiny child held on securely and sweetly to his protector's neck with tears running down his dirty face. Cameron looked as if he was about to cry himself as he wiped the child's eyes. She was convinced that this tenderhearted man was different from any man she had ever seen before. She knew she wanted to know this man and to touch him as the small child was doing. It had been a long time, since she had tried to date anyone because it usually turned out badly after the first few minutes, having only a handful of dates in the last few years. Most of the men she met were selfish and self centered, only interested in taking her to bed. Jazmine was determined to find someone whom she could love for the rest of her life, someone who wanted children and a wonderful happy home, which she would happily provide. As the tall handsome compassionate man walked away, she watched him carefully as he comforted the child, wishing he was rubbing her back instead. Although she could not see his face, she saw and felt the compassion he had for the helpless child and knew that his concern was sincere. *Who was he? What was he doing in Buttermilk Bottom?* She intended to find out. Sighing deeply, she watched the tall handsome man until he disappeared.

When Jazmine reached her mother's house, she had a million questions. Immediately, after kissing her mother on the cheek, she said, "Mother, there was a tall handsome man who defended a child against his abusive father, do you know him? All the children seemed to love him."

Her mother anticipated her daughters questioning and patiently waited for her to ask. "Why do you want to know?" Jazmine smiled, knowing that her mother sensed her urgency and her need to know about this man. Her mother laughed at her embarrassment and said, "It can only be Cameron Fielding. He has brought new life into this old neighborhood. Before he got here, the men didn't even know they had a backbone, let alone knowing that they had the ability to use it. Since he organized them, they have done some wonderful things for this community. Thanks to Cameron, our streets are safe. The men are a security force and because of him. . . No white man comes down here without their permission. After only a week, he had them marching around here like soldiers. They all have to stand watch while we sleep like babies."

"He's very handsome and he sounds wonderful, Mommy. I just wish I could have looked into his eyes. I could have learned more about him."

"If you look into those eyes, baby doll. . . You may never get out of them."

"What do you mean, Mommy?"

"Jazzy, this man. . . He's nothing to play with. . . Stay away from him if you're not serious."

"What is the harm in looking," Jazmine said.

"You'll find out."

"Do you sense something?"

"Baby Doll, I look forward to the day that I don't sense something."

"What is it? Tell me."

"Curiosity killed the cat."

Jazmine knew not to take her questioning any further. Whenever her mother used that old phrase, she knew she had reached a dead end, but she could not help but wonder about the tall handsome man who came to the child's defense and rescued him from his abusive father.

Just six weeks after Blue arrived in Buttermilk Bottom, he came into the main room of the juke joint, carrying his guitar and satchel that he brought with him when he first arrived in The Bottom.

"Looks like you's movin'," Luther said, noticing the satchel he had not seen since the blues singer's arrival.

"Tonight's my last show," Blue said easily.

"You sho don't believe in long good-byes, do ya?" Luther asked, pouring him a farewell drink. "We're really gonna miss ya. We had a packed house ev'ry night since ya came here. Sho' won't be d' same witout you and dat guitar o' yours."

"Thank you," Blue said. Everyone quickly adjusted to his short direct responses. He rarely had a conversation with anyone except Cameron, Jake, and Cora Lee. Everyone else, he felt he would be wasting words. "I have to save my words for my singing," he once said to Jake, when Jake quizzed him about his quietness.

"Queenie's gonna be upset when she finds out ya leavin', not t' mention Cora Lee 'n d' girls," Luther said, grinning.

The blues man walked into the kitchen, placed his small possessions on the floor near the back door, and sat down at the table with Cora Lee for his last meal with her and Addie Mae.

"I want to thank you for feeding me so well while I was here," he said, hugging the two cooks. "I'll dream about your macaroni and cheese and your banana pudding, Miss Cora."

"It wuz our pleasure. If ya git back dis way be sho' ya stop in and be sho you drop us a card now and den t' let us know how you's doin'."

"I will," he said, sitting down to the large plate of food they prepared for him. After packing a lunch for the blues man, Cora Lee and Addie Mae sat down to have an early dinner with the blues man when Jake and Cameron showed up at the back door. Both Jake and Cameron knew their friend was getting restless and needed to move on. They had enjoyed his quiet demeanor, his company, and his remarkable talent, but most of all they treasured the warm steadying friendship that enveloped them like a warm blanket.

The women who worked at the juke joint were still betting on who could get the blues man in bed first. Jake was especially fond of watching them jockey for positions whenever Blue was around. Jake had his money on Blue because he heard and understood him clearly, when he told him that he never slept with professionals, besides Jake knew that Blue was busy taking care of all the needs of every other woman in the Bottom, married and single.

"I thought I was the horniest man on earth until I met you, man," Jake said to the blues man while playing checkers with Cameron. Blue played his guitar that was always with him wherever he went, but he loved spending hours and hours sitting on Cameron's porch that overlooked the entire neighborhood. From time to time, during his six-week stay, Jake would notice him, darting in and out of houses in The Bottom soon after his arrival.

"Jake, I'm a traveling man. I have to get what I can, when I can."

"With your method of advertisement, I know you won't be able to get to all your admirers before you move on." Blue and Cameron laughed. "Have you ever in your whole life ever worn underwear?"

"Not since I found out the difference it made in my tips. The first time I performed without underwear was because I didn't have any. I made a fortune that night. Since then, I've been doing rather well. I then realized that I have two valuable instruments in my show, and I learned to use both of them well."

"The man's got to eat," Cameron said, smiling.

"I haven't been hungry for anything since I was sixteen," Blue said with a quiet smile on his face.

Blue's final performance was one the whole neighborhood would talk about for years. The level of energy in his voice was high, and so were the emotions of the shocked and disappointed crowd when he announced that he was leaving, a loud gasp emanated from the crowd. With his beautiful, shiny guitar in his hand, he began to explain the life of a blues singer as he played his sexy funky music between every phrase and thought he expressed. It was a sad, teary, and intimate farewell.

"I am blessed with the gift of music and cursed. . . Because whenever I find true love. . . I have to leave it behind." There were loud moans coming from the audience. "I travel and I sing. I'm a blues man. . . That's what I do." He hit several deep bass notes to dramatize his words. "My blessing. . . That I bring you and the world is. . . This message. . . That no matter how bad things get here in Buttermilk Bottom." His music became erotic and emotional as the women's screams filled the room. "Somebody. . . . Somewhere. . . Understands what you're going through." He hit an uncharacteristic note and bent it for almost a minute then said, "That's why we're here. . . To understand this pitiful life we live. . . But together we can soar because the message that I bring to the world. . . Is understanding." After a few minutes of intricate, soulful playing on his magical guitar, the blues singer began to sing out the hurts and pangs of heartache and complex human relationships that have mystified mankind for generations. He explained and expressed love and disappointments in heart-wrenching detail. The lyrical pictures that he painted for his enthusiastic audience were heartbreaking and reflected in the tears that streamed from the eyes of the women in the room.

The entire room was on its feet when the blues man sang his last song of farewell and exited the room through the kitchen. Some thought that he was coming out for a final bow, but he placed his guitar in its worn case, picked up his satchel, kissed Cora Lee and Addie Mae then said goodbye. He left by the back door where Jake and Cameron waited and escorted him to the bus station.

As they left the Bottom, Jake asked, "Where to next?"

Blue said, "Out of town."

Months after the blues man left town, an unusual number of women showed up pregnant. Jake was the first person to call attention to it. He planned to calculate the births with the Blues man's appearance in The Bottom then wait patiently to note each child that possessed the chiseled facial features, dark complexion, and long slim body of their friendly blues singer.

"Now I know why that devil doesn't stay in one place too long, and I think he almost overstayed his visit here. I noticed Sally around the corner started showing about three weeks after he left, and I know he was tapping her because I have seen him coming out the back door just before her husband got home. I bet you anything that baby will be long, black, and singing the blues when it comes out." Jake told Cameron as they sat on his front porch.

"Jake, I stopped betting against you five minutes after I met you."

"Now, I am waiting to see if Lula comes up pregnant along with Zelma, Maggie, and Poochie. I will bet anybody that they will show up with big, fat bellies right after Sally. I know one thing. . . You better check the twins downstairs. He may have tapped them, too," Jake said, making his friend laugh. "Ain't no telling who else he got."

"He was a smooth one. That's for sure," Cameron said, remembering their short friendship with the blues singer.

"He eased in and eased out before anyone knew who fucked them. I bet you those women thought they dreamed his horny ass up. I would love to hear them tell their men what distant cousin their babies look like. You watch, the next children born down here over the next nine months after Blue's arrival will be his. You watch. . . Every one of those babies will be long, black, and singing their asses off."

"Jake, you have to have something better to do."

"This is me. . . Watching people be people. When the time comes. . . Say two or three years from now, I'm going to buy me some small guitars just to watch whose babies will crawl over and pick them up. You watch. . . They're going to be long, black with sharp features just like Blue." Jake said, laughing and could not stop. Seeing his friend's sad face, he said, "What's wrong with you?"

"He sang the blues, man. . . . But he brought those women eighteen years of the real blues. They won't ever forget that dude. He was a real blues man alright." Jake continued laughing at the irony of the situation. Cameron laughed then he thought of the long-term impact of the blues man's visit. If Jake was correct, it was no laughing matter, he became quiet as he pondered the predicament that Blue left his women to face alone.

The routine that Cameron established since moving to Buttermilk Bottom was to get up early in the morning and watch the neighborhood wake up. He had his first and second cups of coffee as he observed people over the years going out to work and the children going to school. They all waved at him as they passed by. The children always said, "'Morning, Sheriff." Around nine o'clock in the morning, he would walk to the store on Forrest Avenue to pick up a newspaper and whatever incidentals he might need to complete his day. He had a strong relationship with his downstairs tenants, the elderly twins whom he felt at home with from his first day in Buttermilk Bottom. Whenever he went to the store, he usually picked up items for them as well, but he had to get their requests the night before because they always slept late.

After breakfast, he would sit on his front porch and read one of the many novels he purchased or play checkers with Jake for several hours before laying down for an afternoon nap. Around three o'clock, he was ready to go to work. Most of his work, he accomplished by sitting on his front steps. As people went by, they placed their orders and laid the cash beside him, usually crumbled or wrapped in paper. Around ten in the evening, he would go to the juke joint for a card game. He would also meet with his other clients, who wanted to play the numbers. People were always amazed that he retained everybody's orders in his head and was able to distribute winnings to the appropriate person immediately without getting anything mixed up. People said he was the best number man they ever had because when they won, they did not have to go looking for him. He found them and had their cash in his hands. Most of the time, he would show up before the person knew they had won.

His relationship with Queenie had its moments. For long periods, he chose not to see her because he sensed that she was getting too serious. He never thought of it as being anything except sex and friendship.

Once, he offered her money as compensation, but she took the money off the dresser and gave it back to him saying, "I should be paying you for what you made me feel tonight. Besides, I'm not in the business any more. I'm a real live businesswoman. Taking care of this place allowed me to get off my back. What we do together is not business, it's strictly pleasure."

From time to time, he would buy her very nice gifts. Sometimes it would be clothing and at other times, he would give her jewelry. She always demonstrated great appreciation for whatever gift he gave her. What held him so dear in her heart was the fact that he also bought gifts for her son, who would be seventeen in the fall. Although he did not have a close relationship with her son, he showed affection and interest whenever her son was around him.

"Thank you. The pleasure was all mine," he said, kissing her.

"We should get together more often, Cameron. You know. . . I will always welcome you with my open arms and legs," she said, laughing, still laying under the covers with her leg hanging out, trying to entice him back.

"I'll take that under consideration," he said, trying to get out of the door gracefully.

"Are you still seeing that woman?" she asked.

"Yes and I also like playing the field. The fewer entanglements the better," he said honestly.

"We have been seeing each other for years, don't you ever want to make it permanent. I have a habit of growing on people," she said, batting her eyes.

"I would like to keep things friendly. The last thing I would want. . . Is to have you misunderstand my intentions," he said unmistakably.

"I still love you, Cameron," she cooed.

"I'm still not looking for anyone special in my life. Marriage is out of the question, but if you feel that we should stop seeing each other then I'll understand."

"I want to be with you, whenever I can."

"No strings attached?"

"If that's the way it has to be."

"It does. In the meantime, we can have a lot of fun." He kissed her and left.

Queenie was a professional, although she had not been on the streets for a long time. She knew the game, the Johns, and she knew how to make people do as she wished in and out of bed. Men became easy for her when she took control of her life and her body, but with Cameron, she was not in control, and she knew it. He had a ferocious appetite when it came to sex and so did she. In that respect, they were alike. She wanted to convince him to stop fighting her, which would enable him to be hers alone and forever. In spite of the number of years that they had been having a sexual relationship, she felt in her heart that eventually, she could and would change his mind.

Whenever Queenie attempted to show her seriousness toward the handsome, intelligent number man, which he quickly squelched with a few words filled with a harsh dose of reality. He never thought of her as a love interest, and he made that completely clear. Their strong desire for uninhibited sex had prompted the ten-year relationship, and she was more than happy to oblige him, whenever he was willing.

Jake once asked shortly after Cameron started seeing Queenie, "You don't seem like a man who would like a big woman like Queenie. Isn't she too healthy for you?"

"No. Her size has nothing to do with anything."

"I know what you mean, man. Pussy is pussy and it's all good."

"Jake, you are a little sick in the head."
"I know I am but let it be known by all that I speak the truth."

Late one Sunday evening in June, Cameron was leaving Queenie's quarters just before midnight in the pouring rain. Jazmine was leaving her mother's house, holding onto her brother, Blair's, arm to keep from slipping on the dark muddy road as they attempted to run to the bus stop. They tried waiting at their mother's house until the rain stopped, but it did not. When their mother told them that the rain would not stop pouring from the sky until morning, the sister and brother looked at each other knowingly. Having no other choice, they set out in full rain gear that they found stashed in the hall closet. They kissed their mother and started out for their individual apartments. The lightning began to crack so threateningly that they ducked under the large porch of the juke joint. Just as they ran onto the porch, Cameron was coming out. Because of the blinding rain, they collided with him briefly. Blair tried to apologize.

"Sorry, man, we were trying to get out of the rain," Blair said. Jazmine realized instantly that it was Cameron and noticed that he was more handsome close up than she thought.

The light shinning from windows inside allowed her to see his eyes. Grateful for the oversized raincoat with a generous hood that belonged to her mother, she was happy that she chose it instead of her own because it was raining so hard. Her raincoat would not have covered her so completely. The big hood on her mother's raincoat, allowed her to get a good look at the handsome man without him seeing her. She loved watching people when they had no idea she was observing them.

"Don't worry about it. That's a lot of water falling out there," Cameron said, leaning against the corner post facing them, then he looked out at the downpour feelings frustrated. He looked sad and irritated. Then he thought silently to himself, *Women, what I would give not to have to explain to them that all I want from them is sex. Lots of hot sizzling . . .* She turned away embarrassed that she eavesdropped on his private thoughts.

"In this down-pour, the mud seems like quick sand. You could get stuck out there, and never be found again," her brother said.

"The unfortunate thing is that the wetness never seems to go away. We have such poor drainage down here. It takes days to dry up," Cameron said sadly. *Women,* he thought to himself. *Always trying to stifle you . . .*

always looking for marriage, which I will never do again. Jazmine could not help but tune back into his thoughts. *I love women, but I don't ever want to live with one again. It's too stifling . . . confining.* Underneath his frustrating thoughts, she felt his overriding compassion and strength. It was hypnotic. Her brother looked at her disapprovingly, forcing her to look away. She looked down at her feet.

"How well I know," her brother said slowly.

"It's letting up enough for me to run across the road, so good night to you both," he said, trying to get a glimpse of the person under the wet hooded raincoat. He knew it was a woman from her size and shape and he assumed it was the man's mate.

"Good night," Jazmine and her brother said, but she never looked up.

When the rain stopped early the next morning, it was as if it had been an illusion. The dark muddy street left deep trenches in the roads created by creek-like runoff from the streets above Buttermilk Bottom. It would take several days for the hot sun to soak up the streams of water that flowed steadily into the kudzu-covered forest, surrounding the sunken neighborhood. The sun brought heat, humidity, and children out to play. A group of girls played jump rope in front of Cameron's house. He enjoyed watching them play as they recited witty rhymes to help them keep their pace with the constantly moving rope whipping over their excited heads and under their agile feet.

"Ol' Aunt Kate, she died so late
She couldn't git in at d' heavenly gate.
D' angels met her wit a great big club
Knocked her right back in d' washin' tub."

Then they started another rhyme right after the first one without missing a beat.

"Ol Aunt Dinah, sick in bed,
Sent fo' d' doctor. Doctor said,
Git up Dinah, you ain't sick,
All you need is a hickory stick."

Children took to Cameron like magnets. They loved him because he was always interested in listening to what they had to say. They would sit on his steps for hours talking to him about things that went on in their busy day. No matter how long they talked, he never told them to shut up or go away, and he was never too busy for them. The little girls waved at Cameron as he stood, listening and watching them twirl their swiftly moving rope. He stopped sipping his hot cup of coffee long enough to wave back, as he sat in his favorite spot, the banister on his front porch, listening to their rhythmic serenade.

> Old Mary Mack, Mack, Mack,
> All dressed in black, black, black,
> Wit silver buttons, buttons, buttons,
> All down her back, back, back . . .

There was one little boy, Kenny, who attached himself to Cameron more than any other child in the neighborhood because he needed a safe, dependable friend. Whenever things were going crazy in his house, Kenny would run to Cameron's apartment for comfort and peace. Kenny and his little sister lived with their mother, who had a new, abusive boyfriend who indulged in long bouts of drinking, yelling, and cursing. Whenever there was a fight between Kenny's mother and her boyfriend, Kenny would bring his little three-year-old sister over to Cameron's apartment, sometimes they would spend the night.

The first time, Kenny showed up at his apartment long after midnight. The small boy knocked on his door, holding onto his sister's hand.

"Sheriff, kin we spend d' night?"

"What?" he said, half-asleep and shocked to see the two small children at his door.

"We cain't sleep in our house. My mama and her boyfriend keep yellin' and my sister cain't go t' sleep."

"Does your mother know where you are?"

"Yeah, she told us it wuz okay. Mr. Willie keeps wakin' everybody up," Kenny complained, yawning. Sighing deeply, Cameron looked across the street and saw the children's mother standing on the porch. She raised her hand and waved. Just then, her boyfriend came out and pulled her back inside. He was obviously drunk. Cameron looked down at the two innocent children. The beautiful little girl rubbed her eyes as Kenny waited for him to say that it was okay for them to spend the night.

"Come on, you two. You can have my bed. I'll sleep on the sofa."

"Kin I have some milk?" the little girl asked.

He went into the kitchen, poured milk in two glasses and found a few of the giant cookies the twins always baked for him and gave them each one.

"Thank ya', Sheriff," the little girl said, yawning with sleepy eyes. She had hardly finished her milk before she fell soundly asleep in the kitchen chair. Cameron picked her up, placed her in the bed, and covered her with a sheet.

Kenny said, "Thanks fo' lettin' us stay here. Sometimes, it's hard t' sleep in my house."

"Don't worry, man. I'll talk to your mother tomorrow."

Kenny yawned, hugged Cameron around the neck, and climbed into bed next to his sister. Within seconds, both children were sleeping peacefully. Cameron sat on the sofa and wondered what kind of people would mistreat children so severely, preventing them from getting their precious sleep. It was unthinkable. He stretched out on the sofa and fell asleep, trying to understand the mentality of Kenny's mother who would allow a man to interfere with her raising her children. When Cameron woke up the next morning, the little girl was standing over him, picking her nose. It took him a minute to remember who she was and why she was in his apartment.

After he fed the children a simple breakfast of toast, bacon, and cereal, he went to speak with Kenny's mother, who gave him a long sob story about her situation. He decided to let this issue go and hope that it would never happen again, but it did, repeatedly.

Early on a Saturday morning, Kenny came running over to Cameron's apartment. He was barely able to get the words out of his mouth because he was completely out of breath, trembling, and scared.

"Sheriff, you gotta come. He gonna hit my mama wit a pipe." Cameron did not waste any time. Within seconds, he was at Kenny's apartment and could hear the madness before he opened the door. Willie did have a pipe and judging from the appearance of Kenny's mother; he had already hit her several times because she was on the floor, bloody and crumpled with her hand up in the air, trying to protect her head from being hit again. She had no defense for the sixteen-inch iron pipe that her boyfriend lowered on her head in front of Cameron and her children. Anger propelled Cameron into action as he stepped between Paula and Willie, snatching the pipe from the man's hand. With the same pipe, Cameron beat Willie over the head, running him down the front steps of the building and out onto the dirt road, attracting the attention of the whole neighborhood.

"Don't you ever come back here," he yelled at the shocked, bleeding man. "Don't you ever let me see your face in Buttermilk Bottom again. If you come back, I will fucking kill you."

The man hobbled out of the Bottom the best way he could with blood streaming down his face. When the man reached Forrest Avenue at the top of the hill, the police stopped him. "What d' hell happened t' you?" asked a rookie police officer, who was sitting in his patrol car with his partner, a veteran officer.

"I fell down a flight o' steps," the bloody man responded, trying to avoid the police.

"Did anyone push you?" The young rookie pressured, trying to find out what happened, but the injured man ran down the street.

The rookie jumped out of the car and was about to chase the man down the street, but the older officer stopped him.

Pulling his coat, he asked, "Why in the hell you wanna find out who beat up a nigger?"

Looking embarrassed, the rookie police officer got back into the car with his apathetic partner and drove to their stakeout location just north of Buttermilk Bottom where everything looked peaceful and calm.

A week later, Paula, Kenny's mother showed up at Cameron's door, wearing bandages from her stay in the hospital. Having no one else to care for her children, Cameron quickly agreed to house them until their mother returned. She was carrying a cake to express her thanks. He accepted it gratefully, but not without telling the young mother his thoughts about her life and the situation that she placed her children and herself in by continuing her relationship with her abusive boyfriend.

"Your children need to see you as a strong person, who can protect them and yourself."

"I know,. . . But how kin I? He's stronger than me," she said pitifully.

"It doesn't matter how strong he is. . . You have to find a way to defend yourself. Get yourself, a knife or a rock. . . Whatever it takes, but you have to defend yourself."

"I know. I know. . . I'll find a way somehow," Paula said, too timid to look the number writer in the eye.

"It's disturbing for your children to see their mother abused and not fighting back. They will eventually grow up, thinking that it's normal, and that it's okay to beat people. Your children need to see you as a strong person."

"I try, Sheriff, but dat man never listens t' me," she whined with tears falling from her eyes.

"It's your job to make him listen or get rid of the no-good-son-of-a-bitch. Your children need to see you in control of your life and theirs."

The more Cameron tried to encourage Paula to be strong and to protect her children, the more she played the victim. His last piece of advice for her was to keep the door closed and locked just in case her boyfriend returned. As she walked out the door, he reminded her that her principle responsibility was to concentrate on her children. With those last words, Cameron focused his attention on the children who seemed to be spending more time at his apartment than their own. Since the last incident, their middle of the night visits ceased all together. No matter what was going on, Kenny found the number writer, and enjoyed spending time with him, and grew to love the man whom he and his friends nicknamed 'the sheriff'.

The boy looked at him one day and said, "I want to be jes like you when I grow up."

"No, you don't. You have to go to college and become a lawyer or a doctor. You must get out of Buttermilk Bottom, taking your mother and sister with you. Promise me that you will go to college and learn everything you can," Cameron said with a stern look in his eyes.

"I promise," the child said, seeing the seriousness in his friend's eyes, not sure what the word college meant, but he knew that whatever it was; it meant a great deal to the sheriff.

"Okay, a man's word is his bond," Cameron said, hugging the little boy. With Kenny at his side, the two of them walked to the corner store for a cold soda in a weekly ritual they established, since the first night Kenny and his sister came knocking on his door.

The men of Buttermilk Bottom continued to stand guard over the lives of their neighbors and on the surface, everything appeared fine. Since the disappearance of the police officers, an undercurrent of instability filled the air, which affected everyone who lived in The Bottom. The impact of the disappearances affected everyone but no one was willing to speak of it aloud.

Cameron found plenty of time and space to have an active social life. Finding available women had never been a concern of his because he had plenty of opportunities to have dates and intimacy with a variety of women. Although, Grace and Queenie were the two main women in his life, it never stopped him from seeking the company and attention of other women. Grace, who went to college with Cameron, had become an elementary school principal and her desire to marry him was still a paramount goal of hers. Queenie felt the same way. Believing that true love would never be a part of his life, Cameron had no desire to marry again, and he refused to entertain the idea with either of the two women. Whenever they tried to elicit a commitment from him, he was clear, direct, and often cruel in his assertion that he was not interested in anything more than carefree sex and friendship. When things got too serious, he backed off from each of them. He sincerely did not want to hurt them, but he wanted them to understand that he was not looking for a long-term relationship that included marriage. Each of the women loved him in their own special way, praying simultaneously that in time they could convince him otherwise. They knew he was seeing other women, but they felt that their love was strong enough to change his mind. Despite his warnings to them both, they consistently tried to win his complete love.

Chapter 9

At eight o'clock in the morning, a few weeks after the disappearance of the two police officers, a line of police cars came, thundering into Buttermilk Bottom. The police pulled out their Billy clubs and started banging on doors. Everybody knew that the police were coming, and they were prepared to act shocked and scared. Generally, people slept late on Saturday mornings, but not that morning. Thanks to Jake, they were fully prepared for the invasion. People still in their bedclothes came out onto their porches to make sure everyone could see everybody and that the police did not find a lone person to empty their hatred on, in the form of a beating or something worst.

The door-to-door search took about two hours to complete. No one got hurt but several apartments ended up ransacked. The police seemed angry that they had not found anything. Everyone who lived in Buttermilk Bottom was courteous and cooperative when asked questions about the missing officers. They said nothing because they knew nothing. Those who did have knowledge of the killings remained quiet, elusive, and observant. Detective Bailey Lee waited impatiently by his unmarked car, supervising the impromptu search. Cripple Jake went over to Bailey Lee and shook his hand.

"What's goin' on, detective?"

"We're lookin' fo' anyone wit any information 'bout d' missing police officers."

"Ya mean they were last seen down here in D' Bottom?" Jake asked, knowing the answer.

"No. . . But they were seen not far from here."

"Really? Where? Maybe I kin axe 'round to see what I kin find out fo' ya."

"Somebody seen 'em up on Forest Avenue 'bout three blocks from t' entrance t' Buttermilk Bottom at d' store," the detective said in a heavy southern accent. This was information everybody knew because the storekeeper was telling anyone who would listen that he was the last person to see the two officers alive.

"Ya'll gon searched his sto', too?" Jake asked innocently.

"We gonna search d' whole Fourth Ward 'til we find 'em," the detective lied.

"Well, dat's good. Let me see now, dat wuz on a Wednesday night, right?" Jake asked.

"Yeah, that was around nine o'clock."

"I wuz sittin' on my porch. I didn't see 'em drive through here," Jake volunteered. "Den too, d' police never come down here after dark, less somebody call 'em."

"They said there wuz a group of suspicious lookin' people on d' streets they wanted t' check out. Said, they looked like troublemakers. Ya see any strange groups comin' 'round here?"

"No, sir. People don't usually wander 'round down here after dark, 'less all hell breaks loose. It's real dark 'round here at nine o'clock. There wuz nobody 'round durin' dat time, 'cept a few children sittin' on d' steps, sangin'. Most people 'round here's 'fraid t' come out at night 'cept fo' a few drunken niggers on Friday or Saturday nights. Decent people stay inside, too much shootin' 'n stabbin' fo' most people," Jake said, continuing his habit of talking poorly around the police. He said it made them feel more relaxed when they were in the company of a stupid nigger versus an intelligent, well-spoken, black man.

"Keep an eye out fo' anything suspicious and call me at dis number if you hear somethin'," Bailey Lee said, handing Jake his business card.

"I will. . . I sho' will," Cripple Jake said, smiling broadly as the detective climbed into his car.

The detective signaled his troops to get into their cars and leave. Having found nothing, they quickly left without any of the drama that they entered the sunken neighborhood two hours before. Jake wrapped his fingers around the card, crushing it in his hands and threw it on the ground.

The group, consisting of about fifteen men, that was directly responsible for the missing police officers was standing all around the police. Without any remorse, they took the lives of the two abusive police officers for a very good reason. They deserved it, not only, for what they did the night they disappeared, but also for all the past abuse and harassment they had committed on the residents of Buttermilk Bottom. Over a year ago, the same two officers had raped a fifteen-year-old girl and left her for dead. Almost nude and badly beaten, she crawled home bloody with her clothing torn off her body. When the community tried to protest that incident, nothing happened and three months later, the same two police officers strip-searched a male neighbor.

They laughed while beating the man and said, "All niggers' s'ppose t' be at home 'fore midnight."

When the man tried to explain that he was on his way home from work, the police officers strip-searched him, beat him within an inch of his life, and threw him in jail for three nights. After the man got out of jail, he discovered that he lost his job. He was one of the men standing with the unofficial but very formal police force of Buttermilk Bottom. During that same month, the same police officers pretended they were looking for a criminal, burst into the juke-joint and stole all the money from the gambling tables and the bar, saying that they were collecting evidence. Everyone knew where the evidence was going.

On the night of the police officer's disappearance, one of the sentries spotted the police, harassing the college students and ran to inform Cameron, Jake, and the rest of the men of the incident. The whole neighborhood had fallen in love with the college students who came to register them so that they could vote in the upcoming election. No one had ever come into Buttermilk Bottom before to include them in anything. The students were kind, enthusiastic, showing a great deal of patience while explaining the necessity for every black person to vote. Some of the neighbors invited the students to dinner while others sat and talked with them about the civil rights movement, which the residents of Buttermilk Bottom seemed not to internalize. The students challenged them to participate and told them how they could help create change for the future. Many of the students even took the time to teach people how to write their names. There was new energy in the air because the students were telling them they had power and the students presence added some much-needed excitement to the lives of those living in 'The Bottom'.

When the word spread about the students being in trouble, the men assembled quickly and rushed to where the police had the students lined up against the wall with their backs turned. There was only one light in the area, the spotlight from the police vehicle, and the police had the students poised under it with their Billy clubs drawn. Armed with arrogance and hatred, the two officers hit two of the male students on the head and waited for an excuse to beat another. At Cameron's bidding, the group waited in the darkness to evaluate the situation, knowing that the police could not see them in the shadows with their blackened faces and dark clothing. When one of the two police officers put his hands up one of the girl's dresses, the group began to move in. Within minutes, they hit the police officers on their head with their own Billy clubs, rendered them unconscious then threw their lifeless bodies into the back seat of their patrol car.

The students were visibly upset and in tears as they left the area. They tried to hug the number man and his friends but that was not the time for sentimentality but one or two of them managed to get through, hugging him anyway before he rushed them out of the area. He pushed them away because he wanted them gone as quickly as possible.

The police and their vehicle were in the kudzu, hidden from all-mankind forever. The massive covering of kudzu grew so tall and thick around the community of Buttermilk Bottom that no one dared to enter, unless it was to hide dead bodies. The crew that went into the kudzu to complete the task of disposing of the bodies spent the rest of the evening getting drunk at Queenie's joint. No one spoke about what happened not even in whispers, but they did talk about everything else that occurred in The Bottom over the last fifty years. Cripple Jake was busy spinning his tales, making the men laugh to forget about the incident.

"Once there were two woodpeckers, a country woodpecker and a city woodpecker. They were cousins. The country woodpecker went to the city to visit his cousin, the city woodpecker. The city woodpecker took his country cousin all over the city proudly showing him all the trees that his eyes could survey. 'See what fine work we do here in the city. We all work hard; see all the holes in those trees. We, city woodpeckers, really know our business.' The country woodpecker said, 'That's great, but what happened to that tree over there? Why aren't there any holes in that one?' 'That's a real problem. Everybody has tried to put a hole in that tree, but it's so hard no one can put a dent in it.' 'Mind if I try?' The country woodpecker asked. 'Sure, be my guest,' the city woodpecker said. That country woodpecker jumped on that old tree and bam! In seconds, it was in splinters on the ground. The next year, the city woodpecker went to visit his country cousin, who took his city cousin on a tour of all the trees in his hometown. The city woodpecker spotted an old tree that had not been touched, and asked, 'Why aren't there any holes in that tree?' The country woodpecker said, 'No one around here can put a dent in it.' 'May I try,' the city cousin asked. 'Of course, be my guest,' the country woodpecker said. 'Step aside,' the city woodpecker said, jumping on the tree and seconds later the tree was in splinters." Jake stopped abruptly and waited for his listeners to respond.

"Dat ain't no joke, man. . . Dat's stupid," Sylvester said.

"You're losin' yo' touch, Jake," Moses said, drinking his whiskey down in one gulp.

Enjoying the baffled and confused looks on their faces, Jake said. "But. . . There's a moral to this story." Jake waited until he had everyone's attention, then he said, "The further you get from home. . . The harder your pecker gets."

After a moment to consider his final statement, the room was in uproarious laughter. Their problems faded as they accepted the burden of their joint actions, and because they were all very proud that they had helped the college students. Most importantly, they liberated their community of two abusive police officers. When Jake finished his story, Dellah came over, hugging him tightly.

"Jake, wanna go upstairs wit me," she asked seductively.

"Excuse me, gentlemen, I have work to do," he said, laughing and getting up off the chair quickly and easily as he grabbed his crutches and followed the young woman up the stairs.

Watching their friend in awe as he climbed the steps with Dellah, the men shook their heads in bafflement.

"Dat man gits mo' pussy than anybody I ever seen. . . And he's cripple. If I asked t' pay dat bitch double, she'd turn my ass down," Smoke said, putting out his cigarette in frustration.

"Jake's mighty popular. I wonder what d' hell kin he do wit no legs?" Sylvester asked.

"Not a damn thang. He jes got a pocket full o' money, dat's all," Smoke said, lighting another cigarette.

The next morning the sentries posted on the rooftops of the dilapidated houses spotted a team of police officers and investigators at the entrance of Buttermilk Bottom. No matter where the officers looked, there were no clues indicating what happened to the two men since the night of their disappearance. The officers called in on their car radio to say that they were going to question a group of troublemakers. They were three blocks from the entrance to Buttermilk Bottom that was the last communication from the two missing officers.

Investigators filled the intersection looking for evidence. There was none, no blood, and no sign of a struggle. They did find empty shotgun pellets, which they quickly booked as evidence, but there was no blood on the ground or on the discharged shells. All the men of Buttermilk Bottom wore gloves, so there were no fingerprints anywhere.

After questioning everyone on or near the intersection, the officers interviewed Rev. Freeman, the minister of a local holiness church and a woman who lived in a house right in front of the intersection at the entrance of Buttermilk Bottom. Both people said they had not seen the missing officers. A couple blocks north on Forest Avenue, they re-questioned Ezra Levine and his family at the local grocery store and found out a little more information.

"They came here around seven-thirty. One had an orange Nehi soda, and the other one had a grape," Ezra said. "They stopped here every night about the same time to get a snack and to talk about whatever's going on in the neighborhood."

"Did they mention anythin' t' you 'bout a group o' agitators comin' 'round here?" Detective Lee asked.

"No, not a word but they sure helped me over the years with a few problems."

"Did d' two officers seem nervous. . . Anythang like that?"

"No, they acted normally. I'm sorry to hear that they're missing," Ezra said, truthfully.

"Did you see 'em talkin' t' anyone one after they left here?"

"No. They got in their patrol car and rode away."

"Did they tell you where they were goin' after they left yo' store?"

"Just that they were going to make their rounds. That's all."

"Thank you, sir. If ya think of anythin', please call," Bailey Lee said, giving the grocer his business card.

Time was passing rapidly, yielding no clues. The police knew that the passage of time was not a good sign for them and their ability to solve the crime, if there was one. The news stations and newspapers pondered over the disappearances.

"Not only are the policemen missing, their vehicle is missing," one reporter said.

Everyone speculated over what could have occurred. The news reporter expressed concern as they told viewers about the families of the two men. The officer who put his hands up the student's dress had a wife and two teen-aged girls at home and the other one still lived with his mother.

Chapter 10

Cameron Fielding silently rejoiced as he pondered over his on-going sexual relationships with the two beautiful women in his life. Queenie and Grace, two very different women, and he appreciated the difference. He had no desire to make either relationship permanent because he enjoyed the time he spent with each of them and the other women he happened to date in between. His lifestyle found many opportunities to explore sexual encounters with a variety of women, and he took full advantage of them. His motivations were clear and simple; he loved women.

What stimulated him most about women were those quiet unspoken moments when they did not realize someone was watching. He believed that people were themselves when they were alone, so he watched for those secret and very, private moments. He had no list of things that made him desire one woman over another because he loved all kinds of women, and he took the time to learn how to satisfy each of them in a special way. The joy for him was finding out what each of them needed from him, and he happily obliged them.

The longest relationship Cameron had with anyone was the one he enjoyed with Grace, who worked hard every day as an elementary school principal on the west side of town. After both their short-lived marriages, they met after their divorces and began dating. Their relationship began very deliberately because Grace made it her business to keep track of where Cameron was every minute of every day from the first day she met him on campus. The whole time they were in college, Cameron barely knew Grace was alive, a fact, that never stopped her from following him or dreaming about him. When she heard that he and his wife divorced, she tracked him down and arranged their first encounter. Investigating through her own network of college classmates, she discovered that he hung out at a jazz spot on Hunter Street where an old friend of theirs performed in a jazz trio.

"How many times do we have to come to this place?" her friend Carrie asked.

"As many times as it takes to find Cameron," Grace said, watching the door.

"Girl, this is the dumbest thing you've ever done, dressing up every night and sitting in this place until it closes. Don't expect me to be here tomorrow night, because I have other things to do with my time."

"Lloyd said he comes here all the time."

"Maybe he heard that you were looking for him," Carrie teased.

"He'll be here tonight I just know it."

"You said that last night and the night before. Girl, no man is worth all this aggravation. There are a million men in this world, why you are fixating on this one? I don't understand you. Remember tomorrow is Monday, and we have to be in our classrooms at eight in the morning and functioning like two intelligent human beings."

"I know. I know."

"I'm not staying here until two o'clock in the morning, not tonight. If you want to come out next weekend, okay but. . . ."

"Never mind. . . It won't be necessary," Grace said dreamily.

"Don't tell me you came to your senses at last."

"No. . . Just the opposite. He just walked in."

"Where? Which one is he?"

"The tall one."

"That's Cameron Fielding? Well, my Lord. . . He is the prettiest thing this side of heaven."

"I know."

"Well, get off your ass and go get him. If you don't. . . God help me, I will."

"I'm so nervous."

Cameron walked into the dark smoke-filled room with his co-worker and assistant coach, Lester. The two men stood in the doorway for a while, adjusting to the dimly lit room, then proceeded to the bar where they both ordered whiskey straight and had the bartender pour one for their friend, Lloyd, who was playing in the jazz trio and was finishing the set. As soon as Lloyd saw his two friends, he smiled then went over to join them at the bar.

After drinking down the whiskey, Lloyd said, "Hey man, what's hanging?"

"Not much. It looks pretty busy tonight for a Sunday," Cameron said, looking around the room.

"Yeah, the weekends always seem to start on Thursdays for colored folks and last until eleven o'clock on Sunday night, then everyone disappears," Lloyd said. "Cameron, one of our old classmates is here."

"Yeah, Who?" he said, looking around for a familiar face.

"Grace Preston. She's sitting over there. I think she must have a crush on me because she has been in here almost every night this week. She looks good, doesn't she?" he said, indicating where Grace was sitting.

"She was in our class?"

"Sure, she sat behind you in Mr. Lynch's economics class, and I sat behind her," he said, grinning.

"I don't remember her."

"It doesn't matter. Come on help me out, man. I've been trying to get next to her for years. Come on. . . I'll introduce you."

When the three men came across the floor toward Grace and her friend, Grace began to panic. All she ever wanted since she was a freshman at Morris Brown College was to have Cameron notice her and to have him touch her then ultimately to have him make love to her. Although she was overjoyed that he was finally coming toward her, she was frightened that he might somehow escape her grasp as he had done so many times in the past.

"They're coming this way," she said.

"And who is that with him?"

"I don't know."

"Smile for God's sake," Carrie said as she smiled at Lester.

"Ladies, Ladies. . . May we join you?" Lloyd said, pulling up a chair right next to Grace.

"Sure, please do," Carrie said with her eyes on Lester.

"This is like a homecoming weekend. Grace, you remember Cameron, don't you?"

"Who wouldn't remember him? He was the captain of our football team and the most popular boy in the school," Grace said.

Cameron smiled. "I'm sorry to say that I don't remember you, but it's a pleasure to meet you," he said, noticing her beautiful brown legs, which she crossed in front of him.

"Thank you, this is my friend, Carrie Richardson," she said. Lloyd introduced Lester before he had to dart off to his next set.

"Hold my seat, baby. I'll be back soon," Lloyd said, squeezing Grace's hand as he left the table. Grace looked embarrassed.

"How long have you known Lloyd?" Cameron asked.

"Since our freshman year at Brown," Grace said.

"He's a great guy and extremely talented."

"Yes, he is."

"What are you doing now?" Grace asked.

"P. E. and coaching at Howard. Lester and I work together," Cameron said.

"How long have you been coaching, Lester?" Carrie asked.

"This is my second year. I've learned a lot from Cameron here," he said, popping his fingers to the music as the trio began to play.

"I always wanted to learn about sports, but I never really understood them," Carrie said, lying as she admired Lester's well-built body. Grace sat quietly as Cameron discreetly evaluated her assets.

"Really? Most sports are very simple once you understand the basic principle behind them," Lester said, starting an hour-long conversation with Carrie.

"How long have you and Lloyd been dating?" Cameron asked Grace.

"Dating? We're not dating."

"I thought . . ."

"No, we're not doing anything," Grace said quickly and emphatically.

"He's under the impression that you came here every night to see him," Cameron said.

"No way," Carrie blurted out then realized that she was giving away too much information.

"She has been keeping me company. I've been waiting for my sister to get off work. She works right down the street," Carrie injected.

"Oh, well, somebody ought to tell Lloyd. He has a crush on you. . . Since college," Cameron said, looking at Grace's well-formed mouth.

"This is the first I've heard about it," Grace said, taking a deep breath. "To tell you the truth, Cameron, I had a crush on you."

"Really?" Cameron said with new interest.

"Oh yes, all the girls did. I wasn't alone; there were hundreds of women falling all over you back then. You broke all our hearts when you got married."

"Really," he said, taking time to admire her physical traits. Grace had a beautiful face, and what seemed like a nice body, but he could not give her a full evaluation in the corner where she sat. Grace smiled not knowing what else to say. Mesmerized by his intense stare, she could not believe her luck. "How about you? What have you done since leaving Brown?" he asked, looking seductively at her.

"I'm teaching at Pitts Elementary," she said, smiling.

"Good. How do you like it?"

"I love it, but I'm hoping to move into administration one day."

"Really? It sounds ambitious."

"I want to be where I can do the most good," she said.

For a long time, there was silence between them. The music filled the room and her emotions as the trio played 'Easy to Love' in the background.

"Tell me, Grace. How can I get a date with you? If you're sure Lloyd won't mind."

"Lloyd is not a consideration, believe me, and you can get a date as soon as you ask," she said, not wanting to be coy or pretentious.

"How about tomorrow night?"

"Sounds great."

"Shall I break the news to Lloyd or do you want to do the honors?"

"When did being in the audience obligate anyone?" she said.

"He's my friend."

"Mine, too."

During the break, Lloyd came over to the table and sat next to Grace. Grace got up from the table and said. "We have to go. Teachers have to be at school before the students."

"Will I see you tomorrow night?" Lloyd asked.

"I'm afraid not. I have a date," she said. "The music was wonderful. Thanks." She got up to leave. "It was great seeing you again," she said to Cameron, shaking his hand while discreetly giving him her home telephone number and address."

"Goodnight, gentlemen," Carrie said. Then to Lester, she said. "I'll see you Saturday at seven."

As Grace walked from the building, Cameron was more than pleased with her total package. She was short with a small waistline but had big, beautiful legs.

"Damn, looks like I missed that one," Lloyd said. "How about a drink?"

"You buying?" Cameron asked.

"Hell no."

After several dates, Cameron discovered that Grace had deep feelings for him back when they were in college. He vaguely remembered her, but it did not matter to him in the least. They were getting along extremely well until he was arrested and sent to jail.

Since his move to Buttermilk Bottom, he spent almost every Friday and Saturday night with her in her family's home that she occupied alone. There were times that he could not make it, but he always called her from the pay telephone at the juke joint. Most people who lived in Buttermilk Bottom had no telephone. As the years passed, they became comfortable with each other, lounging in bed for days at a time. He avoided and discouraged any discussion regarding marriage and children. When the subject came up, he was kind but very direct.

"I was like a sick puppy following behind you, and you didn't even know I was alive."

"You should have told me," he said, kissing her.

"I tried. The Lord knows that I tried, but every time I got near you, there would be a group of girls who would descend on you and swoop you away. You were quite the lady's man, you know?"

Admiring her beautiful face, he said, "I had a few good friends."

"Friends? Is that what they're calling them now?"

"Very good friends," he said, smiling from the corner of his mouth.

"Man, you knew you were hot. You had so many girls chasing your handsome behind. . . You wouldn't have noticed me if I had a sign around my neck."

"How you exaggerate," he said, trying to interest her in another round of lovemaking.

"You know I'm not lying."

"We see things differently that's all."

He was right because the difference between them was enormous. It was difficult for her to see him functioning at the lowest level of human existence and living in the worst neighborhood in the city of Atlanta. He never said what he was doing to make money, but she knew whatever it was had to be illegal because he had a great deal of money that he spent generously.

Wanting more from him than their usual Friday and Saturday night encounters, she took a risk and a deep breath, asking, "Cameron, why don't you try to get your certification reinstated so you can go back to work? I know that Carver is looking for a football coach. You could do so much with your life rather than wasting it in Buttermilk Bottom."

As soon as she finished her last statement, she knew she had gone too far. He looked betrayed and hurt by her remarks.

"I hope you understand that I have no desire to go back to teaching or coaching. I have my own reasons, and I hope you can respect that," he said, watching her closely. The truth was he did try twice and had failed both times.

It was a humiliating process, and he did not intend to go through it again. He would never again stand in front of a bunch of pompous white assholes and beg for his job. That part of his life was over.

"If that is your final decision?" she said softly.

"It is. Can you live with that?"

"Yes, I can."

The words that no one heard her say were the fact that she was too embarrassed to bring him around her professional friends. The first question they would ask was, *What do you do for a living?* God only knew what he did for a living, but she knew in her heart that it had to be illegal because the clothes he wore were premium quality. Their love life was excellent because he always showed his generosity, gentleness, kindness, and thoughtfulness in gifts of clothing, recordings, and even thoughtful cards. He was all she ever wanted in a man and more. Very frequently, he showed up at her door with flowers, a book, or a great bottle of wine. At other times, he would surprise her with a new album by Dakota Staton, her favorite jazz singer. When they went out, it was always to quiet, out of the way places that featured local jazz artists. Occasionally, they would go to a movie but on those occasions when she had to attend a formal affair, she would go with a co-worker who was more than willing to step in. Grace and Cameron spent most of their time together in bed in her house where they enjoyed the sweetness of each other's body. She lay in his arms and snuggled up as close to him as she could.

"I love you, you know."

"I love, loving you."

"It's not the same thing," she said, sitting up. "I am deeply in love with you, Cameron. One day, I hope to marry you. I don't think I have ever loved anyone so much in my life."

"Thank you for saying that," he said, kissing her warmly on the lips. "You really know how to make a guy blush," he said, trying to tease her out of the conversation.

"I'm not telling you this to make you blush. I want more out of our relationship. We should be together all the time, every night. . . Always," she said, looking into his eyes for answers.

"It would be a sin to take a beautiful woman like you out of circulation."

"I'm not a newspaper for God's sake, Cameron. I need more from you than weekends under the covers," she said, irritated.

"I wish I could give it to you," he said, sadly.

"Won't you think about it?"

"I have thought about it. I can only tell you what is in my heart." She did not respond so he said, "Maybe, it's time to call it quits."

"Quits?"

"It may be for the best."

"Best for who?"

"You. I'm not going to promise you something I can't give you," he said, looking into her eyes to make certain she understood. "You should find someone who would be better suited for you. Someone without a prison record," he said, staring into her eyes. His career choice embarrassed her, although she never said the words, but he knew.

"I'm in love with you, Cameron."

"I think you are placing unnecessary limits on yourself and your future because marriage is the one thing I can't give you, now or in the future." There was a long silence.

"Then, I will have to be content with what we have," she said sadly.

"Can you do that?"

"I don't think I have a choice."

"You always have a choice."

"Not when it comes to you," she said, kissing him tearfully on the lips.

With regret, he accepted her affectionate kiss and appreciated the love he knew she had for him. Deep inside, he wished he felt more for her, but he did not want to lie to her or himself so he gave her what he knew she wanted. He explored her mouth until he found her sugary tongue and gently stroked it with his until he felt an urgent ripple moving through her body. Pausing to look into her watering eyes, he soaked up the yearning he saw, emanating from them. It made him harder and raised the level of his desire.

Feeling her soft breasts touching his chest, he lowered his head to acknowledge them and to give them the attention they deserved. His lips grew moist as he caressed them, making her nipples stand up in approval, enticing him to continue. The taste of her precious gifts was so sweet that it made him want to rush to get what he needed, because he felt a little moisture from his own body seep out. He wanted to satisfy her and let her know how much he appreciated her honesty and openness. She had taken a risk in expressing her love for him, a feeling he could not return, but he could make love to her and give her all the affection she needed and deserved.

With both of his hands, he pulled her to a sitting position on the edge of the bed. Kneeling down, he opened her beautiful soft legs and kissed each of them, one side, and then the other. The hair on her mound was curly and soft, tickling his nose as he pressed against it to smell the fragrance of her body's sanctuary. As she lay back on the bed, he pulled her hips forward to give him total access to the silky petals leading to the passageway that he ultimately would possess. His lips tingled with excitement as her body moved in rhythm with his moist kisses. What she felt spreading through her body and the movement of her hips was confirmation of her love for him, which he knew and felt as he continued to love her. Suddenly, the sweetness of his lips sent twinges of ecstasy through her entire body, which she hoped would always be his. Knowing the power he had over her and it, she surrendered it to him all too happily.

When he felt her body give into him completely, he knew he could celebrate with her the pleasure and blissfulness of their erotic journey together. His stiffness craved her warmth as he guided his vessel gently into the center of her passion. As he entered her, she sighed deeply and smiled up at him. There was nothing in the world she loved more than feeling him inside of her. They had perfected the act of satisfying each other. Everything matched as he moved, and she moved with him, sensuously and totally committed to reaching the ultimate climax. They stretched the boundaries on their physical aerobics as their bodies flexed and contracted to the lofty peaks of passion. With their bodies weak with pleasure, they drifted off to sleep, twisted and completely entwined while embracing each other.

The morning sun rose slowly as Cameron sat on the edge of the bed, watching the news. He listened as the reporter said, "The search for the two missing police officers will intensify over the next few days. The police have made this case their first priority as Detective Bailey Lee leads a team of experts to discover the whereabouts of their missing comrades."

As the detective began to speak into the microphone, Cameron not only listened to his words; he evaluated the man's demeanor and noted his superior, prejudiced attitude. Standing at the mirror in her bra and panties, Grace noticed how engrossed and intensively Cameron listened to the announcer.

She said, "Please, tell me you have nothing to do with that."

"I have nothing to do with that," he said, pulling her to him, admiring her body.

She could feel his passion for her as he began to nibble on her stomach. *How could a man make love to me so beautifully and not be in love with me?* she thought. *How?*

Chapter 11

All 59,000 square miles of the Georgia land scrape were under a tremendous heat wave in July of 1955, which made Buttermilk Bottom doubly hot because there was no breeze whispering anywhere near its recessed location. Cameron found it easier to stay at Grace's house because her house afforded them an occasional gust of air that could never exist in The Bottom. Around six o'clock in the afternoon, Cameron returned to his own apartment. Just as he was about to open his refrigerator for a bottle of beer, Cripple Jake knocked on the door and walked in.

"You missed all the excitement. The police came back again this morning. This time, they wanted to know if anyone knew about a group of troublemakers hanging around here."

"Troublemakers? In Buttermilk Bottom?"

Cripple Jake laughed, "How about that shit?"

"Was everybody cool?"

"Went smooth as silk, but I have a feeling that they are coming back again and again. I just hope no one gets hurt."

"Let's pray that none of our people get hurt. . . That would be more realistic."

"True. Hey, what about sharing one of those beers with me? It's getting hot out there."

"Help yourself." Cameron walked out on the porch and sat on the banister, Jake came out with his beer in his hand to join him. Jake sat his beer on the small wooden table and sat down in the chair next to it while propping his crutches against the wall behind him. "This is a hot ass summer," he said.

"I'm afraid you're right," Cameron said. They sat quietly for a few minutes enjoying their beers and appreciating each other's friendship.

Jake reached around the back of the chair he was sitting in and pulled out the checkerboard. Seeing this, Cameron picked up the old coffee can filled with checkers off the windowsill and pulled up a stool opposite Jake.

After several animated games, Jake said, "There goes Harlan. He's on his way down to the juke-joint to bang Dellah. That fool has been sneaking down there twice a week to turn her out. When his wife finds out that he's missing work to bang that woman, she's gonna kick his ass. Alberta's one of the smallest and one of the toughest women I have ever met. I would never mess with a woman with a temper like hers, never."

"Maybe he knows what he's doing."

"Harlan? That nigger don't know Jack-shit." The two friends sat quietly playing checkers sipping their beers. "Now, look at that shit," Jake said.

"What now?"

"That motherfucker is back here again."

"Who are you talking about?" Cameron said, looking around.

"That damn insurance man. He's over there, trying to fuck Betsy again. I feel sorry for her. The man's a creep."

"She opens the door for him," Cameron said, unconcerned.

"She doesn't want to. She doesn't have a choice, man. The dude threatens her."

"He's threatening her? How?" he asked, paying close attention.

"He sells her life insurance or health insurance and collects the money every week. After a few months pass, he raises the rates a little each time until she can't make the payments. When she got behind, the son-of-a-bitch offered to pay her premium, and before she noticed it, she was in debt to him for a pretty penny. To make up for the past-due payments, he gets sexual favors. If she refuses to go to bed with him, he tells her that he's going to drop the policy."

"How do you know all this stuff?"

"Shit, it's been going on for years."

"Why would she put herself through that?"

"Because she's got three children depending on her and no family, that's why."

"Damn."

"It's sad, man. You can look at her and tell that she hates it. Every Thursday that ass-hole goes there to take advantage of her. Her next-door neighbor said she gets a glassy look in her eyes. Late at night, she can hear Betsy crying. She told her to go to the witch doctor to get some help."

"You mean the old lady who lives back in the woods?"

"Yeah, the witch doctor, she's the best."

"You don't really believe that stuff, do you?"

"Look, I've lived here all my life, and I've learned not to disbelieve anything. If that is the only way for her to get rid of that bastard, then so be it."

"That's the saddest thing I've heard this year."

"Some mothers will do anything to leave a little something for their children."

"But. . . To put herself through that?"

"Yeah, that. My mother screwed the milkman and the insurance man when she lost her job; I was about nine years old. I never thought about it then because I was accustomed to seeing my mother disappear in her room with somebody she owed money to. Shit, she even screwed old man Ezra at the grocery store to keep food on the table. Hell, he still gives her free center cut pork chops and steaks, whenever she goes in there, just for old-time's sake. She said she did what she had to do."

"I guess I can understand that," Cameron said.

Cripple Jake had a couple more beers while he shared stories about each person who wandered up and down the streets. After he left, Cameron stood on his porch looking out over the community he had grown to love. As the sun descended in the sky, he noticed a figure of a woman walking up the hill away from him, leaving Buttermilk Bottom. He knew he had never seen her before, and he wondered what she was doing there. She reached the top of the hill just as the sun was going down. He caught a stunning sight that gripped his heart and his loins. Her lean shapely frame appeared perfectly womanly as she moved into the dwindling, reddish-orange sun as it fell in the evening sky. Her hips rolled to an unknown rhythm, pulling him away from everything except their round shapeliness sitting upon her long, beautiful legs that peeped out of the slit in the back of her skirt. Jake called him, making him turn away for a second. When he turned back, she was gone.

Chapter 12

The last days of August in 1955 was traumatic for most black people in American because the news of, fourteen year-old, Emmett Till's brutal murder in Mississippi. The husband and the brother of his white accuser drug him from his uncle's home because the woman reported that the teenager whistled at her. A native of Chicago, Emmitt was spending his summer vacation with his uncle. His death brought home the reality of the black man's continued bondage under the Jim Crow laws instituted by segregationist to restrict blacks from participating in the American dream. Black people rushed to newsstands to purchase copies of Ebony and Jet magazines to get the real facts about the murder. At the juke joint, people huddled in various groups reading the accounts to each other and discussing the fate of black people in the South. Churches, colleges, universities, and civil rights groups began to demand changes to eliminate the situation of outright prejudice and abuse of blacks and to punish the persons responsible for the hate crime. The white news media played down the incident until Emmitt Till's mother demanded that the casket remain open to show America how hatred and prejudice affected the black race. Most people were appalled at what they called her 'insensitivity,' but the impact of what she did, had a dramatic effect on outraged whites and blacks all over the country. They saw the reality of racial hatred. Suddenly, racial discrimination moved from being a southern problem to being an American problem.

All lovers of democracy spoke out loudly, demanding immediate conviction of the perpetrators. Buttermilk Bottom, along with the rest of the country, watched and waited to see if the law would punish the murders.

On a hot Sunday morning, in The Bottom, Cameron waited impatiently as he had all week hoping to see the erotic vision he had seen the week before on a Sunday afternoon. The neighborhood was quiet, still sleeping and resting from an emotional weekend of collective mourning for the family of Emmitt Till and for themselves. There was an acknowledgement of frustrations and a high sense of anticipation for what must happen next to grant black people equal rights under the constitution. Many groups, political leaders, and individual freedom fighters wondered what must happen to eliminate racism from the fabric of American life, whether it was in the North or South.

Despite what was happening in the national news, it was almost angelic the way the day began to unfold. Cameron always got up early and had coffee on his front porch. It did not matter what kind of weather it was; he loved watching the neighborhood come alive.

The paperboy came by early in the morning, hollering, "'Lan-a World Paper!" Cameron always smiled when he heard that sound because it reminded him of the many times his aunt made him pronounce the word, At-lanta. This boy sounded very much like he did back then. "Lan-a World Paper!".

"I'll take two," Cameron called out.

"The boy smiled, "'Morning, Mr. Sheriff." The industrious little boy took off his heavy newspaper bag, laying it on the ground. He ran up the steps two at a time and handed the number writer the two papers he requested.

"Good morning. How's the newspaper business this morning?" Cameron asked, giving him the money plus some extra change for a tip.

"Thanks. It's goin' pretty good. It would be much better if people woke up earlier."

"Why don't you come back later?"

"'Cause I gots t' go t church."

"Oh, I see."

"Don't you go t' church?"

"Not anymore."

"Why not?"

"I never thought about it. When I did go, I liked it a great deal."

"I like it." The boy said enthusiastically. "I like d' music 'n d' way d' preacher start jumpin' up and down yellin' at everybody. . . Then d' women start t' cryin', knockin' their hats off and fallin' out all o'er d' place. It's fun."

"It sounds like you have a mighty fine church," Cameron said, enjoying the boy's descriptions.

"It is. D' best part's after all d' yellin' and preachin's over. . . We git t' eat. Dey got so much food laid out on long tables enough fo' everybody. I love t' eat dat church food. It's so good." The boy was so into his talk about the delicious church food he loved that he began to lick his lips, which made Cameron laughed hysterically. The boy said, "Mr. Sheriff, ya ought t' come t' my church. Dey got a lot o' women there lookin' fo' husbands."

"It sounds like that would be a little bit more church than I need right now. . . But when I start looking for a wife, I'll think about it," Cameron said, smiling at the boy's innocence.

"If ya know somebody who's lookin' fo' a wife tell 'em t' come t' my church. Dat's all dey talk about, 'cludin' my mama. She wanna husband real bad."

"I wish her luck," Cameron said, laughing.

"Thanks, I better be goin'. See ya later, Mr. Sheriff." The boy ran down the steps, picked up the canvas bag that held his papers and continued down the street, yelling, "'Lan-a World Paper!"

By ten o'clock, people started stirring in the streets heading for their Sunday worship services. Ladies dressed in their big brim hats and fancy clothes, and the children dressed in their Sunday best had clean faces. A fewer number of men, dressed in suits and ties, started a steady procession up the hill, headed for various churches with their families. Sunday mornings were special; it had a different smell and a calmer feeling. Sundays always appeared to bring a sense of freedom to the residents of Buttermilk Bottom, whether it was conscious or not, it was evident in their mannerisms, their walk, and most visible in their dress. It was so unique, so ethnic, so tribal and. . . So pure.

Almost every Sunday that Cameron lived in the Bottom, he ate Sunday morning breakfast with the twin spinsters, who lived on the first floor of his building. They had adopted him as their son and enjoyed his company immensely. The twins, Gussie and Essie Barnes, cooked a mountain of food for Sunday breakfast, and it was not because their favorite number man was joining them. They had done it all their lives. Sundays were special for them, and they used food to celebrate the Lord's Day. The sisters never got up before ten o'clock each morning during the week because they said it did not make any sense to get up any earlier, but at eleven o'clock every Sunday morning, breakfast was ready. Cameron arrived a little after eleven, carrying the newspaper he purchased for them. He knocked on the screen door.

"Come on in, baby," Gussie yelled.

"Good morning," Cameron said.

"How're you this fine morning," Essie said, wiping her hands on her blue flowered apron.

"Fine. It sure smells good in here. What goodies have you two whipped-up for today?"

"Everything in God's creation," Gussie said, placing a pitcher of orange juice on the table.

"We started cooking one thing then got a bit carried away," Essie said, pulling the hot biscuits out of the stove.

"Sit down, boy. Everything is hot," Gussie said.

The twins placed a bowl of grits on the table with biscuits, eggs, bacon, and a platter full of fried chicken.

"Everything smells and looks delicious," Cameron said.

"It's your turn to say the blessing, Essie," Gussie said. It was their tradition to rotate who said the grace for the table, and Cameron was included in that rotation. He had blessed the table the Sunday before.

"Lord, bless this food and a special blessing for the people at this table, Amen." Cameron loved it when Essie did the blessing because it was always brief and to the point.

They ate in silence for a few minutes, then Gussie, cleared her throat and asked, "Did you hear that that insurance man was over there messing with Betsy again."

"I saw him go in the house. I wish to God that I could do something to help her; she doesn't have a family or anyone to look out for her," Essie said, pouring coffee for everybody.

"It's very sad what women have to put up with to get along in this world. I really feel sorry for those children," Gussie said. They often talked as if no one else was in the room except the two of them.

"Inez told her to go to Cigam for help," Essie said.

"Well, everybody else goes to her. . . No reason for her not to," Gussie replied.

"She might be able to help," Essie said. "I wish she would at least try."

"Do you believe in witchcraft?" Cameron asked.

"I can't say that I don't believe, but I hear some people put a lot of hope and money in it," Essie said.

"There are a lot of things in this world nobody can explain. I'm not all that smart, but I know there's a mess of things that we don't know nothing about," Gussie said.

"From what I've seen and heard, Cigam's got the touch. People say that she knows what she's doing."

"If she didn't, there wouldn't be so many people coming in here to see her. That's what I think," Gussie said.

"There has always been a mystery around Miss Cigam. We're the oldest people around here, and we really don't remember exactly when she moved in," Essie said. "She's been here over fifteen years."

"Not only do we not remember when she came, we don't remember when that house of hers came either. It just appeared out of the kudzu. One day, there were vines all over the place and the next day, there was a house. . . Complete with a rocking chair and that lame black cat of hers with the sparkling green eyes, sitting on the porch," Gussie said.

"For months there was nobody around. We didn't see a soul. Then one night, we saw the smoke coming out the chimney and faint lights flickering inside. When she first moved in the place, it didn't have a drop of electricity until a few years after she moved in," Essie said.

"A couple of months passed before we even laid eyes on her."

"We were sitting out on the porch late in the afternoon, and we saw a woman walking up the road. It was almost dark, so we weren't sure it was a real person or a shadow."

"That's right. My sister and I had just spent the day shelling peas, and we were too tired to go inside."

"We were glad to sit out there and enjoy the sun going down," Essie said.

"When we finally saw her. . . We just stared, trying to figure things out. We finally figured out that it was a person, so we nodded, and she nodded back," Gussie said.

"Then she was gone."

"It was several weeks before we saw her again," Gussie said.

"The whole neighborhood was talking about her and that house appearing out of the kudzu that way. I don't know when we figured out that she lived there, but it took a long time. Matter of fact, people around here generally know everything about everybody, but we never figured out anything about Miss Cigam. It was almost a year before anybody knew her name," Essie said. "Then people, somehow figured out they could go to her when they needed someone fixed. We have never been down there. . . Too many weeds for us, but they say, if you have a big problem with somebody, she's the one to go to. She don't charge much either," Gussie said.

"If you don't have money, you can pay her with other things," Essie related.

"Like what?" Cameron asked.

"Food, clothing, furniture even," Gussie said.

"When she first moved here, some old white woman gave her a brand new Frigerdaire. The house didn't have a lick of electricity. Did it, Gussie?"

"White women can be so crazy. Everybody knew she didn't have no electricity."

"Any fool could have seen that," Gussie said, laughing.

Cameron was strangely quiet and the twins noticed right away. As they wondered what was on his mind, he was thinking of the beautiful woman who walked out of the Bottom as the sun was setting. He wondered if he would ever find out who she was, or if she would ever come back to the neighborhood. Essie did not want to call attention to his daydreaming, so she continued her story, knowing that he wasn't listening.

"Shortly after she moved in, people started coming into Buttermilk Bottom in fine cars and dressed in beautiful fashionable clothes. At first, it was hard to tell where they were going, but it became clear after a few weeks. A steady stream of people, black and white, came to visit Miss Cigam in that house of hers. They came all day long up until the sun went down then nobody comes to Buttermilk Bottom after dark, unless they live here then. . . A body's got to be careful," Essie said. "People here whispered and gossiped til they figured out why people were going there."

"When she walks up and down the road, nobody says a word. Most people cross to the other side of the road. I guess they think she'll do something to them. She only comes out of the house when the sun goes down, and she wears dark colors all the time," Gussie said.

"It makes her more mysterious. . . I think," Essie said.

"People wanted to know who she was and where she came from but everybody was too afraid to ask, including Jake." Gussie said, laughing.

"You know who she is, don't you?" Essie asked.

"Sure, I've seen her many times, but I haven't met her," he said finally participating in the conversation, sipping his coffee.

"Well, we never met her either. She looks like a very interesting person," Gussie said.

"Very interesting," Essie said. "To tell you the truth, I would like to meet her."

"You wouldn't be afraid?" her sister asked.

"At my age, what's there to be afraid of except death? I don't think that scares me anymore," Essie said.

For the rest of the morning, they drank coffee and ate coffeecake that the women baked that morning. They chatted about the missing police officers. They also talked about how upset they were about the police running in and out of their apartment searching for clues.

That evening, a few men met in Cameron's apartment for a friendly game of poker. His second floor apartment overlooked most of the community. He loved the location because of its view. In the business that he decided to pursue, he had to be aware of everything around him and his building afforded him a perfect view of the neighborhood. The only thing behind his building was the mountain of vines that grew so thick no human could penetrate without a few risks. A person could be smothered to death in a few minutes, not to mention the insects, flies, snakes, and God only knew what else was lurking under those thick, smothering vines.

Moses asked, "What do we do if d' police come back agin?"

"The same thing we've been doing," Jake said. "Nothing."

"Ya know, they gonna come back and keep on lookin' fo' dem missin' cops."

"Let them look," Cameron said. "And we will do what we always do, keep silent. When you do what you know is right. . . That justice has been served, you have to stand behind your actions and be proud that you protected your people. In Buttermilk Bottom, we are the law. No one can come here and disrespect our families and friends, and get away with it."

"We have to be like the fucking Supreme Court. Our decisions are final. If we are to survive, we will have to stick together, until the white man respects us as equals," Cripple Jake said firmly.

Chapter 13

The local police precinct was about ten blocks away from Buttermilk Bottom. All the officers were on their toes, making sure that they took extra precautions when it came to their own safety by checking in more frequently on their radios and giving more specifics when stopping cars or investigating crimes. Everyone was baffled when they heard about the missing police officers. It was as if a space ship descended and carried them with their car to another planet because there was no trace of them anywhere.

When Detective Bailey Lee showed up in the Fourth Ward three months after the police officers disappeared, his record preceded him because everyone knew his reputation of hatred towards blacks and against anyone who would harm a police officer. He assumed that the officers were murdered and vowed to find the "nigger" or "niggers" who killed them, or hell will have to pay for the crime. When he expounded on his theory around the police station, his white co-workers were cautious and a bit afraid of his extreme point of view. Although they did not like the black people in their district, they saw no reason to blame them without any proof.

Police officer Bobby Moore and Sergeant Andy Tripp waited until Detective Bailey Lee was out of sight and hearing range. Both officers knew Jake very well and trusted him. If Jake said the officers had not been in Buttermilk Bottom that evening, they believed him.

Officer Bobby Moore said, "I don't mind tellin' you both. . . Dat guy makes me nervous."

"He's scary. He decided what happened down there b'fore he even set foot in d' Bottom. How can anybody make serious accusations witout leavin' their office?" Police sergeant, Andy Tripp asked. "I don't like Buttermilk Bottom either but 'least I try t' do my job."

With the help of other prejudiced officers at the station, he was responsible for beating residents and jailing them for two or three days at a time but eventually, he had to release them because he did not have an ounce of proof. Every day for three weeks, the police went to Buttermilk Bottom and intruded on families as they sat down for dinner or early in the morning as they were about leave for work, always during the daylight hours. Not even the police wanted to be in the Bottom at night. As they stormed through household-after-household, the police officers were rude, displaying their hatred, prejudice, and in some cases, they showed a fierce brutality that everyone expected. Showing little respect for the occupants, they barged in on them without an ounce of respect or consideration. Angry officers abused or ignored those who asked questions. The police had no idea what they were looking for; all the searching was in hope of turning something up that would explain the disappearance of the two officers and their police vehicle but nothing was found.

Months after the incident, Detective Bailey Lee decided that he wanted to search through a few houses in the Bottom personally. When he reached Noitop's house, he asked Cripple Jake, who lived there.

"D' witch doctor."

The man looked at Cripple Jake with questioning eyes. Cripple Jake did not blink. "What do you mean?" the detective asked.

"Jes what I said. Ya know . . . Voodoo, spells, 'n hexes. . . . All dat stuff." The detective started to reach for the gate. Cripple Jake said, "I wouldn't do dat if I wuz you."

"Nonsense," the detective said, opening the gate. He walked up on the porch where a lame black cat was sitting in the chair with its green eyes alert. "You comin'?" Bailey asked Jake, but Jake slowly shook his head no. As Bailey Lee got closer to the door, the lame cat with the sparkling green eyes crossed his path, brushing hard against him. He could have sworn that the cat was trying to block his way. Not allowing anything to deter him, the detective walked pointedly toward the door. As he began to knock hard on the door, his hand began to ache. He knocked again and felt an unusual cramp in his fingers. Angry and upset at what appeared to be happening to him, he knocked on the door anyway in the usual demanding way police officers did to intimidate people. "Open up, police officer," he yelled. The door opened with no visible person in sight. He looked back at Cripple Jake, who merely hunched his shoulders and held up his hands in a gesture as if saying that he too was puzzled.

"Police," the detective yelled into the room as he stood in the doorway. No one answered. He walked inside the extra large darkened room filled with unfamiliar odors. "Anybody home?"

There was no one inside the house and no evidence that anyone was occupying the house. A chill went through him, which made him change his mind about going any further into the dark strange house. Cripple Jake waited outside the gate. "No one lives here," the police detective said.

"You jes cain't see nobody, but they's there," Jake yelled back.

"This place ain't been lived in fo' years," the detective said, backing out the door.

"Dat's 'cause she don't want ya in her house."

"Dat's nonsense, jes a lot o' nonsense," the detective said, walking swiftly out the gate and onto the road where Jake stood.

"You call it nonsense if ya wants, I knows better," Jake said. The police detective grunted and walked to the next building, rubbing his hands. Cripple Jake asked, "What's wrong wit ya hand?"

"Nothing," he said but Jake noticed that he kept rubbing it as he went to other buildings in The Bottom.

While at the police station Jake learned that the police arrested a young high school boy for carrying a small pocketknife that was not even an inch long. 'Pig stickers,' the kids called them. They were not big enough to kill anyone, but they were long enough to hurt someone long enough to get them off you if you were attacked.

As soon as everyone heard about the arrest, they all gathered at the juke joint. The residents were very upset because the boy had hopes of going to college in the fall and in view of the Emmitt Till murder, the month before; people were extremely sensitive and determined to do something about it. He would be the first resident from Buttermilk Bottom to go to college. Everyone was proud of that fact. He was extremely bright, earning a scholarship to three different schools. People were proud of him and wanted to help in any way they could. Reacting to the outrage and anger of the residents, Queenie began collecting money for bail. In no time, she collected over a hundred dollars, and money was still rolling in. As the word quickly spread that the police arrested the boy, more people gathered at the juke joint. Cora Lee fried chicken and made biscuits so that people could eat while they organized and decided what they had to do to help the promising, young man.

"How we gonna git him out?" Pearl asked.

"He will need a lawyer," Cameron said.

"My Madame's son's a lawyer," the boy's mother said.

"You need to call her right away and ask her to contact her son. Tell her you can pay for his services. We need to get him out tonight so he won't have to spend a night in jail," Cameron urged. The mother nodded and went into the other side of the room to make the telephone call. Cameron looked at Jake and said, "Call on Rev. Freeman and ask him to go with you and the mother to the precinct to meet with the lawyer and the judge."

Rev. Leon Freeman was a sincere man who spent most of his time criticizing the lifestyles of those who lived in Buttermilk Bottom. He was quick to judge and slow to act regarding the conditions that threatened and endangered most of his neighbors. He gave no advice to help alleviate the problems affecting the people who lived around him, but he did bombard them with his predictions that they would be condemned to hell and eternally damned.

When Jake knocked on his door, the minister peeped out of his window and asked, "What can I do for you, Jake?"

"We need your help, Rev. Freeman," Jake said, yelling through the door.

The man opened the door far enough to stick his head out. "Yes, what is it?"

"Young Jason Anderson has been arrested. We want you to go to the police station with us to help get him released."

"I'm sorry. . . I just sat down to dinner."

"Rev. Freeman, the boy is only seventeen years old. He wants to go to college in a few weeks. We can't let him get a prison record."

"I'm sure the police know what they're doing."

"Rev. Freeman, all you have to do is go with us. The lawyer will do all the talking."

"I'm sorry, Jake. I can't go."

When Jake got back from the pastor's house and related what happened, people became angry saying, "He jes scared o' white people and wanna stay as far 'way from 'em as he can," Smoke said.

"When Lucy got raped last year by dem missin' policemen, she went t' him fo' help. Do you know what dat son-of-a-bitch told her? He said dat she needed t' pray, and she needed t' axe God fo' forgiveness," Dellah related angrily.

"Maybe she needed prayer but she also needed someone t' help her kick some ass," Moses said.

Cameron listened to people complain about Rev. Freeman and decided to go pay him a visit. When he knocked on the preacher's door, the reverend peeped out again and asked, "What can I do for you?"

"I want you to open this door, Rev. Freeman."

Comfortable in his role as a spiritual leader, Rev. Freeman never went out of his way to change anything. When the college students came into the community for the voter registration drive, he told them that their work would be useless.

"The people of Buttermilk Bottom ain't interested in anything outside of this neighborhood. People need to go to church that's where they will find the answer to their problems, in the house of God," he told the students.

When Jake and several other men tried to convince the minister to help them confront the precinct about abuses against area residents, he said he was too busy and could not get involved. The minister changed the subject to focus on the residents' damnation, stemming from the fact that they did not go to church. The men threw up their hands and left the minister on the steps. This time Cameron was not going to take no for an answer. The minister cracked the door open.

Cameron said, "Come on out here, I want to talk to you." The minister, knowing the number man's reputation, did not dare to ignore him, so he slowly stepped out onto the porch. Cameron spoke softly but clearly, looking directly into the minister's eyes to make certain his intentions were clear and his words understood. "There is a seventeen-year-old boy in jail for nothing. He needs his community's support. You and your church are a part of this community, and you need to step up to the plate. You are aware of what happened to Emmitt Till as we all are, and you know that child can't be left there without some help." The minister started to open his mouth, but Cameron interrupted him. "I did not come here to listen to you, Rev. Freeman. I came to tell you about the situation and to tell you to help this boy." Cameron continued after he made the minister understand that he was not entertaining options. "The lawyer is meeting the mother and family members at the precinct at seven o'clock. You will be there to show support because you know that kid, and you know how hard he has worked to get into a good college. The least you can do is to be there for him to help make sure he gets that opportunity to go to college and not end up in jail." Obviously shaken by the non-verbal threat, the minister did not say a word and Cameron did not give him the opportunity to start babbling his monotonous religious monologue. "When the group comes by here on their way to the precinct . . . Be ready to go with them, or I will be paying you another visit."

Cameron walked down the steps and onto the dirt road, leading back to his apartment. He was angry and wanted to cool off by himself. Back in his apartment, he lay on the bed, wished for a simpler life and his mind floated to the image of the beautiful woman walking in the sunset. For the first time in many years, he thought of his aunt and smiled as he remembered her words, *Do you expect God to drop a mate for you right out of the sky?* His heart filled with longing as he recapitulated the scene that captured his heart. Loving the memory, he prayed that he would one day find someone who appreciated the simple, quiet things in life, someone to share his life with forever. He fell asleep and dreamed of walking into the sunset, looking for the mysterious woman who held him spellbound.

At eleven o'clock that evening, Cameron went to the juke joint to find out if the boy was free and to hear some good jazz and blues. Like all the other residents, he looked forward to the night because there was going to be live entertainment. Since the blues man's departure, there was a void and Queenie tried to fill it, using local entertainers. Sometimes they were good, other times not. When he walked in, everybody was celebrating, because the boy was at home with his mother.

"Man, you should have been there," Jake said excitedly. "The police were shocked when we walked in with a white lawyer, a minister, and the boy's family. All his aunts and uncles showed up. The judge had no choice but to let him go after that lawyer finished with him. It was the best thing that ever happened around here. I tell you. . . It was great."

"Good, I'm glad everything worked out," Cameron said.

"The lawyer wouldn't even accept the money. He gave it to the boy, so he could buy books for school. He was a real nice man."

"Great."

Cripple Jake ordered beers for himself and Cameron just as the light dimmed and a small bashful looking woman came out and stood next to the piano. The pianist introduced all the songs that the singer was going to present to the crowd by introducing all the songs in a masterful musical synopsis. The woman opened her mouth and bathed everyone with her sultry rich voice, a soulful sweetness that hypnotized and healed all the pains of the long arduous day.

The next morning, Rev. Freeman showed up at Cameron's door. "Good morning. May I come in?" the pastor asked.

"Sure," Cameron said, opening the screen door. The minister came inside and stood in the middle of the floor. "Would you like to sit down?"

"Thank you," the minister said timidly, taking the first available chair.

"Thank you for going to the court house with the boy's family. It meant a great deal to them and the community."

"No. You don't need to thank me. I should be thanking you." Cameron was surprised. "I have lived here all my life, and last night was the first time I felt like I was a part of this community. . . Standing there to fight for that child's freedom."

"You weren't only fighting for his freedom, Reverend. You were fighting for all of us."

"I realize that now. For most of my years, I have been afraid to speak out against what was going on in The Bottom, but now. . . I want to help."

"We could really use your help. It means everything when every man stands up as men. We must unite and protect what belongs to us. If we don't value what we have. . . How are we going to demand that others do?"

"I want to ask you one question, Cameron, and I don't want you to get angry or upset."

"I can't promise that until I hear the question."

The minister took a deep breath, "Did you and your group have anything to do with those missing policemen?" He watched Cameron's eyes for signs of guilt or innocence.

"I think those men were a victim of their own behaviors. You know what they did to your neighbors . . . Rapes, beatings, and God knows what else. But to answer your question, no," he said, looking directly in the pastor's eyes.

"Good. I had to be sure. I don't want to get involved in any crime or illegal activities."

"It's a little late for that, sir. You were born black in Georgia. . . In this state and in this country . . . That is criminal."

"I see your point," the minister said, trying to laugh.

"I hope you do," Cameron said, burning him with the truth.

"Thank you again, Cameron. It was very rewarding, even if you did have to force me to be a part of a good deed. Thank you." He held out his hand and Cameron shook it. "Please, call on me for help whenever you need me," the minister said, standing up. Cameron joined him.

"Rev. Freeman, I shouldn't have to call you. You should be leading us. You should be calling us to help you fight for what is right and just."

"I appreciate what you said, but I haven't been very good at fighting. And, this whole, civil rights thing is scary. We have to be cautious. These things take time."

"You try telling that to the next thirteen year old girl who will get raped on our streets, or the next man who will get strip searched. Who knows, the next time it may be you. Don't think for a minute that your collar will protect you."

The reverend nervously touched his clerical collar, as if he forgot he had it on. "I know. I know."

"Look, I don't mean to scare you. . . But this community needs you and your leadership. You need to stop thinking about yourself and think about what's happening to people around you. Jesus did. . . Didn't he?"

The reverend was surprised at the analogy Cameron hurled at him. "Just give me time to work things out in my mind. I'm not sure what I can do."

"You could be a minister for these people in all phases of their lives not just what happens to them on Sunday mornings in church."

"Cameron, you don't bite your tongue, do you?"

"No, sir, I can't afford to and sleep at night."

"I must go but. . . But I will come again soon."

"If you don't. . . I'll come looking for you," Cameron said, unsmilingly. The minister looked worried for a minute then they both laughed, relieving the tension between them.

"Thank you, Cameron."

"Thank you, Rev. Freeman."

Chapter 14

A month after Emmitt Till's death, the murderers were set free. All of Buttermilk Bottom was in an active debate about the fate of the black race if the government allowed the killers to go free. People argued and debated the issue all the time it seemed and Cameron chose to stay away from the constant bickering that re-enforced their sense of worthlessness and apathy for their living conditions.

"Man, you should come over to Queenie's and talk to people."

"Right now, I need to evaluate my own thoughts and feelings. I understand how people can get discouraged because it seems like an endless battle. As soon as we make a little progress, something tragic happens and throws us back fifty years. How can I encourage others when I can't explain it to myself?"

"You always know what to say and people need to hear from you."

"I'll talk to them when I have something concrete to say. Right now, I'm disgusted, too. Last year, we celebrated Brown Vs. The Board of Education foolishly thinking that it would be the law that would integrate the schools. After the Supreme Court said that segregation was unconstitutional and what happened? . . . Nothing. Then this year in a second ruling, the court command that schools be desegregated with 'all deliberate speed' and we are still right where we were before. If the Supreme Court can't mandate the changes we need. . . Who or what can?"

"I don't know, man. But I do know that you were right."

"About what?"

"We can't stop trying."

Cameron looked at his friend, knowing that he was right. "Thanks man. There is nothing more healing than hearing your own words thrown in your face. "Come on let's go have a drink."

"Queenie will be glad to see you."

"I'm not ready for Queenie's tonight. . . Why don't we hop on down to Auburn Avenue?"

"Sounds good to me."

For three weeks in a row, Cameron stopped seeing Grace partly because he did not feel like making love to anyone except the beauty in the silhouette. The other reason was that he did not want anything he did to affect her or her job as principal of a local elementary school, if by any chance the police did arrest him for murder. If it came to that he would not mind going back to jail for taking those two animals off the planet, they polluted. The police were continuing their investigations by searching houses and questioning everyone twice.

Grace was furious that she had not seen her lover in three weeks, so she reluctantly went to his apartment. Buttermilk Bottom was the last place she wanted to be, but she wanted him, and he was there. The only way for her to find out what was going on was for her to go there and see him face to face. When she drove up in her car, Queenie saw Grace as she got out of her car and went up the steps to Cameron's apartment. While the principal knocked on the door, Queenie walked up the steps.

"What can I do for you?" Queenie asked.

"I was looking for Cameron Fielding. I believe he lives here," the principal said, noticing the beautifully tailored outfit the woman wore.

"Why don't you come in and wait for him?" People rarely locked their doors, a fact the Queenie was well aware of.

"Does he live here?"

"Yes. We both do."

Grace felt her legs grow weak and her face drain of color. "You live here with him?"

"What can I do for you, sister?"

"Nothing, nothing at all," Grace said, turning to leave as tears instantly swelled up in her eyes. Not wanting that woman to see her cry, she turned and ran down the steps just as Cameron was coming up.

"Grace, what are you doing here?" he asked.

"I was wondering that myself," she said angrily, rushing pass him down the steps.

He stopped her. "What's going on?"

"Ask your woman. She seems to have all the answers."

"What woman?"

"That woman in your apartment. . . The one you live with. . . Why didn't you tell me you were living with someone? Damn you, Cameron. . . Damn you," she said, hitting him on his chest then she attempted to get by him with tears blinding her eyes.

"I don't live with anybody, Grace," he said, hugging her then kissing her lips. Grace instantly relaxed, enjoying what she needed most. "Now, come on. Let's go see just what's going on. Come on," he said, pushing her back up the steps, in front of him.

When they got to his apartment, Queenie was still there. "What's going on, Queenie?" he asked.

"That's what I want to know."

"Did you tell my friend that we were living together?"

She waited a few seconds, breathing hard and getting angry. Embarrassed, she said, "Yes I did."

"Would you tell her the truth?"

"Tell her your damn self," she said, pushing her way pass both of them.

The principal looked at him and then at the woman's back as she fled down the steps.

"Why would she tell me that if it wasn't true?"

"I don't know, but no one lives here except me. You can look around if you like."

She shook her head no. "Cameron, I came here because I haven't seen you in almost a month, and I was worried. Your phone calls didn't make any sense. Why can't we see each other?"

"Because there is a lot going on around here, and I need to be here. Being around me could get you in trouble."

"Are you in trouble?"

"No, but I could be."

"Is there something I can do to help?"

"Yes, there is. Get your beautiful ass out of here and don't come back. This place is not safe. I don't want you to get hurt in anyway," he said, kissing her on the lips.

"That is exactly what I needed," she confessed, enjoying his lips so much she threw her arms around his neck and kissed him back.

"Come on. I'll take you home," he said tenderly.

As they started down the steps, the twins came out on the porch. "Is everything alright, Cameron?"

"Yes. Gussie and Essie Barnes, I'd like you to meet a good friend of mine. This is Grace Talbert."

"Nice to meet you," Grace said.

"These are my adopted mothers," he explained with a handsome smile on his face.

"It's a pleasure for us to meet you. Cameron doesn't usually have friends over," Gussie volunteered.

"You're the first girlfriend to visit," Essie said. "We knew there had to be somebody somewhere. . . Well, come on in, we have a nice chocolate cake that you can help us eat up."

"I just put on a fresh pot of coffee," Gussie said, smiling.

"No. . . No thank you," Grace said, clinging to Cameron.

"We would love to have you," Gussie tried again.

Grace did not appear willing to join the ladies so Cameron made an excuse for her. "We have an appointment, and we're late already. Can we get a rain check?"

"Sure, anytime," Essie said, disappointed.

"Nice meeting you," Gussie said.

They enjoyed entertaining, and it was a pity that Grace did not want to socialize with them in an afternoon of tea and cake. He wanted Grace to know them. Cameron could see the hesitation on Grace's face, and he understood her revulsion to Buttermilk Bottom and its people, but he would never mention that fact to her. As they got in the car, Cameron ushered her into the passenger seat, and he got behind the wheel of her car and drove off.

Across the street, Queenie was watching.

Chapter 15

A few days later, Queenie was delighted to hear Cameron's voice as she walked into the large parlor, where he sat with the old man drinking a beer. When she saw him, she blushed, feeling guilty about what she did to his 'upper class bitch' as she referred to Grace to anyone who would listen to her ranting and raving after she left Cameron's apartment completely embarrassed. Her jealousy got the best of her as she spiraled completely out of control the moment she saw Grace get out of her car.

"Good afternoon," she said, walking over to him. He did not respond with a greeting or a smile. Luther, the old man sat, watching the interchange between them. His heart was breaking as he witnessed again the love Queenie had for Cameron.

After an uncomfortable moment, he said, "We need to talk."

"Okay. We can go to my room."

"No, this is fine. Luther, would you excuse us?"

"Surely," Luther said as he admitted that he liked and admired Cameron, but he wished he had never moved to Buttermilk Bottom. He also wished that Queenie had never fallen in love with him. For the last ten years, he had not been in Queenie's bed, and he missed making love to her.

"Sit down," Cameron said, holding a chair out for her. She sat looking into his eyes to see if he was angry or not. She could never tell. Luther said he had the best poker face he had ever seen. She could see for the first time what he meant.

"You owe me an apology," he said simply.

"You expect me to apologize to you for trying to get rid of that woman?"

"Yes and for going into my apartment without being invited."

She was embarrassed and hurt, but she listened as he made it clear that he wanted the other woman instead of her.

"Okay, I'm sorry, but I was mad, damn-it. I have been angry with you for weeks because you haven't wanted to be with me. How long do you think I should wait? You know how I feel about you, Cameron. I haven't made that a secret. . . Any fool can see that. Then you have the nerve to let that woman come here and flounce herself in my face," she said, pouting like a little kid.

"What does that woman have to do with you?"

"You."

"What does she have to do with you?" he asked, maintaining eye contact.

"Nothing. . . . I guess."

"What you did was rude and unkind not to mention the fact that you lied to her and disrespected me."

"I know I did, but I had a good reason. I wanted to get rid of her short skinny ass."

Cameron wanted to laugh, but he knew it would be better not to.

"She's my friend. No one can get rid of my friends. No one has the right to interfere in my life."

"So, I noticed," she said, pouting. "But what do I have?"

"You have our friendship," he said, noticing her perfectly done hair. He touched it but was careful not to mess it up.

"Friendship? I never made love with a friend the way I have with you. You can't say we are only friends, Cameron, not when you have ravaged my body the way you have . . . Not after all this time."

"We have been intimate friends, but friends all the same," he said, staring pointedly into her eyes to make sure she got his point.

"Is that all we have?"

"If it's not enough for you then so be it. I won't lie to you, ever. You know how I feel about you, and you know what's going on around here. I have other things on my mind."

"But. . . Are you still going back to her?"

"What I do is my business. The question you need to answer is can we continue to be friends. . . . Intimate friends. If you are looking for more than that, we will have to call it off. I don't feel the way you feel, and I won't be forced to lie to you or anyone."

"I love you, Cameron. Can't you see that?"

"I'm not sure I do. . . Especially when you try to place me in an embarrassing situation."

"Look, I got crazy with jealousy. I'm sorry for what I did. It's just that we haven't had any time together."

"We've spent time together we just haven't had sex."

"I need to have sex with you. It's all I think about."

"Passion is only good when both people feel it, Queenie. I don't want to make love to you, unless I really want to."

"Okay, but the least you can do is try to hurry up a bit. I'm horny as hell," she whined, making him laugh.

He kissed her on the lips. She wanted to devour him, but she was afraid of scaring him off. Therefore, she let him take the lead. If she knew anything, she knew that he was right about two people sharing the same feelings. She respected him for it. After all, she had to lie on her back many times while men took advantage of her body. She would never want to put him in the same position she had been in for years, with no one caring what you felt.

He kissed her again pulling her chair close to his. He began to have deep stirrings in his body for her. She responded readily letting out a little squeal that he loved to hear. He placed his hands under her dress to seek her most intimate parts. He felt the soft velvety tissue that made his shaft throb with desire.

She moaned saying, "Don't you want to go upstairs?"

"Yes, I do, but. . . I think we should wait."

"Why?"

"Your birthday is in a couple of days. Why don't we wait and celebrate together?"

She was touched that he remembered her birthday. "I can't wait."

"I want this to be special, so don't do anything. I'll make all the arrangements."

She kissed him, praying that the time would pass as quickly as possible.

Queenie was a healthy woman, but no one could ever honestly call her fat, but she did have some meat on her bones. *Something for a man to hold on to,* she always said. She made no bones about loving and wanting Cameron, and she had no reservations about showing it. She only desired to be in a solitary relationship with him. Before she saw Grace drive up, Queenie knew he had a long-term relationship with another woman and was not satisfied until she found out all she could about the woman. She saw first-hand that the rumors were true about his friend being a school principal on the West Side. She never spoke to him about it because she did not want to anger him in anyway, but she hated the idea of him sleeping with someone else almost as much as he slept with her.

In running the juke joint, she had to call on Cameron's assistance many times. Most of the time, his presence was enough to instill peace and harmony. She loved having him around. He knew how to undress her with his eyes, and she loved every minute of the attention he gave her when he decided to notice her. One of the things she loved about Cameron was the fact that he did not seem to mind her weight. She tried everything to get the weight off, but nothing worked. She made it her business to look good all the time, including her fingernails and toenails. Her goal was to dress sexy, not trashy, so she purchased the best clothes she could afford, and she could afford a nice selection with the money she took in each week from her business. She loved tailor-made high quality garments with all the matching accessories. She was the only woman who lived in Buttermilk Bottom that did not look like she belonged there.

Queenie's occupation reflected her love of music, laughter, and people. Nothing excited her more than having people around and seeing them have a good time. She had been lucky because she started out selling her body on the street corners of Decatur Street near the '81' Theatre where she first met Luther. Completely in love with her, he helped her purchase the once beautiful house in Buttermilk Bottom. He treated her like a queen, but he was married with several children. Luther committed himself to helping Queenie establish a new life for herself and her son. He taught her about money and business with the hope that she would show her appreciation for as long as he lived.

Riddled with painful experiences, Queenie's childhood was short-lived as her uncle and her stepfather raped her for years in her mother's home. The first time they raped her, she was barely nine years old. By the time, she was twelve; she felt as if she was a seasoned-professional because she learned to make her uncle and stepfather pay her for what they were going to take anyway. By age thirteen, sex meant nothing to her. Pregnant and alone, her mother kicked her out of the house, as soon as she found out who were the possible fathers. Queenie did not know or care which one had actually fathered her child. All she knew was that a baby was growing inside her, and that she could make money selling her body. In order to survive, she prostituted up to her seventh month of pregnancy. With the money she earned, she was able to rent a room, purchase food, and clothing while taking care of herself and her child. Her landlady took an interest in her and helped her out by babysitting. She also gave her tons of good advice like: *Use rubbers wit every man ya sleep wit so ya won't git pregnant agin. Be sure t' tell them up front, so they don't argue wit ya once they git ya by yo'self. Don't pick men up off d' street. Go t' a restaurant, parties, or d' movies . . . That way you kin be sure dat d' men you git, ain't nasty. Don't go wit them make 'em go wit you. Have a place you pay fo'. . . Where people know you.* Queenie listened to all the old woman's advice and took it because it made sense. *Keep yo'self clean and dress well, dat way you kin charge mo' money.* It was the best advice she ever received.

When she met her old man, he treated her like a lady and showed her for the first time what it meant to make love. Before she met him, it was a job, a nasty job, but she had to do it just to make a living. She did it because she knew nothing else while she dreamed of being a beautician, but she never had enough money to enroll in school, so she could earn her certification. Queenie was grateful to Luther for showing her affection and putting her on the right track. It was his idea for her to open a juke joint.

"You kin collect money off d' gamblin' tables, off d' whores, off d' food, and drinks. If ya git someone t' sing and play d' piano, you kin charge people t' come in. You ain't got t' sell yo' body t' make money. You kin keep all dat good pussy fo' me," Luther said, grinning from ear to ear. He found the house, paid for it and helped her buy all the furniture. After the house was all set up, he helped her buy supplies. He was a gambler, so he brought the first group of men to enjoy her hospitality.

Queenie went all out that first Friday night. With the help of her landlord, she fried fish, made coleslaw, cooked collard greens, cornbread, and made a pound cake. The men ate until they were stuffed and played cards until seven o'clock the next morning. As the game was ending, she sold a breakfast of hot steamy coffee, eggs, ham, and grits. Later that morning, she sat down with Luther and counted the money she made after everyone had gone home. Between the game of Georgia skin, the food, and the drinks, she made ten times more money than she would have made in a month on her back allowing men to abuse her body.

That day, she decided that she had found her purpose in life. She had also found a man who appreciated her and loved her and her child. It was not long before she bought a piano, hired a cook, and someone to clean the rooms. The cook and the housekeeper had free room and board; in addition to that, they got plenty of tips. It was a happy home. She continued to dress like a businesswoman and developed a taste for expensive clothes. In the space of a couple of months, she had her very own patchwork family. Her married old gambler came every Friday, Saturday, and Sunday night. He acted as her dealer and cut every game. When there was no game, he worked as the bartender. Queenie's life changed completely, and she fell in love with her own metamorphosis.

Chapter 16

Cameron was looking forward to the upcoming birthday celebration for Queenie. He wanted to make it special, so he talked with Cora Lee, Addie Mae, and the housekeeper of her establishment, asking them to help in the preparations. He wanted to give her an unforgettable day, and they were delighted to be a part of the celebration even the working-women upstairs took time out from their customers to help in some peripheral way to make the day special.

"I want the best steaks you can find, Cora Lee, served with those sliced string beans and almonds you made for me a few months ago."

"You wants me t' make you some macaroni and cheese t' go wit it?"

"No. Just bake a potato with the sour cream topping."

"What 'bout dessert? She loves my banana puddin'."

"Everybody in Atlanta, Georgia loves your banana pudding but no, prepare those brandied peaches. . . They will be perfect."

"You proposin' or somethin'?"

"If I proposed to anybody, it would be to you," he said, kissing her on the cheek.

"She gonna be mighty disappointed."

"She's a big girl."

"You kin say dat agin, but it won't change how she feel 'bout ya."

"No. . . But at least she'll have a nice birthday."

"Well, one thang I kin say 'bout you Cameron. . . You's honest."

"I go out of my way to be completely honest when it comes to that, Cora Lee."

Once he settled on the menu and the wine for the occasion with the staff of the juke joint, he went shopping to purchase the ideal gift for Queenie.

Over the next few days, he looked religiously for the ideal gift. Finding nothing, he continued his search and ended up in Davidson's where he found the perfect lavender suit and a lounge set that he thought would look good on Queenie.

Cameron had a passion for women that surpassed that of most men. He loved women for who and what they were, not how they looked. This he told himself many times throughout his life. His joy was in finding something unique and intriguing about each woman. The only thing that turned him off in a woman was selfishness or one with bad behavior.

While shopping for Queenie's birthday gift at Davidson's, he saw a woman on the other side of the clothing rack where he was selecting the garment for Queenie. With growing interest, he watched her as she chose a dress that he felt did absolutely nothing for her. When she held the dress up to her body, its dull gray color made him laugh because it did not appear to have enough room for her head to push through and would cover her up to her neck. He stood watching her for some time when she realized that he was watching her. She shyly put her head down and turned away. She was a plain woman with no distinguishing features.

"It looks as if you could use some help," he said, looking over the clothes rack. She moved away from him, thinking that he had to be crazy. "Can I help you pick out a dress?" he asked.

"No, I'm okay," she said, continuing to move away from him.

"Are you refusing my help?"

"No. . . Ah, yes. I mean. . . I don't need any help," she said, refusing to look at him.

"I think you do. . . Judging from that dress you chose for yourself," he said, standing right in front of her.

"There's nothing wrong with this dress," she murmured, going to another rack, well away from him. She could not help but notice how good-looking he was, but her bashful nature would not allow her to look at him directly.

"Maybe not but it doesn't belong on your body," he said, following her while noticing that she had nice curves that she was attempting to hide. She almost smiled as she turned her back to him and walked down another aisle, trying to get away from him with her head still pointed toward the floor. He laughed loudly and said, "Are you trying to ditch me?"

She almost looked into his eyes, but her shyness overcame her. He was so tall and handsome that she felt small and insignificant next to him. "I don't know anything about you, Mister."

"My name is Cameron Fielding. Now, tell me your name."

"I have to go."

"Not until you tell me your name," he said, holding out his hand.

"Hope," she said, trembling, but she did not shake his hand.

"Well, Hope, let me see if I can help you find a more suitable dress."

"That's okay. This one is just fine. I just need it to go to work every day."

"Where do you work?"

"In Buckhead. I'm a maid."

"Then you will need a very nice dress. Let me see. . . You are a size twelve?"

"Yeah, but. . . ."

"No buts. Trust me, I'm good at this."

"Mister, I don't need yo' help," she said, unable to stop grinning.

"Come on, stop fussing so much . . ." he said, taking a dress off the rack. "How about this one?"

"No. . . That's too fancy for me."

"But it will look good on your beautiful, smooth skin."

She laughed and said quietly, "You're crazy."

"No, I just like to see a woman dress like a woman. You will look good in this. Try it on."

She looked at the price tag and said, "It cost too much money."

"Okay, okay, let me try again. We don't want to give up too soon," he said, thumbing through the rack. "Stay with me, now. Trust me."

"How you know about women's clothes?"

"I know what makes women beautiful," he said, looking into her eyes.

She quickly looked away and said, "I gotta go."

"Wait," he said, pulling her back to him. "Look at this one . . . It's on sale," he said, holding up a simple dress with a scoop neckline with no trimming.

"I can't wear that," she said, looking shocked at his choice.

"Why not?"

"It's orange."

"It's you."

"No, it ain't."

"Trust me, you were meant to wear this dress."

She laughed loudly saying; "I ain't never heard nothing so crazy in my whole life."

"Well, maybe it's time for a little craziness in your life. It will look great on you, much better than that gray thing, you have hanging on your arm. That makes you look like you're going to a funeral. Are you going to a funeral?"

"No, but I ain't wearing no orange dress."

"If anyone ever needed an orange dress, you do. Here try it on. What can it hurt?" He placed the dress in her hand. She took the dress and slowly walked to the dressing room. "Go ahead, you're going to love it."

While she went off to try on the dress, he pulled several other dresses off the rack that he thought would look good on her. He found three additional dresses and a navy blue two-piece set that was simple and classy. He was inspecting the blue outfit when she reappeared timidly to model the orange dress. He stared approvingly, smiling broadly.

"You look great."

"This ain't me."

"Oh, but it could be. You look beautiful."

"I ain't never owned anything this bright in my whole life."

"Then, its time you did. I would love to see you wearing that dress when I take you to dinner tonight."

"What?"

"Dinner."

"I can't have dinner with you."

"Why not?"

"'Cause I can't that's why."

She walked back into the dressing room with her heart beating rapidly. She prayed that the crazy man would be gone when she came out. She changed into her regular clothes, putting the orange dress back on the hanger and took the gray dress she had chosen earlier. Hoping to escape from the man outside, she sat down in the dressing room and waited for almost an hour, hoping he had gone. She had never in her life attracted a man that handsome. *Why on earth would he want to take me anywhere? I'm plain and unattractive,* she told herself. *He's got to be crazy,* she thought.

Looking at the clock on the wall, she decided it was safe to leave. She picked up her gray dress, her purse, and left the dressing room. To her surprise, he was sitting in a chair, waiting for her, smiling.

"The orange dress would look better on you."

"You need to leave me alone. I don't know you."

"You could get to know me, tonight for dinner at seven, wearing the orange dress," he said, admiring her smooth, dark brown skin.

"I can't do that."

"Why not?" he asked, standing close to her.

"I have a little boy at home."

"Bring him with you." He held her hand because her bashfulness was erotic.

"Man, you're crazy," she said, looking at her feet.

He tilted her head so he could look into her eyes. "You are driving me crazy. I want to see you, tonight."

"I can't."

"You can. Bring your son to Paschal's at seven. I'll be waiting to see you, wearing that orange dress. Don't disappoint me," he said, kissing her lightly on the lips. "I'll be waiting there until you show up. If it takes a week. . . I'll be waiting."

That evening, Cameron arrived at the restaurant fifteen minutes early. He sat in the corner booth and waited thinking about Hope. She looked so scared and vulnerable when he first spotted her. Someone, somewhere, convinced her that she was ugly, and he wanted to help her change that image without changing the sweetness he detected in her.

At seven o'clock, she got out of a cab with her son, and she was wearing the orange dress. He watched from the window as they walked into the building. She smoothed the dress down, took a deep breath, and opened the door while holding onto her son, who appeared to be around five years old. She smiled bashfully when she saw Cameron.

"Hey," she said shyly.

"I'm glad you came," he said, admiring her in the dress for several uncomfortable moments, making her blush. "Hello there, what's your name?" Cameron said, shaking the little boy's hand.

"Neil."

"Hi, Neil. You have a beautiful mother, did you know that?" Hope blushed again, holding her head down, embarrassed by his statement, but there was a beautiful smile on her face.

"Yeah," the five-year old said.

"I don't think she knows how beautiful she is. Why don't we tell her?"

"Will you stop that kind of talk?" Hope said, looking around the room to make certain no one heard him.

"No, because Neil and I want you to know how beautiful you are. Don't we, Neil?"

"Yeah."

"You are beautiful," he said slowly, admiring the way the dress eased over her hips. "Now, Neil, you tell your mother how beautiful she is."

"Mommy, you's beautiful."

"Thank you, honey," she said, kissing him on the forehead.

"Now, do I get a kiss too?" Cameron said seriously.

"No. You're embarrassing me," she said, turning her head, trying not to look at his handsome face.

"Good. You need to hear how beautiful you are. Isn't that right, Neil?"

"Yeah." The little boy said, playing with the paper placemats.

"See. . . Your son agrees with me."

"You're so crazy."

"And, you. . . Are so beautiful."

"Stop saying that. People can hear you." The waitress came over. "Hello, can I help you?"

"Yes, you can. Will you answer a question for me?"

"Sure, shoot," the waitress said, taking a restful stance next to him, holding her pencil and pad.

"I have been trying to convince this young lady that she is beautiful. She doesn't believe me. What do you think I should do?"

"Sweetie, if a man this good looking' tells you you're beautiful. . . . Believe him, he knows. I should be so lucky. Now, what're you folks havin'."

When Cameron reached The Bottom, he took his packages over to Cora Lee to be gift-wrapped then he went to his apartment. He was to meet with Cripple Jake for their checkers game and beer, a daily habit they loved to share between the hours of one and three o'clock. Jake was sitting on his front porch, drinking a beer that he took from Cameron's refrigerator.

"Did you save one for me?"

"Sure, there's plenty. I haven't been here that long." They both laughed.

"Where have you been?"

"Shopping for Queenie's birthday. I wanted to get her a gift before it got too late."

"That'll make her real happy."

"I hope so."

"Did you buy her an engagement ring?"

"No."

"Good," Jake said.

Cameron looked at his friend, trying to study his expression. "What is that look about?" Noticing his friend's thoughtful expression as he quietly drank his beer, he asked, "Are you going to tell me?"

"Tell you what?" Jake asked.

"About that expression on your face."

"Your ass is crazy."

"You still love her, don't you?" Cameron asked.

"Would it make any difference if I said yes."

"No."

Jake laughed and said, "Good because if I'm lucky enough to tap that I wouldn't give you a second thought. Nor do I want your pity."

"Don't worry. I have no compassion for any hard-leg when it comes to me having great sex."

"I know what you mean," Jake said, laughing. "Either you have it or you don't."

"Right."

After several minutes, Jake asked his best friend, "Do you love her?"

"No, but the sex is very good."

"I knew it would be. You're a lucky, son-of-a-bitch."

"I know."

"Could I ask you a question?"

"Depends."

"Have you ever been in love?"

Cameron remained silent for several minutes, feeling a sense of loss for what he never had. He took a deep breath of air and gave his friend a half smile. "No, I can't say that I have." At that moment, Jake felt sorry for him.

"What about Grace?"

"We are friends."

"Like you and Queenie?"

"Yes. . . Exactly."

"One day, you are going to have to pay the piper. All the women you had. . . And you've never been in love? That's hard to believe."

"Some people are just not as lucky as you are, Jake."

"Lucky? Now, that is a double-edged sword, and it depends on what side of the coin you're looking at, I guess." Cameron nodded in agreement. "Oh, shit," Jake said loudly.

"What?"

"There goes Alberta." They watched her march down the dirt road, swinging her arms as hard as she could, heading for the juke joint. "She must have found out that Harlan's in there banging Dellah."

"Oh, shit."

"I already said that. Alberta had a bad temper as a child growing up and now that she's grown. . . It's much worst. Everyone knew this day was coming, and everyone was prepared for it except her stupid-ass, common-law husband."

"What do you think she'll do to him?"

"God only knows," Jake said, shaking his head.

Alberta stormed into the building. People gathered around when they saw her headed down the road in the middle of the day. Everyone knew he was in there, and they knew that he would be in big trouble the minute she found out about his mid-day love affair. For several minutes, it was completely quiet in Buttermilk Bottom; not even a bird dared to chirp. Then suddenly, loud voices filled the air. No one could understand the words, but whatever it was. . . It indicated extreme anger, followed by a loud explosion that everyone knew was a gunshot. Both, Cameron and Cripple Jake ran over to the juke joint and ran up the steps where all the commotion came from. Harlan was lying on Dellah's bed, bloody, holding the gun in his hand while Dellah sat nude in the corner, on the floor, unharmed.

"Somebody call an ambulance," Cameron said, rushing over to Harlan. "Get me a towel and some bandages, quick. Queenie grabbed a towel and ripped up a sheet. "Hold the towel on his stomach as firmly as you can," he said to Jake. "I'll wrap him the best I can." The two men worked fast to wrap the wound up with a sheet before the ambulance arrived. Shortly after that, the police arrived. The officers were busy getting the story when Detective Bailey arrived.

"What happened here?" Bailey demanded. "Who shot you?"

"I wuz cleaning my gun. . . . It went off by accident," he managed to get out before he lost consciousness.

"Cleaning yo' gun?"

"I told that fool about bringing that gun in my house. He's been renting a room here for a week or so. He is crazy about that stupid gun," Queenie said. "I'm glad it happened maybe it'll teach the damn fool a lesson."

"He's a stupid mutherfucker," Luther said, backing up her story. Cripple Jake and Alberta stood at the top of the steps. Alberta started, crying and saying that she was sorry. Cameron tapped Alberta on the shoulder, motioning to her to keep quiet then he took her by the hand, and led her down the back steps to the kitchen. Cora Lee let him wash his hands and gave him a clean shirt to put on. Alberta sat at Cora Lee's preparation table and cried hysterically.

The detective went into Dellah's room and looked around, seeing the whore on the floor, he demanded, "What happened here?"

"We jes' finished makin' love when he started. . . . Playin' wit dat stupid gun. I told him t' put it down, but he wouldn't even listen t' me. I's scared o' guns," she said, crying.

"Get some clothes on. You gotta t' go t' d' station t' make a statement."

"I'll go with you," Queenie said, helping Dellah get dressed.

After the group left for the police station with Cripple Jake along with them, Alberta sat at the bar with a glass of whiskey that Luther poured for her. He re-filled the glass as soon as it was empty. Cora Lee came out of the kitchen with her famous fried chicken and biscuits for people to munch on while going over the unfortunate events.

"I'm sorry ya'll. I lost my mind when I heard he wuz down here fuckin' dat woman."

"Look, we knew you wuz gonna find out. We warned him," the old man said. "The boy's jes' stupid. Who told you?"

"Some lady in d' beauty shop. I wuz gittin' my hair done. I always git my hair done on Fridays. When Miss Mabel told me he was down here, I went crazy."

"Who gave you d' gun?"

"Nobody."

"Where you git dat gun so fast?"

She looked at him like he was crazy, saying, "From my pocketbook."

Luther shook his head and poured her another stiff drink. "Well, drink up, d' damage's already been done. All we kin do now is pray."

"I better git o'er t' Grady Hospital and find out if he's okay," Alberta said.

"Don't you worry, Moses went wit him. You stay out of dis 'fore ya git yourself in trouble. Harlan already covered fo' ya, so leave it be. Drink yo' whiskey 'n sit tight," Luther said.

"No, I gotta go," Alberta said tearfully.

"Sit down, Alberta," Cameron said. "There's nothing you can do, except to get in trouble. Old man's right, drink up." Luther was grateful for his comments and support. "The last thing we need is to have you in jail with children at home, waiting for you," Cameron said.

"I feel bad jes' sittin' here doin' nothin'," Alberta said.

"They're just feelings. They'll pass. Drink up," Cameron ordered. "Give her another drink."

The group of concerned friends sat there quietly until Queenie, Cripple Jake and Dellah returned.

"They bought the story. Everything is going to be fine," Queenie said, sighing deeply.

"These women need to be in the movies. Man, you should have seen them acting and telling lie after lie," Jake reported. "Both of them were automatically backing-up each other's story. It was something to see and hear."

"Did ya'll hear anythang 'bout my husband?" Alberta asked.

"Not yet, but don't worry, Moses is with him, and he'll call when he knows what's goin' on," Jake said.

"I'm scared," Alberta said. "I'm scared he may die."

"Wasn't that the idea?" Jake asked seriously.

Tears fell from her eyes as she hung her head, crying. "I jes' wanted t' scare him. I wanted t' shoot him in d' leg or somethin', but he grabbed d' gun and pissed me off. I didn't mean t' shoot him in d' stomach."

"Damn. It's over . . . And much too late to be wishing for shit," Jake said.

"Eat somethin' and drink yo' liquor, honey," Cora Lee said, patting her on the back.

"I'm sorry, Miss Alberta," Dellah said. Everybody jumped, not knowing how Alberta was going to react. Everyone knew that Alberta also carried a switchblade.

"It ain't yo fault. He wuz fuckin' round on me. . . Not you. This is yo' job. I know dat. . . If I didn't I woulda shot your ass first." Dellah walked backwards slowly, away from Alberta and went upstairs without anyone noticing her except Jake. Hours later, the telephone rang. Queenie picked it up. It was Moses.

"Hello. Yeah, she's right here. Good. You'll call us back when it's finished? Okay. Okay. Goodbye," Queenie said, hanging up the telephone. "They're taking him into surgery. The doctors said he should be okay. The operation will take about five to six hours. Moses will stay there until it's finished, and he'll call us to tell us what's going on."

"Good," The old man said, pouring Alberta another drink, and one for himself.

"If you need to lie down, Alberta, go in my room. No one will bother you there. Somebody go get her kids and bring 'em down here, please. She's in no condition to take care of herself much less anybody else," Queenie said. Azalene and Pearl went to get Alberta's children.

"Well, I'm gonna go put on dinner fo' everybody. It's gonna be a long night," Cora Lee said. "Addie Mae, bring out some coffee and dat black walnut pound cake we made dis mornin'. Bring d' cream, sugar, and a knife t' cut d' cake." Addie Mae went to the kitchen to complete the tasks Cora Lee requested of her.

Cora Lee hugged Alberta and said, "Pray, baby. All you kin do now is pray."

The rest of the group sat drinking, eating, and waiting for the telephone to ring. When Moses finally called, it was almost eleven o'clock at night. Alberta and her kids were all in Queenie's bed asleep. Luther answered the telephone, after listening to Moses' report; he hung up and took a deep breath. Looking at everybody he said, "He's in recovery. They won't know fo' sure 'til mornin'."

Luther shook his head and said "Moses' stayin' all night."

"Well, there is no sense in everybody staying up all night, let's go get some sleep. We might as well close up for the night," Queenie said. Everyone agreed.

"Where you gon' sleep, Queenie? All dem people in yo' bed?" Azaline asked.

Queenie looked at Cameron, who had no expression or comment. Hearing the question as she returned, carrying a hot pot of coffee, Cora Lee interrupted the silence saying, "Take our room, Addie Mae and I kin bunk on d' cot in d' kitchen."

"Thank you, Cora Lee," she said with a half smile on her face.

Cora Lee exchanged glances with Cameron then poured him a cup of coffee. After sitting around reviewing the evening events, everybody disbursed and went their separate ways, leaving Luther to lock up.

The next day, it was all over Buttermilk Bottom that Harlan would recuperate. The doctors told Moses that the first aid he received immediately after the shooting saved his life. Everyone was delighted and began to praise Cameron and Cripple Jake for their efforts.

Jake quickly said, "I only did what Cameron told me to do."

That evening, Queenie and Cameron had another reason to celebrate. With joy and gratefulness in everyone's voice, people were going to the hospital to visit Harlan but could not get in because he was still in intensive care. Alberta was the only person who could see him.

"He looks good considering he got d' shit shot out o' him yesterday. He looked better than I thought he'd look," Moses said, reporting to the group that gathered around him at the juke joint.

"Thank God, he's going to be all right," Queenie said.

"I'm sorry fo' shootin him in yo' house," Alberta said.

"That's okay, girl. God knows that you weren't the first to shoot somebody in here."

"I know. . . But I could've waited 'til he got home."

"If you'd waited 'til he got home, he might've died. Cameron and Jake may not've gotten there in time or at all," Cora Lee said. "Thangs happen fo' a reason."

"What I'm gonna do if he dies?"

"Ain't no need t' be thinkin' like dat, d' doctor says he's gonna be fine. You jes go home wit those chillun o' yo's and take care o' yo'self and please don't worry 'bout nuthin'," Cora Lee said. "Go on. . . Go home." She ushered Alberta out the door. When she was gone, Cora said, "Dat crazy, fool woman is always shootin' somebody. Who wuz dat she shot a few years back, Jake?"

"You remember Johnny Hopkins. . . She shacked up with him for almost a year on Irving Street when she and Harlan broke up the first time. Johnny left his wife and six children for her crazy behind. He owns that barber shop over on Auburn Avenue."

"Oh yeah, I r'member him. He wuz a real nice gent'man," Cora Lee said.

"She shot him four years ago, in the leg for cheating on her. He's still limping around, but he went back to his wife after he quit messing around with crazy-ass Alberta."

"You know what?" Queenie asked.

"What?" Cora Lee said.

"I loved the way Harlan covered for Alberta."

"Dat surprised me, too," Cora Lee said.

"Can ya 'magine. . . Coverin' fo' someone who just shot you in d' stomach?" Pearl asked.

"Hell no," Jake said.

"Me, neither," Queenie said. "It must be love."

"More like insanity, if you ask me," Jake said.

"No one's askin'," Pearl said.

Queenie's birthday celebration was one she would remember for the rest of her life. With great care and thought, Cameron purchased special steaks for dinner, wine, ordered flowers and candy. Her room looked like something out of a magazine, when she walked in. There were flowers and candles all over the room and lying on the bed were two large boxes wrapped with bright red bows. The first box had a gorgeous light lavender suit in it, and the other one had a red negligee in it. Cameron smiled saying, "The first one is for you, and second one is for me."

She laughed. "Man, you really know how to please a woman. Everything is so beautiful," she said, reaching out to embrace him.

"Beautiful things are for beautiful people."

"Thank you, Cameron. . . For all of this. No one has ever done anything so special for me before."

"You deserve it. Now, come on over here and sit down. Cora Lee and Addie Mae went through a great deal of trouble putting everything together for you," he said, ushering her over to the table that he had sat up in front of the window. Dinner was ready and all she had to do was sit-down. "Go ahead, I'll open the wine."

"This is wonderful. You're wonderful."

"You're only saying that because you don't want me to take my gifts back," he teased, making her laugh.

"Cameron, I love you so much sometimes that I get a little crazy. I just want to make you happy."

"Well, you'll get your wish... Right after dinner," he said charmingly. "Now, eat your special dinner. Cora Lee would be upset if she found out you never touched it."

They ate in silence as the sounds of Sarah Vaughn played in the background. Cameron appreciated and loved how elegant she always looked. Queenie loved being a woman, and her personal care routines were legendary from her manicured nails, her perfect hair, and her soft, smooth skin. Over the years, Cameron had spent hours loving and appreciating the beauty and sensuousness of her body. When dinner was over, they sat on the French provincial sofa that sat in front of her bed, enjoying the last of the wine.

As she lay in his arms, she said, "This has been the best birthday of my entire life."

"May you have many more," he said, toasting her. "I have one more gift for you," he said, reaching into his pocket. She prayed it would be a ring, an engagement ring, but the box was long and narrow. She could not help but show disappointment on her face. "I thought you liked receiving gifts?" he asked, reading the expression on her face.

"Oh, I do. What is it?"

"Here, open it up, and find out for yourself."

She opened the beautifully wrapped gift carefully and found a beautiful turquoise and silver necklace. "It's beautiful."

"Come here and let me put it on you." He fastened it around her neck then kissed her on the shoulder. "It's perfect for you."

She turned around, with tears in her eyes. He thought she was crying because she was happy with her gift and her private party, but she was not. Her tears fell because she knew, deep down that she would never get the ring that she so desperately wanted. He kissed her perfectly painted lips and wrapped his arms around her full waist, enjoying the softness and the warmth of her body. She turned around to face him and felt a surge of anticipation, which made her breasts rise up, looking for someone to satisfy them. He unbuttoned the front of her dress exposing the two monuments of pleasure that called silently out to him. She was wearing red underwear, expensive red underwear. The bra did just as the sales lady had promised. It held her breasts up toward the sun and brimming out just enough to drive a man crazy. He reached his hands around to her back, quickly and expertly unfastened her bra, revealing her healthy erect breasts. He smiled and began to kiss each one, welcoming the opportunity to nestle in their splendor. As his suction increased, she began to moan sweetly, making him feel the pressure of his own manhood push hard against the zipper of his pants. Grateful for the dress that buttoned down the front, he was able to maneuver it off her in no time at all. Once she was free of the dress and the bra, he turned his attention to the beautiful red-laced panties that she wore. He took a minute to admire them, as he massaged her big beautiful thighs, then he slipped the red panties off letting them drop aimlessly onto the floor.

He stood up to remove his own clothes and was pleased when she assisted him, kissing him as each part of his taut body was unveiled. They stood in the middle of the floor nude appreciating the love feast they were about to partake. They smiled knowing the exquisite pleasure that was to come. Kissing passionately, they walked to the big high bed where their sexual aerobics would take place.

"I love you, Cameron," she said.

"And, I love. . . Making love to you," he said.

Queenie knew the difference between the two statements, but at that point, she did not intend to question them. She laid down on the bed and waited for him as he stood over her, looking at her body. She loved the fact that he loved her with his eyes before he touched her. Immediately, he pursued what he wanted as he spread her legs open and felt the moistness inside her that made her move with each gentle caress he bestowed on her. When he thought she was going to climax, he stopped and kissed her thighs holding her body close to him. He wanted her to enjoy this part of their lovemaking, because he knew she craved it. When he kissed her special place, it always made her crazy. She could never get enough of his sweet lips. Her whole body was on fire as he teased her with sweet loving moist kisses on the temple of her womanhood. Her nipples stood-up, hard, and straight aching with passion as his large hands explored and soothed her body.

Placing his hands under her rear end, he elevated her for the p'est du resistance. Her hands gripped the top of his head as his moist lips covered her feminine palace, giving her wet erotic spurts of pleasure that isolated her from the entire world. For that time, only the pleasure of their exquisite lovemaking existed.

When her body stopped quivering, she turned her attention to him. His maleness was beautifully shaped, hard, long, and erect. The sight of it made her want him inside her, but she enjoyed the sweetness of him. She did not know when she would get another opportunity to have him so close to her, so she took full advantage of this moment in time. The thick veins that travel from the base to the tip of his desire looked as if they would bust as she took him in her oral embrace. His warm sweetness made her lips contract involuntarily as she tried to take in as much as she could. She found her greatest pleasure in giving him pleasure in that way. He moaned as he felt the full pressure and sensation that her passionate lips evoked. His body became rigid as he tried not to give in to the erotic sweetness that held him captive. After several minutes in her expert hands, he pulled away. She smiled knowing that he was satisfied. The sexual tension between them was at a peak, even before they began. She was slightly annoyed when he stopped to put on a condom. On several occasions, she tried to encourage him to leave it off, but it resulted in him wanting to leave her bed. She never made that mistake again.

The moment he placed his shaft deep inside her, she rejoiced knowing that she could express the raw unleashed passion she felt for him. He was never gentle when it came to intercourse, he was a man possessed by passion and desire, and nothing would deter him from fulfilling his quest for pleasure and satisfaction. He felt out of control guided by his physical need for completion. Enjoying every inch that he explored within her, he pushed harder and deeper, controlled by the rhythm and feel of her body until at last she began to move excitedly, calling out his name. He too began to ignite and give in to all the sensations he had been trying to control as their bodies moved together in glorious moments of erotic celebration. Then it was over. Their energy drained and their bodies laid still and useless, side-by-side, wrapped in each other's arms.

They both slept for several hours. He woke up first and dressed quickly. He hated facing women after it was all over. Queenie was a delight in bed, but he knew that was all there was to his feelings for her. No man could ask for more in a woman, but he held back because he knew she wanted an emotional commitment that he could never give her. With his clothes on, he stood watching her sleep. He placed a rose on the pillow beside her and left the building as quickly as he could.

As soon as Queenie woke up and saw the rose on her pillow, she knew he was gone. Sadness filled her as she clenched the pillow where he slept, smelling his scent. *Why doesn't he know how much I love him? How could he walk away after the magical evening we just enjoyed?* Conquered by grief, she cried herself to sleep.

Chapter 17

The vegetable man came to Buttermilk Bottom almost every Friday morning that it did not rain. He had a raggedy, open truck that held boxes and crates, overflowing with fresh crisp vegetables. He was a black local farmer who could not get commercial buyers for his crop, so he started selling his own produce directly to people in black neighborhoods. This benefited the residents and him because the people had door-to-door service and fresh crisp vegetables at a reasonable price. Once he entered a neighborhood, he began to holler out his trade.

"Vegetable man!
Come 'n git 'em while you can.
Corn, peas, 'n collard greens,
Turnips, kale, 'n string beans.
Come 'n git it!

Hollering out and rhyming was a tradition that he learned from his father, who sold vegetables for his white employer. A century before, the only time that singing was acceptable was when whites forced enslaved Africans to work against their will in the cotton fields and rice paddies, where the work song was born, giving us the first form of African-American music in this country. The words that they used came from the foreign language they learned on their own from their kidnappers and oppressors without any instructions. Sometimes, the words sounded like American words, and sometimes they sounded like a combination of African and American words, but having no choice. . . The enslaved worker mimicked what he thought he heard. The vegetable man often did not understand his father's thick Geechee dialect, but he always enjoyed the sound of his rhymes as he proudly sang out the news about his load of perfectly ripe fruits and vegetables.

> "Watermelons, red t' d' rind'
> You can buy 'em any ol' time.
> I sell 'em t' d' rich,
> I sell 'em t' da po,
> I'll sell t' you when you come out d' doe.
> Watermelons. . . red ripe watermelons."

People came out of their homes and in an instant, Amos' sidewalk store filled-up with smiling faces. To his regular customers, he always gave them something extra to show his appreciation and to keep them coming back for more. The Vegetable Man loved coming to Buttermilk Bottom because the people were friendly, funny, and they bought most of his produce. He loved hearing them brag and praise him for the high quality of his beautiful colorful vegetables.

"Mr. Amos, dem greens look mighty good," his customers would say.

"Man, how in d' world did you grow dem big ass tomatoes," another person said, making him laugh uncontrollably.

They made him proud to be there. He knew most of the residents, and he knew all the children by name. He always had special snacks for the children, a hand full of peanuts, an apple, or a cluster of muscadine grapes. That day, he cut them each a section of sugar cane that they proclaimed was the sweetest they had ever tasted.

His best customers were the cook and owner at the juke joint. They bought more collard greens, tomatoes, onions, string beans, and corn than all the houses put together, and they always purchased everything by the bushel. Although Queenie had a cook, she always took the time to come out and see what was on the truck before any purchasing took place. After she made her purchases, she always invited Amos inside for lunch, which he was happy and grateful to receive. He did not play cards or dice, nor did he drink, but he loved being around people. If he was lucky, he met up with the 'Bug Man' to play his numbers while Jake filled him in on all he had missed since his last visit. Other men would join them for an afternoon filled with stories that he could tell his daughter when he got back home. His wife died several years earlier, leaving him with a wonderful daughter, who stayed on the farm with her husband to help him with all the planting and harvesting. That day like most days that he came to Buttermilk Bottom, he sold out of all his produce. He loved being in Queenie's place and with the people because they appreciated him and his hard work.

Minutes later, Detective Bailey Lee walked in as Jake was telling one of his stories to the Vegetable Man. Bailey Lee looked around the room and satisfied that all the men turned away or held their heads down except for one man, who was sitting in the corner. The detective felt challenged by the arrogance of a black man, who would not lower his eyes or turn away as the others did.

He walked over to the group of men and asked, "Who're you? I never seen you 'round dis place."

"Is that so?" Cameron said, looking into the detective's eyes.

"Where're you from?"

Queenie interrupted, saying, "Detective, this is my cousin on my mama's side. He's visiting me from New York City. Walter, this is Detective Bailey Lee. He's new around here too, but he's a good ol' Georgia boy. Ain't that right, Detective," she said, placing her breasts between the detective and Cameron. "What can I do for you, Detective?" she asked seductively then turned around and yelled. "Somebody bring this man a drink and one of those barbecue rib sandwiches out the kitchen. Hurry up, he don't have all day to wait on your lazy asses. With the detective's attention diverted, everyone seemed to relax. Detective Bailey Lee was smiling from ear to ear. "I swear these niggers ain't no good at all around here. I don't know what I'm going to do with their good-for-nothing asses."

"Kick their asses out," Cripple Jake said, joining the detective and Queenie at the bar. The detective loved talking to Jake because he always knew what was going on, and he felt he could depend on him. Jake placed his crutches on the floor and sat down next to the detective.

"What's goin' on Detective?" Jake asked. "Need me t' help ya wit anythang?"

"We're trying t' find out any information, we kin 'bout a group dat may have come through here the night of the policemen's disappearance."

"There wuz a group of white men dat came 'round here a few nights ago all liquored up. They set fire t' one of dem buildings down d' street. I'll show it t' ya before ya leaves. . . Den they chased a few people wit their cars, almost ran over one o' 'em. But, I keep tellin' people t' keep they asses off d' streets after it gits dark. Ain't no tellin' what may happen," Jake volunteered.

"Ya noticed any other groups 'round here, Jake?"

"No, but I kin keep my eyes wide open. Ya cain't trust most these people, so we kinda stay t' ourselves 'round here. Except fo' Friday and Saturday nights then ya cain't keep none of these fools from actin' up. Ya know how dat is."

"Yeah, I know," the detective said, drinking the bourbon that Queenie ordered for him. She also sent two of her best girls down to give the detective an eyeful. Both girls were good at being sexy without overdoing it. They kept his attention. He licked his bottom lip, showing his obvious interest.

An atmosphere of fear, ignorance, and prejudice prevailed in the household where Detective Bailey Lee lived with his parents and siblings. His drunk and abusive father ruled the rural household filled with dirt-smudged children and a frail, inattentive mother. After his father consumed volumes of homemade beer, he spent the remainder of the day filling the house with obscenities and beating his family. Everyone walked cautiously around his father who threatened to 'beat the shit out' of everyone when his father was fully tanked-up. As a child growing up in South Georgia, Bailey Lee could not remember wearing shoes on his feet until he was well pass age sixteen. The one set of clothing he had, consisted of a pair of over-all. Only during the winter did he have the privilege of wearing a shirt. The only coat he owned, he shared with his younger brother, who was four years younger.

His own verbal and physical abuse contributed to two failed marriages, which he blamed on his two ex-spouses. Finding an appropriate outlet for the mean, abusive nature that his father instilled in him, he excelled in his work as a police officer. It was the one place where he received overwhelming approval. Time after time, his abusive behavior resulted in many rewards and fueled his goal to be a tough cop and years later to be the best detective on the force. With the help of his faithful Comrades in the KKK, he was plotting his way to be the commissioner of the Atlanta Police Department. His reputation was lamented in whispered tones by his co-workers. *No one can kick a niggers' ass like Bailey. He knows how to put 'em down and keep 'em down.* He used his record to get what he wanted. Once he became a police detective, he cut back on attending the big yearly Klan meetings at Stone Mountain with his uncles, cousins, and brothers because of the growing liberalism affecting city and state jobs. Instead, he joined a very conservative businessmen's organization that backed him in his climb to the commissioner's office. His new white collar Klan organization encouraged and paved the way to attain the job as police commissioner, which they felt, once it was secured by one of their own that it could affect the changes they wanted . . . To stop integration at all cost. His associates suggested that he put in a transfer to the Fourth Ward and clean up Buttermilk Bottom because with that feather in his cap, he would be on top of the list when the aging commissioner retired.

At a weekly rally of his white-collar civic group, Bailey cheered when their leaders concluded the meeting with an affirming statement. *You have a divine authority and a God given right to keep the niggra in his place and away from our lily white daughters. We must eradicate every effort to integrate our schools and neighborhoods. We must control our political institutions to make certain that the white man remains supreme, and that we honor our ancestors and our God given heritage of superiority over the niggra race by virtue of our white skin.* The entire hall filled with white men let out a rebel cry that re-enforced their commitment and allegiance to the secret agenda of their brotherhood.

Bailey Lee smiled at one of his fellow detectives as they exited the building and said, "It won't be long now."

"We got the badges and the guns," his co-worker said.

"And the ropes," Bailey said, laughing as he shook hands with other Comrades on the sidewalk.

The detective along with two uniformed police officers cruised around the fringes of Buttermilk Bottom, hoping for a clue that would lead them to catching the person or persons responsible for the missing officers. If he solved this case, he would be on his way to the top office in the police department. He would have the attention of the newspapers, television stations, and city hall. With his high-powered connections in the businessmen's association, he would be a shoe-in for the job. When he first arrived at what he surmised was the crime scene, he took note of all the black faces in the area. Some of them looked to him, as if they were rejoicing because two white police officers were missing. He looked closely at the small group of people gathered at the newsstand, and wondered, which one of them had anything to do with the disappearances. Feeling his throat tighten and his heart beat faster, he resisted the urge to get out of the car and rough up the smiling black faces that appeared to be laughing at him. Instead, he instructed his uniformed officers to question them quickly then get rid of them.

He looked at the area from which the missing officers had made their last check-in. There was nothing there, no car, no blood, and no evidence of a struggle. He looked down the dirt road leading to Buttermilk Bottom and convinced himself that the answer was down there in the gigantic hole called The Bottom. Detective Bailey Lee was determined to find out what happened to the missing police officers, and he vowed to destroy the taboo that plagued white officers in his precinct and made them fear going into Buttermilk Bottom. *I'll get that job as commissioner if it means beating every ass down there,* he thought to himself.

Another month passed with Bailey Lee finding no evidence of a crime, nor could he find the dead bodies of his comrades. His instincts told him that someone murdered them and that someone who resided in Buttermilk Bottom was guilty of the crime. How he was going to prove murder when he did not have the bodies was still a mystery. He went back to the juke joint and looked at the group of men sitting around talking, smoking, and playing cards. *What a sorry bunch of people,* he thought. The man who gave him attitude on his last visit was not there. *It's just as well, I ain't in the mood for kicking some high-class nigger's ass,* he thought, trying to decide which of the whores he wanted to bed. If he was lucky, he could do both of them. He was grateful to Cripple Jake for introducing him to Queenie because he could get all the free food, free liquor, and free pussy he wanted.

In late October of that year, the climate was still very warm. The trees still held their vibrant green color, and people had no use for sweaters or jackets because they were enjoying the benefits of an Indian summer. Early mornings had a hint of a chill in the air, but the afternoon brought warmth and plenty of sunshine, which Cora Lee loved because her garden was still flourishing. After helping her pick her deep green collards from her yard, Cameron was crossing the road to go home and met Noitop Cigam face to face for the first time. He had seen and spoken to her from a distance, but never close enough to see her features. The twins said she only came out after dark and even then. . . It was for a very short time. She fascinated them. When he saw her close up, he understood why. To his surprise, Noitop was a short woman with a robust body. She had dark brown flawless skin that looked soft and radiant.

Smiling broadly as she approached him, he said, "Good evening." She had a pleasant round face and beautiful kind eyes that made him wonder why the people of the Bottom spoke of her, as if she had three heads.

"How are you this evening?"

"Just fine, thank you," she responded with a big smile on her face, as if she wanted to laugh. "Have a blessed day."

Miss Cigam had very long mixed gray hair that hung down her back and on her arms hung hundreds of sparkling gold bracelets, up to her elbow. Each bracelet had a different design etched on them. She wore a large number of gold necklaces, but she had no rings or earrings. The number writer wondered why the clothing she wore was so plain and simple when her jewelry was obviously expensive.

A few hours later, Rev. Leon Freeman appeared at Cameron's door, wearing a big smile on his face. "Good evening, Cameron."

"Good evening, Rev. Freeman, come in."

"Thank you, son. I just wanted to stop by and tell you that my church members would like to give Jason Anderson a hand with his college expenses. I know he's away at school now on that scholarship program, but I'm sure that he needs money for books and clothing."

"That's great news, Reverend."

"We want to help. After all he is the first one of our children to go to college," he said as if Cameron had not quoted those facts to him months earlier.

"I'm sure Jason and his mother will appreciate whatever you can do."

"We're having bake sales for the next three Sundays, and the members are giving fish fries in their homes to help raise the money. In fact, they are planning a few 'Heaven and Hell Parties' to raise the majority of the money."

"Heaven and Hell Parties? I heard about those. How can I help?"

"Well, I was hoping that you and Jake could encourage people to attend and go to the parties held in the apartment designated as 'hell'. Not that I'm saying that. . . . That's . . . Ah, where you belong. . . But . . ."

"Rev. Freeman, I understand," Cameron said, laughing and putting the minister at ease.

"There is no way I can attend the 'hell' parties, but I will plan to attend those designated as 'heaven'. With you and Jake attending, we are guaranteed to have a good turn-out."

"Look, I am not offended. I'd be happy to do whatever I can to support the church and Jason. You can count on both of us."

"Good, we plan to have one in two weeks and every month during the winter so that Jason will have all the money he needs for expenses. If it goes well, we'll do the same thing next summer."

"Sounds like a great plan. I look forward to helping out."

"Thank you, Cameron, and thanks again for setting a fire under me."

"It was my pleasure and I would gladly do it again," he said seriously. After a few nervous moments, the minister realized that he was teasing him again. They both laughed.

The first 'heaven and hell party' took place on a Friday night in a building up the street from Cameron's apartment. It was a four unit building with two apartments on each floor. In one of the second floor apartments, a member of the pastor's congregation conducted the 'heavenly party'. They had punch and cake, sang hymns, played games, sold fish sandwiches and fish dinners with potato salad and greens. The pastor gave a lengthy sermon, which got the heavenly party guests just as loud as the party group in the apartment just below them that was designated as 'hell'. Downstairs, in the 'hell party', people were gambling, selling whiskey, drinking, and dancing. They sold fish sandwiches and dinners over the gutsy sounds of the blues that were in direct competition for the hardy sounds of the heavenly gospel songs, sang by the holy-rollers in the upstairs apartment.

Amos, the Vegetable Man was on his way upstairs to the heavenly party when he ran into Lucille on the first floor porch. Lucille was drinking a beer from the bottle when she spotted the Vegetable Man.

"Amos, where you goin'?"

"I'm headed upstairs, Lucille," he said, trying to appear in a hurry.

"What d' fuck ya going up there fo'. . . D' real party's down here."

"Sounds like everybody's having a good time, but I promised Rev. Freeman, I'd meet him upstairs."

"You kin come down here and have a beer wit me b'fore you go up there, cain't ya?"

"No, Lucille, I don't drink."

"Den what d' fuck do you do?"

"I work hard during the week and go to church every Sunday."

"What 'bout a woman? Don't ya need a woman?" Drunk and unsteady on her feet, she slithered over to the banister where he stood.

"I had a real good woman 'fore my wife died."

"Shit. . . Her ass been dead fo' years," she said, grabbing his reluctant hand. "Don't ya need somebody now t' make ya feel good?"

"I gotta go upstairs, Lucille. I'll see you later," he said, breaking the tight grip she had on him.

"Go d' fuck on den. Don't nobody want yo'. . . . Black-ass anyway. You old black-ass mutherfucker," she yelled.

"Lucille, what in the world is wrong with you? We're trying to raise money for the church and for Jason. Why do you have to start all that cursing around here?" Queenie asked, coming out of the apartment on the front porch when she heard Lucille's loud voice.

"I'm goin' back t' d' juke-joint. I'm sick o' dese uppity actin' mutherfuckers 'round here. Everybody's actin' like fuckin's out o' style or somethin'. Ain't no men 'round dis place worth a shit 'n d' first place."

"You're looking for a man, Lucille?" Queenie said, laughing.

"I's always lookin' fo' a fuckin' man and if you know what I know. . . You better do d' same damn thang."

"What on earth are you talking about?"

"Talkin' 'bout you pretendin' you got d' Bug Man all locked up. D' truth is. . . All you got is a man dat wants t' fuck yo' brains out. . . Dat's all. You jes like d' rest of us stupid-ass women down here. Dat nigger ain't gon' marry yo' fat ass."

"What have you heard, Lucille?"

"Same damn thang I been hearin'. . . . Dat man ain't gon marry yo' fat ass, no mo' than I is."

"Lucille, you need to shut your nasty mouth," Queenie said, trying to keep from getting angry.

"You gonna make me, bitch," Lucille said, staggering with her hands on her hips.

"What's going on out here?" Jake said.

"What's going on is. . . Lucille is about to get her ass kicked."

"Bitch, carry yo' heavy, fat, ass back 'n d' house. Don't nobody want ya. Not d' Bug Man, not anybody. . . Ya fuckin' big fat-ass bitch."

"I'm going to fix that mouth of yours once and for all." Queenie was moving toward Lucille, but Jake stood squarely in front of Queenie, preventing her from passing. Lucille walked down the steps and started walking down the street, stumbling as she went.

"Fuck you, Queenie. Fuck all o' you uppity actin' mutherfuckers."

"If you hit her, you won't be hitting much," Jake said.

"I'll at least have the pleasure of kicking her ass."

"Then what?"

"I don't know. She makes me so damn angry. . . I just want to hit her in that big mouth of hers."

"That's because she's crazy and a drunk. You should know better than to get into a pissing match with Lucille. You're smarter than that. What did she say to get you all worked up?"

"Nothing."

"Nothing, huh? You were ready to beat up that skinny, little, old, drunk woman for nothing?"

"She talks too fucking much."

"Everybody knows that and you most of all. Now, tell me. . . What did she say about Cameron? I heard her mention the 'Bug Man'."

"It's nothing."

"You can talk to me, you know," he said, taking her hand.

"Are people talking about Cameron and me?" she asked, pulling her hand away.

"No more than usual."

"What are they saying, Jake?"

"What do you care?"

"I don't. . . But I hate to think that people are talking about something that's none of their damn business. We're both grown, and we don't need anyone's approval."

"Who said you did?"

"It's just that. . . As crazy as Lucille is. . . She may be telling the truth. What if he never marries me, Jake?"

"Then I'll marry you," he said seriously.

"Jake, I'm serious."

"So am I," he said, leaning on the banister with his crutches still under his arms and holding her hand again.

H. Victoria Hargro Atkerson

"You know I love Cameron and. . . Let's be real, Jake. There is no way I could be interested in you."

"Not even a little bit."

"Hell no. I have needs," she said, touching her hair and neck.

"I can take care of those needs. Believe me. . . I can give you what you need, Queenie."

"Don't be silly, Jake."

"Just give me a chance, Queenie. I am very serious about you," he said, leaning toward her, feeling his passion for her begin to swell.

"Well, you don't have to be any more because here comes my man right now." Jake turned around to see his best friend, crossing the dirt road. Breathing in all of her sexual tension, she said, "He's all the man I need."

Disappointed, Jake felt his heart break once more and said, "Well. . . I'll be around if you change your mind."

"I won't," she said, rushing to greet her handsome lover. "Hey, baby, it's about time you got here," Queenie said, hugging Cameron around the neck.

"Hey," he said, kissing her on the cheek. "Jake, how's it going?"

"Everything's going fine. We should have raised enough money for ten children to go to college with all the money the church is raking in tonight. They have a good poker game going on out on the back porch."

"Let's get to it." Cameron kissed Queenie on the cheek again and said, "I'll see you later, time for papa to go to work."

The two best friends went off together, leaving Queenie frustrated and alone to ponder her future as Lucille's words reverberated in her ears.

Both parties made enough money to fatten Jason's college account by several hundred dollars. The best part of the whole evening was that everyone came together for a good cause with Rev. Freeman emerging for the first time as a positive leader in the community.

Chapter 18

In November of 1955, Jim Crow laws continued to restrict and inhibit the movement of blacks in and around the city of Atlanta. All the educational institutions, transportation, and recreational facilities imposed limits that continued to isolate blacks from the main stream life-styles that would afford them decent housing and jobs for themselves and their families. Restricted to the back of buses, Blacks had separate and unequal restrooms and drinking fountains in public places and made to subsist on minimal income with little to no public services. In spite of the depressed conditions, black civic groups and strong church leaders forged ahead to insist on changes that would benefit Atlanta's black populace. Although integration had been the order passed down by the Supreme Court the year before headed by an Eisenhower appointee, Chief Justice Earl Warren, the white political structure, stressed gradual change and slow to no improvements in the life of black communities in the South.

Despite the oppression by the white only government in Atlanta, the black community strengthened its economic base with black owned businesses taking center stage in the 'Sweet Auburn District' where the Atlantic Life Insurance Company grew into a multi-million-dollar business. Black owned newspapers, radio stations, nightclubs, mortuaries, restaurants, and many other black businesses benefited from the segregation imposed on the blacks.

For several months, the bashful Hope and Cameron dated regularly, and they frequented many of the restaurants and nightclubs on Auburn Avenue and a few new black owned entertainment spots that began to emerge on the West Side along Hunter Street. They often went to the movies, but they both loved to go dancing and when time and opportunity allowed it, they went places that they could share with

Hope's son. Cameron even talked Hope into going shopping. He treated her to several very feminine outfits and ignored her protests about the amount of money he spent with a series of wonderful sensuous kisses.

Whenever they were out together, Hope always noticed people staring at them. Seeing the wonderment on their faces, she surmised that they, like her, wondered why he wanted to date her, but at his request, she stopped asking him why. It was uncomfortable, but it felt good to hear the hundreds of compliments that he bestowed on her. She never had anyone to praise her before, especially someone so good looking. Cameron was extremely kind to her and her son. Never in her life had anyone treated her so affectionately or so royally. From the beginning of their courtship, he kissed her constantly but never asked her to go to bed with him. She wanted to, but she would never ask. In all her life, no one had made her feel so special. It felt good just being with him. In all her life, she only had one serious relationship with a man and that one was very short and ended badly when she got pregnant. From that moment on, she focused on her child, and her only concern was getting what he needed to survive.

Cameron called her early one Saturday morning and asked her to arrange for Little Neil to spend the night with someone. "I would like to make some very special plans for the two of us. . . With your permission."

"What kind of plans?"

"Special plans, just for you and me. Is that okay with you?"

"I guess so."

"Maybe, we should wait a little longer? You don't seem sure."

"I'm sure," she said quickly.

"I don't want to rush you."

Helplessly blushing, she said softly, "You're not rushing me."

"Are you sure?"

"Yes."

"Then I'll pick you up at eight."

It was finally going to happen. The only problem was that she felt extremely nervous about being intimate with anyone, especially Cameron. Hope had only had one sexual relationship and that was with her childhood sweetheart, the father of her child. She was not sure she even remembered how to, but she was eager to try, especially with Cameron. At eight o'clock, Cameron picked Hope up and took her to a small hotel on the West Side. It was the first time she had ever been in a hotel room, and the fancy environment intimidated her. Once they were in the room, he gave her a large, beautiful bouquet of flowers and a chilled glass of champagne. It was the first time she ever tasted champagne. He turned on the radio to some very soft music and pulled her into his arms.

"Let's dance," he said, holding her so closely that she could hardly breathe.

"I'm so nervous. I'm not sure I can," she said, bending her head down toward the floor to watch his feet.

Taking her chin in his hand and tilting her head up, he looked into her eyes. When she tried to look away, he said, "I want to look at you. Don't worry about your feet, just hold on to me." They danced to several songs, including a bop, which she had no idea how to do, but he was teaching her, and she was getting better at it since the first time she tried it months before. She tried harder because it was fun, and he seemed to love to dance so much. Laughing at all her mistakes, she forgot all about being self-conscious.

There was a knock on the door, which made her jump.

"Don't worry. It's room service. I took the liberty and ordered dinner for us. I hope you don't mind."

Hope was speechless. Why would she mind him being so wonderful to her? She could not believe how kind and considerate he was. He always asked her if she minded or cared about what he wanted to plan for them. No one had ever asked her what she thought or what she cared to do before him. When Cameron opened the door, there was a waiter in a sparkling white jacket, pushing a large table full of food. All the special treatment surprised and delighted her, knowing that he had done so much to plan the evening for her. Things like this only happened in the movies or on the pages of the romantic novels that she read constantly.

"Cameron, you shouldn't have done all this."

"I wanted to, for you."

"Thanks," she said shyly.

"You are welcome, Hope." He watched her, as she was so near tears. "Let's eat. Grits, anyone?"

"You ordered grits for dinner?"

He opened the cover on the plates to reveal chicken breasts stuffed with wild rice, green beans, and slithers of carrots decorated with a thin green onion wrapped around them. She looked surprised and delighted that there were no grits. They both laughed.

"That sure is pretty."

"Let's eat."

They ate at leisure then talked for hours. Cameron was asking her questions about what she wanted for her future, and he made suggestions regarding a few choices she could explore.

"I really think you should go to school."

"Me?"

"Yes, you. You could get a grant to help you pay for it, and you could still keep your job. College isn't like high school. You can take classes whenever you want, and you don't have to take them all at once. Do it at your own speed, then little by little, and you will finish. One day you will have your degree and a chance at a bright future for yourself and Neil."

"Does that mean you won't be there with us?"

"It means. . . That I will be very proud of you for taking control of your life."

"But, what about us?"

"My wish for you is that someday, you will find a man who will love and appreciate you and Neil. Someone you can be proud of and love for the rest of your life."

"This is beginning to sound like goodbye."

"It will last as long as it lasts. I can't promise you any more than that. I wish I could, but I can't." She was silent for a long time. He waited purposefully knowing the full impact of the choice he offered her. He would not put any pressure on her in anyway. If things became intimate between them, it had to be her choice, knowing, understanding, and accepting all the facts.

"There is no future for us, is that what you're saying?"

"Yes."

She was quiet again. He waited. Then suddenly, she said. "At least, you're honest and this time, I know how I'm supposed to feel and think. Can you kiss me now?"

Laughing at her innocence, he said, "Are you sure you want me to?"

"Yes, I really do."

Standing up, he held her by the hand and looked at her long and hard saying, "You are a beautiful woman, Hope."

She smiled bashfully as he kissed her tenderly on her forehead and said, "You make me feel beautiful."

"Hope, you don't need me to make you feel beautiful because you are," he said, kissing her deeply as he unzipped her dress then allowed it to fall on the floor, which he quickly picked up and placed on a chair.

She placed her arms around his waist, hugging him and trying desperately to get closer to him. They remained in a warm comfortable embrace for a long time because he wanted to take his time and treat her as gently as possible. Her body shivered as he removed her slip, bra, and then her panties. When she was completely nude, she looked as if she was ready to run and hide. He smiled because she covered her breasts with her arms. After admiring her body for too long a period for Hope, he finally picked her up and laid her on the bed where he continued to admire her physical attributes. He knew she was uncomfortable because she tried several times to pull the covers over her body, but he removed them each time.

"I want to admire you," he said softly with his eyes, moving up and down her body. Since she did not know what to do with her eyes or her hands, she lay perfectly still with her eyes closed. The idea of someone admiring her body was new to her. No one ever had. In her one failed relationship, she had never been completely nude in front of a man. Cameron placed his hands on her body and felt her respond to his touch. He smiled and said, "There is nothing more satisfying for a man than having a woman do what you just did."

"I didn't do anything," she said timidly.

"You responded to my touch."

"I couldn't help it."

"I know. . . That's what makes it so special and nice," he said, kissing her on her soft plump breasts. Her nipples were already hard and pointed towards him. As his tongue whipped around her nipples, she began to tremble, feeling out of control, not certain what to do as her breathing became more rapid and erratic. Taking his time, he kissed each of her breasts delivering feelings of passion deep within her that shook the foundation of her being. It was wonderful and amazing. He was creating a new erotic world for her and for the first time, she knew first hand, what those feelings were all about that she read in those romantic novels, which consumed so much of her time because she was fond of reading them.

He nibbled on her stomach and shocked her as his lips touched her very private parts.

Like a bullet, she sat straight up and asked, "What are you doing?"

The shock on her face was amusing, bringing a smile to his. "I'm making love to you. Haven't you ever had oral sex?"

"What?"

"Has anyone ever kissed you down there," he asked, touching her vagina lightly.

"Heavens no, never," she said, alarmed that he would even ask her that question.

She refused to look at him as she pulled the covers over her body. He waited then held her face so that she could look nowhere but into his eyes, holding her attention.

"I would like to be the first," he said softly and sweetly.

His words made her shiver with uncertainty and wonder.

"I don't know nothing about that," she said, shaking her head no. Allowing more time to pass so that she could think about what he had proposed, he made sure she wanted to before kissing her again on the lips and giving her time to feel comfortable again. When her body relaxed, he touched her breasts with the tip of his tongue and elicited a deep moan from her.

"Hope, do you like it when I kiss you on your breasts?" he asked, applying more pressure and pushing her back down on the bed.

"Yes. . . Yes I do," she said, feeling sensuous for the first time in her life.

"Hope. . . You are going to love it when I kiss you right here," he said, touching her clitoris. Please trust me. Will you trust me?"

"I don't know about that. . . It don't seem right."

"It's perfectly normal between lovers who want to satisfy each other. Let me show you just once, how wonderful you are. If you don't like it. . . I promise you, I will stop."

After several long suspended moments as his gaze held her in suspense and filled her with wonder.

She took a deep breath then heard herself say, "Okay." When she saw him lower his head, she shut her eyes tightly and held her breath as he started nibbling on her navel then on each of her thighs. She partially opened her eyes and said, "Okay," so softly, he barely heard her.

When he tried to separate her legs gently, she unconsciously tightened them to avoid any intrusion. He stopped.

"I'll only do this if you want me to," he said tenderly. "You don't have to do anything that makes you feel uncomfortable."

Thinking about all the wonderful things that he shared with her and how excellent he made her feel, she took a deep cleansing breath of air, and said, "I trust you. I'm ready."

Cameron waited patiently until he was certain that she had made up her mind. Slowly, she began to open her legs to him. When he lowered his head to touch the inside of her thigh with the tip of his tongue, her body trembled against his lips. When she felt his tongue touch the crest of her womanhood, she jumped; he stopped but did not remove his tongue or lips from her. As gentle as a lamb, he gently kissed the peak of her womanhood, until he felt her relax. Slowly and warmly, he suckled, massaging away all her inhibitions and fears, taking time to make sure she appreciated the exquisiteness of her own body. Slowly and deliberately, her hips began to move in response to his artful manipulations. She began to enjoy the pleasures and excitement that her body revealed, moving faster and faster until she cried out in complete satisfaction.

Completely embarrassed, she smiled at him then quickly looked away, surprised at what she felt.

"You can rest a while, and we can do that again if you would like," he said. She did not speak, but the look on her face said she was more than willing. He got up, crossed the room, and poured them a glass of champagne. "Wine compliments good sex like nothing else can. Here drink this. It will make you feel better," he said, handing her a glass.

"I don't think anything can make me feel better than what you just did," she said with an air of complete innocence.

He laughed aloud and sat down on the bed next to her, sipped his wine and began removing his clothes. She watched him as he revealed his fine muscular structure.

When he took off his shorts, she looked quickly at his enlarged shaft then turned away.

"Don't tell me you have never seen an aroused nude man before?"

"I've only been with one man in my whole life and the few times we were together. . . It was always in the dark. He didn't take his clothes off or anything like that."

"I feel sorry for him," he said, kissing her thirstily. "He missed a wonderful opportunity to make love to you. Having sex and making love are as different as night and day. The experience has to be shared completely."

He emptied his glass of wine and waited as she sipped hers, but she was taking too long. Staring down at her, he grasped both of her legs, finding no resistance; he began kissing her high on the inside of her warm thighs. He paused for a moment to make sure she was cooperating then finding her body responsive; he began kissing her womanhood again. Before she could securely place the glass on the end table, the glass fell onto the carpet as she began to moan in reaction to his warm moist lips that penetrated every layer of her being. A few minutes later, she began to beg for more.

Chapter 19

Noitop Cigam was originally from Haiti and came to this country when she was twenty years old. As long as she could remember, she had knowledge and abilities that far exceeded her peers. The existence of the occult and all the mysteries it held were second nature to her as she grew in her innate ability of prophesy, which was discovered by her mother and grandmother when she was only five years of age. As rumors spread of her psychic gifts in the tiny country, people began asking her to tell their destinies before she entered first grade. As their ancestors had done before them, her grandmother and mother trained her in the craft and monitored her progress while protecting her from over-zealous people who were anxious to use her gifts before they were fully developed. Noitop was not always happy to have special abilities, but she never turned anyone away who needed her help.

Marrying late in life, Noitop found that she only had to hold her suitors' hand to tell what they were feeling and thinking. Before she had the opportunity to fall in love with them, she knew they would cheat, lie, or grow afraid of her and her gift. The one man who overcame all her readings died only seven years after their marriage, leaving her with two beautiful children. Both of their children had the same gifts as their mother, but they chose to ignore them, and she allowed them to do so because she knew the burden that accompanied the unique gifts that they were born possessing whether they wanted to or not. The gift was strongest in her youngest child, a daughter, who studied nursing while her son, who was trying to make it in his own business, running a small clothing store on the West Side. He chose to ignore his unusual abilities. Both children loved her, but they were relieved that they no longer had to live with her in her obscure and lonely manner with strangers coming and going all day long. When they started their teenage years, they went to live with their grandmother. When their friends discovered that their mother was a 'witch doctor', they made fun of them and their mother, but no one could make them ashamed of her because they knew how valuable and special her gifts were. People, their mother had taught them, do not like things they do not understand. Both children learned that very early in life.

As mother to Jazmine and Blair Cigam, Noitop never forced them to do anything because she believed that character and destiny were predetermined. She felt better when they were away from her because it freed her from the emotional attachment that she had with them from birth. It was difficult being a parent and having the gifts that she had. She saw and felt things about her children that were private and personal, which she chose not to share with them. Some things, she knew she could never share with them.

Both her children visited her on Sunday afternoons; they talked continuously about their lives and asked questions about the people of Buttermilk Bottom. Being a private person herself, their mother told them very little about other people's business except for general information where people lived, how many children they had, and sometimes what they did for a living. If their occupation were illegitimate, she would tell them nothing. Jazmine knew when her mother held back information. She could always tell what her mother was thinking and feeling, and she knew that her mother was completely aware of her abilities. They had a non-verbal agreement to never to speak about their gifts, unless Jazmine or Blair decided that they wanted to develop it. Her son's gift was not as well developed or as instinctive as his sister's was, but it was there, lurking below the surface. He chose to ignore it and bury it. On several occasions, he had to acknowledge it because he sensed danger and had to act on it.

As a teenager, Blair found that he had to rely on his senses because he felt that his younger sister was in danger. He immediately ran to where he knew she was playing at the swimming hole on the creek near their home. Her friends teased her about not swimming.

A group of boys, who did not believe that she could not swim, tossed her in the water and said, "If you can't. . . It's a good time to learn."

They were laughing as she fought for survival. Blair jumped in the creek and pulled her out just in time. Then he went over to the boys who did it and knocked them both down. He knew instinctively who had done it. After he made certain that his little sister was okay, he took her home. The next week, he spent hours and hours teaching Jazmine how to swim.

Noitop knew that the people of Buttermilk Bottom were afraid of her. It amused her and gave her many hours of laughter at their expense. She used their fear to guarantee her the privacy she needed. The fewer people she interacted with the better and the more peace she had when she laid her head on her pillow at night.

The old house sitting in the kudzu was a gift, complete with the deed, from one of her grateful clients who had all the vines removed one day and her furniture moved in before daybreak the following day. The house was not much to look at, but it was all she needed and with a little care, she soon made it a comfortable home. For the first few years that she lived in Buttermilk Bottom, she had no electricity. It did not bother her because she rarely used electric lights anyway. She preferred candlelight instead. Darkness scared most people, but for her, it was where her soul lived. The house had indoor plumbing, a good solid cast iron cooking stove, and fireplaces in the living room, dining room, and in both bedrooms.

Noitop loved helping people. She thought of herself as a minister or a doctor trained to heal those invisible parts of the human soul. Taught by her mother and grandmother that there were places within the body no doctor could reach and no minister could understand. She was an ardent believer in the power and the miracle of prayer, believing strongly that special people had special gifts, and that she was one of them. For her there was never a choice. Possessing her God-given talents were a part of her family's identity for as long as she could remember.

A new client came to Noitop early one morning, a young girl about seventeen years old, saying, "Miss Cigam, I needs yo help."

Noitop did not respond. She looked at the young woman, creating more anxiety in the young woman about being with a witch doctor because the girl did not understand that the process of her reading had already started.

After a while, Cigam said, "Sit down, and place your hands on the table." The girl did as instructed, placing her shaking hands on the table. Cigam looked at her hands, back, and front. Then said, "You have a lot of worries for a young woman."

"Yes, ma'am."

"Why did you come to me?"

"Well, I came t' axe you if you could gimme somethin' dat'll make my boyfriend marry me? Or, could you tell me somethin' t' do."

"I see two men in your life, which one are you talking about?"

"Which one? I only see one man," the girl lied.

"If you want my help you must be truthful. Otherwise. . . Take your business elsewhere."

The girl looked up at Noitop with tears in her eyes. Instead of words, a mountain of tears flowed out of her eyes, and deep moaning emerged from her mouth. The old woman sat and waited. When the girl regained her composure, Noitop said, "Reach into that bowl and give me a hand full of bones, place them on the table in front of you." The girl wiped her tears and obeyed, placing the bones on the black velvet cloth that covered the table. Miss Cigam looked at the bones then into the girl's eyes. "Before I tell you what these bones told me, I'm going to tell you something. Crying won't make your problems go away, so get a grip on the truth and from there your problems will be eliminated." She studied the girl's teary face then continued. "The baby, you're carrying belongs to your mother's husband. If you tell her, she will hate you, and she will disown you for the rest of your life. If you tell your stepfather. . . He will call you a liar and a whore. Your mother will believe him."

The girl's tears ran freely down onto her flowered dress. "Your boy friend suspects that you're pregnant. If you tell him, he will be angry, but he will support you. He loves you, but he won't marry you, unless you do something that will make him believe in you. He is a nice boy. Do you want to trick him?"

"No, no ma'am," she cried, wiping her eyes.

"Then go home, find yourself some work, and a place to live away from your mother. Raise your child and hold your head up high. You have nothing to be ashamed of here. Be strong for your child."

"But who's gonna take care of me?"

"Take care of yourself, girl. It is the only way for you to go. Be proud, everything will work out."

The young girl placed a five-dollar bill on the table and walked out with her head hung down. Noitop knew that the girl had the ability to make it on her own. She saw love in her future, but she did not share it with the girl because she believed that things of the heart should happen naturally and unexpectedly.

November brought with it the promise of winter and cold air that suddenly permeated the landscape, making leaves turn brilliant colors and drop from their branches, which refused to release them only weeks before. For the first time, people found the warmth of an extra layer of clothing to shield them from the colder air that finally reached into the southern state of Georgia. The frigid air was a prelude of a day, which would mark the beginning of a new lifestyle for many people in the country. It was certainly true for Cameron, as he started the month out unaware that fate would touch his life.

By the end of the workday of that first day of December, astounding news spread all over America. A black woman, in Montgomery Alabama, refused to relinquish her seat to a white male on a bus ride home from a hard day's work. This simple act of defiance made history for several reasons. It was unheard of for a black person to defy a white person in the South. The fact that the woman was well-dressed and displayed a gentle disposition made everyone look on in awe. Plus the fact that it was the perfect timing because the NAACP was looking for a case that they could use to fight the segregation laws governing transportation. The incident involved a person who was no stranger to the fight for civil rights. Mrs. Rosa Parks was a long-time activist, who had an innate sense of her own worth as a citizen of this country. With a strong sense of integrity, she responded the only way she could have reacted at that moment with a resounding and unequivocal answer to the unreasonable request, 'no'.

Even in Buttermilk Bottom, the air was lighter, sweeter, cleaner as the sun rose the following Sunday morning, when Cameron saw Jazmine for the first time up close. Everyone was elated over the Rosa Parks incident and prayed for her as they saw pictures in the newspapers of the police fingerprinting her for objecting to an unjust law. People huddled in front of the small black and white Motorola television screen that Luther purchased for the juke joint only days before the incident. Watching as the short, quiet woman defied hundreds of years of discrimination gave everyone a sense of pride and honor, knowing that what she did, captured an abuse, they all had endured. She was not the first person to object nor was she the first person the police arrested and fingerprinted. At that moment, she represented every black person in the South, who lived under the unjust double standards set in place by an oppressive system of white Jim Crow laws.

Following a big breakfast with the twins, Cameron went up the hill to the grocery store as he did most Sunday mornings. After picking up a copy of the Atlanta Constitution and a sirloin for dinner, Cameron realized that it had been weeks, since he visited the juke joint. Cora

Lee missed him and often sent him dinner when he failed to show up. As he walked out of the store, heading back to Buttermilk Bottom, he saw the beautiful dark woman that he admired and dreamed of since he first saw her walking in the setting sun on top of the very hill he was standing on. Filled with deep longings, he admired her beauty, up close. She was on her way to visit someone in The Bottom. Her presence paralyzed him; he stood, taking in all her features and almost drowned in her stunning good looks. For months, the silhouette of this woman haunted him. He knew that body well because he went to sleep every night, remembering it and slipping it into his dreams. Being so close to her made his heart pound hard and loudly in his chest. The light wintry air suddenly became too heavy to breathe, as he walked helplessly and instinctively over to her.

"Hello."

"Good morning," she said, looking into his eyes but what she saw in them, frightened her. It was raw lust. She lowered her head and picked up speed as she started walking down the hill.

My God, you are beautiful, better looking than I ever dreamed, he thought. "Good morning, my name is. . . ." he said not realizing he had stopped talking. *What I would do to get you in my bed.*

"Excuse me," she said angrily, interrupting his thoughts and walking around him, avoiding his eyes all together as she felt the hair on the back of her neck rise up.

"Can I please talk to you for a minute?" he said, trying to keep up with her. *I won't let you get away from me,* he thought, keeping pace with her steps.

"No," she yelled, refusing to look at him again, afraid what she might see.

Without missing a step, she hurried down the dirt road that led into Buttermilk Bottom because she did not intend to be a notch on his belt. She remembered all too well that he only wanted sex from women and nothing else.

In his dreams, she was a dark mysterious woman with the most smooth, and perfect skin he had ever seen. In real life, her skin was so perfect that it looked artificial. She had her long wavy hair tied up in a roll on the back of her neck.

Cameron tried again, saying, "Can I walk with you? It seems as if we are going the same way."

"No, I prefer walking alone," she said, cutting him off dryly as her contradicting light gray eyes pierced his heart as she continued on her way down the hill. *The only direction you're going in is the bed, and you're not using me the way you use other women,* she argued to herself as she hurriedly walked away from him.

Feeling his heart beat rapidly in his chest, he wanted to run after her, but he also wanted to enjoy the sight of her walking away from him with her hips and buttock rolling to the beat he felt in his heart. He walked behind her and was not surprised when she passed right by his house. Her beauty had captivated him weeks before, long before he saw her face. Like a hungry animal, he followed helplessly behind her mesmerized by her shapely body, her angelic face, her flawless dark, brown skin, and her exotic physical traits.

When he reached his building, the twins were sitting on their front porch. They watched him as he sat on the steps, watching the tall beautiful woman until she disappeared around the corner. A sense of urgency came over him as he made up his mind to find out everything he could about the beautiful woman, and where she was going.

"He's obviously been struck by the love bug," Gussie whispered, smiling.

"I think so," Essie said, trying not to let him know they were watching his lovesick behavior.

After she was out of sight, he turned to ask the twins about the beautiful young woman.

"Who is she?" he asked the twins, still looking down the empty street. When they did not answer, he turned and saw them smiling at him. He smiled, knowing that they caught him at a weak moment. "Do you know her?"

"We don't know, but she comes here every Sunday about the same time. She's very friendly," Gussie related.

"She dresses real nice and has the prettiest smile," Essie said.

An hour later, Cameron went to look for Jake at the juke joint to question him. Jake was proud and delighted to share the little knowledge he acquired about her.

"She goes down to see the old woman every Sunday, a man joins them around noon. They both stay down there until well after dark; then they leave together. I tried to talk to her myself on several occasions without any luck. She always gave me a beautiful smile, but she made me know to keep my distance." He played it off by saying, "I guess she's not into cripple guys."

Cameron smiled because he now knew how to track her down. The man who joined her may or may not be a threat. He had to find out if they were married. If they were not he would attempt to get her full attention. If she was married, maybe he could try to interest her in a long-term affair. Either way, he wanted her. He wanted her as he had never wanted anyone in his whole life.

It was an obsession, which he knew began the day he saw the beautiful silhouette of her with the blazing colors of the setting sun radiating around her. Cameron was determined to intercept the dark beautiful woman who haunted him every night in his dreams for the past few months. All he had to do was to close his eyes to see her walking up the hill framed by the sunset. It gave him a warm feeling inside. He stationed himself on his front porch to keep watch, when he noticed from his front porch that the police were staking out and watching for anything suspicious. A patrol car stationed at the entrance of the community remained there throughout the day. Cameron called a meeting of his friends and sets up a surveillance team to watch the police. The men spread the word for everyone to be especially careful that the police might be looking for a reason to come in and shoot up the neighborhood.

Cripple Jake climbed up the steps and said, "Give me a beer man."

"Go get it yourself," Cameron said, looking for the beautiful woman to appear. He waited impatiently to see her as she left the Bottom.

"My legs hurt. How about helping me out?" Jake lied.

"Okay, okay." Cameron said, frustrated, knowing that he could miss the beautiful woman when she passed by. Hurriedly, he went into his kitchen for two beers and was about to head back when he heard a knock on his rear door. No one ever came to his back door. The vines were too deep and menacing. He looked out the window and saw a man standing on the landing in a chain gang outfit.

He said, through the windowpane, "Cripple Jake told me to come here."

"What?"

"Cripple Jake told me to come here," the young man said, looking behind him. Cameron took a deep breath and opened the rear door, which had several intricate locks on it. When the young man was in the house he said, "Thank you, Mister."

"What is this all about?"

"Is Jake here?"

"He's on the porch. Wait here, I'll get him." Cameron stuck his head out the front door and said, "Jake, get your ass in here."

"I think it'll be best if you come out here with that beer," he said, seeing a police car drive by the apartment. Jake waved at the officer in the patrol car, and the officer waved back.

Cameron was not happy about leaving a stranger in his house, but he trusted his friend. "Wait a minute," he went back inside and told the young man in the prison uniform to sit down at the kitchen table. He gave him a beer and took another one out of the refrigerator. He was about to leave the kitchen when he asked, "Are you hungry?"

"Yes, sir." Cameron gave him the fried chicken that the twins gave him that morning at breakfast. "Thank you, Mister."

Cameron smiled and said, "Don't mention it. I'll be right back." His unexpected guest began tearing into the chicken before he could turn around. On the porch, he gave Cripple Jake a beer and then looked up and down the street to see if he missed his dark, beautiful woman. "What's this all about?"

"That's Johnny Mason. Since the day he was born, he lived a few doors from me. The police picked him up four years ago and threw him in jail. There was a robbery and someone said it was a black man. He was the first black man they saw, so they threw his ass in jail."

"Are they looking for him?"

"I don't think so."

"How do you know that?"

"Because when Johnny was arrested, he gave them a phony name and address. He was a smart little kid when they arrested him. He's a man now."

"They took his finger prints."

"Yeah, so what? They can't go around the whole city finger printing every nigger in Atlanta to make sure they catch some convict."

"They can't?"

"Well, he's willing to take the risk. He's a good kid. They caught him in the wrong place at the wrong time. It's the same old fucking story; guilty of being black in America."

"Well. . . Tell me. What are we going to do with him?"

"Give him a bath, some regular clothes, money, and a place to stay until I can get him a job and a room somewhere."

"So, you want me to keep him here? A Stranger?"

"Yeah. Do this for me, man. The boy is a nice kid. He just got a bad break."

Cameron looked at his friend and wondered what he was getting into. The possible consequences of his decision flashed in his mind, but just as quickly, they disappeared.

"Okay, but I'm holding you responsible," he said, pointing his finger at Jake.

"No problem. He's a good person. . . Honest."

Cameron went back into the house took out a fresh set of clothes complete with underwear and gave them to the boy. "Sorry, I can get you some new underwear tomorrow, but at least you can get some clean clothes on. The bathroom is over there. Put your clothes in a bag, I'll get rid of them later. After you're dressed, come on out on the porch."

"Thank you, I sho' appreciate this, Mister."

"Don't mention it."

Cripple Jake and Cameron sat on the porch, talking about the police stakeouts. When Johnny appeared, he hesitated at the door, looking in all directions then retreated backwards.

"If you had the nerve to break out of the chain gang, you should have the nerve to come out here and sit down," Cameron said, looking at a much younger man, figuring he had to be no more than twenty-two years old.

Vacillating for a few minutes, Johnny came out, sat down immediately, looking up and down the dirt road. As soon as he sat down, Cripple Jake said, "Go back in the house and bring us some beers." The young man hesitated. "Go on," Jake urged.

"All we have to do now is to get him to stop walking, as if he still has chains on his feet. He looks like a completely different person without all that dirt and hair all over him," Cameron said.

"He'll look even better when you give him a haircut."

"Shit, is there anything else you want me to do?"

"Yeah, don't forget to give him some money. The boy is broke."

"Okay, okay. Where is the boy's family?"

"They moved away. They know he's here, but they are going to wait a few weeks before contacting him. . . Just in case."

"Well, I'll be damned," Jake said.

"What?"

"It's Big Money."

"Who?"

"Big Money Banks, he is the biggest gambler around here. He cheats like hell, but he has more money to cheat with than anyone in Buttermilk Bottom."

"I don't remember seeing him."

"He left just before you moved here. I see he has a brand new Cadillac. It's a beauty."

"Must have cost him a fortune," Cameron said, admiring the big automobile.

"Don't worry, he's got plenty of money. I'm glad he's back. We can look forward to some big games, and I'm talking about some real money, man."

"I thought you said he cheats?" Cameron asked.

"He does but he has a lot of friends with big pockets and when he's around, they're around, which means more opportunities for all of us. I wonder where he's been all this time."

"Does it matter?"

"No, not to me but he left his wife and four children behind," Jake reported.

"I'm surprised that she let him back in the house after so many years."

"I'm not. She's a plain woman and rather old fashioned."

"Still, that's a long time to be without a father and a husband," Cameron said.

"Shit, most of the families around here don't have fathers or husbands, but they make out okay. They're still here," Jake said.

"It's sad."

"It's life," Jake said.

That evening as Johnny laid down on the sofa, sleeping like a baby. Seeing how soundly he was resting, Cameron decided let him sleep and not wake him up for dinner. After quickly eating his own dinner, Cameron rushed back to his perch on the porch to look out for his beautiful, live dream of a woman who walked all over his heart that morning. Unable to think of anything else, Cameron stared down the hill hoping to see the woman that made his heart boil. He thought of his pitiful behavior and had to smile at himself, but he was unashamed because he wanted to know her and hold her in his arms as long as she would allow it. What he felt was real, evoking new feelings that he once thought impossible. He would continue to wait for her to appear no matter how long it took.

Hours passed before Cameron saw the beautiful, dark woman who penetrated his thoughts for the past few months. He did not remember ever being so excited about a woman. Usually, he could take them or leave them. Even his wife had not been the woman of his dreams. They were best friends, but he was not in love with her. In fact, he thought that being 'in love' was a bogus concept. What he was feeling about this woman was unusual for him, and made him feel completely out-of-sync.

When he caught sight of her as she was leaving The Bottom with her male companion, he felt something strange pulling at his chest. Then he realized that his heart was beating so loudly that he could feel it in every part of his body. The couple seemed familiar, busy laughing and talking together as they made their way up the dirt road. The sound of their laughter got louder as they walked close to his building. He felt a strange heaviness in his heart. *God, she is the most beautiful woman I have ever seen. Just give me one chance to be with her, and I'll love her for the rest of my life. Look at me. Don't you dare ignore me. Woman, you know I love you. Look at me, please.* Suddenly, she looked up at him as he stood watching her and her companion. He was not sure what her expression meant except that it made him feel like he was eavesdropping on a private conversation. Her companion turned and looked at him for a moment then he smiled and nodded his head. Cameron had no choice but to nod back. He had been guilty of watching another man's woman. He felt childish and foolish, but he watched her and the way her body moved until she was completely out of sight.

It only took a few days before Jake arranged for Johnny to work and have a room at the juke joint. Jake figured that with Johnny living and working there, it would reduce his chances of being arrested, and taken back to jail.

In order to experience Sunday again when Cameron would see the woman he loved, he had to rush the coming and going of each day as it slowly passed. He had to find a way to make her listen to him, talk to him, and if he was very lucky, he could touch her beautiful smooth skin or place his arms around her small waist. *Love,* he thought to himself. *Was that what I'm feeling? Could I have fallen in love with a woman whom I have not touched? How could that be?* Then he thought of how Grace spoke of love and how Queenie begged him to commit to her.

For the first time in his experience, he truly felt sorry for them because if they felt anything like he felt at that moment; they were in danger of being hurt and hurt badly. Something deep inside him told him that he needed to be with that beautiful dark woman, which was evident in the ache he felt deep inside his body when he thought of her. In a fit of jealousy and desperation, he thought about going to see Mrs. Cigam to get any information he could from her. He started down there twice, but changed his mind, realizing that he was out of his mind. Impatiently, he paced the floor, but he decided to wait until the following Sunday.

On Wednesday, he was pacing the floor because the days would not pass fast enough. Each day seemed like a year, reminding him of the time he spent in prison, waiting for his life to begin again. That week tormented him in the same earthshaking way.

The twins watched him moping around, going in and out of his apartment slamming doors or sitting on the porch in the chilled air all day staring up the hill. Because he had not been to the juke joint all week, people came by the house looking for him. When he was not pacing back and forth, he was walking the streets, sometimes very late at night.

When Jake came over because he was concerned about him, Cameron told him, "I think I'm going crazy, man."

"What is this all about?"

"If I tell you, will you keep it to yourself?"

"You only have to ask."

"I think I'm in love, Jake." He waited for Jake to react.

"In love? What the fuck does that mean?"

"I know it sounds crazy but that woman I asked you about, I haven't been able to think of anything but loving her since the day I first saw her. I feel so helpless."

"Damn, man," Jake said, scratching his head.

"Yeah. . . Damn."

"What are you going to do?"

"I have to talk to her. So far, she won't give me a minute of her time. She practically ran from me last week."

"Shit."

"I was tempted to go down to Mrs. Cigam's house to ask her for her address, but I changed my mind. . . She may think I'm insane."

Jake shook his head saying, "Well, I know how you feel man. It's bad when a woman doesn't return your feelings."

"I'm not giving up. I'm going to make her talk to me when she gets here Sunday morning."

"Do you think she'll want to?"

"I don't know. I can only try. I'll continue, trying every Sunday until she does, if I have to. I love her."

"You really do have it bad."

"Yes, I'm afraid so."

"Let me know if I can help in any way. Perhaps I could distract her long enough for you to hit her over the head and drag her off," Jake said, laughing.

"Don't laugh. That might be the only way for me to talk to her," Cameron said sadly.

That afternoon, Kenny was walking up the street crying. Cameron watched him for a few minutes before he stopped the little boy, who seemed to have a world of problems resting on his tiny shoulders.

"Kenny, what's wrong?"

When the child saw Cameron standing in front of his house, he ran over to him and grabbed him around his legs. Cameron sat his groceries on the steps then sat down allowing the boy to cry as he held him in his arms. It was a cold day, but it felt good sitting outside enjoying the fresh air even under those circumstances. Patiently, he waited until Kenny stopped crying. When he did, Cameron offered the little man a Butterfinger that he had in his shopping bag. The boy wiped his eyes with his dirty hands, leaving smudges of dirt and tears on his face, and started opening the bright yellow and blue candy wrapper. Smiling at his little friend's dirty face, Cameron took his handkerchief out of his pocket and wiped the boy's face. They sat in silence for a long time.

Half the Butterfinger was gone before the boy began to speak, saying, "My mama's boyfriend is mean," he said finally. "He threw some hot water on my mama fo' nothin'," he whined with tears falling from his eyes. "I'm gonna kill him one day."

"You're not going to kill anybody, Kenny. You promised me that you would go to college and be a lawyer or a doctor, remember?"

"I kin still kill 'em."

"No, you can't. Doctors and lawyers help people. They don't kill anyone."

"He need t' die, and I need t' kill 'em," the boy said with his lips trembling as he spoke.

"You need to leave Mr. Willie up to me and the other men around here. We will deal with him. All you need to do is come tell Jake or me. We will take care him. I promise you that, and I don't make promises I can't keep. A promise is a man's word, and his word is what makes him a man. Understand?"

"Yeah."

"You promise to come for Jake, or me, if you need any help?"

"Yes, I promise."

"I don't want you to worry about this. Okay?"

"Okay. I'll come and git you. I promise."

"Good."

They sat there for a long time. Cameron reached in his bag and pulled out a quart of milk, opened it and gave it to Kenny to drink. They continued to sit on the steps in silence, basking in the warmth of their friendship.

"Why Mr. Willie's always hurtin' my mama?"

"I don't know, Kenny."

"He tried t' hit me and my sister, but we ran out d' house."

"That's the best thing for you to do Kenny. Always take your little sister and run. Take your mother too."

"She won't go. She's scared o' him. Why he so mad all d' time?" the little boy asked with a worried and puzzled expression on his face. "Why do Mr. Willie wanna hurt people?"

"I don't know the answer to any of those questions, Kenny. The only thing I can tell you is that people who hurt other people need help. It seems as if they may have something wrong in their brain, or maybe someone hurt them, and that makes them want to hurt other people. Either way, it's wrong."

Kenny's mother, Paula, was afraid of almost everything, even breathing. Everything scared her. Paula was one of three children in her family who lived with her parents and two brothers in Buttermilk Bottom. Afraid of being overwhelmed by a world outside the borders of her life-long community, Paula never considered moving anywhere else because the neighborhood felt protective and familiar despite the poverty-riddled conditions that continued to trap her and her children. Both of her parents had been hot-tempered alcoholics who fought every Friday and Saturday night while the whole community watched and gossiped about their many, violent flare-ups. Her mother ended up raising her and her two brothers, but both boys left Atlanta for places unknown before they reached age sixteen. No one had ever heard from them again. Their absence left Paula alone with the two people she feared most in the world, her parents.

Once in a drunken stupor, her father beat her with an ironing cord because she did not make dinner. Since her mother was in bed drunk, it meant that all her mother's duties fell to her. She was only nine-years-old at the time. When she complained to her mother, her mother slapped her in the mouth and called her lazy.

Spending most of her time hiding from her parents, she rejoiced briefly when her father abandoned them. Someone said he ran away with a woman with five children. This infuriated her mother who launched an endless series of beatings on the nine-year-old for the slightest infractions. Trapped by her life and afraid of change, she did not have the comfort of friends or family to ease her pain and frustration; instead, she kept it all inside her troubled, depressed mind. Her mother's bad temper quickly manifested itself in daily beatings and verbal harassment that lingered long after she left her mother's home.

Her mother yelled, "If it wuzn't fo' yo no count lazy ass. . . Yo daddy would still be here."

On more than one occasion, her mother locked her in a closet for several days at a time, only allowing her to come out to use the bathroom. Paula never knew a time when she was not afraid. Things did not change for her when she began her adult life at age thirteen when her mother married her off to an older man, who also abused her. She suspected that her mother received money for her hand in marriage, but she could never be sure. The thought of asking her mother about it was out of the question. The older man left her while she was pregnant with their second child. When her husband abandoned her, Paula managed to get work only three days a week in three different homes in the white community as a maid and a cook. The money she made was barely enough for her to feed and shelter her children. When she met her boyfriend Willie, she had a rush of financial freedom. Her euphoria lasted only a few weeks when she found her new boyfriend, standing over her with a balled fist, which he used to punish her for not cooking his eggs done enough. She was back where she started in her mother's house, trying to find a place to hide.

Chapter 20

It had been weeks since Grace saw Cameron because of the increased police investigation and the activities in Buttermilk Bottom, none of which he shared with Grace. When Grace complained of spending so much time without seeing Cameron to Horace, knowing that Grace was alone on weekends, he began to stop by. In the beginning, Grace would not allow him to enter her home, but after weeks of not hearing from Cameron, she began to relent. Not wanting to stay at home alone, Grace began accepting Horace's invitations. They went out to movies, to dances, and socialized regularly with friends.

Late on a Saturday afternoon, Cameron showed up at Grace's door while Horace was busy, making small repairs around her house. It was Horace's intention to take Grace out that evening thereby spending the whole morning and evening with her. Cameron's sudden appearance halted all his plans, and Horace could tell from the expression on Grace's face that his presence was no longer needed or desired. Quietly, and discreetly, Horace gathered all his tools and headed for the front door.

"Horace Singleton, this is Cameron Fielding, Cameron. . . . This is my friend Horace from school," Grace said to Horace's disappointment as she held Cameron around the waist. It broke Horace's heart to see how happy she was to see her 'convict lover'. It made him angry, knowing that Cameron dated Grace for so many years and had not committed himself to her, which he was more than willing to do because he truly loved Grace.

"Hello, happy to meet you," Cameron said, smiling.

"Hello," Horace said, shaking his rival's hand. "I have to go, Grace. I'll see you on Monday."

"Thanks for everything," she said, unaware that she was hurting Horace's feelings. He smiled, feeling the weight of his broken heart.

"It looks as if I interrupted something," Cameron said, watching Horace leave.

"No, you didn't. I'm so happy to see you," she said, jumping in his arms. "Why didn't you call me?"

"There's a lot going on."

"I was so worried."

"At least you had good company," he said, nodding toward Horace, who was driving away.

"Don't be silly. Horace and I are friends."

"I think Horace wants to be more than just a friend," he said, looking at Grace closely.

"We are friends. . . That's all."

"Grace, maybe you should explore changing things between the two of you. From what I saw, he's willing, and you would be better off with someone like Horace. He's stable and has a good career."

"Why are we talking about Horace? I haven't seen you in weeks," she said, kissing him while remembering the hurt expression on Horace's face, but she could not help what she was feeling. She was honest with Horace, and she hoped that he would understand and accept things the way they were. Helplessly, she clung to Cameron and the love she knew she wanted.

For a time, everything seemed quiet in The Bottom. Life was calm but no one expected it to remain that way, because it was Buttermilk Bottom.

"Johnny is all settled in at the Queenie's juke-joint," Cripple Jake said, sitting at his best friend's kitchen table. "I really appreciate what you did for him."

"Don't give it a second thought. We have to stick together," Cameron said.

"Thanks to you, people are really looking out for each other."

"No one can be safe if we don't."

"Guess what Ole' Johnny Boy is up to?" Cripple Jake asked.

"I have no idea."

"He's fallen in love. . . Trying to get close to Betsy."

"Isn't Betsy still involved with the insurance man?"

"Oh, yes. . . She wishes she wasn't, but yes. . . It's still going on."

"She should get rid of that creep."

"I know. She needs help. I told her to go see Miss Cigam."

"Why?"

"Why the hell not. What would it hurt?"

"There should be another way."

"The girl needs some serious help. If she came to you, as she wanted to, you would only go over there and pistol-whip that white motherfucker. Then where would we be?"

Cameron did not respond because he knew Jake was telling the truth. "Pistol-whipping is better than shooting."

"Not if you beat the man to death and get thrown in jail."

On the first day of December, Rosa Parks refused to give up her seat on a bus in Montgomery, Alabama. It was not the first time a white man asked a Negro to get up and stand in the rear of the bus. It was not the first time that they jailed a Negro for not obeying the unjust laws that attempted to govern him into a sub-human status. A spirit of inevitable circumstances mobilized civic and religious groups to denounce segregation on buses, insisted on respect from drivers who had police-like powers over black riders and to insist on the employment of black drivers for black neighborhoods. The black community celebrated when they heard that Dr. Martin Luther King, Jr. was going to lead the fight against the discrimination practices of the bus company in Montgomery, Alabama. He was one of their own, and they were proud. The people of Buttermilk Bottom celebrated too, but the neighborhood felt fear and dread for the young minister who had just begun his career at the Dexter Street Baptist Church. While hopeful, people expressed their fears for him and his young family.

"They gon hang 'em."

"They don't care 'bout him goin' to college and gittin' a education. They don't care 'cause he's black."

"I won't be surprised if we wake up t'morrow and find out dat they done hung him, too."

"Alabama's worse than Georgia. They got a law dat says, blacks and whites cain't even play cards or checkers together. Dat's how much they hate us."

On Friday nights, Queenie decided to convert the juke joint into a dazzling dance hall. She did it to please the women in the area. Normally from Friday night until Sunday morning the place would be flooded with gamblers, and she encouraged it because that was her big money maker. The ladies complained about the men taking over the juke joint until Queenie came up with the idea for a dance. Moving the tables and chairs away from the center of the floor, she hired a band to play for three hours.

In preparation for the dance, Queenie sent Johnny out to pick up supplies, a job he took seriously and cherished. Not only did he feel good because Cora Lee and Queenie placed their trust in him, it meant that they saw him as a part of the household, the family. Since his escape from prison, he had nothing to do but work, and he loved it because he could do what he wanted most in the world, to go through any door anytime he felt like it. To Cora Lee's displeasure, he would sit on the back porch for hours, enjoying the rain and natural elements once denied him behind the thick forbidding walls of prison. Sunshine, rain, and green plant life were the things he missed the most.

Cora Lee would yell at him, saying, "Boy git back in dis house and out o' dat lightin' fo' you git struck in d' behind."

"Don't worry, Cora Lee. I'll be alright."

"Not if dat lightnin' strike you 'n d' ass," Addie Mae injected.

He laughed and did as they requested, knowing that they were deathly afraid of lightning. As soon as the bolts of electricity flashed through the sky, Cora Lee closed all windows and doors. She turned off all the electricity then found a quiet place to sit. Not only was she cautious, she made everyone around her take the same precautions. If a person ignored her warnings, she would recite a storehouse of stories about lightning striking people, resulting in death or dismemberment. She considered lightning to be a mysterious phenomenon that God used to punish the disobedient. In the quiet kitchen, she sat at the table praying and telling numerous tales of disaster to anyone who would listen.

"You know why Mr. Brown, who lives down d' street, limps all d' time?"

"No," Johnny said.

"'Cause he went out in d' thunder 'n lightnin' witout no shoes on his feet. Then d' fool went and stood under dat old lonesome pine tree on d' hill. . . Said he wanted t' keep out o' d' rain. Any fool knows you cain't stay dry under no pine tree."

He should've known better," Addie Mae said. "That's d' first place lightnin' strikes."

"Then there wuz d' time Miss Campbell got killed by lightnin'. Dat wuz long b'fore you came here. Any fool knows lightin' follows a draft and dat fool woman had her front and back d'or wide open. Lightnin' came rumblin' through her house and fried her black as my cast iron fryin' pan ov'r there," Cora Lee said. "Dat's why I close all d' doors and windows. . . 'Cause lightnin' follows a draft."

"The chance of being struck by lightning is about a million to one," Johnny offered.

"Dat's only true if you obeys d' rules," Cora Lee said. "Stay out of a draft, stay 'way from trees, stay 'way from water, and cut off all 'lectricity."

"How do you know all this stuff?" Johnny asked.

"'Cause I knows people dat's been struck, and Dey ain't here t' tell you d' natural facts. So, I'm tellin' you, mark my words."

Johnny knew there was no reasoning with Cora Lee when it came to lightning. He also knew that if he continued to tell her that he doubted her tales, she would continue the whole night telling one pitiful disaster after another. Cleverly, he sat quietly with Cora Lee as she and her lifetime partner sat shelling peas and recounting tragedies while they waited for the storm to pass.

Betsy was going out to work early the next morning as Johnny was coming back from making purchases for the weekend festivities at the juke joint. They smiled at each other as a sign of their mutual attraction. Without a word spoken between them, they entered a silent agreement of mutual admiration and praise. Their subsequent meetings resulted in mere smiles, acknowledging their presence across a street or while shopping in the local store. Johnny was not quite sure how to approach a woman after his stint in prison. Several months passed with neither of them making an overt move to speak with the other. They merely smiled bashfully, and kept their private feelings and interest a secret between them. Johnny still saw himself as a jailbird, unworthy of anyone's love or attention. Without their gossipy neighbor's knowledge, Betsy quietly admired him with hopes and reservations of her own because she was still involved with the insurance man, while he shied away, hoping she would not discover that he was a convict. Despite the fact that he did nothing wrong, the fact that he spent time in prison was humiliating for him and his family. Finally, Betsy gave him a brilliant smile, removing all his doubts and reservations. He knew he had to speak with her, even if he failed, but he had to try. Curiosity got the best of him, as he waited for Jake to come into the joint to seek his advice. As soon as Jake came in the door, he balanced himself on his crutches and began to pull money out of his pockets for an informal game of poker with Luther, Dellah, and Azalene. Before Jake could sit down and get comfortable, Johnny began asking questions about Betsy.

"Betsy works as a waitress at a luncheonette down town," Jake said.

"Is she married?"

"No, but she's datin' somebody," Dellah said, laughing.

"What's goin' on there ain't datin," Luther said, smoking a cigar that hung loosely from his lips.

"Is it serious?"

"Serious and sad," Jake said as he explained the whole affair with the insurance man.

"I sure would like to talk to her," Johnny said.

"Save yourself the aggravation and find somebody else," Jake advised.

"There is no aggravation if she's not married. She's fair game," Johnny said.

"You better watch yo'self wit dat white man. He could cause you a lot o' trouble. So, go slow wit dat one," Luther said.

"My favorite speed," Johnny said, smiling.

The dance turned out to be a celebration of black unity because spirits were high and hopeful for the boycott of Montgomery's buses. Many people in Atlanta stopped riding the buses in sympathy for those walking for miles every day in Alabama. They knew that the success of the boycott would also benefit them if Martin Luther King and his followers attained their goals. No one imagined that the strike would last more than a few days, and they were hopeful that they would have some progress, especially with all the sacrifices of so many. Inside the juke joint, people were smiling and talking about the events in Montgomery.

On the night of the first Saturday night dance at Queenie's, Betsy made special preparations in her dress and makeup because she anticipated meeting Johnny. She convinced her next-door neighbor, Miss Inez, to go with her because she did not want to go alone. Knowing that Betsy was attracted to Johnny, Miss Inez prayed that somehow her attraction to Johnny would motivate her to rid herself of the insurance man.

"I don't drink or gamble, but I kin look," Inez said.

"You mind if I drink somethin'?" Betsy asked.

"You grown wit chillun. . . You ain't got t' ask nobody nothin'."

"Miss Inez, you sho' is nice t' me and my kids. . . I don't know what I'd do witout you."

"You ain't got t' think 'bout it, baby, 'cause I ain't goin nowhere."

"I hope we's doin' d' right thing. I ain't never been in no juke-joint b'fore."

"Honey, it ain't nothin' but a party-house wit gamblin', whorin', and dancin', all d' thangs people do already. There, it's jes all under d' same roof. Dis one happens t' have d' best food in town. I use t' hang out in a juke-joint all d' time when my husband wuz alive, but since Henry died, it didn't seem right. We'd dance all night long," Inez said with a smile on her face.

That night at the juke-joint, the room set the mood for fun, romance, and sizzling hot music as the sounds filtered into the streets, welcoming Betsy and Inez as they walked through the doors. Excitement rushed through both women as they entered the building. Dressed in their fancy outfits, the two women sat in a corner just inside the door and listened to the sweet sounds of soulful music played by some local musicians. The house soon over-flowed with people from The Bottom and the surrounding neighborhoods. The word had spread about the dance, attracting strangers who before that night had never dared to enter Buttermilk Bottom. Queenie counted heads and quickly calculated how much money she was making off the door alone.

Luther looked at her and said, "Looks like you got yo'self a hit." They both laughed at their new joint success. There was no written agreement between them, but the two partners had a lasting airtight agreement from which they both profited handsomely.

"Queenie, I could clean out d' basement and run a special game wit our best customers and make a mint while people up here is dancin'."

"There won't be any card playing in this house while dancing is going on. We want our men in the same room with us."

"But, we kin make a fortune, Queenie."

"I know, but I promised the ladies this would be their night, and I'm not pissing them off for a few extra dollars in our pockets."

"They ain't got to know about it."

"There is no way anybody can keep a secret in Buttermilk Bottom. No one ever has, and no one ever will. Get those dollar-signs out of your eyes and pour me a drink," she said.

The room was bustling with activity. People were drinking, eating, talking, and dancing in the crowded room when Cameron walked in, pleased to see that all of Queenie's plans were realized. As he moved through the crowd, speaking to a few people, he noticed all the new faces

he had never seen before. When Queenie saw him, her face glowed with
hope that the evening would culminate in making love to the handsome
figure approaching her, loving the mixture of danger and sex appeal he
exuded.

Smilingly, he stood in front of her not touching her, but she could
feel him deep inside her body. Handsome and reeking of masculinity,
he took her hand and led her out onto the dance floor, attracting the
attention of envious women in the room. Their dance was slow and
organic. The temperature in the room raised by several degrees as all the
women looked on, some fanning themselves as they watched Cameron's
love-dance with Queenie. Betsy and Inez sat watching the romantic
couple along with everyone else in the room. Several dancers stopped
and watched as Cameron stared lovingly at the bar owner while cuddling
her in his generous arms. The neighborhood's most admired couple found
themselves alone on the dance floor. Queenie felt special, knowing that
every woman in the room wanted to be in her lover's arms.

"Wow, he sho' is good looking," Betsy said dreamily.

"Dat kind o' man don't grow on trees."

"I know that's right," Betsy said, imagining what it would be like to
be in the number writer's arms.

"Don't fret too much. . . There's yo' little hunk comin' dis way. He's
mighty cute, too," Inez said, smiling.

Suddenly, Betsy became very nervous, seeing Johnny walk into the
room.

"Cute? He's down-right good-lookin', if you ask me."

"I kin see you got d' bug already. Well, git ready. He jes saw you, and
he's comin' dis way."

Johnny had on a white apron because he was helping Cora Lee and
Addie Mae with the big crowd of people who showed up for the dance.
When he saw Betsy and the old woman sitting in the corner, he could
hardly contain himself. It had to mean that she was interested in him.
At least that is what he prayed, and he made up his mind that he would
find out.

"Hello, ladies, can I git you anything?" he asked. "We have d' best
fried chicken in town."

"I think I'll have some," Inez said. "What comes wit it?"

"Collards, potato salad, and bread pudding for dessert. . . D' best in
town."

"Good, I'll have dat."

"What about you, beautiful?" Johnny asked.

"I'll have d' same thang," Betsy said shyly. "Do you have cornbread?"

"Sure do . . ."

"D' best in town," they all said together.

They all laughed together, "My name is Johnny. After I place your order, I would like t' dance with you."

"Okay," Betsy said, blushing.

"Good, I'll be right back," he said, dashing off to the kitchen.

"You think it'll be alright?" Betsy asked Inez.

"It sho will, but you r'member, you gotta git rid o' dat white man 'fore you start messing wit somebody else. Nothin' worse than a woman messin' wit two men at the same time."

"What's I gonna do about him?"

"I already told you. . . Go see Cigam. She'll fix his ass fo' sho'."

"That's what Jake said, but I ain't never messed wit no voodoo."

"Well, you ain't never been in dis kinda mess b'fore."

"I gots t' think about it. 'Cause my mama told me t' stay away from stuff I don't understand, and I don't understand nuthin' at all 'bout no voodoo."

"Make sure you don't go on a Sunday. . . Nobody in their right mind do dat kind o' bizness on Sunday. It's bad luck."

"Well, if I go. . . It won't be on no Sunday. Lord knows, I don't need anymo' bad luck."

"Queenie, did you hear. . . A rat bit Miss Pauline last night. Dey rushed her t' Grady Hospital, but she lost her lil' baby," Dellah said.

"That's too bad."

"Dey gonna keep her a few days," Dellah reported.

"I'm sorry she lost her baby, but the woman's got ten chillun already," Azalene said.

"It's always sad when a woman loses her baby, and it don't matter how many she got. . . She gonna miss dat one," Cora Lee said, overhearing the conversation and serving platters at the same time.

"We had so many rats in our house dat we had t' nail d' traps to d' floor t' keep d' mutherfuckers from walkin' off wit 'em," Moses said, laughing.

"Now look here, Moses, we ain't having none of your rat stories tonight. So, shut the fuck up and go dance with somebody," Queenie said, laughing and taking his drink out of his hand. Moses slipped away onto the crowded dance floor and grabbed a dance partner.

"Would ya look at what d' cat drug in?" Dellah said.

Lucille walked in the door in a beautiful, red dress and perfectly executed make-up on her face. She was dressed in a beautiful dark red dress with jewelry to match, and her hair was beautifully styled on top of her head. Everyone made positive comments as she entered the music-filled room.

"She looks real nice," Azalene said, smiling because she never saw Lucille look so nice.

"It won't last," Dellah said, laughing.

"What you mean?" Pearl asked.

"B'fore d' evening's over. . . She'll be so drunk, she won't know she put on that dress," Dellah said. "You watch. I know 'er."

Knowing that she looked beautiful, Lucille walked in, sat at the bar, and said in a sweet voice, "Luther, gimme me a drink, please."

She felt wonderful and hopeful that she may meet someone special in the room full of people, who were all dressed up and looking amazing. It took her a long time to prepare for the dance because she wanted to look ravishing like the old days when men fell over themselves just to speak to her.

"Look at you. What you all dolled up fo'?" Luther asked, laughing.

It annoyed her that Luther was teasing her about her appearance. She tried to ignore him, but his laughter made her want to fight back, but she smiled and looked out at the crowd in the room, looking for a potential partner. If it was only for the evening, even that would be fine with her, but she hoped for more.

"It's a party, ain't it? I came t' dance all night long," Lucille said, popping her fingers to the music.

"Look like you washed yo' face t'day."

"Luther, you better mind yo' own bizness 'fore I tell ya what I really think 'bout yo old fuckin' ass," Lucille warned, irritated that he would not leave her alone.

Frowning, Luther looked at her wondering what she meant. He poured her drink then went on to wait on other customers while Lucille scouted the crowd to find who she was looking for.

Before Betsy could say another word to Miss Inez about going to see Miss Cigam, Johnny was standing over her with his hand extended, inviting her onto the dance floor. She looked at Miss Inez, who smiled with approval and watched the young couple join the group of slow draggers already engrossed in Roy Hamilton's hypnotic tune, "You'll Never Walk Alone." For Inez, the music rekindled memories that she held in her heart from years past, and she was happy for her young friend and the possibility of her finding happiness, even if it was only for one night.

Johnny felt he had died and gone straight to heaven as he held Betsy in his arms because she fit perfectly. He stood a few inches taller than she did. Before the dance ended, she laid her head on his shoulder, which triggered urges, he denied for too many years. Since his arrival back in Buttermilk Bottom, he only had sex with the whores in the juke joint, but that was business, and there was nothing personal or loving about it. Holding Betsy in his arms was different because it was the kind of touching that he needed so badly. She looked up at him and smiled, melting his heart as the song ended.

When she turned to walk away, he said, "Don't go. Let's go out on d' porch."

Not waiting for her to answer, he led her out the door. Betsy looked at Inez, who was smiling from ear to ear.

"I hope you don't mind me takin' you 'way from d' party?"

"No, it's alright."

"I know you know dat. . . I've been watchin' you, tryin' t' git yo attention."

"I saw you, too."

"What 'bout you and me dating? We could go t' a movie or something," he asked anxiously.

"I got kids and it's hard fo' me t' find somebody t' keep 'em. Besides, I'm seein' someone now, and I cain't do nuthin' 'til I git rid o' him."

"I heard dat you're seein' dat insurance man."

"No. . . He's seein' me. I don't wanna see him at all. . . But I'm trapped, and I got t' find a way out of it."

"Lemme take care of it fo' you."

"No, I don't want nobody t' git hurt. I'm tryin' t' git up my nerves t' go see Miz Cigam. Miz Inez thanks she kin help me, but I'm scared o' dat voodoo bizness."

He laughed. "I'm scared o' it too, but I heard a lot 'bout her. If she cain't help ya'. . . Nobody kin."

"Kin you axe me agin when I git rid o' dat old, nasty, white man?"

"Kin I see you? It don't matter when or where, I jes wanna see you."

"I don't know about dat. It's no good fo' a woman t' see two men at one time."

"We don't have t' do anything except talk and maybe kiss a little if you don't mind," he said, placing his lips tenderly on hers.

Feeling consumed by the raging emotions that stirred inside him. He began to lose control of his desire to love her, and she enjoyed the urgency of his passion as she responded anxiously to his touch and his wonderful lips.

"I guess a little kissing won't hurt since I never kissed him on the mouth."

"Good," he said, kissing her again.

"We'd better stop. I'm gittin' kind o' carried away," Betsy said, breathing hard.

"Yeah. . . Me, too," he said out of breath. "How long do you think it'll take to git rid of dat old white man?"

"I don't know. I got t' git up my nerves first, but I'll let you know."

"Where can we meet?"

"I kin come here, or you kin come t' my house."

"What 'bout dat old white man?"

"He only comes on Thursdays."

"Then I'll come every day but Thursday," he kissed her again, this time allowing his hands to feel her waistline and the shape of her hips. He purposely did not touch her well formed behind because he knew he would not be able to stop himself if he did. He took her by the hand and led her back inside and to her table.

"Hey, Vegetable Man. Come dance wit me," Lucille said, smiling and hopeful.

"No thank you, Lucille. I jes promised dat' lady in d' corner," he lied, walking away from her quickly.

"Fuck you then," Lucille said, going back to the bar. "Luther, you old asshole, gimme a hit."

"I thought you came here t' dance?"

"I did and I'm gonna dance when I git damn good and ready," Lucille said, throwing the drink down her throat. Looking around the room for anyone who would be a possible candidate for her to spend the evening with, she felt isolated. Fighting the tears in her eyes, she said, "Luther, gimme another one." As Luther was pouring her drink, she said, "Make it a double." After pouring her drink, Luther shook his head and walked away.

There was no one at the table when Betsy returned, making her look around the room and say, "Miss Inez must've gone t' d' bathroom."

"No, she didn't. Look, she's out on d' dance flo'," Johnny said, pointing to Inez, who was dancing with Amos, the vegetable man. "Who's dat?"

"It's the vegetable man," Betsy said, smiling. "Well, well, ain't dat somethin'?"

"It sho is. I guess, old, don't always mean old," Johnny said, laughing.

"I guess you right 'bout dat."

"I'll git your dinners, and I'll be right back. Maybe we kin dance again if thangs slow down. I cain't leave Cora Lee stranded on her busy night."

"It'll be okay. I ain't goin' no place."

He placed his hand on the back of her neck, sending chills down her entire back. He felt her response and smiled saying, "You better not." He leaned down to kiss her on the lips before scurrying off to the kitchen.

Amos walked Inez back to the table. After he walked away, Betsy said, "Now. . . Jes look at you . . . Dancin'."

"I guess I ain't lost it after all. Besides, dat old coot wouldn't take no fo' an answer."

"Miss Inez. . . He's still lookin' at you."

"Don't be silly, girl. We's both too old fo' dat mess."

"Maybe old ain't old," Betsy said, laughing at her friend's obvious embarrassment.

"I ain't thinkin' 'bout nuthin you sayin' chil', so jes shut yo' mouth." The two women had a good laugh together, but when Inez looked up, Amos was still looking at her, making her body feel warm inside.

The special evening of dancing gave many the feeling of being in a grand ballroom where everything seemed festive and enchanted. Betsy and Johnny danced every chance they got, and Amos, the vegetable man, came back every time a slow record played on the jukebox. Cameron stayed at the dance long enough for the crowd to die down then he disappeared, leaving Queenie alone and frustrated. Both Cripple Jake and Luther wanted what Cameron refused, an opportunity to be intimate with Queenie. Lucille danced wildly by herself, stopping only to drink her corn liquor and to eat the pickled pig feet that she loved so much. She laughed uproariously, remembering a time when she was the center of attention and surrounded by men who wanted her.

"What the hell is she laughing at?" Jake asked.

"How the hell do I know?" Luther said, looking on in amazement.

"It was a great night, seems like everyone left satisfied," Jake said.

"Almost everybody," Luther said, looking at Lucille, who still stumbled around the room, dancing by herself.

"It was a magnificent evening, Queenie. You did a good job," Jake said in praise.

"Thanks, it was nice," she said without enthusiasm.

"Are you okay?" Jake asked.

"Yeah. I'm fine. . . Disappointed but I'm fine," she said.

"Gimme another drink, you old mutherfucker," Lucille yelled, laughing and swaying with the music.

"I think you had enough, Lucille. Why don't you go on home like ev'rybody else?"

"Fuck you. Gimme another drink, bitch."

Luther poured her a drink and went to the other end of the bar away from Lucille.

"See, I told ya. . . She wuz gonna fall 'part like a wet cookie. Dat corn liquor gits her ev'ry time. Now, look at 'er," Dellah said.

"She looks like shit," Azalene said.

"Who d' fuck you bitches talkin' 'bout?" No one answered because they were afraid of a verbal battle with Lucille. "Lil' young pussies. . . Sittin' 'round here. . . Makin' fun o' me, 'cause. . . I'm old and drunk. Don't laugh at me. . . 'Cause you gotta git old, too. Shit, I use t' be pretty. . . Better lookin' than you skinny ass bitches," she said, strolling over to the prostitute's table. Both Azalene and Dellah moved back from the table a few inches as Lucille leaned on the table, placing one hand on the table and the other one on her hip. "Men. . . Use t' love me. Fo' years, they chased my ass all over this stinkin'. . . Hole we live in. Shit, I couldn't turn 'round witout some nigger. . . Tryin' t' git in my drawers. Back then. . . We danced," she said, moving around the floor again. Then she yelled, "Lord, we use t' dance all-night long! Drinkin' and. . . Dancin'. We use t' have a ball," Lucille said loudly, raising her voice and both of her arms. "Dey jest loved me."

"They'd like you now if you wuzn't drunk all d' time," Luther said.

"I wuz drunk when I wuz young and. . . Dat never stopped nobody from. . . Fuckin' my brains out. My drinkin' ain't got shit. . . To do wit nuthin'." Sadly, she said, looking at the young whores, "I thought I wuz gonna be. . . Young forever . . . Jes' like you smart-ass bitches," she said, stumbling over to the young prostitutes. "But . . . Time fucked me up. Jes like it's gonna. . . Fuck yo stupid asses up, too. You think. . . You gon look like dat all yo' life," she said, pointing to their breasts. "Well. . . You ain't. You's gon wake up n' see yo fuckin' wrinkled asses. . . In d' mirror jes' like I did. Nobody told me, my skin wuz gonna sag and drag. . . On d' fuckin' ground. I had pretty. . . Hair, too. It fuckin' fell out," she said, laughing as tears fell from her eyes.

"Lucille, nobody wants hear dat o' drunk shit you talkin' 'bout. Drink up and go d' fuck home," Luther said, annoyed.

"What you tryin' t' do? Git rid o' me? Luther, you 'fraid I'm gonna tell everybody dat you's been sneakin'. . . Down t' my house. . . Fuckin' me when you cain't git it. . . Anywhere else?"

The room went completely silent. All eyes focused on Luther, who appeared to shrink a few inches as Lucille continued her true confessions. "What's wrong? D' fuckin' cat got. . . Yo' fuckin' tongue? Tell 'em. . . Go ahead. . . Tell 'em." Luther said nothing. "You make fun o' me when. . . You 'n front o' yo' fuckin' friends. . . But since Queenie dumped yo' old ass and. . . These lil' bitches turn ya down. . . Ya come creepin'. . . 'Round my house, looking fo' my ole ass pussy. Fuck you, Luther. Fuck all o' you." Lucille drank the whole glass of corn liquor and stumbled to the door. Before she left the building, she said, "Fucking, bitches."

All eyes focused on Luther, who had a sheepish grin on his face. When everyone waited for his explanation, he had none. Jake saved him.

"Pussy is pussy, right Luther?" Everybody laughed.

After everyone left the building, Azalene said, "Look what somebody left."

"What d' fuck is dat?" Luther asked, looking into the crumpled newspaper Azalene was holding.

"Somebody left their false fucking teeth," she said, holding them out for all to see.

"How d' fuck somebody leave a dance witout their fuckin' false teeth?" Luther asked.

"Shit, I don't know . . . But here it is," Azalene said, placing them on the bar.

"Shit, don't give 'em t' me. What d' fuck I'm gonna do wit 'em ?" Luther barked.

"What d' hell do I care?" Azalene said, walking away.

"Shit," Luther said loudly.

"What's that?" Queenie asked, walking into the room.

"Some stupid mutherfucker left their fuckin' false teeth," Luther said in disgust.

"What? How the hell could someone forget their teeth, Luther?"

"How d' hell I know?"

"What are you going to do with them?" Queenie asked.

"I ain't gonna do shit wit 'em."

"You just can't throw them out."

"Why not? They did."

"What if they come back looking for them?"

"Then they's shit out of luck. I ain't keepin' no nasty ass false teeth behind my bar," Luther said, chunking the teeth, wrapped in a newspaper, into the trashcan.

During the entire month of December, all eyes were on Montgomery, Alabama and the bus boycott. Black people walked miles to and from work, to schools, to churches, and wherever they needed to go, but it was always at the expense of their shoe leather. The white paternalistic government and business leaders relentlessly enforced the stifling Jim Crow laws that excluded blacks from interacting with whites and having the same privileges as whites. With winter facing the blacks boycotting segregation on public transportation, officials began to speculate that blacks would soon give up and ride the buses because January and February were the coldest months of the year. They waited, knowing they would win. The colder the weather became the more the walkers hugged their frail thin coats and continued walking with more determination than ever. Sympathetic citizens with cars organized to assist the walkers, but the majority of the demonstrators walked. Winter came and went but the boycott held, supported by the entire black community with the inspiring leadership of Martin Luther King, Jr., who was gaining prominence in the national news. The people of Buttermilk Bottom felt that he was representing them because he came from Atlanta's Fourth Ward, just as they did. They talked about him, as if he was a member of their family.

The dogwood trees began to bud, and the weather turned warm with the kudzu vines gaining strength as it covered more of the Georgia landscape. Early on a Sunday morning, Cameron returned to his perch to wait for the beautiful woman to appear. Resuming his vigil, he steadfastly refused to move all day although several people invited him to join them in various activities. It was not warm enough to play checkers outside, but

Cameron insisted on maintaining his watch so Jake gave in and played a few games before it became too cold to continue. Jake suggested that they go join the guys in a high-stake poker game at Queenie's, but he refused. Jake went away, knowing that his friend was obsessed. It was midnight when Cameron finally went to bed without seeing the woman of his dreams, but in his dreams, he craved to touch and hold her in his arms. Tormented by visions of her in his dreams, he awakened soaking wet and completely out of breath, so he got up and went back out on the front porch and sat there until daybreak. Realizing that he had to wait another week before he could possibly hope to see her, he prayed for the first time in years for God to give him an opportunity to be with her and love her.

On the first Monday morning in April, Betsy made up her mind to go to Miss Cigam for advice at Jake's and Inez's constant urging. She was extremely nervous about going into the intimidating little cottage in the most isolated part of Buttermilk Bottom, but knowing she was in desperate need of help; she took a deep breath then bravely opened the gate. On the porch of Noitop's house, the young woman cautiously knocked on the door. A beautiful brown woman with a devastating smile opened the door.

"Miz Cigam, my name's Betsy. I live up d' road wit my chillun. I hope I'm not botherin' you, but Cripple Jake n' Miz Inez said you might be able t' help me."

Noitop smiled putting the girl at ease. "Come in and sit down," Noitop said. She liked the girl immediately.

"I don't know how I got myself in dis mess, but I sho need t' git out o' it as soon as I kin."

Ushering her into the sparsely decorated living room, Noitop invited her to sit at a small table draped in black.

When Betsy sat down, she said, "Place your hands on the table."

Betsy placed her hands on the table and continued her tale, saying, "I paid my insurance man all d' money on my bill, and he still say he's gon cancel my policy if I don't keep sleepin' wit 'em. I ain't got no other insurance. My kids needs t' have money if somethin' happens t' me, 'cause my mama and daddy's dead," she said as Noitop inspected her hands back and front.

"Put your hand in the jar and take out a hand full of bones. Place them on the table in front of you."

Betsy reached in the jar and pulled out all she could manage and placed them on the table, and said without considering whether she should place her hand in the jar or not, "I jes hate it when he puts his white hands all ov'r me. I don't know what t' do. I tried t' git rid of 'em, but he keeps comin' back, tellin' me that I gots t' do what he tells me. He said my chillum got t' go t' d' po house when I die. I jes don't know what t' do."

Noitop listened as the girl told her all the details of her forced relationship with the insurance man. She felt the tension easing out of the young woman with every word she spoke.

"Betsy does the man drink or eat at your house."

"Sometimes."

"Does he sit in a special place?"

"Oh, yessum, he's always sittin' in my big chair. He act like he owns it. He gits mad if one of d' chillun sit in it, and it's they house not his," she said, annoyed.

"Can you afford to throw that chair out when he leaves?"

"If it'll git rid o' him. . . I sho' can."

"Do you have anything that belongs to the white man?"

"He left his tie at my house jes last week."

"I want you to take a hair from the back of his head and bury it with his tie anywhere away from Buttermilk Bottom."

"I'd be too scared t' take hair outta his head."

"If you want to get rid of him, you will need that hair."

Betsy thought for a minute, taking in a deep breath of air, she said with certainty, "I'll git it. I'll be scared t' death. . . But I'll git it," she said, making Noitop smiled.

"Take the chair he sits in and clean it with Clorox then sit it outside for two days. Don't let anyone touch it. . . Just you. Bring it inside and place it facing the door. Take this powder and place it in the chair. . . Let it sit there overnight." Noitop gave her a small bag with purple powder in it. "Clean the chair with clear water the next morning. After you sleep with that white man. . . He sleeps a little afterwards, doesn't he?"

"Yessum, he sho do. I gots to wake 'em up t' make him go home."

"Put this powder in his shoes while he's sleeping." She gave Betsy another small bag with black powder in it. "He won't bother you again." Handing her a bottle, she said, "When he leaves drink this liquid it will take away any pregnancy that might start inside you. Then be sure that you take a nice hot bath after you sleep with him; the hotter, the better."

Betsy looked at the bottle and the two bags in her hands, then she looked at Noitop with tears in her eyes. She jumped up from her chair then rushed to hug her around the neck and said, "Thank you, Miz Cigam. I'll do everythang you said. I promise. Thank you, thank you." Betsy left money on the table and asked, "Is dat enough? If it ain't I kin bring you some mo' next week."

"It's plenty," Noitop said, smiling.

"Miz Cigam?"

"Yes, Betsy."

"You ain't nuthing like people said. You's real nice. Kin I come back 'n visit wit you? Not fo' advice or nuthing like dat. . . Jes t' talk. I kin bring my chillun too. . . If you like chillun?"

"I like children just fine, Betsy. That would be nice," Noitop said, smiling warmly as she walked the young woman to the door.

"Thank you. I'll tell you what happens whenever it happens. Okay?"

"Okay, Betsy. Goodbye."

"Bye." Betsy hugged her again and ran all the way home.

Jake came into the juke joint noticing the demurred atmosphere and smiled broadly. Everyone was sitting around quietly talking.

Acknowledging his love of storytelling, Jake said, "Well, it looks to me like nobody in here has heard about what happened to Gus, the Ragman." He captured his audience instantly, and he smiled at his great introduction to one of the best stories he would ever tell.

"What?" several people said at once.

Everyone began crowding around Jake as he laughed; taking his time to set the stage for what he knew was going to be one of his all-time favorite stories.

"What happened?" someone asked.

Jake, having a flare for drama, took his time placing his crutches on the floor beside his chair.

"Luther, I'm going to need a drink to tell this one. In fact, everybody's going to need a drink to hear this shit. . . Give everybody a drink on me and keep them coming."

Luther placed a bottle of whiskey and glasses on the table as everyone pulled chairs up to get close to Jake. They knew from experience that he had a good story to tell. Jake waited until everyone settled down around him and had a drink.

The skillful storyteller drank down his whiskey and said, "The police arrested Gus, the Ragman, for drunkenness and disorderly conduct up on Forrest Avenue. He was at Reuben's corner store raising hell because they wouldn't take back the five pounds of neck bones, they sold him. Gus said they were bad, and I believe him. After Gus cursed everybody out, he took a brick and broke their big window out." Jake waited for everyone to express their shock. "It took eight policemen about an hour to get that fool in the paddy wagon. After they got him in the wagon, Gus started yelling at the top of his voice for the police to let him out because he had to go to the bathroom. There were two white officers in the front, one sitting in the driver's seat and one sitting in the passenger seat. They ignored him, so he started banging on the sliding door between the two compartments. 'Let me out. I got to piss, motherfucker.' You could hear him yelling to the top of his voice all over the neighborhood. The police officer in the passenger seat yelled, 'Shut d' fuck up,' but Gus kept banging and yelling, 'I got to piss. I got to piss.' As the paddy wagon was rolling down Forrest Avenue, the officer still sitting down in the passenger seat, slid the door opened, and yelled, 'Didn't I tell you to shut the fuck up?' Gus stood up, pulled his dick out, and pissed right in the man's mouth." Everyone sitting around the table with Jake screamed, moaned, and made sounds of disgust. Some made sympathetic comments for the police officer. Jake loved the sounds and comments coming from his audience. "Not only did he piss in one officer's mouth; he pissed on the driver too. The officer crashed the paddy wagon into that large oak tree right at Hilliard Street, trying to get away from Gus' urine that seemed as if it would never stop flowing. Of course, the two officers beat the shit out of Gus. He's up at Grady Hospital, but they tell me that he's okay, except for a few knots on his head from the Billie clubs that came crashing down on his hard-ass head.

As Jake's audience wiped the tears from their eyes, he sat back and enjoyed the fact that he had maintained his reputation as a good storyteller. All the facts, Jake told his group at the juke joint, he overheard while sitting at the sergeant's desk at the local precinct, and he saw the piss-soaked officers when they walked in the precinct. When he left the precinct, he went to the hospital to check on The Ragman, who was still drunk.

In spite of the fact that he had knots all over his head, he told Jake, "They should have stopped the fucking truck and let me go take a piss like normal people."

Chapter 21

Racism in the city of Atlanta was multi-layered and complicated by an intricate system of Jim Crow laws based on color that solidified and defined the role of each race. While whites hated blacks, making their lives difficult and less than humane in isolated areas of the city that were allocated for blacks only, whites depended on them to care for their children, cook their meals, and to do the menial tasks that they thought were beneath them. They also displayed hate and distrust for the Jewish community as well. In many cases, they systematically restricted Jewish businesses, encouraging them to operate only in the black community because whites often refused to serve blacks. As white hatred for both races continued, synagogues and black churches were bombed and burned. They vandalized Black and Jewish graveyards throughout the South. The abuse toward Jews was not as overt, but it was there affecting the fabric of their lives as they lived and moved throughout the city. Unintentionally, there developed a hierarchy of prejudice that affected these three major racial groups, which also reflected the socio-economic status of each group with blacks at the bottom of the scale.

The atmosphere of hatred and violence created an obscured love-hate relationship between African Americans and Jews. That complex relationship, while sympathetic and friendly, was at times supportive, but the white establishment often manipulated, interrupted, and made it difficult for the two races to get along. The two groups became accustomed to the interference and developed coping-skills that would usher them through many difficult situations. There were times when whites made it impossible for the two unwanted groups to co-exist in a peaceful manner at other times, it became suffocating.

While black businesses on Auburn Avenue gained national attention due to Forbes's magazine proclamation that it was "The Richest Negro Street in The World," despite the fact that most corner stores in black neighborhoods throughout the South remained owned and operated by Jews. The storekeeper, Ezra Levine worked hard with his wife, his brother, and his three children in the corner grocery store a few blocks from the entrance of Buttermilk Bottom. They had worked hard to keep the store clean and stocked with supplies that they knew their black customers would want to buy. Bags of black-eyed peas, butter beans, cornmeal, bread, milk, and an assortment of fresh vegetables the locals loved, like yams, collard greens, and turnips, 'nigger vegetables,' as Ezra's brother referred to them. Ezra admonished his younger brother, whenever he overheard any racial comments, and it did not matter who was in the store when he corrected him. For the convenience of having a well-stocked store in their neighborhood, the customers paid almost double the price that stores charged in white neighborhoods for the same products. When people argued about the prices, the Jewish storekeeper just smiled and ignored them. If his customers' complaint became offensive, loud, or rude, he would put that person out of his store, or on very rare occasions, he would call for police assistance as he did with Gus, The Ragman.

For almost twenty years, the Jewish storekeeper maintained a profitable business in the community, and he knew everybody and their children by name. His was a face everyone knew and one of the first persons the police interviewed when the police officers were missing. As it turned out, he appeared to be the last person to see the two police officers before they disappeared off the face of the earth. Ezra Levine knew both officers, since he encouraged them to come by his store to get free sodas, candy, donuts, and other snacks. Ezra knew that the officers did not like him because he was Jewish. Despite their obvious hatred, he handed out daily freebies to the officers. He also knew that they hated blacks much more than they hated Jews, so he had an edge in his relationship with the officers because they used his store as a safe haven. The police were Ezra's security blanket in the neighborhood and for many years, the storekeeper enjoyed listening to the officer's escapades with the locals in Buttermilk Bottom.

About six months before the two patrol officers disappeared, there was a robbery at Ezra's store. The missing police officers responded immediately and caught two suspects within two blocks of the store. The only problem was that Ezra was certain that the men they caught were not the men who had robbed him.

When he voiced his doubts, the first officer said, "They robbed someone, somewhere. . . . We just cain't prove it."

"It wuz just a matter of time b'fore we'd have t' arrest them anyway," the short fat officer said. "You might as well help us git these no good niggers off d' street."

Ezra was afraid to oppose the determined and prejudiced officers, so the storekeeper kept his mouth shut out of fear that his store would mysteriously catch fire, putting him out of business. The burning of Jewish establishments was a normal occurrence, and they too went without any disciplinary action.

By the time Detective Bailey Lee appeared at the store, weeks after the disappearance, he was completely aware that time was slipping away from him and his ability to catch the murderers. He knew that the longer it took him to solve the case of the missing police officers meant that his success in apprehending the responsible party was nil.

"Mr. Levine, how you doing t'day?"

"Fine, just fine."

"I've been thinkin' 'bout you and yo' statement," Detective Bailey said in a strong southern accent.

"Yes, like I said they were here just before I closed."

"What direction did you see 'em go after they left here?"

"I don't know. When they left, I closed up shop and went home."

"Is it possible dat they went t'ward Buttermilk Bottom?"

"I guess it's possible, but I never saw where they went," Ezra Levine admitted.

"If we called you t' be a witness, you would be able to say dat they went t'ward Buttermilk Bottom, right?" the detective said pointedly.

The storekeeper hesitated and thought about it for a minute, knowing that if he refused there would be consequences, so he said, "I guess. . . I could do that." He said almost inaudibly, not wanting to contradict the calculating detective.

"Good, 'cause that's what we may need you t' do."

"Whatever. . . I have to do to keep the streets free of crime," Ezra said nervously.

"We're gitting closer t' d' criminals dat did this," Bailey lied.

"Just call on me when you need my help."

"Don't worry. I will. Good night."

"Good night, Detective," Ezra said, wiping his brow.

"Why did you tell him that?" his wife asked, angrily.

"Do you think he gave me a choice?"

Around two o'clock on Thursday afternoon after Betsy's visit to Miss Cigram, Mr. Tom, the insurance man appeared, knocking on Betsy's door as she stood inside in a state of panic. She was nervous and afraid of completing the tasks her new friend, Noitop Cigam, gave her to do. Determined to rid herself of the irksome and disgusting man, Betsy needed to claim her independence, the love, and the life she wanted with Johnny. All during the week, she enjoyed Johnny's visits because being with him restored her sense of dignity and made her feel respected. It had been a long time, since she could enjoy a man's company without feeling soiled and depressed. He made her laugh all the time, and his kisses brought her nothing but pleasure. Taking her neighbor's advice, she knew she had to end it with the insurance man, before thinking of sleeping with the new love in her life. What made her extra sure about the direction of her life was the fact that her children loved Johnny, and he showed nothing but care and concern for them. To make certain everything would go as planned; she memorized everything Noitop told her to do. With her complete faith in Miss Cigam's abilities, she knew nothing could stop her.

The big rocking chair, she had carefully prepared the night before, was in the front room, facing the door. She moved some of the other furniture around to make it look as if she rearranged the room. Remembering the tie the night before, she placed it in a brown paper bag, where it waited for the last ingredient, a hair from the back of the white man's fat greasy head. After the torturous sexual encounter, he forced her to endure for months and months, she planned to take a long bus ride to bury the two items as far away from Buttermilk Bottom as her money would allow, to make sure he stayed away from her forever. The small envelope of black powder was on the kitchen table ready to go into the insurance man's smelly run-over shoes and the liquid Miss Cigam gave her to drink was sitting in the refrigerator when he knocked on her door. The tall, fat, white man walked through her door, acting as if he owned the apartment and everything in it, demanding to know where the children were.

"They's outside playin'."

He sat down in his favorite chair not even noticing that it was in a new location. "Come here, gal. Take my shoes off," he said rudely.

"You want me t' rub yo' feet," she asked, knowing it was the last time.

"No, I cain't stay long. My wife got some damn fool dinner party t'night, and I got t' go home on time."

"Dat's too bad," she said softly, but she celebrated inside.

"Hurry up. . . Take yo' clothes off, gal."

"Yessa'."

As soon as she had her clothes off, he placed his sweaty, slimy hands on her breasts.

"You colored girls sho' got some pretty chocolate titties," he said, getting wet around his mouth. "I jes love yo' titties. Big and pretty jes' like I like 'em." He stood up and slipped his pants and shorts off then pulled her into the bedroom that she shared with her children. He sat on the edge of the bed and said, "Come on now, I told ya. . . I'm in a hurry. Let's git on wit it." He then placed his partially deflated, uncircumcised penis in her mouth, which always made her want to gag.

I'm gonna do it hard and quick, so I kin hurry up and finish. Then I kin git his big, sloppy-ass out of my house fo' good, she thought. It took a while but he finally got hard enough to consider having intercourse. An act, she did not mind because she could pretend that she was not there. *God make me feel dead inside, so I won't feel nuthing. Please, God, make me feel dead.* It was a prayer that she prayed once a week for months. Sometimes he yelled at her for not groaning and making noise. That day, he did not seem to care. She blocked her mind out so that she would not feel his presence. This was not hard to do since his penis rarely stayed hard. He humped a couple of times and took in one and two deep breaths, and then he humped a few more times and paused for one big breath of air.

Then right on schedule, he started his usual chant, singing, "I luv black pussy. . . Yes I do. I luv black pussy, yes I do." His words fell in with his labored series of humping rhythms. It was getting close to the end. She knew because the whole sordid affair lasted only five to ten minutes, but they were the longest and the most disgusting minutes of her life. Finally, he humped, humped, and humped in secessions of threes, then a few seconds passed, and it was all over. Sweaty with his white shirt and tie still on, he fell fast asleep on top of her, snoring so loudly it hurt her ears.

"Thank you, God," she said aloud, knowing that he was out for at least an hour. "Git yo' white. . . Fat ass. . . Off o' me," she said, rolling him over.

As tears fell from her eyes, she snatched a hand full of hair from the back of his head, making him complain. She froze out of fear that he would wake-up, but he did not. She thought about it and snatched several more hairs from his head. He uttered a muffled sound, making her jump off the bed, but he barely moved.

With her treasures, she went into the kitchen, threw the straight oily hair in the brown paper bag with his tie, and went to the sink to wash her hands before going to the refrigerator to drink the liquid that Noitop gave her. With tears falling from her eyes, she prepared herself for what she thought would taste horrible, but to her surprise, it tasted like a soft drink without the fizz. After she drank the liquid, she went into the bathroom to clean herself up, but the tears kept running down her face.

When she was fully dressed, she went to the kitchen and got the bag of black powder that was to go in his shoes. Wiping the steady flow of tears away, she went into the front room, where she found his shoes, and she poured the black powder inside each shoe. To make sure the process worked completely she grabbed his pants off the floor and put some of the powder in each of his pockets. She smiled through her tears and laughed out loud, feeling better about the whole situation she had been trapped in too long. Going to the bathroom, she took a towel and washed her face. Turning around slowly, she felt empowered and marched angrily into the bedroom, and stared at him on her bed. Feeling liberated for the first time in months, she slapped the insurance man hard across the face. As soon as she slapped him, she panicked.

"Wh. . . What happened?" he asked, still half asleep.

"Mr. Tom, ya told me t' wake ya up right away so you kin git home t' your wife," she said innocently with her head down. "It's gittin' late."

"Okay, okay. . . I got git outta here. What time is it anyway?" he asked, feeling a sting on his face where she slapped him.

"I don't know. . . My clock's broken," she lied.

"Gimme my pants and shoes," he ordered.

She went in the living room and picked up his pants carefully. "Let me put 'em on fo' ya. You still sleep," she said, wanting to make certain that nothing fell out. She went back to pick up his shoes and helped him put them on. After she gave him his jacket, she walked him to the door.

"See ya next week," he said, grinning.

"Not if I got anything t' do wit it," she said, slamming the door in his face as hard as she could and fell against the closed door. "Thank ya, Jesus," she cried. "I won't ever have t' see dat miserable bastard agin."

The insurance man looked at the closed door in shock and was about to bang on it to demand an explanation until Miss Inez appeared, saying, "It sho is gitting cold, ain't it? D' day ain't long enough fo' me t' do nuthing."

Knowing that he had to get home, the fat insurance man ignored her and rushed to get home before his wife could complain. Tears started to fall down Betsy's eyes, but she did not bother to wipe them away. Instead, she went into the bathroom, brushed her teeth, and washed her mouth out as hard as she could. She took a scalding hot bath after placing a capful of Clorox in the water because she always felt filthy when her ordeal was over. After she dressed, she grabbed her jacket and the bag with the tie and hairs in it then told her neighbor, she was on her way to complete her mission.

"Go right on, girl. I'd be happy t' watch yo' chillun. Go on now, so you kin git back b'fore dark."

"Thank you, Miz Inez, thank you!" Betsy said, turning to run down the wooden staircase and onto the muddy, dirt road.

Smelling her freedom, she ran as fast as she could up the hill to the bus stop. Taking two buses, she took the insurance man's possessions on a journey that would keep him out of her life forever. She sat on the bus, grinning and laughing, as tears fell from her eyes, attracting attention from other passengers, but she did not care about how foolish or crazy she seemed. All she cared about was completing her mission and getting that fat, greasy, white man out of her life. The trip seemed to take forever, and she knew she was almost insane as she wrestled with the pain and humiliation she felt because she allowed herself to get in debt with a ruthless man. The pain she endured made her physically ill and no amount of soap, bleach, or water could remove it. Following her weekly torture, she tried to wash the memory away but nothing helped. It took days for her to feel normal but before the memory faded, he was back, claiming her as his own personal sex slave. Suddenly, joy filled her heart because the prospect of a happy, joyous future was near. No one would ever force her again to surrender her body against her will; especially to someone she loathed. Getting off the second bus at the end of the line, she walked until her legs ached. Finding an open field, she placed a rock and some dirt inside the bag that held the insurance man's hair and tie.

"Miz Cigam, you didn't tell me t' do dis but m'ybe it'll help send it t' hell," she said, near hysteria as tears poured from her eyes.

Looking around, she found a stick and started to dig a deep hole. The red clay dirt was difficult to remove, but she did not care how long it took because she wanted to bury that white man's possessions as deep as she could. She looked up at the sky. It was getting late, but she kept on digging until sweat dripped from her forehead and her hands began to hurt. The pain did not stop her, but the threat of darkness did because she had to find her way back to the bus stop. She was in an unfamiliar area and did not want to linger much longer. After placing the bag in the hole she dug, she covered it with a large stone that she found close by and replaced all the dirt on top of it.

As the hole filled up, her tears fell from her eyes, she uttered, "May you burn 'n hell. . . You nasty-ass, white maggot! Burn 'n hell!" She let out a blood-curdling scream as tears fell helplessly from her eyes. Standing on the grave of the objects she buried, she stamped her feet on the loose dirt then she began jumping up and down on the grave in a fit of anger, as she made certain that it was firmly packed. Seeing a huge stone a few feet away, she rolled it on top of the white man's possessions. She screamed, "You nasty stankin' white cracker! Burn in hell! You filthy son-of-a-bitch! Burn in hell!"

On her return trip home, she began to feel lighter and stronger. The further she traveled away from the burial location, the more liberated she felt. For the first time in two years, she felt free. Although, there was no proof that the magic stuff worked, she could not remember when she felt so good. Before she knew it, she was back in the Fourth Ward, getting off the bus in front of Mr. Ezra's corner store. Laughing all the way, Betsy skipped and ran down the hill on the jagged, uneven, dirt road that led to Buttermilk Bottom, feeling happy and in control of her life.

When she reached her apartment building, the children were sitting on the porch with Miss Inez. With a beautiful smile on her tear-stained face, she ran up the steps and kissed each of her children then hugged and kissed Miss Inez, who celebrated right along with her.

"I'll put my babies t' bed, and I'll be right back. Is Mr. Amos comin' by t'night?"

"No, he's comin' by t'morrow."

"Good, 'cause I got somethin' special jes fo' you and me," she said, smiling from ear to ear.

"What is it?" Miss Inez asked with a huge smile because she loved seeing her young friend happy.

"Wait right here. . . I'll bring it back in a minute. Come on, kids, it time fo' beddie-bye," she said, smiling at her neighbor devilishly, then she went inside to put her beautiful children to bed. The job took longer than she expected, but she finally came out with a gallon bottle of red wine, two glasses, a cake, and tea sandwiches like the ones her mother made on special occasions when she was alive.

Surprised with all the treats that Betsy brought out on the porch, Miss Inez asked, "What's all dis chile?"

"It's our celebration, yo's and mine," she said with her arm stretched out. "Thank ya, Jesus! Thank ya," she yelled. "Miz Inez, if it wuzn't fo' you and Jake. . . I wouldn't be free t'day. I wouldn't have another happy day in my whole life. I jes wanna thank ya fo' tellin' me t' go t' Miz Cigam. It wuz d' best thang you could've done fo' me and my babies." She handed Miss Inez a glass and filled it to the brim.

"What kinda wine is dis?" Inez asked.

"Hell, I don't know and I don't care. It's wine and I wanna git drunk wit you t'night, Miz Inez." She touched her glass to Miss Inez's; spilling some on the porch then drank the whole glass of wine at once. It was very sweet, but she did not care. "Today's my birthday, Miz Inez. I wuz born all over agin t'day."

"Do ya think dat stuff worked?" Miss Inez asked.

"I sho' do. It feels like it worked right away 'cause I got real bold wit Mr. Tom b'fore he left here. I don't know why I felt so good and strong. . . But I did."

"You did?"

"Sho did."

"I slapped d' shit out o' him while he wuz layin' down sleepin' on my damn bed. I got so mad. . . I jes hauled off and slapped d' pure d piss outta him," she said, getting mad all over again. "Then I started feelin' devilish, so I put dat black shit all over dat man." She laughed hysterically until a river of tears fell from her eyes and cascaded down onto her clothing. Miss Inez could not help but join her teary joyous outburst because she knew how much Betsy suffered over the past two years. "Then ya know what I did?" she asked, crying and pouring another drink from the gallon jug for each of them. "I slammed d' fuckin' do'r in his ugly white face. Ain't dat somethin'?" She laughed so hard she had to sit down, but instead of sitting on the chair, which was behind her, she sat on the floor by mistake. Miss Inez thought she hurt herself, but Betsy's loud laughter made her relax and laugh with her. "I wish I could've seen his fuckin' fat face when I slammed dat d'or," she said angrily.

"Well, I did and dat man looked shocked and scared," Miss Inez said. "I wuz sittin' right here on d' porch."

"He did?"

"Yes, he did," Miss Inez said, laughing at the memory. "Chile, you slammed dat d'or so hard all d' windows shook."

Betsy started laughing again and could not stop herself. When she calmed down, the tears flowed helplessly, and consistently down her smooth brown face, she said, "Jes' thank about it. . . Lord, I don't have t' see dat white wrinkled-up dick ever agin. . . Wit dat dried up skin hanging all over d' place! And. . . Guess what, Miz Inez? Guess what?" she said as tears continued to roll down and wet up her clothing.

"What, honey? What?"

"I don't have t' put up wit dat limp-dick, mutherfucker ever again." She laughed so hard that Miss Inez could hardly understand a word she was saying. "Lord, thank ya! No mo' hump, hump, hump" she said, exaggerating and mimicking his breathing, "Hump, hump, hump. Den he'd go hump, hump, hump. . . And den he'd give out o' breath agin and go hump, hump, hump." The tears rolled down her face until she actually started crying.

Miss Inez held her hysterical, young friend in her arms and said, "Hush now, hush. It's all over now. No need to worry 'bout dat animal ever agin. He's gone forever, Betsy. He's gone, baby. He's gone."

"Ya really think so?"

"I sho' do. I'm beginnin' t' feel it jest like you did. Dat devil's gone fo' sure. Hallelujah," Miss Inez yelled out as if she was in church on Sunday morning.

Feeling the wine take its full effect, Betsy said, "Here, Miz Inez try some of dese sandwiches and let's eat us some cake." Then she yelled," We's gon celebrate all night long."

"Lord chile, I ain't got drunk in almost twenty years."

"Well forgit 'bout dat now. . . 'Cause you and me gon have us a real party," she said, standing at the banister and yelled as loudly as she could. "'Cause t'day's my birthday."

Jake and Cameron were sitting on the porch, watching Betsy and Miss Inez. The two women waved at them, and they waved back.

"What do you think they're celebrating?" Cameron asked.

"I don't know, but it looks like Betsy and that old lady are pretty drunk."

"Looks like it," Cameron said. "Whatever it is, they look like they're having fun."

"No one deserves to have fun more than Betsy. The last couple of years have been hell for her."

"Maybe she got rid of that old white man," Cameron suggested.

"That old man's not gonna leave that young thing alone without a fight."

"Maybe he gave her some money or something."

"Maybe."

Just then, Big Money Banks rode up in his brand new Kelly green Cadillac. He stopped the car in front of his house, let the motor run, and stayed inside.

"What the hell is he doing?" Cameron asked.

"Keeping cool."

"In the car?"

"He doesn't have a fan in his house, so he sits outside in his car because it has air conditioning."

"What about his wife and kids?"

"The children aren't allowed in the car. The only time his wife is allowed to ride in it. . . Is when he takes her grocery shopping."

"That is the most selfish shit I have ever heard," Cameron said.

"Hey, this is Buttermilk Bottom, not Buckhead."

Another Sunday finally arrived and Cameron waited impatiently for his beautiful dark goddess to appear. At five o'clock in the morning, he could not sleep for tossing and turning in his bed. When he closed his eyes, he imagined kissing her beautiful lips and holding her around that narrow waistline of hers. His desire for her was so intense he could not believe the feelings that moved inside him. What he felt was parallel to what he normally experienced while making love with a woman, not from wanting one. This was different. He thought of nothing but the beautiful woman with the curvy hips, the gorgeous face, and the most seductive eyes he ever experienced looking into. She consumed his thoughts since the moment that he saw her leaving the Bottom surrounded by the beautiful glow of the yellow and orange sunset. His feelings intensified when he saw her up close; the day she rejected all of his advances, which crushed him, but it also stimulated him beyond anything he ever thought could be possible. He had to try again.

Sitting on his front porch in the fragrant spring air, rubbing his hands together, rushing time, he waited impatiently for her to appear. Finally, he saw her at the top of the hill and began to sweat as he rushed inside, putting on a clean white shirt. He ran down the steps and waited. She was hypnotic as he watched her stroll sensuously down the dirt road toward him. Her body moved and swayed with ease and grace as she placed one foot in front of the other, bringing her closer to him. Anticipating her nearness to him, he could feel a warm tingling sensation moving around his waistline, traveling up toward the back of his neck. He took deep breaths of air as she came closer. She saw him sitting on the steps in front of her; she slowed-down then crossed the street to avoid contact with him. Angry and frustrated, he was not about to allow her to get away with that, so he waited until she was close enough then he crossed the street to intercept her.

He stood right in front of her, looking at her, unable to speak. *Damn you, woman. I've been waiting months just to get a look at you. You thought crossing the street was going to stop me,* he thought, not trusting himself to speak at that moment.

"Excuse me," she said politely.

"No, I won't. Not this time," he said, feeling his anger and frustration building. She did not respond verbally to him, but she tried to get around him. Each time, he stepped in her way. *You smell so amazing,* he thought, inhaling her scent.

"What is your problem?" she asked, looking into his brilliant eyes.

"You. I want to know you," he said hardly able to get the words out. *I need to talk to you . . . And love you for the rest of my life.* When she looked into his piercing eyes, she had to take a step back, not believing what she saw in them.

"I'm sorry, but you are in my way," she said, trying to regain control of the situation.

"I don't mean to bother you. . . But I really would like a chance to talk to you," he said, trying to convince her to stay for a few moments. *Please, God, make her talk to me . . . Please.*

Before she could respond, Little Kenny ran up to Cameron crying. "Sheriff, my mama's boyfriend, he's back," he said, panicking with tears running down his dirty face.

No, not now . . . Please, not now, he thought looking at the little boy, then at the woman of his dreams. *I want you more than I have wanted anyone in my whole life. God, please don't make me lose her now, please.*

"Sheriff, please. . . My mama needs help."

She smiled, "It looks as if someone needs you," she said, looking down at the crying little boy.

Damn him for needing me now, he looked angrily at her beautiful smile, feeling that she was making fun of him. Kenny was pulling his shirttail, trying to get him to respond and follow him.

"You had better go," she said gently, looking at Kenny's desperate face.

"I need to talk to you," he said. He thought, *What I really need is to hold you and make love to you slowly for the rest of my life. I feel like I'm having an orgasm, and I haven't even touched you yet.*

"Sheriff, please. . . Come on," Kenny said, crying, pulling him away from the most beautiful woman he had ever seen.

Looking at the distressed little boy, she said, "He needs you now." He looked down at Kenny, who was pulling his hand, pulling him away from the one person he wanted most in his whole life. "Go on, the child needs you," she said, seriously. He touched her hand as he walked away and felt a shock of energy, coming from their brief contact. After several moments of hesitation, Cameron went with the boy.

When he arrived at Kenny's apartment, no one was there except his mother and Kenny's little sister. He checked all the rooms then he went back into the kitchen where the mother and daughter were sitting and crying.

"Did he leave?"

"Yeah," Paula said, trembling in her seat at the kitchen table.

"Did he hurt you?"

"No," Kenny's mother said, not looking at him.

Wanting to go find the beautiful woman, he said, "Well, he must have taken off. If he comes back. . . Let me know." Cameron was about to leave until he caught the eye movements of the little girl. She was standing in the doorway of the kitchen, staring at the sink. "Are you sure you're alright?" he asked Paula.

"Yeah, I'm alright." She was obviously upset, but he could not help but focus his attention on the little girl who had not stopped looking at the sink. He stepped in front of the sink and opened the cabinet door only to find Mr. Willie curled up in a ball, hiding. Surprised to see a grown man hiding in such a small space, he began to laugh. The man tried to come out, but he was stuck. Cameron continued to laugh and the children joined him. The man was frustrated because he could not get out without help. Within minutes, Cripple Jake and Johnny arrived after seeing their friend run toward Kenny's apartment, to see if their friend needed any help. They, too, laughed until tears rolled down their faces at the sight of the grown man stuck under the kitchen sink.

They eventually helped Willie out from under the kitchen cabinet and ushered him out of the apartment.

"I told you once that I was going to kill you if you came back here. I won't ask you why you came back because that has to mean you're stupid or retarded. Now, you listen to my last warning," Cameron said with his finger stabbing the man's chest. "I'm only telling you this because you made us laugh today. In the future, if you put one foot in this neighborhood again, I am going to kill you as sure as you can piss and shit."

"Man. . . I was just trying to . . ."

Opening his mouth was a tremendous mistake, because Cameron hit the man on top of the head with his pistol. "Shut the fuck up! Don't let me catch you around this family ever again. Do you understand me?"

"I won't. I promise . . ." Wham! Cameron hit the man again with the pistol. "Didn't I tell you to shut the fuck up?" This time, the man shook his bloody head, yes. "Now get your stupid-ass out of here."

Moses and several other men appeared in time to escort the beaten man out of their neighborhood and to make certain that he was far enough away before they returned to hear what happened. Looking around and not seeing the beautiful woman, Cameron sighed then asked Cripple Jake and Johnny to keep the children outside while he went inside the apartment to talk to their mother. Sitting down at the table across from Kenny's mother, he looked at her for a long time before he spoke.

"You know what?" She sat there not saying anything. "A woman like you can get a lot of people killed. You refuse to stand up for yourself because you're lazy, and you like being sorry. . . But I'm telling you, starting right now. . . That you better find a backbone to stand up for you and your children because I'm not coming here again to rescue your pitiful ass. You have children to raise and protect. If you can't protect yourself, protect them. I'm putting the word out on you. If that motherfucker ever comes back here, we are calling someone to take these beautiful children away from your sorry ass. He can kill your ass if he wants to. . . No one will give a shit, since that's what you seem to want. You didn't have to let that piece of shit in this house. The second you saw him, you could have sent someone for us. . . Or the police, but you didn't. From now on, sister, you're on your own. There is nothing in this world worse than a sorry-ass mother. I'm not going to jail for you; no one should. It's your job to protect yourself and your children. Stop letting his ass in the house," he yelled. Seeing her cry pitifully, he said, "You are better than that. You can be stronger than that. Wake up and take care of your children," he said, sighing deeply then he got up and left.

When he reached his apartment, he sat on the porch disappointed that he had missed a perfect opportunity to become acquainted with his mysterious goddess. When he stood next to her, he felt his passion rising out of control, and he saw something in her eyes that made him want to reach out and grab her, claiming her for his own. Then as fate would have it, he missed another opportunity to get to know her because Kenny needed him. Feeling sick inside, he wondered how he could want someone so much, before he even had a chance to kiss her or even know her name. He remembered the shock he felt when he touched her hand.

"She felt it too. I know she did," he said aloud.

That evening he waited for her to pass by with her companion. He stood on his porch as they walked toward his building. He looked down at her, hoping she would look in his direction and give him some kind of signal, but she did not. When they were right under his porch, her companion looked up and nodded his head.

"Good evening," the man said while holding the hand of the woman Cameron wanted to cherish for the rest of his life. Seeing them together made him crazy with jealousy.

"Good evening," Cameron responded, praying for a glance from the dark beauty who made his desire for her explode. "Look at me, damn it," he said aloud, knowing she could not hear him. *Hide from me now,* he said to himself as she walked away from him displaying her beautiful body as she moved. *But I am going to have you for my own. I promise you that.' Just then, she turned around and looked at him. His heart stopped. 'I love you, woman. I love you.* He finally confirmed his feelings, and he finally could admit it to himself. She turned and looked into his eyes then grabbed her companion's arm and walked away, sending a stabbing pain through his heart.

Chapter 22

Horace Singleton, the counselor at Grace's school, continued his infatuation with Grace and tried everything he could to establish an on-going relationship with her instead of just filling-in for what he called her 'gangster' boyfriend. Knowing that Grace only called him when she needed a formal escort for public appearances, he bristled at the thought of leaving her again, without her realizing that he was more deserving of her love. Horace had a legitimate job and could move in her circle of friends as well as professional gatherings, but what he did not have was her love. He was her official escort only when she needed one. Despite the fact that Horace dated co-workers from school and other women from various social settings, he still had strong feelings for Grace. Over the years, he tried to lure her away from the gangster she was involved with and the inappropriate relationship that they shared to his constant disgust.

"Horace, thank you for taking me tonight," Gracie said, trying to encourage him to leave, but he did not move. When he stood in the door, staring at her, she moved away and tried to make polite conversation. "The party was wonderful. The Hendrickson's always give the best parties in Atlanta. Everyone who is anybody was there."

"Their home was quite a showplace, the perfect environment for a formal party."

"I loved having those wonderful servants waiting on us hand and foot. That was a first for me, and it was a real class act. They were handsome in their sparkling white uniforms and gloves. It really gave the evening a very special air."

"Yes, it was classy," he said, looking at her with love in his eyes. "You were the most beautiful woman at the party," he said, admiring the white beaded dress that accented her well-developed body.

"Thank you, Horace. I really appreciate you taking the time to escort me."

"I don't want your appreciation, Grace."

"Well, you have it anyway. Thank you."

"Grace, isn't it time for you and I to be perfectly honest with each other?"

"I think it's time for us to say goodnight, Horace," she said, knowing what was coming next. "Besides, aren't you still dating Susan from the music department?"

"I love you, Grace, not Susan," he said softly, trying to make her listen. "I know you don't want to face the facts, but it's painfully obvious that this man you've been seeing is not willing to commit himself to you. He will never marry you."

"Good night, Horace," she said angrily, opening the door.

Filled with anger and passion for her, he walked inside, and closed the door behind them and held her in his arms. When he attempted to kiss her, she turned away. "You have to stop seeing this man. He's a convict, and he lives in Buttermilk Bottom, Grace. For goodness sake, you have to stop seeing him."

"I can't."

All she could do now was to pray and try to convince Cameron to change his lifestyle and his address, especially his address. She pushed Horace away. Over the years, they became good friends, and she learned to depend on him being there to listen to her and give her support, whenever she needed it, but his constant declaration of love made her uncomfortable.

"No one with any self-respect would go to Buttermilk Bottom, let alone live there," Horace said, walking pass Grace into the living room.

"It's a deplorable place. I can't understand why he continues to live there," she said, remembering her only trip there.

Grace never spent the night there, and she knew he would not invite her and for that she was grateful. As ashamed as she was of his circumstances, she felt blessed each time she was with him, and every time they made love. Her only hope was to get him to change his lifestyle and marry her. If that happened, she would be the happiest woman on earth.

"You have to stop seeing him," Horace said, consumed with rage and jealousy as he pleaded his own case. She knew he made perfect sense because all the words he spoke were exactly the same ones that she related to Cameron. "What you need is stability and assurance. You need someone you can be proud to be with, not some loser from the ghetto. He's no good for you."

Grace acknowledged her shame and disappointment with what Cameron had become, but she did love him. He was the one she craved, and loved.

"I know."

"Then let him go, Grace," Horace said, reaching out for her, holding her to him, rocking her in his arms. "We could be happy together. We have everything in common, music, dancing, and friends. Grace, you know how I feel about you. If you would give me a chance, I could love you like no one ever has." She turned away from him. "I'm begging you, Grace." When she did not respond, he became quiet. Taking a deep breath of air, he said. "I can't continue being your escort when it suits you, or seeing you when he doesn't show up. If you want to see me again, you will have to call me and tell me that I am the only man you want, but you will have to give him up, completely. I won't be second in line ever again," he said, holding her by the shoulders. "I love you too much for that." He kissed her on the lips with all the passion he had in his body and soul, hoping to make her understand the depths of his love for her. Seeing no change in her demeanor, he picked up his coat off the back of the sofa, he said, "I won't wait forever, Grace. Even I have my limits." He was gone, but all she could think about was Cameron.

Grace loved Cameron long before he knew she existed, back in college when he was oblivious of her presence on the planet. He was tall, strong, and beautiful. It was hard for her to describe him as handsome because he exceeded handsome. His beauty came not only from his good looks; it extended to his dress, his kindness, and the way he moved. His walk was enticing and kept her hypnotized long after he faded out of sight. She watched as he courted and married a fellow classmate and silently rejoiced when she discovered that they had divorced. Her own marriage ended in less than a year because her husband was not the man she wanted. There was no other place for them to go except in their separate directions. Finally, she could love and touch the man of her dreams, but she was unable to confirm him as her own. Due to an unfortunate incident and a year in jail, their lives took them in opposite directions.

On the other side of town, Queenie was also in need of Cameron's company. She tried to imagine what would make him satisfied with her. Knowing that Cameron was not ready for any type of serious relationship, she did know that he enjoyed making love to her, but something always held him back from committing to her or to any women.

As lovely as her birthday celebration was with Cameron, Queenie found herself at square one, where she had to fight for his attention then try to entice him back to her bed so that he could make love to her. She had a bigger problem; he had not come around the juke joint at all since the dance, months before. *Why does it always have to end up this way?* She felt sad and abandoned.

Late in the afternoon, Dellah came into Queenie's limping, barely able to get in the door. When Luther noticed that she was in tears, he rushed to assist her.

"What d' hell happened t' you?"

"Some stupid, mutherfucker stomped my foot," she said tearfully.

"What?" Azalene asked, "Who'd do such a stupid thing?"

"Some man, wearing a pair o' big ole' ugly combat boots," Dellah said. "He jes walked up t' me like he wanted t' talk t' me. . . D' next thang I knew. . . . Wham! He stomped my damn foot," she said, outraged.

"That must've been dat 'foot stumper' d' police been lookin' fo'. They bin lookin' fo' him all year. Seems like d' man hates t' see women walkin' 'round wit their toes hangin' out. He's been stompin' ev'rybody's feet who wear them open toe shoes," Luther said.

"Who in the hell does he think he is. . . Going around stomping people's feet?" Queenie said, helping Dellah to her seat. "You need to go to Grady. Your foot may be broken."

"It sho feel like it," Dellah said.

"Call Core Lee to take a look at it. She'll know what to do," Queenie said to Azalene.

"The police say he wears d'em steel-toed combat boots," Luther said. "They really wanna git his ass 'cause he's stomped 'bout twenty women on d' feet, and he don't care if they's white or black."

"They's not d' only ones dat wants t' find him," Dellah said with tears in her eyes. "If I see him agin. . . I'm gonna kick his fuckin' ass."

Chapter 23

Normally, on a Saturday night, Cameron would spend the night at Grace's house, but since his encounter with the beautiful woman, he wanted only to see and touch her. Knowing that she was coming to Buttermilk Bottom on Sunday mornings, he stayed home and waited for the dawn to break. The aroma from the Southern Bakery filled the air when he awakened extra early to wait for her to appear. Cameron knew that she came early to visit the old lady, and stayed the whole day until her male companion came to take her home. Needing to see her and talk to her, he intended to intercept her before she got to Noitop's house and before her boyfriend or husband came to interfere. This time, he would make certain that she would not escape.

He had thought of nothing but her, since he first saw her silhouette walking up the dirt road in the sunset, and the awesome image of her tormented him in his dreams. When he first looked upon her face, he was surprised at her startling beauty, which took the breath from his body and reduced him to a helpless idiot. As the morning sky brightened, he knew that he could not stay away from her because his desire for her was too strong. In the middle of the night, he found himself again in the midst of a wet dream centered on loving her. Even in his sleep, his desire for her consumed him. All week, he wandered the streets aimlessly or sat on his front porch wanting and waiting for her to return.

Mystery surrounded her as his mind filled with questions. He had no idea why a girl who was that beautiful would need voodoo or magic when she had everything to create her own. *Why did she need to see a witch doctor every week? Was she in some kind of trouble or was that man she was with giving her problems?* If so, he would gladly take him out of the picture for her. All his unanswered questions only added to the mystery.

According to Jake, she came every Sunday morning to see Mrs. Cigam. What was disappointing, to him, was the fact that she met someone there and left with him every Sunday night. If he was going to make an impression on her, he had to do it between his house and Mrs. Cigam's house, before her friend appeared. He sat on the steps with a newspaper that he was not interested in reading. Looking up the hill every few seconds in full anticipation of her appearance, he pondered over his feelings of urgency and the raw desire that monopolized his conscience and his unconscious mind. He had no idea what he was going to say to her or how she would react to another unwanted encounter. For the first time in his life, he prayed that he would be able to make a positive impression on a woman.

"If God is in heaven, He will grant me this one wish," he said aloud.

This time, he would not let her go no matter what happened around them, and he was not taking a negative response from her without pleading his case first. He continued to pray, hoping that he had not scared her away.

After a few skeptical moments, he looked up in time to see her turn the corner at the entrance to Buttermilk Bottom. It was a magical and wonderful moment. Helplessly, his heart fluttered as she walked down the hill toward his building. It was eight o'clock in the morning, a whole hour earlier than the week before. *Is she trying to dodge me?* He was beside himself with passion and desire for the gorgeous creature whose vision haunted him night and day. The site of her strolling down the hill was amazingly beautiful, an amazing scene that kept his heart in a state of captive bliss. Her hips swayed to an internal rhythm that made his heart quake, bringing warmth, and moisture to his body.

She spotted him and slowed her stride. After working a double shift, Jazmine did not want to deal with his strong feelings so early in the morning, and she did not want to face her own feelings for him, which had escalated since she last saw him. The fact that she hesitated broke his heart, but he was determined to speak to her and ultimately claim her for his own. *Don't even try to cross the street, woman,* he said to himself, acknowledging that he was completely out of control. She slowed down and started to cross to the other side of the dirt road, but she knew he would only run after her as he did before. Knowing that she had to face him, she took a deep breath and walked slowly toward him. *You won't get away from me today or ever . . . Not on this earth.* His heart fluttered. His breathing labored as his hands began to sweat, and his throat became dry. The closer she came to where he was standing, the more nervous he became. An adolescent could not have been more in awe of the magnificent sight before him.

"Good Morning," he said, standing directly in front of her, nervously hating his lack of control over his emotions.

"Good morning," she said, attempting to walk around him, but he did not attempt to move, making her look at him inquisitively.

"I would like to speak with you for a moment. . . If you don't mind?"

"I am in a bit of a hurry," she said, walking around him, appearing not to show any interest in him whatsoever. The look in his eyes was so intense that she needed to move away from him, and she attempted to get pass him.

"Not this time," he said, reaching out to grab her hand. Her eyes pierced his soul like an arrow, making him release her, but he could not help himself. She continued walking down the hill. "Look. . . Please wait, I need to talk to you," he heard himself say after taking a deep breath. "Please." She stopped, turning around to look back at him. "I have been waiting since sun-up to see you," he said honestly.

"Why would you be waiting for me?" she asked, looking directly in his eyes.

"I wanted to introduce myself and. . . Find out your name. I want. . . To talk to you." There was a long pause before she began to speak as he silently prayed, *God, please allow me this chance to know her and to love her.* A smile came across her lips, as if she was about to say something, but she changed her mind because his sincerity shone through, peaking her interest. "May I walk with you?" he asked, praying she would not chase him away. She smiled generously, giving him a rush of feelings that caught him off guard then she laughed and continued to walk. She had not said no, so he joined her. They walked for almost a block before he asked, "Are you going to tell me your name?"

After they had walked several more feet down the dirt clay road, she slowed-down, smiled broadly and said, "My name is Jazmine."

At first, he could not respond. He was lost in her smile as he imagined kissing her lips, which he could not stop himself from admiring. Then as if someone had shaken him awake he said, "My name is . . . Is? " He drew a blank.

"Cameron Fielding, I know."

"How did you know my name?"

"You are a hero around here. . . From what I hear," she said.

It surprised him that she knew anything about him. "Who told you that?"

"My mother."

"Your mother? Do I know your mother?"

"No, but she knows you. I think it's about time that you two met, don't you?"

"If you say so," he said, looking into her strangely beautiful gray eyes that took the breath out of his body.

Smiling at his infatuation with her, she said, "I do." Smiling inside, she led him on down the dirt road and inside the picket fence. As she stepped inside the gate, he realized that her mother must be 'Miss Cigam'. On the first step to the porch, she turned, smiled and said, "Don't be nervous. She doesn't bite." They both laughed.

"Maybe I do," he said seriously, looking down at her breasts that peeked out ever so slightly from her blouse. *If I get the chance, I'll never let you out of my sight, woman,* he thought, grabbing hold of her hand, but she pulled away after several seconds. *I'll have to take it slow, so I won't scare her away,* he thought, cautioning himself in face of a near disaster.

Noitop Cigam lived in the most isolated house in Buttermilk Bottom. It was a single stone structure that sat alone with the dense covering of trees, brushes, and kudzu vines as her closest neighbors. It could have used a good painting around the shutters and windows. Curvy smothering kudzu vines could be seen everywhere. The house was hardly visible from the dirt pathway leading to it. The residents stayed away from the small isolated house that lay snuggling quietly in the kudzu, hidden from the world for a very good reason. They were afraid.

When people came for help, they rarely spoke her name or mentioned money. She used her eyes to indicate whether they paid enough, but most people overpaid her out of fear that her potions would backfire on them. They simply laid the money on the table, making sure that they walked in and out of her house quietly, being careful not to slam the door.

The inside of Noitop's house was very unusual. It did not look like anything Cameron had ever seen before. There were herbs hanging from the ceiling, a round table with two chairs was in the center of the room with a black cover on it. There was a large fireplace, which looked unused with all kinds of pots and bowls sitting inside. Dark drapes and six straight back chairs were the only other furniture in the large parlor.

"This is my mother's office," she said, watching his reaction.

"You mean. . . ?"

"Yes, Noitop Cigam is really my mother."

As they walked to the back of the house and down a narrow hallway, he could not help but watch and appreciate Jazmine's well-built body. Once they reached the end of the hallway, they entered a beautiful, brightly lit kitchen and sitting room. There were beautiful, fresh flowers and plants everywhere. He smiled in relief. When Noitop came into the room, she looked different from the times he saw her on the streets. Except for the long natural locks of hair that hung down to her waist, she did not look like a witch. Looked like a normal woman with nothing to do with voodoo or black magic.

"I am not a witch doctor, and I don't engage in black magic," she teased in a wonderfully refreshing, island accent as she read his mind while extending her hand for a firm handshake. Her smile covered him like a warm blanket. "Welcome to my home where I practice white magic. . . There is a huge difference. Why don't you come outside into my garden and have a seat, Cameron?"

Cameron was shocked to see the beautiful flowers, decorative ground covers, a vegetable garden, and herb garden in her back yard that was surrounded by an old stone wall, made of the same stones that the house was made of. The stone wall was a natural barrier to the kudzu that monopolized the area beyond the wall. There were beautiful trees and shrubs, strategically situated in the large yard and under a gigantic oak tree was an old large wooden table with four chairs. It looked like a scene from a magazine.

"Thank you, Miss Cigam. This is a wonderful place. . . So unexpected," he said, looking around."

"Noitop would be fine," she said, leading the way to the oak tree where she invited him to sit. Feeling privileged to be there, he watched as she poured him a cup of tea and gave him a huge slice of black walnut pound cake. "I'm happy to finally meet you, Cameron. This neighborhood was in big trouble until you came. You taught our men how to stand up and fight back."

"I helped a little," he said as his eyes searched for Jazmine, who instantly disappeared after their arrival.

"Don't bother being modest, boy. Everybody knows what you've done. They were nothing but a bunch of weaklings before you got here. When people experience poverty and degradation in such gross circumstances, they begin to believe that they are useless and have no value. You gave them courage, purpose, and direction."

"I think they were ready to take a stand," he said as Jazmine reappeared, making his body heat up as she brought out a bowl of fruit.

She poured herself a cup of tea as he stared, appreciating her every movement. He could not help but want her, and he felt embarrassed sitting with her mother feeling so intensely about her daughter. Their eyes met, making his heart pound louder as he silently prayed, *I hope with all my heart that her look means that she's interested in me. I don't know what I'll do if I'm wrong,* he said to himself. She smiled generously at him, which made him relax. He took it to mean that there was hope.

"This community lives in the shadows of wealth and success, minutes from the city's financial center while putting up with foul air, brutality, practically no city services. . . And substandard housing conditions, but we have survived. . . Because we must," Noitop said. "Oppression, hatred, and discrimination are cancerous symptoms of a dying society, but we can't allow them to prevail. In your own way, you have started the process of rebellion in our neighborhood. Our men wouldn't have done anything without your assistance. If we can get over this crisis, everything will be fine, and you will be free to live the lifestyle you want and deserve. Have you thought about leaving Buttermilk Bottom?"

Cameron smiled appreciating the fact that she used the word 'we' as she interpreted the problems facing Buttermilk Bottom.

"All the time," he said honestly not taking his eyes from her daughter.

Jazmine felt his deep yearning and felt her body heating up because she had a crush on Cameron, since she first saw him. Despite her mother's words of caution, she continued her fascination with him.

"It will happen. I get a very good feeling about you," Noitop said, keenly aware of his feelings for her daughter. Her daughter asked about him constantly, after she saw him rescue the child from his abusive father. Her infatuation with Cameron started long before he ever noticed her. As a mother, she was very protective of her daughter and wanted her to go slowly in regard to her feelings for the number writer, but every week for months, Jazmine bombarded her with questions about Cameron. "I have one concern, Cameron," she continued as if she was not aware of his acute interest in her daughter or his constant gazing at her. Since she knew he could not help himself, she excused him for being so distracted.

"Ah. . . What's that?" he asked, forcing himself to pay attention to the wise woman sitting before him. His eyes loved the vision of beauty in front of him, making him force himself to listen to Noitop's seasoned advice.

"There's a detective who is looking for you, but he doesn't know who you are. It is important that you stay out of sight until the time is right for you to challenge him."

"I'm not sure I can orchestrate how we meet, but the next couple of weeks will tell."

"During the next few weeks, you should conclude your life here because your destiny lies elsewhere. The most important thing you have done for these people was to get them involved in the world outside of this neighborhood. That will continue as stronger leaders emerge in this community. They must own their destinies and work toward using their personal resources, which will benefit them most in the long run. The time has come when we, as a community, can no longer hide from the world. We must get involved and stay involved. Buttermilk Bottom, as you know it will ultimately exist only in our memories."

When Noitop went inside to get more tea, Cameron quickly turned to Jazmine. "Come over here and sit by me," he said, wanting her near him.

She shook her head no, but she gave him encouragement by rewarding him with a big beautiful smile. He thought, *She is the most beautiful woman God ever made.* He beckoned her with his finger to come to him, which only made her laugh and move further away from him. He was about to pursue her when her mother returned, continuing their discussion about the direction of the neighborhood and its people.

Just as Cameron was getting comfortable in his conversation with Noitop, her daughter's companion walked in, causing him several nervous and anxious moments. He began to worry as he watched her companion greet the woman he loved, kissing her on the cheek, throwing his arms around her shoulders. They laughed easily together as they did months before when he watched them from his front porch. Heartbroken, Cameron closed his eyes, trying not to see the two of them together. Feeling the pangs of anger and jealousy grow stronger in his chest, his face became warmer and tense as he watched the two of them walk toward him arm-in-arm. When the smiling man walked over to him with his arms still wrapped around the woman he loved, he prayed for strength not to give into his instincts, to knock the man out and grab Jazmine from his grip. His jealousy grew stronger and more unstable the closer they got.

"Hey, man. I'm Jazmine's brother, Blair. I see you finally tracked her down," Blair said, smiling and extending his hand in a friendly shake.

Cameron was not sure he heard him correctly. *Brother? Did he say brother?* "Hello. . . . You are her brother? That's . . . That's very nice, man. I am really happy to meet you," he said, laughing and letting out a huge volume of air that he did not realize he was holding, making everybody laugh aloud together.

To relieve the tension he felt, he grabbed hold of Jazmine's hand and in doing so, it calmed him in ways he could never explain. Taking a deep breath of air, he felt his heart pound with excitement as his need for her soared. Holding her close to him, he realized that he indeed had a chance to love her, and keep her with him for the rest of his life.

"We thought we had better let you off the hook before you knocked me out," Blair said, laughing.

Cameron could not speak because he was so relieved. All he could do was smile and hold onto the woman he loved. Feeling her hands and fingers as they both sat side by side, talking with her mother and brother, which completed him as nothing else on earth could.

Noitop turned out to be the most fascinating person he had ever met. Her knowledge of politics, the drama between the police and Buttermilk Bottom, civil rights, and the direction for the black race was astounding. The four of them shared the entire day together and concluded the evening with a wonderful dinner while pondering the fate of Atlanta's Black community and the world as they shared generous portions of candied yams, string beans, fried chicken, and his favorite macaroni and cheese. All during their conversation, Cameron could not keep his eyes off Jazmine. She moved to sit across from him, which tormented him because he wanted her close to him. Under normal circumstances, the time that he spent with her family would be the most stimulating and thought provoking moments of his life, but all he could think about, and want, was Jazmine. Their discussions were phenomenal, but in view of the fact that he craved only to be with Jazmine, he could not fully participate because his mind and his heart was consumed by her presence. He shared breakfast, lunch, afternoon tea, and dinner with them, stealing moments to hold her hand, to touch her face, and to find slices of time to convey his feelings for her. Following dinner, they all sat in the backyard long after the sun went down. Blair poured brandy for each of them, followed by cups of hot steamy coffee.

Intoxicated with desire, Cameron watched Jazmine constantly. His eyes could not land anywhere else; it did not matter where she went, he watched her longingly. Finally, after dessert, which they also served outdoors, he was finally alone with her. Without any prelude, he walked over to her the moment her mother and brother went inside the house, pulling her to the side of the house where no one could see them. Her lack of protest encouraged him, as he wrapped his arms around her waist, embracing her for several minutes to enjoy the fact that she was in his arms. *Please, love me, woman. Please, just love me back. I'll do anything to have you . . . Anything,* he thought, tightening his hold on her. Looking into her eyes, he touched the smooth skin on her face then kissed her lovingly and completely on the lips. Finding no resistance, he kissed her repeatedly, losing himself in the feel and taste of her lips. When he paused to look into her beautiful gray eyes, he felt dizzy. *So . . . This is what it feels like to be in love,* he thought to himself as he tried to control his breathing. He had no idea where all his feelings were coming from. He only knew he could not be away from her even for one second. Jazmine felt her body ignite with a blazing fire that she never wanted to calm down as he did in her nightly dreams since she first admired him. His brilliant eyes filled her with a love that she knew was hers forever, making her relax in his arms.

"You are the most beautiful woman I have ever seen. These past few months. . . Have been almost unbearable. It was difficult to think of anything but you. . . It was impossible for me to breathe until you appeared at the top of the hill, coming towards me," he said, kissing her so deeply that he forgot where he was. The feel of her lips and the sweet taste of her mouth made him feel deep stirrings in his loins, which he found almost impossible to control.

She pushed him away breaking his heart . . . Then finally, she said, "It's getting late, time for me to go home."

"Where is home?" he asked, holding on to her.

"I live on the West Side, off Hunter Street."

"Do you have to go now?" he asked, kissing her again on her well-formed lips.

"I have to be at work in the morning at six o'clock. Walk me to the bus stop?"

"Sure, I'd be happy to," he said, kissing her again. This time he placed his hands on her behind, but he quickly took his hands away when he felt his Johnson stiffening.

Holding her hand tightly, he said good night and thank you to her mother and brother then placed his arms around her small waistline, and escorted her out the door. On the porch, he took her in his arms, squeezing her and kissed her wonderful sweet lips that felt intoxicating and deeply erotic.

He paused, looking into her eyes, needing her and feeling the passion build up in his body, he said, "We should go."

She smiled warmly allowing him to lead the way. He held her around her waist as they walked up the hill to the bus stop. He did not speak because his only thoughts were of the overwhelming passion he felt for her. Now, he could relate to the feelings women expressed to him about needing someone and loving them no matter what. Finally, he understood because he was in the same position as the many women who professed to love him, despite the fact that he was unable to return their affection. Finally, he understood their desperation because he felt that way about Jazmine. He felt so at home with Jazmine in his arms that he never wanted to let her out of his sight.

At the bus stop, they kissed not caring if anyone was around. When the bus came, he could not leave her to ride home alone so at the last minute, he jumped on the bus with her.

"Where are you going?" she asked, laughing.

"With you," he said, taking her hand and leading her to the back of the bus where he could hold her and have some privacy.

He felt like a school-boy, sitting with her wrapped safely in his arms. He could not get close enough to her sweet smell to satisfy what he knew was his raw desire to make love to her. Realizing how special she was, he made up his mind not to rush her. Yet, he could not ignore the deep, demanding passion that raged deep down in his body. He had to control himself if he wanted to build a life with her, loving her. As the bus passed Five Points, she looked at him and smiled. All of her instincts were confirmed in his eyes as he conveyed his deep passion and need for loving her. Grateful that he pursued her, it delighted her to know that he did not want to leave her side. Her mother's words came true because she knew that she would never be able to get away from him because his needs were emotional and spiritual as well as physical. All of his needs she would be willing to fulfill because she loved him for many months, long before he knew anything about her.

"If you only knew how deadly your smile is to me," he said, not wanting to scare her off with his deep erotic need that he was attempting to harness while trying desperately to convey his feelings for her.

For the first time since he went to prison and lost his job, he wanted to make changes in his life. First, he needed a car. Since the boycott in Montgomery, he had not ridden on a bus. He felt strongly about the Jim Crow laws that made segregation possible and demanded that blacks sit in back of the bus while allowing whites to take seats from blacks who paid the same fare as whites. He vowed to get a car as soon as possible. On the bus, he kissed her, held her hand, and played with her precious fingers. They did not speak because there was too much sexual tension between them. He felt it and he hoped she felt it too.

Jazmine lived in a rooming house close to the hospital where she worked as a registered nurse. When they reached her house, he refused to release her, so he pulled her under a huge magnificent, magnolia tree that stood in front of her building; it hid them from the world. Holding her in his arms, he explored the feel and smell of her, while noting the roundness of her hips and the thin waistline that drove him crazy with cravings that were too raw to allow them to surface. What he really wanted to do, was to unbutton her blouse and taste her breasts, but he pulled himself away. He wanted nothing to spoil her impression of him, not wanting to do anything that would risk losing her. She smiled at him and kissed him so lovingly, he wanted to cry out to her because his need for her was so great.

"I must see you again," he said with his lips nestled on her hair, and his arms wrapped completely around her warm, shapely body.

"How about a movie and dinner this weekend," she suggested.

"That's too far away. Tomorrow. . . I'll pick you up tomorrow after you get off work. I want to be with you," he admitted. "I really need to be with you." He held her so close that she was barely able to breathe.

"We have a lot to find out about each other," she said finally, pulling away admiring his handsome face, which she caressed with her delicate brown hand.

He kissed her hand, loving the feel of it on his face and craving much more from her; so much, it hurt him to think about it.

"I want to know how you feel about me," he said with his heart in his mouth.

"We need to get to know each other first," she said, pulling away.

"We can start right now if you'd like," he said, kissing her on her neck.

"Tomorrow, we can start tomorrow. . . Then I want to know everything about you, from the time you were born, up to the time you will pick me up tomorrow, everything," she said, stepping away from him.

"My life is an open book," he said, pulling her back into his arms.

"Good. I love to read," she said, kissing him lightly on the lips, but he responded by smothering her with a barage of passion-filled kisses.

"Are you certain you want to know me?" she asked.

"Yes," he said, closing his eyes in a silent prayer of thanks to God.

"I hope you will want to know me as time passes. People change when they find out who, and what I am," she said, making it sound like a warning.

"What I am. . . Is crazy about you. You must know that by now and that will never change," he said, speaking from his heart.

Then to himself, he said, *The last thing I want to do is scare you off because I need you and love you. I never thought it possible for me to feel this way about anyone.* She looked into his eyes with such passion and feeling that he wanted to take her with him and make love to her at that moment. He felt his passion building, and his hardness was evident. This time, he knew she felt it, but she did not push him away. Instead, she laid her head on his shoulder and held him tightly. Her throat tickled with the urge to tell him that she knew exactly how he felt. Instead, she just smiled. He finally summoned enough strength to withdraw from her strong erotic presence.

"You had better go inside," he said, barely able to breathe.

"I'll see you tomorrow?"

"Nothing will stop me," he said, kissing her again, alarmed at the amount of feelings he experienced just from kissing her.

Desperately needing the connection he had with her, he kissed her again.

"Good night, Cameron." She walked away from him as he stood watching her.

I'm going to marry you and make love to you as I have never made love to anybody in my whole life. I can't wait to make you mine. Then, I will never let you go, he said all this to himself as he watched her walk toward the building.

"I love you. God, help me, I love you," he whispered, feeling his heartbreak as she walked away from him. She turned around and stared at him, then walked swiftly back to him, giving him a final kiss. That kiss was so magnificent that he felt his body quiver with desire, making her want him. "You had better leave before I end up taking you with me," he said seriously, not trusting his ability to turn her away a second time. She smiled, kissed him again then walked swiftly toward the door, waved, and went inside.

The minute Cameron walked Jazmine up the dirt road, arm-in-arm to the bus stop, the residents of Buttermilk Bottom started talking. Someone saw them kissing at the bus stop. When the word got back to Queenie that he was kissing a tall, dark, strange woman on the street, she went berserk, crying, screaming, and knocking objects over in her room. No matter how many times he told her that their relationship was friendly, she always hoped for more. Now, she knew she was in jeopardy of losing him forever, but she tried to convince herself that she could out last this woman as she had done with the principal. Deep down, she knew that his overt behavior of demonstrating intimacy in public was a dangerous sign, and she had to think of something quickly.

When Cameron arrived back home, he suddenly did not feel comfortable in his apartment or in his lifestyle. They did not fit any more. Sleep evaded him as Jazmine, a vision of black erotica, consumed every corner of his mind. At age thirty-eight, he was in love for the first time in his entire life. Wanting desperately to deserve her love, he spent a sleepless night planning ways to make everything perfect in his life so that she would want to spend the rest of her life loving him.

The next morning, he got up early and went shopping for a car. After spending the whole morning looking, he finally negotiated a good price and bought a four-door, white Buick with a red interior. As he drove around the city, he began thinking about finding a new place to live away from Buttermilk Bottom. Since moving to The Bottom, he saved almost every dime he earned off his illegal occupations of gambling, and the numbers. He also had the profits from the rents he collected from the three apartments in his building. Aside from paying a few bills, and purchasing a few gifts for the women he dated, he saved practically every penny he earned. Until that moment, he never thought about how he would ultimately spend his savings.

If granted the privilege of making love to Jazmine, he would make their first time together special. He did not want any hotel room because he used so many of them in the past, seducing other women. He did not like the idea of using a bed that others had slept on. It was revolting to him. It had to be a special place, but what he wanted was to marry her and spend the rest of his life loving her. Yet, he knew that he had to stay in The Bottom until all the trouble was over regarding the missing police officers. He also knew that he was principally responsible for all the conflict and suspicion cast on the neighborhood. He thought, *Me . . . And my sense of justice.* Being invisible was no longer an asset to him or the future that he wanted with Jazmine. He had to figure out a way for him to re-enter society and make a living legitimately.

The sun was shining brightly at three o'clock in the afternoon as Cameron waited for Jazmine outside McLinden Hospital where she worked as a registered nurse. He arrived early and waited for her to appear, praying that he did not dream the night before, or that he had actually touched her, kissed her and held her in his arms. Time stood still until she walked out the door dressed in her white uniform, taking off her nurse's cap, as soon as she exited the door. When she saw him standing by a new car, she stopped, smiled broadly, and laughed enjoying her own sense of humor. With his heart pounding throughout his aroused body, he watched passionately as she walked toward him. Her movements made feelings stir deep inside his body, feelings he never felt before meeting and wanting her. When she reached him, he devoured her in a long penetrating kiss, making a prayer request to God that he would never have to let her go. Opening the door for her, he admired her big perfectly formed legs as she slid into the front seat of his new vehicle.

She said, "I like your new car." As soon as he got in the car, he kissed her again, hoping and praying that she felt just a little of what he felt for her. If she did, he would be the luckiest person in the world. She looked into his eyes and said, "I think you are the luckiest person in the world." He looked at her wondering as she laughed not wanting him to know how in-tuned she was to his thoughts and feelings. She had to go slowly out of fear that it would frighten him. "Anyone who can go out and buy a new car like this must be sitting on God's shoulder." He laughed and kissed her again, pulling her close to him.

"I need to be close to you," he said softly into her hair.

"You've made that very clear," she said with her breath shallow and labored.

"I have never been a person to play games or to pretend something that I don't feel, but I have to know something. I don't want to force anything on you or rush you. . . But do you think you could learn to love me?" he asked with his heart in his mouth.

She laughed and moved away from him, wanting to make sure she could look into his eyes. "Are you certain, I'm the person you want to love? After all, there are a few people in line ahead of me from what I understand."

"There is no line. I am certain that I love you, and I need you to love me," he said not sure where those words came from, but he was not sad that he said them.

Reaching out and pulling her close to him, he thought, *Nothing in heaven or on earth can be as sweet as this.* For the first time in his life, he knew, what he craved was a deep spiritual and emotional connection to Jazmine, and his need was so pronounced that he doubted he could ever live without her loving him. She wanted him too, but she had to be certain that he could deal with her odd lifestyle and the gifts that went along with it. Her past experiences told her that she should go slowly.

When Jazmine first saw Cameron, she fell in love with him and his compassion for people. Her heart ached for him as he demonstrated his sympathy for the little boy whom his father abused. Instinctively, she knew he was a good person because of all the accolades she heard from all the children who cheered when he rescued their little friend. Children, she felt were excellent barometers in judging character and good people. She trusted their innocence, which she learned to do while working in the children's ward at the hospital. From the moment that Cameron laid eyes on Jazmine, she had never felt a man's love so deeply. At first, his feelings scared her, but no matter what happened around them, she could not avoid or deny her feelings for him. Once his sincerity came through that day when Kenny interrupted them, she relaxed, knowing that they would ultimately be together. Without doubting his love for her or hers for him, she remained cautious because there was a question that she had to ask him, *Could his love transcend all the oddities, usual and unexplainable behaviors he was bound to encounter if they were to live together?*

Once he had Jazmine sitting by his side, Cameron acknowledged that his passion for her was pure, raw, and undaunted, but it also had the potential to reel out of control. Rather than try to put his hands under her dress or on her round full breasts, as he desperately wanted to do, he simply held her close to him, not wanting to let her go even for a second. She knew he was in uncharted waters, and that he had no idea what he should do next. The evening passed by quickly. After taking her home to change clothes, he took her to dinner then to a jazz spot to hear a local artist who was drawing a large crowd and building a reputation as a great jazz singer with a terrific jazz trio to back her up.

Over the next few days, he met her every day after work and took her out to dinner, to movies or nightclubs and then home, when he could not keep her out any longer. They were together constantly. After a week, he asked her to marry him.

She said, "I can't answer you until I tell you something about myself."

He smiled, kissed her, and said, "Nothing you can tell me will make me change my mind."

"I'm not so sure. It scares most people," she said, seeing the concern build on his face.

"What is it?"

"I have gifts like my mother," she said, looking into his eyes to see his reaction.

"Okay," he said, laughing. "Is that all? You scared me for a moment. Now, will you please marry me?"

"Wait. Listen to me, Cameron, you have to understand, what I'm trying to tell you."

"I understand what I need to understand," he said, pulling her to him.

"No... You don't," she said, pushing him away. "This is important. I can, at times, read people's thoughts," she said finally then waited.

"Okay," he said slowly, kissing her tenderly on the lips. She knew he did not understand.

"Cameron, I can read your mind," she said quickly.

He looked at her, "You can do what?"

"There are times when I can read your thoughts, Cameron," she said seriously.

"Everything I think about, you will know before I say it," he asked.

"No, not everything, but I can, at times, pick up thoughts and feelings from people if those thoughts are strong enough."

"How does that work?"

"No one really knows... Least of all me. As near as I can tell, it's a mixture of mental telepathy and emotional transference."

"That sounds crazy and erotic," he said, teasingly, touching her face, wanting only to kiss her lips and experience total completion.

"It is also a pain in the ass. It can be impossible living with a person with my gifts. It can put a strain on a relationship no matter how good it is," she tried to explain.

"Anything else?" he asked, taking the pins out of her hair so that it fell down onto her shoulders. He touched it lovingly.

"Yes. I get strong premonitions and I can sometimes tell the future. I'm not as good as my mother, but I can do it. . . At times," she said, waiting for him to respond. All she felt from him was the intensity of his love for her.

"Anything else I should know?" he said, still playing in her hair.

"That's enough, don't you think?"

"Will you marry me?" he asked, thinking, *Please, will you marry me before I go crazy? I can't wait to get between those big, beautiful, brown legs of yours.* She smiled broadly then held her head back and laughed. "What is it?"

"I. . . Can't wait. . . For you to lie between these big, beautiful, brown legs of mine," she said aloud.

He looked at her in surprise and shock. After several seconds, he laughed. "Oh, shit," he said, looking at her with his eyes wide open. "This is going to be great."

She laughed and said, "You are crazy."

Will you please marry me, he thought, knowing that his love was eternal.

"As soon as you give me a ring," she said, smiling and kissing him on his sweet sensuous lips. Returning her kiss and exploring all that she was, he took a deep breath then pulled a diamond ring out of his pocket, and placed it on her finger.

"You are serious?" All he could do was to kiss her with all the passion he felt rushing through his body. When she tried to pull away, he kissed her longer and deeper.

She cried and began to kiss him all over his face and neck, unbuttoning his shirt because she wanted to make love to him, but he stopped her.

"When we make love for the first time, I want it to be special. I want you to remember it. . . Forever."

"Don't worry, darling, I will," she said, still trying to unbutton his shirt.

"No. I really want to wait," he said, holding her hands still.

"Only if you insist. We don't have to wait, honey. . . I'm not a virgin, you know?"

"Neither am I. Believe me, there is nothing I would enjoy or appreciate more, but there have been too many casual relationships in my life, but this isn't one of them."

"You mean. . . Casual sexual relationships?"

"Yes. I don't want this one to resemble anything in my past. It's important to me."

"Okay. Then, we'll wait," she said, kissing him completely. "If you're sure that's what you want."

"I'm sure."

As blacks continued to walk on the streets of Montgomery, Alabama, individual achievements continued despite the turmoil of oppression that stifled blacks from reaping the full benefit of their citizenship in The United States. Colorado elected its first black state senator. The stage play, "Mr. Wonderful," starring Sammy Davis, Jr. opened on Broadway. Althea Gibson won the women's title in tennis at the French Open. Floyd Patterson held the World Heavy Weight Championship belt. Nat King Cole's National Network Variety show aired in homes across America; Geoffrey Holder joined the Metropolitan Opera as a dancer. Frank Robinson became Rookie of the Year with the Cincinnati Reds. Don Newcombe, a pitcher for the Brooklyn Dodgers, and became the National League's Most Valuable Player. The previous year, Marian Anderson became the first black person to perform at the Metropolitan Opera in New York. Willie Mays and Hank Aaron played on National League baseball teams.

As Roy Wilkin, the NAACP, A. Philip Randolph, Martin Luther King, Jr. led the struggle for civil rights; anti-black protests were staged by whites all over the South to prevent integration. The National Guard was called upon to enforce the laws and protect students who wished to attend historically white institutions. In Alabama, the NAACP was ordered to close down and turn over their membership list to punish the agitators and to abolish jobs of those who worked for the city and state, which included teachers in the public school system. In Buttermilk Bottom, the police presence on the streets surrounding the community increased. The police arrested people at random and questioned them about the disappearance of the two police officers.

At Queenie's juke joint, gambling was better than ever with Big Money Banks and his friends, circulating large rolls of money in every game for over a week. The games of choice were poker and Georgia skin, which afforded a skillful player an opportunity to win huge amounts of cash. Both Jake and Cameron sat in the midst of the men, gambling and winning a substantial share of the money that circulated around the room.

Before the gamblers assembled for the games, Queenie turned the whole house upside down, making sure everything was in perfect order. It was as if a major tournament was about to take place. Every piece of furniture was polished to a high shine with floors mopped and waxed. There were special small ashtrays adorning the corners of each table so that each player had his or her own. Cora Lee prepared special foods and was available for early morning breakfasts because the games continued around the clock. At one table, a skin game lasted four days and three nights. Queenie had special cots brought in for men who wanted to get a little sleep between hands.

This series of games, Queenie knew, could net her a few thousand dollars, so she gave away free breakfasts to the players as long as they played. The last thing she wanted them to do was to leave and go home for any reason. Her job, which she did to perfection, was to see to it that they had everything they needed including women. She stocked their favorite drinks, foods, and cigarettes, along with a place to lay their heads and bathe if necessary. The more they gambled, the more money she made because every game they played, she got a cut of the pot.

The jukebox in the corner of the room blasted out the blazing hot sounds of Chuck Berry's new hit song, 'Maybellene' and Ray Charles' new hit 'I got a woman'. The players always sang along or popped their fingers with the music, even if they were losing their rent money. The music transcended all the problems in their lives for the two or three minutes that the music played. For those few minutes, the music served as a musically induced retreat from reality because the cursing and the accusations returned in full force at the conclusion of each song. Several times during the games, Queenie tried to engage Cameron in a conversation, but he totally ignored her as he had done over the few months that he dated Jazmine, except for a brief greeting when he walked in or out of the door. On the first night of the games, Queenie came downstairs and found him sitting at the bar with Luther and Jake while the other men sat at the tables engrossed in their night's work.

"Can I speak with you a minute?" she asked Cameron.

"What about?" he asked coldly.

"About us," she whispered.

"Queenie, there is no us, remember? There never has been and you know that."

Her heart began to beat out of control as she watched his harsh demeanor harden and listened to the coldness in his voice.

"Cameron, please. . . I need to talk to you," she said, trying to keep the panic out of her voice.

"We're in the middle of a game," he said. "Come on, Jake. Let's hit it." The two best friends took their drinks and went back to the tables where she knew not to interfere or interrupt them.

Twenty-four hours later, to break the monotony of the card game, the men started shooting craps. Gathering around a long rectangular wooden table that they pushed against the wall, they were able to throw the dice against the wall and allow the falling dice to land on the padded tabletop that Luther had cushioned with a blanket. Building their enthusiasm for the roll of the dice, they snapped their fingers to confirm the release and called out the number that they prayed would show. With dollar bills clenched tightly in their fists, the men placed their bets on the table in front of them. Moses who normally won at craps was having a bad run of luck. No matter what he did, when he threw the dice they crapped out.

"Dis is bullshit. I ain't never crapped out three times 'n a row 'n my whole life. Hey you. . . Come here." Sylvester was changing his child's diapers at a table in the corner of the room. Unable to resist the opportunity to win some extra money, Sylvester chose to gamble while his wife was at work, and since he could not leave the baby with anyone, he brought his six-month-old son with him. "Bring me dat fuckin' baby." The young man knew Moses well and did not think twice when Moses called out to him. "Gimme that boy," Moses said. Sylvester handed his son to Moses, who turned the baby over and kissed the baby's naked behind. "Now, my luck's gonna change," Moses said triumphantly. "Come on dice, Daddy's naked ass baby gonna change my luck ret now," he said, throwing the dice as hard as he could. The dice fell on eleven. He fell down on the floor in celebration, "Hot damn, gimme my fuckin' money."

"Ya better stop while you kin," someone warned.

"Oh no, dis is my roll. I jes kissed a baby's naked ass. . . I'm hot. Gimme those fuckin' dice." Moses held the dice close to his ear and shook the dice in his hand for several seconds, saying. "Come on now, git yo' money on the wood, 'cause daddy is hot t'night." He threw the dice and a five showed up. Grabbing the dice as his companions threw money against him increasing the pot by several hundred dollars. "Put yo 'fuckin' money on d' table, big mouth, 'cause I'm gonna own yo mama when I'm finished."

Jake and Cameron placed their money on the table to ride with Moses, "We're betting on that baby's ass," Jake said, laughing.

Moses picked up the dice and rolled, "Come on, baby. Poppa needs a new pair o' shoes. Gimme a five." The dice landed on four. "Dat's good. Dat's real good. . . I'm still hot."

"Yo' ass gonna crap out. . . Better quit while you kin," Big Money said, betting against Moses.

"Quit? Shit, man. . . I'm jes gittin' started. Come on, baby. . . Tell daddy what ya need. . . Gimme a five." Moses shouted and rolled a four.

"I say you cain't make it," Big money said, placing a big roll of money on the table to bet against Moses, followed by several of his friends. "Yo luck's bad. . . Been bad all day."

"Been dat way all yo' life," someone else jeered.

"You didn't hear a word I said, man. I jes kissed dat naked baby's fat ass and my luck's strong. . . Pay close 'tention now." He shook his hands, wrapping them around the dice and holding them up to his ear, as if they were talking to him. "I cain't lose dis mutherfucker. Hey, Sylvester, tell your son when he git old dat a grown-ass man kissed his natural black ass. He can be proud of dat 'cause he gonna make me a whole lot o' money, hot-damn-it." Moses threw the dice and a five rolled out. "What I tell you? I cain't loose. Gimme all dat fuckin' money, nigger. Gimme my money ret now. I'm a rich mutherfucker." Moses raked in all the money due to him then turned to Sylvester and said, "Here, buy dat baby some new diapers and bring his nasty ass back here t'morrow so I kin kiss his ass agin," Moses said, giving the father a fist full of money. Everybody laughed and enjoyed drinks on Moses because he won the largest pot of the night.

The games were an important part of the black male experience. They often gave them the edge that they needed to meet the cost of raising a family in an economy that froze blacks out. The average income of a black male during that time was $195.16 per month, while white males averaged $332.16 per month. When the gamble paid off, it raised the living standard of that family considerably but when they lost, it was crippling.

There were two tables of six men playing Georgia skin and poker.
The stakes between Wolf and Hunter had risen to over twelve hundred
dollars. Luther was in his groove as he won the last few hands played,
but the next pot was the one he wanted. He and Big Money made a
side bet of five hundred dollars and laid the money between them. Big
Money took the five hundred that he had bet with Luther and made
an additional side bet with Moses, who sat on the other side of him.
He lost the bet with Moses right away. Moses put the five hundred
dollars in his pocket. At the end of the game, Big Money lost the bet
with Luther, but when it came time to pay off Luther, Big Money had
no money.

"How ya gonna take our bet money and bet it wit somebody else?"
Luther wanted to know.

"Man, I thought I wuz gonna win Moses' money."

"You thought. How d' fuck you gonna thank wit my fuckin'
money?"

"I had a good hand," Big Money explained.

"You bet me first, and you gon pay me my money, mutherfucker."
Old man Luther pulled out a gun. "Gimme my fuckin' money," he yelled
with the gun pointing at Big Money's head. "Every time you come
'round here ya start fuckin' wit people. You ain't fucking wit me t'night."
Johnny who was sitting behind Luther grabbed Luther's arm that held
the gun, making the gun fire into the ceiling.

Big Money did not wait around. He ran out the back door with
Luther following behind him. Moses held Luther back, but Luther got
away in time to fire two shots at Big money before he jumped over the
back fence and ran out of sight.

"Man, you cain't go 'round shootin' people," Johnny said.

"Dat nigger thank he kin walk my money and git away wit it. . . He's
fuckin' crazy. He better not bring his ass back here witout my fuckin'
five hundred dollars." Everybody went back inside the juke joint where
Jake and Cameron sat still playing cards and collecting their share of the
winning poker hands.

Both whores, Dellah and Azalene, made more money than they ever
expected. Business was always good when the games were going on.
The men gambled freely, seeking the comfort of the women if they lost
and celebrating with them if they won. Both ways the whores made a
fortune.

"Oh, Lord . . ." Dellah said.

"What's wrong?" Pearl asked.

"It's d' cat lady. Why does she have t' come in here stinkin' up d' place?"

"She stank?" Pearl asked. It was the first time she saw the woman.

"Honey, hold yo' breath 'cause you gon be in fo' it. She got a hundred cats. They crawl all over her house and d' whole damn neighborhood. If ya see a stray cat. . . It b'longs t' her."

"She really loves cats."

"The pity is. . . Dat woman got a lot of money, and every penny go on dem damn cats."

"How you know she got money?" Pearl asked.

"'cause I know somebody who use t' work fo' her. . . You 'member Bertha? She said dat she had to git drunk jes t' walk in d' woman's house. . . It stank so bad."

"That's nasty."

"Sho is." Just then the nicely dressed, rather attractive old lady came over to the bar and sat down. Seconds later, the odor emanating from her was overwhelming. "I gots t' go," Azalene said, getting up, walking to the other side of the room. "I ain't got t' smell dat. . . . Lord have mercy."

Luther went over and served the woman, who was kind and very soft-spoken.

"Dat r'minds me," Dellah said, "Did ya'll hear 'bout Mr. Tom, d' insurance man?"

"No. What happened t' him?" Luther asked.

"He lost his job. We gon git anuther one and dis time, they's sendin' a woman. . . A black woman, she wuz here t'day," Dellah said, laughing. "I saw her myself. She tried t' sell me insurance."

"You mean Betsy don't have t' put up wit dat ole' white mutherfucker no mo'?" Azalene asked.

"Dat's right. They said 'fore they fired his fat ass, he came t' work on crutches. D' new insurance lady said, he wuz stankin' somethin' awful, smelled up d' whole office. She said it wuz comin' from his feet and his ass. She said it wuz awful . . . Said he still on crutches, can't even walk," Dellah said.

"Ain't dat a shame," Azalene said.

"Hell no, it ain't. Dat mutherfucker been comin' down here takin' our women and gittin' way wit it fo' years. I'm glad his ass's gone,'" Luther said.

"Dat's one mo' white man we don't have t' look at," Azalene said. "I know Betsy's glad."

"Shit, she ought t' be," Dellah affirmed. "Somebody said she and Miss Inez wuz out on d' porch all night drunk as skunks."

"Good fo' them. Maybe they heard somethin' bout it," Luther said.

"Maybe they's d' one's dat did it t' dat man," Azalene said.

"Well. . . Somebody said they saw Betsy goin' down t' old Cigam's place," Luther offered.

"Oh, shit. She don fixed d' damn man," Dellah said, laughing, banging her hand on the counter.

"How ya know dat?" Luther asked.

"Ya ever heard o' anybody gittin' dat sick in two days. . . Losin' their job and needin' crutches? It ain't nuthin' but voodoo, fool. Dat Miss Cigam's somethin'. . . . People better stay d' hell outta her way if dey know what's good fo' 'em," Dellah said.

"Voodoo?" Azalene asked.

"Voo. . . Doo. Dat's what it wuz," Dellah said.

"Shit," Azalene said.

"Piss too if ya eat right," Dellah said, not looking up as she polished her nails a vivid red. Azalene touched Dellah on the shoulder and said, "Look, d' cat lady's leavin'."

"Thank God," Dellah said. She grabbed a salt shaker from the bar. As soon as the cat lady was out the door, Dellah loosened and took the cap off the shaker then threw the contents behind the woman as she walked out on the porch and down the steps to the dirt road.

"What d' hell you do dat fo'?" Luther asked Dellah.

"Dat's my own special hoodoo. I'm makin' sure dat damn stankin' bitch never comes back in here."

Chapter 24

For two months, Cameron and his beautiful dark fiancé looked for an apartment to live in, but nothing they saw satisfied Cameron. Without Jazmine with him, he contacted an old college friend who was in the real estate business and found a house on the West Side that he loved in a new development built by a black builder for blacks. After he picked Jazmine up after work, he took her to see it. He had asked the twins to prepare lunch for them with a blanket, champagne, sandwiches, fruits, and cheese in a basket, just in case she loved it as much as he did. If she liked it, he planned to have a picnic in the back yard of their new home. His friend, the real estate sales representative, met them at the house. After showing them around, he stood back and allowed them to roam freely and talk it over.

"Please take your time and look the place over. I'll wait outside for you," the salesman said, walking out the door. "Just take your time."

Everything was brand new with thick carpeting on the floor. After looking at all the rooms, Jazmine said quietly, "Cameron, I love it."

"Good. I was hoping you would."

"There is plenty of space for children,' she said, looking around.

"Children? You want children?"

"Six sounds like a good number," she said, walking from room to room.

"When do you want to start?"

"When I first laid eyes on you," she said, surprising him.

Wow! That means I don't have to wear any condoms, he said to himself, smiling.

"You are so nasty," she said, laughing at him.

Realizing she had read his mind, he laughed and hugged her around the waist then said seriously, "And. . . You didn't answer me. How soon are we starting our little basketball team?"

"As soon as God blesses us. There is plenty of room for us to have our privacy and the large room in the basement will be perfect for your office."

"What office?" he asked.

"For the business you're planning to start. I know you haven't decided what that's going to be, but that space will work well for an office, at least temporarily."

He laughed remembering that words were not always necessary between them. "You are really something."

"I hope you will always remember that," she said seriously.

"I will always love you. Let's put this man out of his misery and send him home. He has the contract, and we can sign it today."

"Really?"

"Really."

They called the real estate person inside and went into the kitchen to sign the contract. After Jazmine and Cameron signed the bill of sale, Cameron gave his friend a check and the agent gave him the papers and keys, which he gave to Jazmine.

To celebrate, he went to the car, took the picnic basket out of the trunk, and laid the blanket on the floor because it was beginning to rain. Sitting on the blanket, they began making plans for their new home and their future. Admiring her beauty, he took her in his arms and held her close to him. Overwhelmed by his feelings and need for her, he pushed himself away from her because he wanted to make love to her right there on the floor, but he wanted to wait so that he could plan something special for her.

"Cameron, it's okay. . . Please, don't pull away. . . Make love to me."

"What?"

"I want you to make love to me, now. I know you want to."

"No, not like this. I want to wait."

"Cameron, I appreciate that you are accustomed to making special arrangements and planning liaisons with other women, but this is different. This is the first day in our new home. What could be nicer?"

"It's important to me that our first time together is not ordinary. I want it to be special for you."

"Nothing between us will ever be ordinary. Darling, I'm not as strong as you are. I have needs just like you do and making love is for both of us. You can't always set the stage for loving someone, especially when that someone needs and craves to be a part of you. I don't want to wait any longer, please," she whispered in his ear. Feeling his desire for her thunder through his body, he responded by smothering her with his lips. "Please."

Tears filled his eyes. "I love you," he said. For the first time in his life, he had someone he loved who loved him back. "Jazmine, I love you."

"I know, darling. I know. Just make love to me, now," she whispered softly in his ear.

With no fancy hotel room, no flowers, no negligees, and no bed, he began to fulfill his life-long dream to love and possess a woman of his very own.

She started to undress, but he said, "No don't. Allow me." He stood her up on the blanket in front of him, took a deep cleansing breath, and prayed to God to allow him to do everything just right. Her smile let him know that she knew what his prayer request was. Shaking his head, he said, "This is going to be so different and so wonderful."

"Thank you for loving me, Cameron," she said, kissing him fully on the lips.

He pulled her blouse over her head and quickly unfastened her bra to get a full view of her perfectly formed breasts, which up to that point he had only dreamed of loving. He caressed them gently, kissing her lightly on the lips. While unfastening her jeans, he felt a surge of passion rise up in his pants as he uncovered her small waistline and perfect hips, which eased into her long beautiful brown legs. She helped him undress, feeling his hard muscular body and rejoiced in his beauty. Feeling a wonderful peace wash over her, she succumbed completely to the intense affection she knew he felt for her. His feelings for her were so overpowering that they evoked sensations so deep that it made him crave to be inside her more than he ever imagined possible.

When his lips touched her breasts, she gasped at his tenderness, as sensuous feelings rippled through her entire body. It was so sweet that they were almost painful. She loved looking at his masculine hands on her body as he explored every inch of what would always be his to love, caress, and enjoy. He laid down on the floor and pulled her to him, placing his lips on her special secret place. He moaned, as he tasted her natural feminine flavor as she moved her hips slowly, responding to his wonderful erotic exploration and his gentle manipulation of her body. When she raised up, turned around, and began to give him pleasure at the same time, his heart soared as he relished in loving her. Captivated by the feel of his hard shaft on her beautiful lips, and pleased with her aggressiveness, he thanked God for blessing him with such a sensual and alluring woman. Her movements stimulated and charmed him and made his body shake uncontrollably as she used her hands and her electrically charged oral parts to bring him pleasure. She was so good at loving him that he felt himself losing control, so he pushed her away.

"We have to slow down," he said. "I won't last if we don't."

"Let's not wait, Cameron. I want to feel you inside me now," she whispered in his ear. "You are big, beautiful, and hard. . . I can hardly contain myself."

Her breathing was soft, shallow, and reflected wonderfully in the movement of her breasts as she continued loving his maleness. He looked at her, amazed. Her words were so full of passion and lust that he grabbed her in his arms and kissed her deeply, trying to make her a part of him. *God, I love this woman,* he thought.

"Then, show me how much you love me. Come on, babe. . . Show me," she whispered in a deep sexy voice that drove him mad.

When he began placing his hardness inside her, there was a little resistance, so he pulled back and slowed down, but she pulled him into her, holding his buttocks tightly.

"Don't pull away, darling, you won't hurt me. I need all of you. . . deep inside me," she said barely loud enough for him to hear her, but he strained to listen. Between the warmth and excitement of having his electrically charged and throbbing shaft inside her warm moist body and the erotic way she spoke to him. His passion ignited as he quickly spun out of control. For the first time in his life, he had no control over his body or what was happening to him. Having no choice, he gave in and surrendered to her completely. His body quaked and shivered, making him cry out loud and long as he reached deeply for the sweetness and love, he never knew existed.

Cameron had no master plan or any stage of execution that he normally performed when he made love to a woman. With Jazmine, he was a victim, poised helplessly to experience loving her as each moment unfolded. He could not think pass what was happening at that moment. Making love to her required voluntary actions and that was all he could manage, no matter how much he attempted to control the situation. He failed. For the first time in his life, while making love to a woman, he was only able to react to the sensations that moved through his weakened state of mind and body. Giving in to the passion, which he restrained since meeting her, he discovered a new vulnerable side of his sexual nature. She unexpectedly overwhelmed him with the force and intensity of her movements that left him quivering and praying that it would never end. Satisfied in a suspended state of passion, he was far beyond anything he had ever known before. Not only were the physical rewards of sex his aphrodisiac, he experienced an undeniable and an unbreakable bond with this amazing woman. He was home, a place he desperately needed and a place where he belonged. As her body moved, he reacted like an inexperienced school boy. Within seconds, his overly aroused body flared hot, ejaculating his pleasure all at once. He lay on top of her shuddering blissfully out of control as he tried to plunge deeper and deeper into her soul, lost in loving her.

"Oh, no," he cried, burying his face in her neck. Completely drained, he held on to her desperately for several long minutes, then he uttered, "I'm so sorry." Exhausted from the most pleasurable climax he had ever experienced and embarrassed that he did not perform well enough to satisfy her, breathing heavily he said, "That's the first time. . . That has ever happened to me. I'm so sorry. I just. . . Couldn't stop myself," he said, trying to catch his breath.

"Don't worry, darling. I will always be here for you anytime you want me," she said, kissing him hungrily. "We have a lifetime ahead of us."

Embarrassed by his lack of control, he lay back, trying to catch his breath. Looking at her, he said, "I don't know what excited me most, your body or your words." Feeling the blissful aftershocks of loving her radiate through his body, he kissed her and held her tightly, saying, "Darling, I'm so sorry. I ruined it for you. I wanted our first time to be just right."

"It was perfect for me. I loved it because it was filled with your passion and love for me. It overflowed. I felt all the love inside you. That's what I wanted, Cameron. . . To feel the passion you had been holding back all this time. I felt it and I will never forget how much you wanted me."

Still out of breath, he said, "This is the first time. . . I received praise for not doing my job."

"Don't worry, my love. I'll give you a rain-check." They both laughed, holding each other. "Jazmine, I want you to move in here right away. You can start decorating the house the way you want it. By the time we are married, it will all be complete."

"I will only move in. . . If you move in with me."

"I can't," he said, kissing her moist lips. "I still have some unfinished business in The Bottom."

"Cameron, you go. Take care of your business and when your workday and obligations are finished, You come here. Come home to me, every night."

He looked into her seriously beautiful gray eyes and felt her determination.

"I'll come home to you every night for the rest of my life if you'll have me," he said, giving into her.

"I will have you," she said, taking hold of his deflated penis. "I will have you."

He smiled and kissed her again but could not stop because his lips needed hers. Suddenly, he felt his passion rising, and placed his hardness inside her again, desperately kissing her. This time, he was purposeful in executing his skills. He felt every sweet curve and corner of her sensuous well as he raised and lowered his hardened vessel inside her. With his lips still glued passionately to hers, his body moved in harmony with hers and the world around them. It felt like an itch left unscratched his whole life then finally; someone came to rescue him, and scratched until his soul was satisfied. Never in his life did he need his lips on another person because her lips were his lifeline. Her sweetness propelled him into having feelings he had never experienced before as he lovingly continued his penile exploration. As her hands explored his body, he began to breathe heavily, feeling his lungs burst into flames, his body moved and quivered in ways it had never done before. She matched him in every movement and every stroke, propelling the sensations that roared through their bodies to greater heights, exceeding both their expectations. Inside her, he felt an intense muscular tightening around his overly aroused apparatus, which drove him crazy, creating new sensations that washed over his entire body. Physically, they became one exciting sensuous unit as waves of love induced screams and moans of blissful pleasure. Her orgasmic movement pulled and massaged the muscles of his hardness. For the first time in his life, he felt complete love for the person he made love to because for the first time, he was truly making love. With her wrapped tightly in his arms, he vowed never to let her get away from him, because he needed her to be complete.

He was the luckiest man alive to have a beautiful sexually aggressive woman who enjoyed making love and was not afraid to show it or to speak about it.

He was trying to be gentle, afraid he would hurt her, until she whispered, "Harder," she urged in his ear. "Fuck me harder," she whispered. She screamed and convulsed under him. "You are so big and sweet, Cameron. I don't think I can hold it any longer," she whispered so low he had to strain to hear her words.

Her hips moved impetuously in what seemed like several different directions at once, causing the muscles in her vagina to contract so tight around his shaft that he gradually began to swell to an extended climax as her muscles pulled at his sensuous tool then released him only to pull harder again. It drove him crazy with deliciously sweet pleasures that were genuinely erotic. Again, he experienced the longest climax of his life as their bodies shuddered, twisted, and melted together.

Laying wrapped snugly in each other arms, he whispered his most private feelings in her ear. Enchanted by her, he languished in a state of complete bliss, happy and satisfied with her legs still wrapped firmly around his body.

"I'll be home every day and night for the rest of my life. In fact, I will never leave home."

They laughed together, smothering each other with moist succulent kisses. With their beautiful brown shapely bodies intertwined, they fell soundly and deliciously asleep.

"Cameron, wake up. Wake up."

"What is it?"

It was dark outside.

"Something's wrong. That little boy who loves you... He's in trouble or his mother is. Hurry and get dressed, please."

He looked at her baffled, still half-asleep.

"Are you sure?"

"Yes. Hurry, you must go now."

He put on his clothes and fastened his belt.

"What about you?"

"I'll be fine. Please, hurry," she said, wrapping the blanket around her body as she saw him to the door.

"I'll be back as soon as I can," he said, kissing her, not wanting to leave her alone.

"Hurry... Go, please," she said, kissing him goodbye.

He got into the car and rushed off to see what was going on in Buttermilk Bottom. As soon as he reached the dirt road at the top of the hill, he saw police cars everywhere. When he drove in front of his building, he looked over at Kenny's apartment, and saw Kenny and his sister sitting on the steps with a female police officer. The police were coming out of their second floor apartment with a body covered from head to toe. He became weak in the knees when he tried to get out of his car. When Kenny saw him, he broke loose from the police woman and ran crying hysterically to Cameron, his sister, Missy ran behind him.

Jake saw Cameron when he drove up and went over to meet him in the middle of the road where the children desperately held on to Cameron's leg crying. He knelt down and hugged both children as they cried pitifully on his shoulders.

"What happened here?" he asked Jake.

"That son-of-bitch came back and strangled her," Jake said.

"Did the children see it?"

"No but Kenny found her when he got home from playing at the creek with the other kids. There was nothing anyone could do."

"Did they find the son-of-a-bitch?"

"No."

"Get the men together," Cameron said.

"Sure. We'll meet you at the juke joint in an hour."

"No, meet me in my apartment."

"Oh. . . Okay," Jake agreed, realizing the need for the change.

The female officer came over to him as he comforted the children. He stood up to greet her but the children continued to hold onto Cameron's legs crying.

"Are you a relative?" she asked.

"No, a close family friend."

"The children seem to love you," the policewoman said.

"It's mutual."

"I understand that there are no family members."

"That's right."

"The children must go to an orphanage until a suitable home can be found."

"They have to go right now? Can't that wait until after the burial?" he asked, frowning.

She looked at the crying, heartbroken children clinging frantically to Cameron and said, "I'll check with my captain."

She walked away and talked to a man in a formal looking uniform.

"Kenny, you're going to be alright. Don't worry."

"Are we gonna find Mr. Willie and kill him?" he asked.

"No. We're going to find him and turn him over to the police, and they are going to lock him in jail for the rest of his life. That's what we do when people act like animals and hurt other people."

"Okay. . . Okay," the boy said between his tears. "We'll put him in jail. . . That's what we're gonna do. Put him in jail," he said, hugging his sister while continuing to cry with his arms wrapped around Cameron's leg.

The police captain came over and asked, "Who are you sir?"

"My name is Cameron Fielding. I'm a close friend of the family," he said, looking into the man's eyes.

"I see the children are very attached to you. And, I understand you want to keep them until after the funeral?"

"I don't think they need to be with strangers right now. Not after this."

The captain looked at the children clinging to Cameron's leg and hearing their heart-wrenching cry, he said, "I have grandchildren their age. I think you're right. Tell you what . . . Give the officer your name and address. We'll get in touch with you in a week or two. Don't worry, I know the judge on duty tonight. I'm sure he'll agree. We have a murderer to catch."

"Thank you." Cameron extended his hand in a firm handshake.

The address Cameron gave the police officers was the new address on the West Side of town. With the children still clinging to him, he went up the stairs to his apartment to pack a few of his belonging in a bag and placed the bag in the trunk of his car. He waited on the steps holding both children in his arms until the female police officer came with as many clothes and toys as she could find for the children that he also placed in the car.

"I took all I could find. I'm sure they won't be going back there." Kenny looked at the officer and started crying again. Missy joined him creating a sad duet. "Will you take care of the funeral arrangements?" the policewoman asked.

He thought a moment and said, "Yes," as the children continued to cry and hold on to him. Missy walked in front of him and held her arms up for him to pick her up, which he did, kissing her on the cheek. As she cried on his shoulders, Kenny cried, holding onto on his leg. Wherever he went, they stuck to him, refusing to let go.

Jake came over to let him know that the men were waiting for them. Cameron took the children to the twin's apartment and told the children to wait for him there.

They began to protest in loud screams until Cameron took Kenny by the shoulders and explained, "Kenny, I have business to take care of. I have to find Mr. Willie and see that he goes to jail."

"No, no, I wanna go wit you," Kenny screamed. Seeing her brother panic, Missy joined in the frantic screaming.

"Look at me, Kenny," Cameron said calmly, holding him firmly by his small shoulders. "You know what we have to do. I need you to be the man and take care of your sister and these ladies until I get back. Can you do that?"

"Ah, ah. . . Yes," he said with his little lips trembling.

"Can you be the man here until I get back? I need you to be strong, Kenny." The little boy wiped his eyes, trying to appear stronger. "Okay then. Hold down the fort until I get back. I'll come back as soon as we catch him. Do you understand what I'm telling you?"

"Yeah. Okay. . . Okay, Sheriff," he agreed, wiping his eyes, trying hard to control his grief stricken body. He took his sister by the hand and went inside the twins' apartment.

The men of The Bottom met in Cameron's apartment to talk about their plans. They assigned each team of three men a special territory to search for Willie. They all knew where the man lived and where he hung out. Going their separate ways, they set out to find him. The search did not last very long because the word went out on the streets that the men of Buttermilk Bottom were looking for him to kill him. Before ten o'clock that evening, Willie had turned himself into the police.

Jake, Rev. Freeman, and a few other men went to make sure that what they heard was indeed true, and it was. The small committee went back to Buttermilk Bottom to confirm with everyone that he was indeed in jail.

It was almost midnight, when Cameron went to get the children. Emotionally, and physically exhausted, the children fell asleep. The twins agreed to keep the two children overnight not wanting to wake them. As Cameron was about to leave the twins' apartment and return to the house to get Jazmine, she drove up in a taxi.

"Where are the children?"

"They're with the twins. They offered to keep them overnight."

"Go get our children," she ordered with tears in her eyes.

"What?"

"They can't wake up in the morning and not see you. Go get them," she said in a strange voice.

Looking at her as she tried to keep the tears from falling, he grabbed her and kissed her, trying to soothe away the pain he saw on her tormented face. With his arms wrapped around his chosen partner, he went back inside the twin's apartment, introduced them to Jazmine, and took the sleeping children from their bed. He picked up the sleeping boy, and Jazmine picked up the little girl. They kissed and thanked the twins then placed the sleeping children on the back seat of their car.

Feeling Jazmine's compassion and sympathy for the children, Cameron pulled her in his arms, leaning on the car for support. He kissed her with all the passion and feeling he possessed. "Let's go home," he said. She got into the car on his side of the vehicle. They paused to embrace and smother each other with warm passionate kisses for several minutes before he said from a place deep in his heart, "I love you." He turned the key and drove away.

They went to their new home after stopping at Jazmine's rooming house to get her clothing, some sheets, pillows, and blankets that they used to make a bed on the carpeted living room floor for the children and themselves. Cameron held Jazmine tightly in his arms and slept with the two children at his side. *What a way to start our lives together,* he thought, thinking about the burden he was placing on Jazmine's shoulders, thinking that she was sound asleep.

"What better way to start our lives together than to give a loving home to two beautiful children, who love you? If it gets any better than this, I don't want to know about it," she said.

He kissed her deeply, trying to taste all her sweetness, understanding and appreciating the generosity that she demonstrated that night. With his lips covering hers, he could not get enough of her and he knew he never would.

Chapter 25

At the juke joint, things were on-edge. Johnny got up early in the morning to start organizing the kitchen and preparing for the Friday night activities. There was always a huge crowd on Friday nights. He listened as Cora Lee, Addie Mae, and the housekeeper gossiped about Cameron and Queenie.

"Honey chile, I know what's wrong wit her. She's upset 'cause Cameron ain't been 'round here," Cora Lee said.

"I know. He ain't been here since d' dance and d' last time they wuz t'gether wuz on her birthday months b'fore dat. Dat ought t' tell her somethin'," Addie Mae said.

"Guess it didn't go too well 'cause he ain't been back since," Cora Lee said. "I know d' food wuz good 'cause we spent d' whole day gitting ev'rythin' jes right."

"You'd think somebody died 'round here d' way she's actin'," the housekeeper said.

"Somethin' died," Cora Lee said.

"Do ya think she knows 'bout him and dat other woman?" Addie Mae asked.

"If ev'rybody in d' Bottom's heard 'bout Cameron and dat woman... What makes ya think she didn't?" Cora Lee said.

"I jes feels sorry fo' her, dat's all. I made her some chicken noodle soup. Maybe dat'll help cheer her up," Addie Mae said.

"She sho' didn't eat nuthin' I took up t' her, but what she needs cain't be found in nobody's soup," Cora Lee said.

Queenie was beside herself with grief and yearning. Everyone tried to be extra nice and considerate, whenever she came around, but she rarely left her room. She had painfully watched the dramatic union of Jazmine, the children, and Cameron as they placed the children in their brand new automobile. When she saw him kiss her so passionately, her heart broke into a million pieces.

Queenie was devastated knowing that Cameron had lost interest in her completely. Over the previous weeks, she tried everything to get his attention but nothing worked. In the beginning, she thought that the principal had won, until she heard about some woman he was kissing at the bus stop. She had no idea who the person was, but it was clear that Cameron had abandoned her. It left her on a desolate tract with no one. The night of the murder, she saw first-hand that her loss was complete. Sheer stubbornness ruled as Queenie decided to attempt to win him back. As she laid hugging her pillow and wiping the tears from her eyes, she had no idea how she was going to get him back in her bed. She only knew that she had to try. Spending the last few days crying, she prayed that he would just once come to her of his own freewill without her prompting him in any way, but deep down, she knew that it would never happen. The night of her birthday celebration, she felt he was committed to her, loved her. She could not believe he was gone when she awakened the next morning. To make things worse, he never returned. She felt used and discarded, but she wanted to be used again as she pictured his strong muscular body standing over her and imagined the feel of his lips on hers, and the feel of his lips on her body.

Downstairs in the juke joint, Queenie was irritable and appeared angry all the time. For the first time in anyone's memory, she was rude and mean to her staff. They all understood because they knew why she was so upset and her mood got worse when she looked up and saw Lucille walking into the juke joint around noon, talking loud and wrong. She apparently started her weekend early.

"Queenie, what d' fuck's wrong wit ev'rybody in dis fuckin' place? Feels like a damn graveyard in here," Lucille said with a frown on her face. Luther tried to tell their unwanted customer to simmer down, but she would not hear it. "Who died?" No one answered. "Who d' fuck died?"

"No one, jes keep it down," Luther urged.

"I came here t' have me some fuckin' fun. Where d' fuck's d' fun?" she asked, stretching her arms out in a questioning manner, missing the music and the laughter.

"It's early yet. Why don't ya come back later?" Luther asked quietly.

"I'm sick of dis whole fuckin' place. Buttermilk Bottom ain't what it used t' be. Gots d' fuckin' police bustin' in on ya ev'ry other day, tryin' t' fuck people up. People 'round here killin' people . . . Got dat fuckin' witch-bitch down d' road scarin' d' shit out o' ev'rybody. . . Dis whole place stinks. Somebody ought t' take a machine gun and shoot dem fuckin' police off dat damn corner. Somebody oughta be a man and shoot they fuckin' asses."

"You need t' go home and go t' bed, Lucille," Luther said.

"If I had a gun. . . I'd shoot they asses. I ain't scared 'em. I ain't scared o' nuthin'. . . Then somebody needs t' go down dat road and burn dat nigger witch out o' dat fuckin' voodoo house o' hers. Gots all kinds o' white folks comin' n' here all damn day long gittin' shit t' fuck people up. What kinda place is dis t' live in?"

"Lucille, please . . . Jes go home," Luther said.

"Don't worry, I'm gittin' d' fuck out o' here. . . It's dead in here anyway. Fuck all o' ya'll! Shit, I don't need yo' sorry ass. Shit."

Lucille stumbled out the door onto the dirt road, just as Noitop was making her way up the black, dirt road to do her late afternoon shopping and like a bear drawn to honey, Lucille intercepted Noitop and stood right in the woman's face, wobbling and unable to maintain her balance. Noitop stepped back immediately because the smell of alcohol was all over Lucille.

"You fuckin' witch. I'm sick of you and all dem fuckin' white people comin' 'n here lookin' fo' yo' voodoo ass. You needs t' take yo ass back where ya fuckin' came from wit all dat black magic and voodoo shit. Git d' fuck out o' Buttermilk Bottom, bitch, or I'm gonna fuck ya up," Lucille yelled as Noitop smiled and kept walking on her way. "You nappy-head, voodoo bitch." Everybody was standing on their porches watching and waiting for something else to happen. When it did not, they went about their business. Lucille stumbled drunkenly on home, cursing everybody she saw. "What d' fuck ya'll lookin' at?" she barked at the twins, who were sitting on their front porch, minding their own business. "Nosy ass bitches."

During the first three days in their new home, Jazmine and Cameron moved all their belongings into the house. Cameron gave her the new car and purchased a second hand car for himself. He wanted her to buy all new furniture, but she opted to buy a mixture of the old and new furnishing. Shopping all over the city, she purchased a new bed for everybody but the dressers she purchased from used furniture stores and received other antiques from her mother. He did not argue with her because he wanted her to be happy in her new home. The children refused all their attempts to be separated or to be placed in their own private rooms. For now, Jazmine said it would be best to keep them together. Wisely, she bought them separate types of furniture that she knew they would need later when they became more secure and at home.

She frequently asked for Cameron's opinion about the decorating, but he had none. He loved watching her carefully place furniture and accessories in each room. He and the children helped her hang the drapes and took pleasure in moving furniture whenever the mood hit her. The house was taking shape beautifully. It felt and looked like a warm, comfortable home that had been in existence for years instead of weeks.

Anxiously, every night, Cameron returned to their warm and loving home. He could not wait to get inside the door where he knew she would be waiting for him. Sometimes they ate at home. With Jazmine's work schedule, they ate at local restaurants most of the time.

"I don't want you to spend your time cooking for us."

"My family needs good home cooked foods," she said, thumbing through one of many new cookbooks she purchased to experiment with.

"What I want to eat, doesn't need to be cooked," he said, nibbling at her neck and knocking the cookbook on the floor.

"Boy, you are so nasty," she said, laughing.

"You call me nasty? You, the queen of dirty-talk, with your whispering. . . 'Do it to me harder, baby.' Do you think because you whisper it makes it less dirty?"

"You love it."

"Yes, I do. I thought I had myself a nice church lady when I first met you," he said, looking down at her breasts that were bulging out of her blouse. "That's a wonderful surprise. Every man dreams of having a perfect lady in public and a beautiful wild beast in bed, lucky me. I love you, Peaky and Sweetie," he said, nibbling her breasts that he nicknamed.

He swore that one breast got harder than the other one and that one was sweeter than the other one was, hence Peaky and Sweetie. He pulled her breasts out and placed them in his mouth, sending a multitude of pleasurable sensations throughout her body. His lips slid down to her belly and down to her pleasure zone where his passion consumed her, demonstrating his deep and abiding love for her. In minutes, she was pleading with him to enter her. When he did, she went wild, holding on to him, and moving her body with such a fervor that he became obsessed and fixated on the act of loving her. She always wanted him and responded to him with such animation that he could hardly believe she was real. Even when he was not with her, he only had to think about her, and his Johnson would get hard instantly. It drove him crazy when they separated because he craved to be close to her. Finally, he knew and understood what being in love was all about.

Relaxing in his arms, Jazmine said, "Cameron, I discussed our living together with my mother and brother."

"What was their reaction?"

"They already knew it, but they wished us well."

"Both of them?"

"Yes. They know how much we love each other."

"Do you love me, woman?"

"Shall I show you how much?"

"No. You're going to kill me," he said still out of breath. "But I'll take a rain check . . . For later tonight."

"You're on. Cameron, there is something we need to talk about."

"Sure, what is it?"

"Don't you think it's time for you to talk to your friends about us?"

"I'll tell them when I'm ready. Right now, I don't want anyone to know we are together. It may sound selfish. At this moment, you are all mine. I don't want anyone even talking about us. I need to enjoy this time with you. I hope you don't mind. Since I can't take you on a honeymoon, I can at least carve out the time and space just for the two of us. The rest of the world can wait," he said, trying to kiss her concerns away.

"Thank you, darling, but you have some loose ends to tie up. There are women in love with you, and you know that. The least you can do is tell them that it's over to their faces. If I were in their shoes, I wouldn't want to hear it from a second party."

"Maybe, you're right."

"I am. It is always a good idea to be truthful and kind. . . No matter what the circumstances. You owe them that much."

An hour later, they walked into the family room where the children were watching cartoons and playing with their toys on the floor.

"We are going to have to get them ready for the funeral," she said. "The police called today. They are ready to release the body. The funeral home will pick it up in the morning."

"Do you think they should go?"

"I don't know. Let's talk to them then I can tell."

Cameron led Jazmine over to the sofa that faced the television. "Kenny, we need to have a serious talk," Cameron said. Kenny got up and took his sister by the hand bringing her along with him to where Jazmine and Cameron sat side by side. After the kids settled with Missy sitting on Jazmine's lap, Kenny sat next to Cameron.

"Is dis 'bout my mama?"

"Yes. In a few days, we will have a funeral. Do you know what a funeral is?"

"Yeah. I went t' my grandmama's funeral."

"Well, we need to have one for your mother."

"Den we kin bury her?"

"That's right," Cameron said.

"Will she go t' heaven?" the five-year old asked.

"Yes, sweetie," Jazmine said, kissing her on the cheek.

"What we want to know is. . . If you want to go to the funeral and the burial?"

"You gon be wit us?" Kenny asked.

"Yes, we both will be by your side the whole time," Cameron promised, hugging the little boy.

Kenny thought a minute then kissed his sister. She screamed and wiped away his kiss. He laughed too, "Yeah. . . We wanna go."

"Kenny, when the funeral is over . . . Jazmine and I would like to adopt you and Missy. Would you like that?"

"Dat mean we kin stay here wit you?"

"Yes. It means we will be your new mother and father."

"Yeah, dat would be good 'cause we don't wanna go back t' d' Bottom," Kenny said.

"Okay then, it's a deal. We are now a family. The four of us," he said, kissing Kenny and hugging him in his arms. Jazmine kissed Kenny and Cameron kissed the five-year old. She quickly wiped his kiss away. When he tried to kiss her again, she tried to get away from him while screaming and laughing all at once. Cameron grabbed Missy and began tickling her, making her cry out to Jazmine for help. When Jazmine tried to make Cameron stop, he started tickling her and the two children jumped on his back, laughing and screaming. They all ended up on the floor, laughing and hugging each other.

Chapter 26

As summer 1956 ended, Detective Bailey Lee commenced an all out campaign to get the job of his dreams as police commissioner. There were two obstacles, he had to find someone to pin the disappearances on, and he had to show that he had complete control of Buttermilk Bottom. Although, he did not have bodies to prove that the two police officers were murdered, he knew that he had to blame someone for it to get the praise and the job he wanted. First, he had to find someone to take the blame, so he stepped up the arrests and detainment of residents in The Bottom. The incidents of beatings and arrests by the police increased as the detective called strategy meetings at the precinct to get everyone hyped up about catching the person or persons responsible. Sergeant Tripp made an unwelcome suggestion that they cancel the whole plan, but his coworkers met him with disapproving stares. He had worked in Buttermilk Bottom for a long time, and in his experience, nothing came out of there, unless people want it to come out. Besides there was no proof indicating that Buttermilk Bottom had anything to do with the missing officers or their car. Two older officers reminded, Detective Bailey that he did not know the area or the people well enough to do what he was planning. Angry and disgusted with what he interpreted as insubordination by nigger-lovers, the detective became more determined to disrupt Buttermilk Bottom's reputation in order to protect and highlight his own reputation for being a bloodthirsty, fierce, and cruel police officer. Bailey was so prejudiced, and so empowered by his hatred of blacks that he ignored the warnings of those who had worked in the precinct for years before he arrived. Bailey Lee vowed that he would be the first police officer to conquer the notorious Buttermilk Bottom.

Bailey Lee and his supporters had another problem that they seriously misjudged. The office of the mayor was not interested in placing a hard nose segregationist in the office as police commissioner. William B. Hartsfield served as mayor for six terms and was known for his ability to circumvent trouble between blacks and whites. He skillfully ushered both groups through hours of negotiations, encouraging tolerance to the frustration of both groups. His progressive eyes were on building the business structure for Atlanta and making it the center of travel and commerce for the entire Southeast region, maintaining the position that Atlanta was just too busy to hate anyone. While listening to the problems and conflicts of blacks and whites, he sold his dreams to both groups and made them a part of his vision. He artfully kept businessmen, civic groups, and politicians focused on making Atlanta great and being the transportation hub of the Southeast. He made them visualize a complex system of highways that stretched across the city landscape, and he made them see jumbo jets commanding the skies all the while he urged moderation allowing the process of integration to enfold slowly but surely. Of course the pace was much too slow for the black community that was directly affected by the policies of his administration and the pace was entirely too fast for the staunch bigots and racists who wanted the blacks to be kept in their place and separated from whites.

Driven by hatred and blind ambition, the detective wanted to put himself in line for the ultimate job on the force as police commissioner. Since the department had a history of hiring from within, he knew he had a chance. All he needed was more publicity as he plotted his way to the top. The Fourth Ward held his destiny, and he felt the job he craved was in his grasp, as soon as he proved that he could handle the toughest neighborhood in the city and win him the reputation he needed. After lengthy questioning of Ezra Levine and his family at the corner store, Detective Bailey Lee uncovered the lead he was seeking.

"The children talk about a man in Buttermilk Bottom known as 'the sheriff', who tells everyone what to do. He's some kind of hero to those people. If you find him, you may be able to find out about that group you're looking for."

Detective Lee became incensed and excited about this new information. It renewed his convictions and he became more determined to succeed. If this 'sheriff' was not guilty, he would make certain he was, by the time he found him. Bailey Lee immediately started laying his foundation for false and circumstantial evidence. He told other officers about 'the Sheriff' and the group that he commanded, making up a few facts to egg some of the more reluctant officers to action. To confirm his story, he documented rumors and lies in his report. The stage was set, and he was ready to act out his plot. He would need a team of reliable men to back him up, and he sat down to scribble the names of those he deemed worthy for his special force, which would capture the sheriff and his outrageous gang of criminals.

Cripple Jake sat at the front desk talking to Sgt. Tripp and observed the detective as he walked around the station, as if he owned it. Noticing the sneer on the desk sergeant's face, Jake said, "Man, he sho' look like he knows what he's doin'."

"That son-of-a-bitch thinks he knows, but all he's gonna do is git somebody killed." Sergeant Tripp said, reaching for one of the warm Krispy Kreme donuts that Jake brought in a double box. The remnants of the crème-filled donut were all over the sergeant's mouth. He wiped his mouth with the sleeve of his shirt, which sickened Jake, but he did not say a thing. Knowing that something was stirring, Jake was not going to leave until he found out what the detective planned so he grabbed his crutches and went to get the sergeant a cup of coffee, after offering him another donut.

Almost everybody attended Kenny's mother's funeral from Buttermilk Bottom, many of the children's playmates attended with their parents. The services took place at Rev. Freeman's church. He gave a very touching eulogy in a simple service that he made short just as Cameron requested. Queenie sat with her staff in a beautiful tailor-made black suit with a gorgeous black hat trimmed in white feathers. She tried unsuccessfully to get Cameron's attention several times, but all he saw was his new lover. Jazmine and the little girl wore beautiful white dresses and Kenny and Cameron had on black suits. They looked like the perfect family with Jake, Noitop, Blair, Johnny, Betsy, Miss Inez, Amos, the vegetable man, and the twins sitting with the family. Cameron had asked Cora Lee and Addie Mae to join them, but they opted to sit with Queenie instead.

"She's got enough heartbreak witout havin' me addin' t' it. You understand, don't ya?"

"Sure as long as you know that we wanted the two of you to be with us."

"We thanks you. We really do thanks you," Cora Lee said, hugging Cameron who had come to the back door of her kitchen to extend the invitation.

The burial was at Lincoln Cemetery because it was closer to Cameron and Jazmine's new home. They figured it would be more convenient for them and the children to maintain the gravesite on their side of town. Only a few people attended the burial but afterwards, everyone went back to the church near Buttermilk Bottom for a wonderful meal where everyone in the neighborhood gathered for the children's sake. After trying to get Cameron's attention unsuccessfully, Queenie stayed out of the way because his cold, steely eyes told her it was over and to stay away. Hurt and embarrassed, she walked away with tears in her eyes. As she was making her exit, she bumped into Jazmine and the little girl and clumsily dropped her purse. Jazmine picked it up and looked into her eyes. Seeing how much she loved Cameron, she smiled to let her know that she understood. Queenie tried to smile back but could not manage a proper response, so she turned, leaving with a broken heart and went to the juke joint where she could mourn in peace.

Most of the neighbors brought food in covered dishes to spread out on the picnic tables behind the church. The children were busy running and playing. Cameron watched Jazmine as she kept a keen eye out for the children, his heart filled with love and pride. He had been lucky to find her, no. . . Blessed, because only God could have made his life so complete. "I love you too," she whispered as he placed his arms around her waist. "We are both blessed."

As Cameron and his new family buried Kenny and Missy's mother, the South celebrated in burying the long, sufficating segregation laws that forced African Americans to sit in the back of the bus while paying the same fares as white riders. The Supreme Court denounced segregation on public transportation and public places. Blacks all over the South took immediate advantage and for the first time rode on buses with a new sense of dignity, although the law would not go into affected until later that year, December 21, 1956.

Weeks passed with September growing hotter instead of cooler. People spent more time quietly sitting out on their porches, chatting with their neighbors. The front porch remained the center of every household. It was where they plaited their children's hair, played cards, gossiped, snapped beans, picked collard greens, cut up old clothes to make quilts for the winter, played checkers, and told stories. When the nights became extremely hot, people slept on their porches, where their bodies could cool off, allowing them a cool blessed night of sleep.

Buttermilk Bottom was quiet. No one talked too loudly, and no one was cursing or drinking in the middle of the dirt roads. The Ragman got out of jail, ambling through the streets, quietly, and lazily pushing his cart. Then suddenly a breeze blew through the wooden shacks and the dirt roads of Buttermilk Bottom, raising dust to an unusually high level for a late summer day and restoring life back into the emotionally and physically depressed community.

On a Friday night, two men were sitting at a corner table, casing the juke joint. The two men came in for one reason only, to rob the place. There were two tables for gambling and both of the tables had a pile of money in the center. The kitchen was busy filling orders for their pig feet, potato salad, cornbread and collard green dinners and the money from both the gambling tables and the kitchen flowed all night long. When the two men, saw the biggest pot of the night on the tables, they pulled out a shotgun, and a pistol then made everyone lay on the floor. Queenie heard the commotion and sent her son, Tony, who was by then a healthy teenager, to get Cameron, then she went downstairs, praying that Cameron would be home.

Cameron went to his apartment to pack the final items of his personal belonging to carry to the new house. No one knew of his plans, and he wanted to keep it that way. He had just placed the last bag in his used car, when Queenie's son came running to him out of breath, to tell him about the robbery.

"Two men with shotguns," Tony related out of breath.

Cameron sent the boy to his apartment then he crossed the street to the juke joint. He looked through the window and saw the man with the shotgun in the parlor with everyone on the floor except for Queenie. She was standing on the steps with her hands raised. The other man was not in view. He circled around to the kitchen and saw the second man with a pistol. Johnny and the other helpers were lying on the floor. The man had his back to the rear door. Cameron managed to get Johnny's attention.

"Man, let these ladies go," Johnny begged.

"Shut d' fuck up," the man yelled. "Where's d' rest of d' money?" he demanded.

"Over there by d' door, on d' top shelf in d' Crisco can," Johnny volunteered.

The man went over to the cabinet and reached up for the can as he did, Cameron came in quietly and knocked him in the back of the head with his pistol. Johnny ran and caught the gun before it hit the floor.

"Tie his ass up and gag him," Cameron instructed Johnny, who was more than happy to oblige. "Take his gun and join me in the parlor when you finish.

"Luther's shotgun is inside the cellar steps," Cora Lee volunteered.

"Come through the front door," Cameron said quietly to Johnny as he helped Cora Lee and Addie Mae up off the floor.

Cameron walked through the kitchen door into the parlor with his gun drawn, shocking everyone. The man with the shotgun could not believe it.

"Your friend is dead. If you don't want to join him, I'd advise you to put that gun down and get out of here." Cameron said, not smiling or moving his eyes from the man's eyes.

The man with the gun began to shake, "You, git back, or I'm gonna blow a hole straight through ya."

"If you do, you're dead." Cameron said simply. Johnny was in place directly behind the man. The man heard the click from Luther's shotgun. The robber held up his hands, appearing to give up and pretending to relax the gun in his hand. When Cameron walked close to him to take the gun out of the man's hand, he pointed it again at Cameron and pulled the trigger just as Cripple Jake hit the man from behind with one of his crutches, the bullet missed. Cameron knocked the gun from the man's hand then took his own gun and smacked the man upside the head, dropping him to the floor. Everyone cheered.

Queenie ran and threw her arms around Cameron's neck, kissing him on the lips, noticing that he did not even try to return her affection.

"Thank God you were home. Where's my son?"

"He's in my apartment," he said, pushing her away.

"I'll send someone over to get him." She turned asked one of her girls to go get Tony and bring him home. When everyone crowded around Cameron, she could hardly maintain her position at his side as she struggled to throw her arms around his neck again. The women came out of the kitchen, thanking Cameron and singing his praises, pushing Queenie aside.

"Drinks on d' house fo' ev'rybody," Luther said. Everybody cheered as the music played loud again and customers recanted the evening's events.

Cameron turned to his men and said, "Tie his ass up and get the one out of the kitchen, you know what to do." The men did as he asked and disappeared with the would-be robbers. When he broke loose from Queenie, he went to hug Jake and Johnny. "There is nothing in the world like having friends you can depend on," he said, holding each of them in his arms.

Queenie smiled feeling a little jealous, but she understood that she owed just as much to Jake and Johnny as she did to the number man. She went over and hugged them both, thanking them for helping them out of a potentially fatal situation. After everything had settled down, Cameron sat talking with Cripple Jake and Johnny. Jake reported that the police was looking for someone called 'the sheriff' in Buttermilk Bottom, making Cameron smile.

"This sheriff person is supposed to be some kind of super hero or something," Jake related. "They have a big investigation starting up soon, couldn't find out when, but it's gonna be a doozy."

"What do they know about this man?" Cameron asked.

"Nothing just that he's black and lives in The Bottom," Jake said.

"Maybe we can help by giving them a few helpful descriptions."

"Why in the hell would we want to do something like that?" Jake asked.

"Everybody could have their own unique opinion. You know how niggers never get anything right," he said, smiling.

"Oh, I see. Niggers can't remember shit. Right?"

"Right. And the more you have. . . The more mess you gonna get," Johnny said, laughing.

"That's right," Cameron said.

The three men began to laugh loudly, attracting Queenie's attention. She loved to see her man laugh. It was a rare sight. Then she remembered that he was not hers anymore, but he was hers at that moment and as far as she was concerned, she had the advantage. She was grateful for his help, and she planned to show him all night long.

"I am so grateful to the three of you for saving us tonight. Everyone loved what you did," she said honestly. "Please, take this as an offering of thanks." She sat a bottle of aged liquor on the table. The women in the kitchen came out with three plates complete with steaks, potato salad, and greens.

"There a big ol' lemon pie when ya finish dat," the fat cook said, smiling from ear to ear. She kissed the three of them on the cheek, as if they were little boys.

The three men ate the food and plotted their next move while basking in the center of everyone's attention. There was a parade of people passing by their table, giving their thanks.

When the meal was finished, Cameron got up to leave. "Jake, I am going to need to speak with you, business."

"Sure, tomorrow?" Dellah came over to Jake and put her arms around his neck, giving him a big hug. "Hey, babe," Jake said to Dellah.

Cameron laughed when he saw the woman hugging up to Jake. He smiled and confirmed, "Around noon?"

"Sure. Noon it is," Jake said, but he had already turned his attention to Dellah.

"Where do you think you're going?" Queenie asked.

"To take care of some business," Cameron said then he turned and left.

She was standing there in the middle of the floor fuming mad. Everyone watched her as she tried to conceal her broken heart. To prevent anyone from seeing the tears that were about to fall, she ran upstairs to her room. In the privacy of her own quarters, she cried as she had never cried before. A few days passed and Cora Lee was fed up with the fact that Queenie had taken to the bed again. She was sick of her not dealing with reality.

"Queenie, sit up," she said as she entered her room without knocking. "Sit up."

Queenie slowly raised her head. Her makeup smeared with tearstains on her face. "I don't want to talk, Cora Lee. Please, just leave me alone."

"You ain't gots t' talk. All you gots t' do is listen."

"I can't right now. I lost him."

"Lost him? Baby, you ain't never had dat man, and ya knows it. Dat man had sex wit you n' nuthin' mo'. Queenie, you been 'round and I know ya knows d' difference. You's tryin' t' make mo' of it than it wuz. You cain't make a person love ya, honey. Either he loves you or he don't. . . It's jes as simple as dat."

"I can't talk to you about this. . . You like women. How in the hell can you tell me anything?" Queenie yelled.

"No, Queenie. . . I loves one woman. Only one."

"But it's different with a man. You could never love a woman the way you love a man. Some man probably raped or beat you, and that's why you ended up sleeping with a woman. When my stepfather and uncle raped me, it didn't turn me against men. I learned how to get what I wanted from them and empty their pockets at the same time."

"Jes so's you knows. . . I ain't never been wit no man. I ain't never been wit but one person in my whole life and dat's Addie Mae. You cain't make me feel bad 'bout what I do and who I loves."

"You never been with a man?"

"No, I sho ain't."

"Then how do you know you can't love a man instead of a woman?"

"I never said I can't. . . I said I never did. No man ever wanted me or me dem. I guess by me livin' in d' white folk's kitchen all my life put me out o' reach o' men folks, but I never thought 'bout it. Addie Mae and me worked hand 'n hand fo' 'most three years b'fore we fell in love. After dat, we couldn't help ourselves. . . We wuz in love."

"Haven't you ever wanted a man, Cora Lee?"

"Can't say I did. . . But I did want some chillum, but dat all changed when me and Addie Mae got t'gether. I ain't got chillun o' my own, but I got chillun all 'round me and dat's a blessin'. All love comes from God, Queenie. Don't matter where it comes from or wit who. . . I know dat God sends us what we need, and I ain't ashamed o' me 'n Addie Mae."

"And I'm not ashamed of my feelings for Cameron. I need him and I know that if I could talk to him. . . He would come around."

"Dat man told you long time ago dat he only wanted t' go t' bed wit you 'n you allowed it fo' years. He didn't give you no ring or axe you t' marry him. He told you d' truth, but you didn't wanna believe him. Now, you's sittin' 'round here, feelin' sorry fo' yo'self and being mean t' people. It ain't gonna change nuthin'. He still fell in love wit somebody else, and you's gotta live wit dat. You might as well git out dat bed and find yo'self somebody else, 'cause he ain't comin' back. . . Ever."

"We could have been good together. . . If only he had just given us a chance," Queenie said with tears falling from her eyes.

"You had all d' chances you needed, as many times as you slept wit him? You had plenty time t' figure out ev'rythang."

"But I love him," she cried.

"D' cold facts is he nev'r loved ya, baby. Did he ever tell ya he wanted t' build a life wit you? Or wanted t' have chillun wit ya?"

"No."

"You wuz dreaming, wishful dreams, and it jes didn't work. He loves someone else. A person don't choose who they loves. They jes love 'em. Ya needs t' stop all dis cryin' and git yo b'hind back t' work. There's plenty o' men who'd giva million dollars t' be wit you."

"I don't want any man. I want Cameron."

"Well. . . You kin cry fo' d' rest o' ya life. . . But it won't bring him back, dat's fo' sure. I gots dinner t' put on and a kitchen t' run. You git yo behind outta dat bed and start running dis' place again."

After thinking about Jazmine's words, Cameron decided to go over to Grace's house and tell her personally that it was over, and that he loved someone else. He did not relish the idea, but he knew it had to be done. Grace was overjoyed to hear his voice on the telephone because it had been months since she last saw him. It was their habit to stay in and spend the evening in bed, and she was looking forward to that again. In preparation for a night of complete bliss, she ran to put a bottle of wine in the refrigerator to chill, and she instantly thought of what she could make for a special dinner for the two of them. As soon as he arrived, he asked her to sit down. He did not want to wait to tell her what he had on his mind. Feeling the pressure from the life he wanted to settle into with Jazmine and the children, he saw no reason to put off what he had to do.

"I've met someone special. I fell in love for the first time in my life."

Grace thought she was dreaming. Those words did not come out of his mouth. Her heart started beating so rapidly, she could feel it pounding on the bottom of her feet. "What did you say?"

"I said, I've fallen in love with someone."

"What?" She shook her head in disbelief. "Who?"

"That doesn't matter. I wanted you to know as soon as possible."

"Is it because I put too much pressure on you to get your job back?" she asked, feeling herself panic.

"No."

"Because I didn't like where you lived?"

"No. It has nothing to do with any of that."

"What does it have to do with then? I love you. I have loved you for so many years."

"The only thing I can tell you is that it happened suddenly and completely. I never knew what it felt like to love another person until now. Nevertheless, it happened. It changed my life."

"Why couldn't you have changed for me? What does she have that I don't?" she asked, feeling herself losing control.

He took a deep breath and told her the truth, "My love." She knew he was right because she saw it in his eyes. He hugged her and said, "I hope you will find someone who will love you as much as I love her." He kissed her on the forehead then he got up and walked out.

It was time to come clean with everyone. He owed that much to the women in his life, whom he was intimate with over the past years. He did not feel as if he owed Queenie an explanation because he was brutally honest with her from the beginning. He felt he was honest with Grace also, but he owed her for standing by him over the years, especially when he was in jail. Her attitude toward his lifestyle had not hindered them from getting any further in their relationship. The simple fact was that he never loved her.

The only other person he felt he owed an explanation was a sweet, bashful, young woman, Hope. She was a true innocent, although he had told her that he had no intentions in getting serious about her. Out of fear that she might revert to her old behaviors, when she hated herself and lived life without tasting its richness, he wanted her to grow as a woman. Hope had a beautiful body, and she was attractive when she held her head up and straightened her back so that people could admire and appreciate her. With that in mind, he dialed her number and asked that she meet him at Paschal's restaurant on Hunter Street.

Hope arrived on time in a taxi, looking like she believed she was beautiful. He was proud of her and all the progress she made since the last time he saw her. As she walked from the taxi to the restaurant, she had a rhythm to her walk, which said she was a woman ready for womanly things. He felt proud that he had a little to do with the change in her attitude and her appearance. She wore a lavender dress that showed off her shape and her beautiful brown skin. As she walked through the restaurant, several men turned to watch her as she passed by their tables. Memories of their first time together brought a broad smile to his face as she approached him.

Rising from his seat to greet her, he said, "You get more beautiful every time I see you." His comment brought a smile to her face. In it, she displayed confidence and charm.

"Hey, Cameron," she said, sitting in the seat across from him. "I'm glad to see you. It's been a long time since I heard from you."

"A lot has happened, that's why I wanted to meet with you," he said.

"I wanted to talk to you too, but I didn't know how to reach you. I was glad to hear from you. I wanted to tell you that I met somebody real special."

"Really?" he asked, sitting back in the booth, looking at her anew.

"Yeah. I guess I should say that I've gotten to know him better. We work together. He's the chauffeur for the lady I work for."

"That's wonderful. He's a very lucky man."

"His name is Charlie. He's very nice to me and my son."

"Does he satisfy you?"

At first she did not answer, then she smiled broadly, showing some of her old bashfulness and said, "Yes. He satisfies me just fine."

"In every way?"

"Yeah."

"Hope, I hope that means you are settling for someone who knows how to make love to you, the way you deserve to be loved," he said, looking into her eyes.

She met his eyes for a brief moment, saying, "He knows what to do." Her sheepish demeanor, reminding him of the first time he met her at Davison's.

"Are you sure?"

"Oh yes, I'm sure. He does everything you did and some other things too," she said softly.

"Good. A man is supposed to know how to satisfy his woman and anticipate what she needs."

"I know that now."

"This guy, Charlie, does he keep the lights on?"

"Yeah and he lets me see him, too," she whispered.

"And he looks at you?"

She laughed, "All the time. You ain't got t' worry 'bout me. I'm doing alright," she said, blushing. "Cameron. . . He wants t' marry me."

"So soon."

"Well, t' tell you d' truth, I been knowin' him fo' five years. I was jes too scared t' talk to him. . . Before. . . Before you came along. When I didn't hear from you. . . I thought. . . Maybe, I should talk to him. You said you didn't want t' get serious. . . Right?"

"Right."

"You're not mad or anything?"

"No. I'm very happy for you. Just make sure you get what you need from him or any man you decide to be with," he said, sounding like a father. "You deserve to have someone who can love you, all of you. You really like this guy, don't you?"

"Yes, I do and he loves me. He said he's been lovin' me a long time, but I wouldn't give him a chance. I was scared t' talk t' any man 'cause I thought I would get pregnant again, and I didn't want that."

"You're not afraid anymore."

"No, I did what you said. I went to a store and got myself some of those rubbers, and they're working out jes fine," she said, smiling beautifully.

"Good. I'm proud of you."

"Me, too. Sometimes, I don't even know who I am. I changed so much."

"The change was good for you. You are a beautiful woman, Hope."

"Thank you."

"Does he tell you that you are beautiful?"

"All d' time. I'm real happy now."

"Good. I'm happy for you."

"You're not mad?"

"No. I am very proud of you, and I can see that you are in love. I wish you the best."

"Thanks," she said. He held her hand across the table and enjoyed the fullness of their brief friendship. After a few minutes, she looked out the window and said, "I gotta go now. He came to pick me up." She indicated his car parked across the street. She waved at him with a big smile on her face. She stood up to go. "Thank you, Cameron. Thank you so much."

"It was most definitely . . . My pleasure. You are welcome, beautiful lady. You are very welcome," he said, kissing her on the cheek.

She walked away and waved back at him when she got to the car. The man got out of the car to open the door for her, and then he got in on the driver's side. Once Hope got in the car, Charlie waved at Cameron, and he waved back. It felt good knowing that he did not hurt her feelings. Instead, he felt proud that he had something to do with her transformation. Then his attention turned to Jazmine and the love they shared, which gave him a new sense of urgency. He wanted to enjoy the feeling of his lover in his arms. He paid the bill, leaving a large tip on the table then got up to go home to his family.

It was ten o'clock when Cameron arrived home. The house was quiet and the children were nowhere in sight. Walking into the kitchen, he saw the love of his life and smiled. Even standing over a pile of dishes, Jazmine was ravishing and the most beautiful woman he had ever seen.

She heard him drive up and move about the house, but she waited for him to come to her because she knew he was seeking and needing her the minute he walked in the door. Smiling at the certainty of him loving her, she completed her duties quickly, knowing that he was observing her quietly.

"Hello, my darling."

Turning to face him, she smiled that devastating smile that always overwhelmed him. He could not believe that he shared his life with a creature so completely sensuous and smart.

"I love you too," she said, reading his thoughts and rushing into his arms. His arms held her so closely that she hurt, but she remained quiet because she loved it. "I'm late cleaning up after dinner because Mama came by and had dinner with us. She loves the house."

"Great, I wish I had known. I would have been here to welcome her." Looking into her eyes, he said, "I missed you."

"I missed you." Staring into his eyes, she knew that he had met with two of the women he was dating before they met, and she saw that he was satisfied with the outcome. She sensed that the woman would be fine, but she knew that one of them was greatly hurt but would have happiness once she accepted the situation for what it truly was. In her talk with her mother, who told her that after hurt the healing would begin for two of the women and that the other one was already in love with someone else. It was rare that her mother interfered with her children's affairs, but sensing that her daughter needed reassurance she planned to be there to make certain she was emotionally able to deal with Cameron and his past. Since she was expecting her first child, Noitop wanted to make certain that her child was going to have a smooth and healthy pregnancy.

Chapter 27

Lucille showed up on the streets several weeks after she confronted Noitop Cigam, looking like a lost dog. No one had seen her since the incident and her absence in the juke joint made everyone worry because no one could remember a day that passed that she did not come in for her shot of corn liquor and her favorite pickled pig feet. When the people in the juke joint spotted her, she was walking around talking to herself, but she did not appear to be drunk. Almost instantly, people started gossiping that Miss Cigam fixed Lucille and people avoided Noitop more than ever before, giving her the complete right of way on the shabby streets of Buttermilk Bottom. No one would dare bother her or impede her in anyway. If they found themselves on the same side of the street as she, they hurriedly crossed the street to get away from her. They feared that if she got angry; she would place a hex on them, as she did with Lucille.

The children of The Bottom were always sharing the gossip that they overheard from their parents, but they had their own network for spreading rumors and lies. They played games where they acted out real life scenarios using real-live people as their characters and role-models. All the boys wanted to be The Sheriff, and all the girls wanted to be either Miss Cigam or Queenie. Cripple Jake was another favorite role-model to emulate and someone even pretended to be Johnny.

As they played, they began to make up their own stories and situations. The children loved their time together. It made them feel special. The children acted out the latest neighborhood drama, an impromptu skit about how Miss Cigam fixed Lucille.

Someone said, "I bet ya won't go down there t' her house." The 'I bet ya' thing always trumped everything in play.

"I bet I will," another child responded. "You's d' one dat's scared."

"No, I ain't. I betcha you won't go down there," the challenger said demanding proof. There was only one way to settle the dare and they all knew it.

As the group began to creep down the dark pathway to Noitop Cigam's house, someone said, "I heard somebody say if ya see a witch b'tween nine o'clock 'n midnight she won't have no skin on. But, she gots t' put it back on, right after midnight, or she won't ever be able t' put it on agin."

"No skin. . . What you talkin' 'bout?" one of the children asked, shocked and scared at the new information.

"Witches, they cain't be in their own skin too long 'cause it gits hot from d' inside, and they have t' take it off."

"Dat's stupid," another listener said.

"It may be but dat's what my mama say." Once a child used their mother's word as the consenting authority, it was as good as quoting the bible. The group became quiet and thoughtful.

Silhouettes of the tall pine trees reflected on the dark blue sky as nightfall sank into the sunken community of Buttermilk Bottom. A group of sixteen children waited in the dark behind the bushes until it got dark enough for them to complete their noble mission. They gathered at the corner behind the building just in front of Noitop Cigam's house. Under normal circumstances, none of the children would have dared go down the path leading to Noitop's house, but it was a genuine honest to goodness dare challenge that had to be satisfied in order for any of them to hold their heads up again.

Sensing that something was about to happen, Noitop got up from her kitchen table went into the living room and looked out the window. She saw the group of children tiptoeing toward her house. Totally amused, she smiled and went to put on her long black robe and a green witch's mask that she had set aside for just such occasions. She stood in front of the window and the closed drapes, after placing candles just behind her so that the dimmed light would frame her body. When she heard the children creeping on her front porch, she laughed and waited patiently to make sure they were right in front of her window then she flung open the drapes and let out an inhuman blood-curdling scream. On seeing her horrific green face and hearing sounds that made their skin crawl, the startled children screamed and ran, falling over each other, trying to get away from her. She opened the front door and stood with arms stretched out and let out another scream that sent the children running down the dirt road falling over and into each other, screaming and crying for their mothers. With her lame cat on her lap, she sat on her porch and laughed for an hour, loving every minute of the torment she imposed on the innocent, scared children.

It was Saturday night and something interesting always happened on Saturday nights in Buttermilk Bottom. Three strangers came in the juke joint. People were on guard this time, just in case there was trouble. A few of the men with guns positioned themselves around the room so that if the strange men tried something, they would be ready to disarm them. Someone went into the kitchen and told Johnny about the strangers. He came out to monitor the situation along with Cripple Jake. The men ordered a bottle of liquor a piece then ordered platters of food from the kitchen. Suddenly, the strangers saw the men standing around the room, quietly watching them.

"What d' fuck is dis?" one of the strangers asked.

"You niggers' sho' actin' kinda funny," the other stranger said.

"I thought dis wuz suppose t' be a friendly place," the first stranger said.

"Look. All we wanna do is spend some money 'n have some fun," the third man said, looking at the serious faces around them.

"Where's your money?" Johnny asked.

One of the men smiled and put his hand inside his pocket. The men were ready if he produced a gun. He drew out a hand full of cash and placed it on the bar. It had to be over five hundred dollars in the pile. Everyone was shocked seeing that much money at one time.

The stranger said, "Shit, dat's jes what I got 'n dat pocket," and he pulled out another handful from his other pocket.

"Do you know how to play poker?" Jake asked.

"Sho' do. Dat's why we came here," the first stranger said, smiling.

"Where's all dem women y'all suppose t' have?"

"I'll call 'em," Luther said, wanting to do anything he could to get his hands on some of that cash for Queenie.

As it turned out the three men had just robbed a bank and got away with several thousand dollars. They sat down to play cards and lost most of the money in a matter of days. The rest they spent on women, food, and alcohol. For almost three weeks, they roomed at the juke joint, paying ridiculous amounts of money for the royal treatment. For a short time, they were the talk of Buttermilk Bottom, big spenders that everyone loved and wanted to take advantage of. When the money ended so did the attention. The three strangers left smiling and broke, leaving Buttermilk Bottom rich by several thousand dollars.

The police began asking questions about the sheriff and discovered that he was the most elusive man in the world with the characteristics of a clever ghost. Only his closest friends knew his real name, and they could not find any of them. They searched everywhere to no avail. By the time they got to Cameron's apartment, they found Cripple Jake occupying it, ready with stories and beer for his friends in blue. When the bad detective asked for a description of the sheriff, there were too many discrepancies. He was tall, short, light-skinned, and very dark. He was fat and skinny. Some said he was very muscular while other said he was nothing but skin and bones. As for the group, he commanded; nobody knew anything about them.

The police even questioned the children about the sheriff, since each of them saw him differently; their descriptions were just as varied as their parents were. Being children of the Bottom, they knew better than to give the police any information about anyone who lived in their neighborhood, especially the teenagers in Tony's peer group.

"Mama, the police tried to make us tell them about the Sheriff," he said to Queenie.

"They did?"

"Yeah. We didn't tell 'em nuthing. They cain't scare us. We got rights. The white man ain't gonna boss us around."

"Tony, you stay away from the police. You and your friends better stay out of trouble."

"We ain't doing nuthin' bad. We were jes sittin' 'round talkin'."

"You mind your own business and stay away from those cops."

"They were trying to git us to rat on Sheriff. We ain't gonna do that, not in a million years."

"Look, you take care of yourself. Sheriff can take care of his own damn self. . . He's real good at doing that. So, stay out of it and stay out of trouble," she yelled.

"But Mom . . ."

"But nothing. You take care of your own business and leave the Sheriff to take care of his. Now, get out of here and leave me alone," she yelled. "You worry more about that damn number man than you do your own mother."

"It's true then."

"What?"

"You and the Sheriff broke-up."

"Who told you that?"

"I hear things."

"Well, don't worry about my business. You just keep your little narrow ass out of trouble. Now, get out of here."

Tony went where he always went when he was confused, to Cora Lee and Addie Mae.

"It's true," Cora Lee said. "But don't fault nobody, 'cause d' heart is d' only thang on dis earth dat cain't be controlled."

"But didn't he love my mama?"

"No, not like she wanted, but he wuz honest wit her and dat's all you kin ask of a man."

"That's sad."

"It's jes life, boy. Your mama gonna find what she's lookin' fo' as soon as she stop tryin' t' make d' world d' way she wants it. . . 'Stead o' d' way it is," Cora Lee said.

"Here," Addie Mae said, placing a large bacon, lettuce, and tomato sandwich in front of Tony. "You gotta be hungry."

The children and youth of Buttermilk Bottom ran around the sunken community like a herd of wild horses, galloping from one area of the neighborhood to the other. In keeping with the tradition of minding everybody's business, the children carried gossip from one household to the other. At age sixteen, Tony and his group burst into the juke joint to tell everyone that a fight was about to start. All the customers ran outside, not to stop the fight, but to watch it. It was Friday night in Buttermilk Bottom, which meant that anything could and would happen, and it did. The neighbors watched attentively as a man and a woman came out of the juke joint arm-in-arm to discover that the man's wife was standing by his car with a baseball bat in her hand.

"What d' hell you doin' here?" the husband asked, not noticing that his wife had broken the window on the passenger side, waiting for him to appear. Neither of the three lived in The Bottom, but the man came every weekend with his female friend to dance, gamble, and have fun at Queenie's.

The wife yelled back, "I wanna know what you doin' here wit dat bitch?"

"Go home, Mattie. I'll talk t' you when I git home," he said, taking a step toward the car with his girlfriend still on his arm. The angry wife lifted the bat high in the air, over her head and smashed the front windshield. "What da fuck you doin'?" the man yelled.

"Fuckin' up yo' car. . . Dat's what I'm doin'."

Moving away from him, she smashed the other window on the passenger side. As he chased her around the car, more people gathered to see the spectacle. With her husband close behind, she smashed the rear window and ran to the front of the car where she broke both headlights. For a moment, he stood there in shock. When all the windows were broken, she started hitting the body of the car with the baseball bat, placing dents, wherever she slammed the bat. The man chased her around the car several times until he finally caught up with her and snatched the bat from her hand.

"You 'n yo bitch ain't ridin' in dis car," the wife yelled. "Ya limp dick mutherfucker."

The man was completely enraged and swung the bat, as if he was playing baseball and smashed it across his wife's leg, making her scream out in complete agony.

"Fuck you," she yelled, falling against the car.

He raised the bat again, hitting her on the other leg, and she crumbled to the ground. People watched in horror and disbelief but nobody moved. Everyone could see the fiery rage on the man's face, as he growled something unintelligible. He lifted the bat high over his head while standing angrily over the fallen woman with her legs crumbled underneath her. As he was about to lower the bat on top of the woman's head, Cameron snatched the bat away from him. The man turned to hit the number man but Cameron intercepted it. The number man pulled out his pistol and hit the man up side his head, knocking him out cold.

Slowly, Cameron turned to the crowd angrily and ordered, "Somebody call an ambulance for this woman," as he kneeled down to help her. He placed his jacket under her head then he ordered someone to go get a blanket. He walked over to the unconscious man lying on the ground and spits out, "Get this piece of shit out of here."

The man's girlfriend ran up to the number man and yelled, "What you do dat fo'? She started it."

Cameron stopped and turned around; his eyes burned the woman where she stood as he towered angrily over her. "It was only a car. She's a human being for Christ's sake," he said, pointing at the fallen woman. "Now, you get out of here and take this piece of shit with you," he yelled, pointing at the man. "And don't come back, ever."

Chapter 28

Everyone was on alert for the police, who were busy looking for the man referred to as 'the Sheriff'. They had the roads blocked, and the houses searched, taking every precaution to make certain that no one could get in or out without their detection. The people who lived in Buttermilk Bottom knew how to get around the police and anyone else who would forbid them the freedom of moving in and out of their own community. There were ways to move in and out of Buttermilk Bottom without detection and those who needed to come and go did so without interference or detection by the police.

Cameron was in Buttermilk Bottom when the police posted the stakeouts and started their search teams. Hot on 'the sheriff's' trail, Detective Bailey Lee gave instructions to the officers he recruited.

"I know that d' person we're lookin' for ain't no ordinary nigger that you meet on d' streets. This man is cagey and well informed. I know because I kin feel his presence as I walk around dis filthy-ass place." The detective's career depended on finding this man and nothing on earth would stop him from getting a scapegoat for the alleged crime of murder. "Murder is what we're dealing with, and I have enough experience to know that. Police officers would not just disappear without a hint of what happened to them or their car. Something sinister happened here and this man is the ringleader. I can feel it in my guts, and I have fifteen years of experience to prove it."

When the word circulated that Cameron was getting married, and that the object of his affection was the voodoo woman's beautiful black daughter, Queenie became enraged, breaking furniture, throwing objects all over the house. She even cursed out old man Luther and Dellah, who were her most devoted followers. She became so depressed that she refused to talk to anyone as she retreated to her bed, crying and refusing to eat or drink anything. No one could approach her much less talk to her. Her son was upset and so afraid that he went to Cora Lee for help. He had never seen his mother that distraught.

When the detective and the police officers reached the juke joint in their search for the elusive 'sheriff', they started a room-by-room search, overlooking nothing. When the police reached Queenie's darkened room, she was laying on the bed crying. She sat upright when the police entered her quarters without knocking.

"What the fuck is going on around here?" she demanded.

Looking around the elaborately decorated room, the officers knew her, and said, "Sorry, Ms Queenie. We're looking fo' d' man they call 'the sheriff' Do you know anything about him?" Fire and jealousy consumed her, and she was about to speak when the old man entered the room, holding her tongue with his steely eye-to-eye gaze.

"Who?" she muttered, looking at Luther. He had a determined look on his face.

"We're lookin' fo' someone called 'd' sheriff'," the policeman repeated. "We have t' search ev'ry room and ev'ry crack in Buttermilk Bottom."

"Queenie ain't been feelin' well gentlemen, she been under d' weather. Go ahead and search but please allow her t' lay down, quiet like and rest, please." Luther's eyes never left Queenie's.

The police searched every corner of the room as old man Luther, who had been silent during her affair with Cameron, eased over to Queenie and whispered, "It's over, let him go. He's in love wit someone else." She began to cry deep and mournfully for a love that she knew was never hers. It was a love that she knew she would miss and crave for the rest of her life.

Cameron found that he was playing cat-and-mouse with the police, dodging all their traps and had literally walked around their stakeouts. He knew there would be a time when he had to face the bad detective, but he also knew that he had to win. He had one advantage. The detective did not know who he was and in addition to that, his friends kept him informed so that he knew who and where the policemen were at all times.

Feeling that he needed to give Noitop an explanation about his living arrangements with her daughter, Cameron went to Noitop's house and was surprised to find her waiting for him with the door opened. Knowing that the police were close by, she waved him inside. He sat in the kitchen for several minutes before the police knocked at the door. Not wanting to cause his future mother-in-law any trouble, he exited her house.

Before he left, she said, "You must face that detective. It is inevitable that you meet. What you have to do is choose where and when that will be." She kissed him on the cheek and said. "My daughter loves you and I know you love her. Your future is set, all you have to do is to get pass this hurdle, and you will be home free forever. No one can do this for you, and no one can help you. God be with you." She kissed him on the cheek and pressed in his hands a bag of black powder. He looked at it.

"What is this?" he asked.

"Let's just say, it's a gift. It can render a cow unconscious for at least six hours. All you have to do is give it to a person in a drink, or you can blow it in their face." He smiled and gave her a big hug before he left.

Cameron went back to his old apartment where Jake was sitting on the porch waiting with Johnny. Cameron saw the crazy detective from where they were sitting. They had already searched his whole apartment building, so he felt relatively safe, but Noitop's words haunted him. He knew he could leave Buttermilk Bottom at anytime, but he wanted the situation and the circumstances around them settled.

You have to choose the place and the time, he heard Noitop's words to him. He looked at Jake thoughtfully and said, "Tell that bad ass detective that I'll meet him behind the juke joint tomorrow night at midnight."

Cameron waited for the appointed time after a brief meeting with his men's group. He knew that the detective would not play fair so he had his men watch the detective and his crew of police officers over the next twenty-four hours. At nine o'clock, police officers started coming in and posting themselves on rooftops and in windows where the rear yard would be in plain view. Cameron knew that as soon as he showed his face, they would shoot him dead. He waited and plotted his revenge.

It was finally sinking in Queenie's brain that Cameron was lost to her forever. She knew that she was no competition for the hauntingly beautiful dark woman he had chosen over her and the school principal. What's more, the woman looked like someone she may have liked as a friend, but she knew that it was impossible because her feelings for Cameron were too strong. She sat in the corner of the large parlor for the first time in several days. The tears stopped flowing but the feelings of abandonment and sadness were still there. She knew that most people pitied her, but she did not care. Thankfully, the place was empty when she descended the stairs. It was too early but by the time seven o'clock came around, the place would be jammed with fun-seeking customers.

Cripple Jake came in and purchased six sodas and six beers.

"What you gonna do wit all this? Plannin' a party wit some young girls somewhere?" Luther asked, laughing.

"Something like that. Could you put them in the icebox? I need you to keep them real cold."

"Sho' nuff, I'll take care of it," Luther said.

"I don't need them until tomorrow. Moses will pick them up. We're going fishing early Sunday morning."

"These fish got two legs?" Luther asked with a smile on his face."

"They sure do."

Luther laughed and asked, "What you drinkin'?"

"I'll take a beer for now," Jake said.

"Okay," Luther placed the beer on the bar and went in the back room.

"Queenie, how about a beer? My treat," Jake asked.

"Hey, Jake. No thank you," she said, despondently.

"You still mooning over Cameron," he said, strolling over to where she was sitting, placing his crutches under his chair in one smooth move.

"What the fuck you got to do with it?" she snapped.

"I'm just surprised that a woman as fine as you are. . . . Is wasting your time crying over some nigger who doesn't want you."

"I wish everybody around here would stay out of my fucking business," she shouted, lighting a cigarette.

"That's hard to do, because everybody loves you, Queenie, and we don't like seeing you unhappy," he said seriously.

"It's hard not to be unhappy when you lost as much as I have."

"What you have left is a lot of people who love you, and you still have old man Luther. He loves the ground you walk on, and you know that."

"He can never give me what Cameron gave me."

"What's that?"

She laughed and blew smoke out of her mouth as hard as she could. "You just wouldn't understand." She smiled, remembering.

"How do you know? Try me."

She looked at him seriously for a moment then decided to tell him the truth. "Well, let's just say. . . Old Luther is particular where he puts his mouth."

"What?" She lowered her head and looked at him in a naughty way, smiling in the corner of her mouth. "Oh, I see," Jake said.

"Do you really see?" she asked. "Cameron was an artist when it came to a woman's body. It is rare to find a man who knows how to love a woman completely, not just the act of loving but the mood, the feeling, the touching and the kissing. It all has to come together just so. . . In order for it to be right. Cameron knew how to love a woman. He did it with his eyes, his smile, his fingers, and God bless him for his soft sweet lips," she said, letting out a big breath of air. "I was in the business for years, and I know that kind of loving doesn't grow on trees. Lord knows, I'm gonna miss that man."

There was a long silence between them. Then Jake said what was on his mind. "How do you know that Cameron is the only man who can satisfy you?"

"What?"

"How do you know?" he said seriously. "You never gave me a chance."

"You?" she looked away, laughing.

"There you go again," he said, hurt by her attitude because he wanted her.

"Jake, what are you talkin' about?"

"You've been around, you know damn well what I'm talkin' about. You make the mistake most women make when it comes to me. I'm crippled, so I can't possibly know anything about satisfying a woman."

"I never said that," she retorted.

"No. . . But you constantly turned me down."

"The girls like you, Jake. You have a good reputation with them."

"There's a good reason for that. . . I know what I'm doing," he said.

"I always wondered if they were lying about you," she said, looking at him, appreciating for the first time how handsome he was.

"Don't you want to find out?"

"Not really."

"I think you do. What the old man won't do for you, I do extremely well."

"Jake, you are crazy. Get out of here," she said, looking at him differently.

"If you need what I can give you. . . Call me. Check out your girls, you don't hear them complaining, do you? The only thing that doesn't work on me is these legs."

"I'll admit that I've been wondering about what you do with them. They don't do much talkin' about you, but they do an awful lot of whispering."

"There's nothing to talk about when you get what you need. If you decide to try me, I'll be close by waiting for you to give me a chance. I've waited for you this long. I can wait another day, or week, or year, if I have to, because you're worth it to me," he said seriously. He finished drinking his beer, staring at her the whole time then got up on his crutches and left.

As soon as Jake left the building, Queenie felt a warm stirring in her body and could not believe Cripple Jake caused it. She called Dellah and Azalene downstairs.

"Come here. I want to ask you both something."

"You want us, Queenie?" Azalene asked.

"I sure do. Both of you have been with Jake, right?"

The girls started grinning, "Yeah, sure. Did he ask for both of us t'night?" they asked anxiously.

"Both of you?"

"Yeah," Dellah said. "We done it many times. . . . And it wuz fun."

"You mean to tell me, he can handle two women?" They both laughed and shared a private joke. "Well, what is it?" Queenie asked.

"If he had an extra tongue, he could handle a couple mo'," Azalene said, laughing and slapping her friend on the back in a teasing friendly manner.

"You don't say?"

"Yeah, we say. Did he axe fo' both of us t'night?" Dellah asked anxiously.

"No. I was thinking about checking him out. I been kinda bad off these days, I need a 'treatment' for myself."

"Well, it's 'bout damn time you started livin' agin," Azalene said, slapping her hand against Queenie's.

"I tell ya one thang. . . That's a good way t' git back in d' swing o' thangs 'cause dat cripple man gots a Johnson on him, and he knows how t' move those hips of his," Dellah said.

"I always thought you like going with him because he paid you such good tips," she said, making them both laugh.

"Oh, he gives us good tips. But, he don't have t'. . . When we ain't busy, we gives him freebies, 'cause he knows a lot o' thangs. . . 'Bout women," Dellah whispering as Luther came into the room.

"Sometimes, we jes' wanna relax wit somebody who knows what dey's doin' and Jake knows exactly how t' give us what we needs," Azalene said, laughing.

"Everything?" Queenie asked.

"Yeah, girl, ev'rythang plus some. He wore both o' us out last week. I wuz so tired I couldn't move fo' hours. I love's it when he stays over night," Dellah volunteered.

"We have us a ball," Azalene said, hitting her friend's arm playfully.

"My legs wuz so sore I couldn't walk last week. You r'member, Queenie, when you kept askin' me what wuz wrong wit me?"

"You mean?"

"Dat's right. Jake wore my ass. . . Out," she said, jumping up and down, laughing with her friend.

On the West Side of town, Grace Talbert retreated to her bed, crying for the love denied to her by a weird twist in her unlucky life. She could not understand how such a tragedy could have happened to her. The news about Cameron's love life that did not include her was shocking and left her without enough energy to complete the simplest of tasks. The day Cameron left, closing the door behind him, she fell to the floor and cried until she fell asleep then crawled to her bed and stayed there, only getting out to find a scotch bottle or to go to the bathroom. For days, she refused to leave her bedroom, answer the door, or talk to anyone on the telephone. She was to report to school the second week of August, but she called in sick. Two weeks later, she still had not returned to work. School opened the first week of September, and she needed to be at school to prepare for the upcoming school year. Whenever the telephone rang, she refused to answer it and when she heard a persistent knocking on the door and the doorbell ranging at the same time, she got up to see who was there and always found Horace or her old friend, Carrie standing on her porch. Not wanting to see either of them, she went back to bed. Nothing mattered any more as she lay in bed feeling hurt and sorry for herself, trying to figure out why Cameron did not love her. When she thought about how honest and harsh his words were when he told her that he loved someone else, she would take another drink and cry herself to sleep, wishing that she could start all over again. If she could, she would never complain about anything he did or where he chose to live. She would sleep with him anywhere if he would only take her back and love her as only he could. Knowing she would never love him again, she began to drink heavily, and she continued to drink until she passed out. The harsh reality she had to face was that the only place her love for Cameron could exist was in her dreams.

Chapter 29

A week before the teachers was due to report to work, Grace still had not returned. Most of the scheduling and reports that she was expected to do were completed by Horace, and her secretary, but time was running short, and Grace needed to be on the job if she expected to retain her position as principal. Feeling he had no choice, Horace went by Grace's house as he had done many times before, but this time, he was determined to get inside, one way or another. When he arrived, she was still refusing to answer the telephone or the door, so he felt he had no choice but to break the window and crawl inside. The house was quiet and dark at eleven o'clock in the morning because the shades were still down. His heartbeat was out of control because he feared what he might find. He looked around the house and found everything in disarray, and he began to panic. Grace normally kept an immaculate house but what he saw was uncharacteristic and extremely unsettling. Cautiously, he walked into her bedroom, found it dark and totally disheveled with no sign of Grace anywhere. There were so many clothes, papers, books, and household objects covering every surface, on the bed, in the chairs, on the dressers, and the floor. He could not see a clear surface anywhere in the room. His heart raced, pounding hard against the walls of his chest. There was no trace of her.

"Grace?" he called out, but there was no response. A sense of terror and panic ripped through his body as he contemplated what could have happened to the woman he loved. Nearly hysterical, he called out again and prayed that she was alive somewhere. "Grace? Grace. . . Where are you?" he cried out with tears forming in his eyes. "Oh, God, please. . . Where are you?" He was about to turn and leave the room when he saw the clothes on the bed move. He rushed over to the bed and found the form of her shapely petite body under a pile of clothing and bed linen totally hidden from view. "Grace?" With his heart in his mouth, he called out again, "Grace?" He touched her and was relieved to discover that she was breathing normally. He began to shake her. "Grace, wake up," he said, but she did not move. Horace began to panic and shook her harder.

"What?" she uttered, annoyed that anyone was disturbing her.

"Grace. . . Wake up. For God's sake, what has happened to you?" he asked, alarmed that she was in such dire circumstances. "Grace, sit up. . . Please."

"What is it? What do you want?" she asked angrily, pushing his hands away.

"I want you to get up," he said, worried. Then he smelled her breath after stumbling over an empty liquor bottle. "You're drunk."

"So what? What are you doing in my house?" she asked. "How did you get in here?"

"Never mind. The question is. . . Why are you lying in here drinking and not coming to work? Everybody is worried about you," he yelled, releasing his frustrations.

"That's nobody's business," she said, remembering that Cameron was lost to her forever. "Get out," she yelled, pulling the covers back over her head. "Just. . . Get out!"

"Why are you doing this to yourself? You have a job to do. Why are you throwing everything away?"

"Get out," she screamed with tears flowing down her face. "Just get out of my house. . . Now."

"I'm not leaving until you tell me what the hell is going on. Sit up," he ordered, angrily. "Grace. . . Get up. Now."

She refused to move. "Leave me alone and get out of here," she screamed to the top of her voice.

Not knowing what else to do, Horace went into the bathroom and filled the tub with cold water, and he returned to her bedroom and picked her up out of bed. It shocked her that he ripped her from the comfort of her bed, stripping her of the isolation and comfort she needed since Cameron's visit. Angry at his intrusion, she began kicking and screaming in her wrinkled, alcohol-soaked, yellow flannel pajamas. Her hair looked as if no one touched it in weeks.

"Put me down, you oaf. Put me down," she screamed, trying to hit him.

"I'll put you down, alright," he said, carrying her easily into the bathroom and dumping her in the frigid bath water that made her scream louder and longer.

The sound of her screams and outrage filled the house as the cold water soaked through her pajamas, freezing her body. "How dare you?" she yelled, trying to keep the water out of her mouth.

"How dare you break in my house. . . And treat me this way? I'm going to call the police," she yelled, attempting to stand up.

"You will do no such thing," he said, pushing her back in the cold water, making her scream again as she thrashed her hands and feet, trying to get up.

"I hate you. Get out," she screamed, swinging her hands, trying to hit him but slipped backward into the cold water that made her let out another loud, blood-curdling scream.

Sitting on the edge of the tub, Horace held her head under the water while appreciating the seductive impression of her breasts showing through her wet garments. He felt his heart beating faster because her nipples were hard and stood-up, pressing through her pajama top.

"Get out and leave me alone," she yelled at the top of her voice. "Damn you, Horace. Damn you."

He pushed her head under the water again and yelled, "It's time for you to sober up and get to work. You have a job to do." He was angry that she allowed herself to fall so low. "People are depending on you."

"I'm resigning. I hate my job. . . And I hate you. Now, leave me alone," she yelled, stepping out of the cold tub, grabbing a towel as she stomped her feet and left the bathroom.

"You are not resigning. You are going to get yourself together and be at work first thing Monday morning, or so help me God. . . I will come here and drag your sorry ass out of this house," he yelled, making her stop and think.

The reality of living without Cameron flooded her mind as she attempted to think about leaving her house to live without any hope of loving him again.

"I can't do it. I can't," she cried as tears fell uncontrollably from her eyes, and her nose began to run. Not caring, she wiped her nose on her sleeve. "Please, just go away and leave me alone." She sounded pitiful and defeated.

Sensing that Grace was suffering from a broken heart, he felt empathy for her, but he could not afford to allow her to continue destroying her life and her career.

"I'm not going to leave, but you are going to take a bath and clean yourself. . . And this nasty house. On Monday, you will be sitting at your desk acting like you have some damn sense," he yelled at her. She slid down the wall in the hallway and sat on the floor, crying. "Get up and put on some dry clothes," he said, talking as if he was speaking to a small child. "Get up."

"I can't."

"You can and you will, damn you," he said, pulling her to her feet and holding her in his arms, squeezing her. He attempted to kiss her, but her bad, foul-smelling breath, reeking of alcohol, made him push her away.

"You stink. Go get a fresh set of clothes, I'll draw you a proper bath." She went into her room, sat on the edge of the bed, and held her head down, crying. Horace, seeing what bad shape she was in, went to her dresser drawer and pulled out her underwear then he went into the closet and selected a blouse and a pair of slacks. In the bathroom, he filled the tub with fresh warm water. Seeing bubble bath on the counter, he picked it up and poured some into the tub, making a mountain of fragrant bubbles. When he went back into the bedroom, Grace was laying down, curled up in the fetal position, crying.

"Oh no, you don't," he said, standing her up, undressed her then took her back into the bathroom and placed her in the hot sudsy bath. For almost ten minutes, she just sat there not moving so he picked up a washcloth and began to bathe her. It broke his heart to see her that way, but he was determined to get her on her feet and functioning again. After her bath, he helped her dress then took her into the kitchen and made her a bowl of soup, buttered a slice of bread for her and made her eat it. After brewing a pot of coffee, he poured a cup for her and one for himself then sat watching her.

She was too embarrassed to look at him, so they sat in silence while she tried to eat.

"Thank you for what you've done. I do appreciate it. You can go now," she said without looking at him.

"I'm not leaving, but you. . . Are going to get up, comb your hair and brush your teeth then clean up this nasty house of yours." She looked at him in disbelief. "That's right. I'm staying until I know you are functioning like a normal person, so you might as well relax and get use to me being around." Without any conversation, they spent the rest of the day cleaning and getting the house organized. Horace never left her side as they went from room to room cleaning. When all the work was complete and the house was back to its normal pristine condition, Horace sat down in front of the television to watch an old movie. Feeling embarrassed and depleted about her alcoholic stupor, Grace entered the room quietly and sat down on the sofa next to him. Her pitiful, hopeless stance was so out of character for her that he felt sorry for her. Seeing how exhausted she was, he reached for her and let her lay her head on his lap, within seconds she started crying.

"Are you ready to tell me what happened to you?"

"No."

After several minutes, he said, "He dumped you, didn't he?" She did not speak because she could not, the words stuck in her throat. "I'm not happy you're hurting, Grace, but I am happy he finally let you go since you couldn't let him go. You may not appreciate it now, but he did you a favor."

"How can you say that? . . . I love him," she said, wiping her tears away.

"That was the trouble. The two of you should have been in love, Grace. . . Not just you."

"I would have made him a good wife."

"How can you think of marrying someone who doesn't love you? Don't you have any pride?"

"No. I would have done anything for him, but. . . He wouldn't let me," she said with silent tears falling down her face.

"Well, I guess I can thank him for that."

"He said. . . He fell in love. . . For the first time in his life. All those years and he never loved me. . . ? Never? How could he make love to me and not love me?"

"Men are different. Let me ask you this. . . Did he ever tell you that he loved you?"

She had a severe pain rush through her body, taking a deep breath, she said, "No. . . But he loved me. He did. . . I know he did."

"Grace, you made the mistake most women make. . . Sex is not love. Sex is just sex. It has nothing to do with anything else. A man can and will have sex with a woman as long as she allows him, but love. . . That's an entirely different matter." Grace was quiet and she finally stopped crying. "You're lucky you didn't end up pregnant."

"I wanted to have his children, but he refused. He always used protection. I couldn't talk him out of it. . . When I tried, he would leave."

"Well. . . At least one of you had some sense." It made him sad to hear how much she loved him.

"Obviously, it wasn't me." After a long pause with the television, as the only noise in the room, she said, "Thank you, Horace, you saved me from losing my job. . . I don't know what I would do without my work. I know I have a lot of catching up to do. I appreciate everything you've done including breaking my window to get in here."

"Do you think that was all this was about? Your job?" he said, showing the anger he felt. She started to speak but did not because she saw that he was in pain. "I love you, Grace. I have always loved you." He looked as if he was about to cry, but he did not. He simply held his head down with his hands clasped together. He looked up then made sure he had her attention and said, "Grace, I was worried sick about you. I didn't know what to expect when I came in here, but I had to find out because I love you, and I needed to know that you were alright." He grabbed her and held her close to him, wanting to kiss her but did not.

"I am sorry I worried you. I am sorry," she said with her eyes watering again.

"I don't want you to be sorry, Grace. You needed help. . . So I helped you," he said, kissing the top on her head. "There's no shame in any of that but . . . What I did, I did out of love for you." He held her head up so that she could look into his eyes, hoping she would see all the passion he felt for her. He kissed her deeply, exploring all the precious sensations that emitted from his heart and tried to convey it to her through his lips. She was open and available to him for the first time. He could tell because her lips were more pliable and ready for his tongue as it explored the far reaches of her sweet, oral cavity. Feeling a rush of passion about to overwhelm him, he pulled away from her and said, "I think you should go to bed."

"Don't leave. . . Please, don't leave. I don't want to be alone," she begged, holding on to him.

"I'm not going anywhere, Grace. I'll be right here on the couch. Go on. . . Go to bed," he said, getting up and pushing her out of the room.

"Why don't you come with me?"

"Because if I do, I will want to make love to you, and I don't want you, unless I know you love me. I told you before. . . I want it all or nothing. I won't be second and I won't be the guy you fell back on because you couldn't get who you wanted. You have to love me for me, first. . . And only me, Grace. Those are my conditions. I love you too much to settle for less. Now. . . Go to bed. . . Please." She kissed him then went into her room thinking about his words, remembering the look on his face and admitted that he was right not to accept less as she had done for years with Cameron. Horace had the right to expect true love, and she wished that she had been that strong with Cameron. If she had, she would not be hurting as much as she was at that moment.

Grace woke up to the smell of coffee and bacon cooking. For a moment, she forgot that Horace was in the house. She quickly showered, and dressed and went into the kitchen where he sat reading the morning paper. The sight of her beautiful face standing in the doorway made him feel warm inside. To him, she was the most beautiful creature on earth, and he loved her so long he did not know exactly how he would ever function in life without her by his side. He was grateful that Cameron finally told her the truth because he knew that it would never work out the way Grace wanted it to. He knew that his infatuation with Grace was complete and that what he felt for her would last a lifetime.

"You didn't have to fix breakfast. . . I would have done that," she said, smiling and warming his heart.

"I love to cook, besides. . . I want to take care of you," he said, trying not to sound too emotional. "Now, sit down and let me serve you. I made a big pot of grits."

"Grits? I haven't had grits in years."

"Well, get use to them. They will make you stronger and put some meat on your bones."

"I have enough meat on these hips already. After this meal, I will have to run a mile to get the pounds off," she said, looking at all the food he prepared. "I would be fat as a pig if I ate like this every morning."

"Maybe so, but I wouldn't worry so much about your weight. You could stand a little rounding out," he said, looking at her with love in his eyes. "Well. . . Eat up. We have to purchase the glass and repair that window, then I'm taking you shopping for food. You don't have a thing in this refrigerator. Tonight, I'll prepare dinner for you at my house," he said, looking at her for a reaction.

When he heard no objections, he continued giving her his plans that included her spending the whole day and most of the night with him. As she sat eating the grits, eggs, toast, and bacon he prepared for her, he filled up with love for her, which he planned to express to her for the remainder of his life, giving her many pleasurable nights of lovemaking. Ultimately, he planned to feel, touch, and love every muscle on her body as he made deep passionate love to her. When he bathed her the day before, it took all his strength not to touch her in an intimate way because the sight of her naked body excited him. He thanked God that she was too out of it to notice the stiffness in his pants as he washed, dried, and clothed her. Nothing would have given him more pleasure than to take her nipples in his mouth and caress them or to touch her vagina in a loving way.

He took a deep breath and smiled at her from across the table, "How's the food?"

"Delicious, I didn't realize how hungry I was."

If you only knew how hungry I am for you, he said to himself. Taking a deep breath, he said, "Eat up. There is plenty more waiting for you." He was not referring to the food.

Chapter 30

While Grace and Horace were settling into their day, things in Buttermilk Bottom were heating up. Cameron spent time instructing his men while the police busily staged the capture of a vicious felon, whom they deemed guilty of murder without a shred of evidence. The neighbors whispered their expectations and dread regarding what they thought and hoped would happen that evening. Parents kept their children off the streets, just in case there was trouble, but the children's absence left an eeriness to the normally active neighborhood. Inside the juke joint, people spoke in whispers and the music was playing low and mellow, waiting for something to occur, but only a few trusted friends knew what was about to unfold.

On Saturday night, the trap was set with every detail planned to perfection, which the police reviewed several times during the last twenty-four hours to make certain that they would end up with an arrest or a dead body. The bad detective, Bailey Lee, felt secure because he had eight men pointing guns on the spot where he was to meet the notorious 'Sheriff of Buttermilk Bottom' as he had renamed him. Over the past forty-eight hours, the police took turns, standing-watch. Another shift was in place by nine o'clock that evening in plenty of time to keep 'the sheriff' from detecting their presence.

Cameron and his men distributed the black powder in sodas and beers and were surprised to see that the powder turned clear once mixed in the drinks. They gave the drinks to women and children in the area to give the police officers at their post. Around ten o'clock, the officers were beginning to get thirsty and the children and women of Buttermilk Bottom came to the rescue.

A child asked, "Mister, you want a soda?"

"Thanks, kid, I sho' would." The child gave the officer a tainted soda.

There were two men on Jake's roof. He gave them both beers to quench their thirst then he returned to sit on the porch where he could see the whole neighborhood. From there he knew he would not miss a thing. Other members of the community offered tainted beers and sodas to the police officers. By eleven P.M., the police officers were all sleeping soundly.

At midnight, Cameron stood back in the darkness, watching Detective Bailey pace back and forth, thinking that he had coverage for everything he planned to do. The air was still, and the night was extremely quiet. The crickets were louder than normal, and the late September air was thick and humid. The detective heard something scurry in the bushes and used his flashlight to see what it was and his flashlight hit upon the tail of what must have been a huge muskrat. He hated rats more than he hated black people. He moved around more, trying to make noise that would scare off any other possible crawlers. Hearing more noise coming from the kudzu covered bushes, he turned on his flashlight again. This time he saw a gigantic rat, the size of a small dog.

"Oh shit," he said aloud, pulling his gun out of his holster. He was about to shoot it when he thought better of it. Not wanting to foul up his well-laid plans, he stamped his feet, trying to scare it away. "Damn-it," he complained. The only light, other than his flashlight was coming from the back porch of the juke joint. He was grateful for that, but his patience was growing thin. At ten minutes, past midnight, the bad detective became very nervous. Just as he was about to call his men, Cameron appeared, stepping out of the darkness into the light, surprising the detective.

"I should've known it wuz you. You're under arrest," Detective Bailey Lee shouted.

"For what?"

"For murder," Bailey Lee said with confidence.

"Who did I murder?" Cameron asked calmly.

"I knew it wuz you. I should've seen it the first day I laid eyes on you. Fuckin' nigger, trying to stare me down. You made a fatal mistake by comin' here. Now. . . Put your goddamned hands up and turn d' fuck 'round, now," Bailey ordered.

"Who's going to make me?" The bad detective signaled for his men to fire, but nothing happened. He signaled again, nothing. His face turned white. "It seems that we are alone," Cameron said. The detective looked around where he knew he stationed men with rifles. It was too dark to detect anything.

"Shoot him," he yelled. There was no response. The detective, realizing that he had no assistance, went for his gun. Before he could pull it out, Cameron was on top of him with his gun drawn and hit the detective up side his head with the butt of his gun, drawing blood with the first blow. The detective struggled to take out his gun, but Cameron took it away from him and threw it in the kudzu.

"You black. . . Fuckin' nigger," the detective uttered.

The number writer smiled, smashing the detective again up-side his head with the butt of his gun and saying, "Don't you ever fucking forget it." At that moment, Cripple Jake, Johnny and the other men stepped into the light.

"Jake . . . Jake, take his fuckin' gun," Bailey Lee ordered, but Jake didn't move. "You boys take his fuckin' gun."

"Shut the fuck-up," Jake said to the detective who looked at Jake in shock

"And, who d' fuck you callin' boy?" Moses said, stepping closer to the downed detective. Bailey crawled backwards to get away from Moses.

"Goddamn you, Jake, I'm warning you. . . ."

"I'm warning you. . . Shut the fuck up," Jake said angrily, hitting the detective across the mouth with one of his crutches. "Yeah. . . You stupid motherfucker. If you haven't noticed, I'm black, and I live here, too," he said, then turning to Cameron, he said, "You better get out of here."

"I'm not leaving."

"Yes, you are. This is our business. We'll take care of this."

"I'm not leaving until this is finished."

"It's finished, man," Jake said. "Now get your ass out of here. We know what to do."

"You fuckin' niggers gonna to burn in d' electric chair!" The bad detective yelled. "Help! Somebody help!" One of the men hit him on the head, rendering him unconscious.

"Cameron, get out of here, now. You taught us well and we know what we have to do. Besides, you have a family at home. Get out of here," Jake urged.

Noitop was waiting on the fringes of the lighted area. "Come on, Cameron, it's time for you to leave Buttermilk Bottom. Your job here is done."

"What are you doing here?"

"Protecting my son-in-law," she said, smiling.

He looked at his friends, who were standing over the bad detective. "Go on, man, we can take care of this," Cripple Jake said, pushing him in Noitop's direction.

He smiled broadly. "Thanks," he said, hugging his best friend.

"You're welcome but we should be thanking you," Jake said. "Now, will you get your ass out of here?"

"Thanks, man," Johnny said, patting Cameron on the back.

He walked over to Noitop and placed his arms around her shoulder. "Did you know that daughter of yours can read my mind?"

"That's not all she can do," she said.

"Don't tell me there's more."

"She is capable of many things. . . But she is not ready for all that is in her power to do and know."

"Magic, huh? That sounds very mysterious."

"It is, boy. I know that my girl loves you and the male child she's carrying," she said only telling him half of the real story.

"Really? Holy shit. Really?" Noitop smiled. "When did she tell you?"

"She didn't."

"Tell me, how do you know these things?" he asked, walking to the car with his mother-in-law-to-be.

"Some people say I'm a witch," she said, making him laugh.

As soon as Noitop saw that Cameron had gotten in his car and was heading out of Buttermilk Bottom, she turned around and went back to the rear of the juke joint where Jake and his men were dragging the Detective Bailey Lee off into the kudzu-covered woods.

"Jake," Noitop called out.

Jake saw her and said, "Don't worry Miss Cigam. We'll take care of him. You can go home now."

"You can't kill him, Jake."

"The hell we can't," Jake said, and the men with him mumbled in agreement.

"If you kill him, you will bring more pain and suffering down on these people. It's time to put everything to rest."

"It will be, as soon as we kill his ass and put him where no one will ever find him."

"Jake, Cameron tells me that you are a smart man, wise beyond your years. If that is true, you must stop and think about the results of your actions." Jake silenced the men who were losing patience with the old woman. "Kill him and Buttermilk Bottom will have no peace."

"This motherfucker is going to die tonight," he said in anger, hitting the detective with one of his crutches as he began to wake up.

"There are many ways a person can die, Jake. Be smart. These men have families, and you are starting a new amazing life for the many children who will follow," she said with such certainty that she held his attention. "Jake, sometimes it's not about avoiding the storm, sometimes. . . It's about learning to dance in the rain." Realizing that he needed to vent all the anger that he held in check for so many years, Jake stared at the wise woman and took a deep breath of air. Feeling the pain of his injuries, Bailey Lee was confused, looking around him, he realized where he was and whom he was with, so he shouted, "You fucking niggers' gonna die . . ." Jake hit the detective hard with one of his crutches, eliciting a deep groan of pain from him. "Jake, take this and give it to him in water. He won't bother anyone anymore," Noitop said, handing him a small bag.

Looking in the brown paper bag at a vividly red powder, Jake said, "What's this?"

Smiling mischievously, Noitop said, "A solution to your problem."

For a few seconds, Jake evaluated their options then said, "Miss Cigam, this shit better work."

She smiled and said, "It has already. . . All you have to do is to give it to him." With that, she walked off into the darkness, leaving the men staring as she disappeared into the night.

"What the fuck is everybody standing around for? Somebody go and get a glass of fucking water," Jake yelled.

Johnny left quickly for the kitchen to get the glass of water, which he held while Jake poured half the powder in the glass.

"What d' fuck you doin', Jake? Put it all 'n there," Moses said, watching intensely.

Jake poured the remaining powder in the glass. Johnny took a spoon out of his pocket and stirred the liquid. It was bright, red, and thick with small fine bubbles forming on the top, making the men frown. The bad detective saw the men coming toward him with the liquid and tried to get away but Moses knocked him down quickly. "Hold him still and pour it down his throat," Jake said. "And. . . Hold his nose to make sure he swallows it."

With several men, holding him down, they forced Bailey Lee to drink the thick, red, blood-like liquid. When he had all of it in his body, they stood watching him.

The detective started laughing, saying, "You niggers cain't hurt me. I'm gonna string your fuckin' black asses up, hang ya upside down, and beat d' shit outta every fuckin' one o' you." A thick white liquid drooled from his mouth, making the men step back. "Go git me a rope boy. . . Go git me a fuckin' rope, damn-it," he yelled as loudly as he could while the dribble flowed heavier and thicker from his mouth and became airborne creating a scent that made the men step back from him. "I'm gonna peal d' fuckin' skin off every last one o' you black, greasy bastards. That's d' way, you gotta treat a nigger. You give me dat can of gasoline. . . We gotta git rid o' all d' fuckin' evidence." Suddenly, the detective farted loudly and lost complete control of his bowels. The men made a collective gasp and retreated as far away from the crumbling detective as they possibly could, but they were unable to look away, not sure of what they were witnessing. "Strike that damn match. . . Goddamn-it, boy. . . Burn their black asses up," the crazed detective yelled as the smelly dribble and excrement continued to ooze from his out-of-control body.

Jake could not believe his eyes or his ears as he remembered what Noitop had said about there being more than one kind of death.

"I think we can just leave him alone," Jake said to the men who were still in shock at the drastic change in the man's behavior and appearance. "Come on, let's get out of here."

"Kill dem black motherfuckers . . . Fuckin' niggers . . . Kill 'em," they heard the dead man say as they walked away into the blackness.

Around one o'clock in the morning, the men's committee walked into the juke joint with Jake and Johnny leading the pack. They were in a sober mood and wanted to hear music and laughter to take their minds off the horrific sight they had just witnessed. As soon as Jake entered the bar, the two whores came over and sat beside him as they always did. They considered themselves friends of Jake's, and they had turned enough tricks for the night to 'pay the rent', so they were out for fun and laughter, knowing that Jake could give them what they both needed. Jake smiled knowing that he needed their company more than ever.

"Where d' hell you been?" Luther asked.

Looking at his co-conspirators, Jake laughed and said, "Dancing in the rain."

"It ain't raining," Luther said.

"You're right, not anymore," Jake said. "Give everybody a drink."

When Jake attempted to pay for it, the old man said, "It's been taken care of." The men were all drinking beer and whiskey with the money Cameron left with Luther with instructions to pour until they fell on the floor.

"By who?" Jake asked.

"A friend."

"Would that friend be our friendly number writer?"

"It could be."

"He's too much. Shit, if he's buying. . . Give these ladies whatever, they want."

"Thanks, Jake," the two whores said together.

"Cora Lee stayed late to fix you men some grub. All you gots to do is let me know when you want it. She went t' bed 'cause it wuz a slow night. I'll fix it when you's ready."

Jake looked at Johnny, who spoke up quickly, "I'll serve the men, Luther. Don't worry about a thing. You keep those drinks coming, and I'll take care of the kitchen."

"We have a very good friend looking out for us," Moses said, toasting his drink to his friends, who did the same thing.

"Yep, you sho' do," the old man had to admit.

As the men completed their meal and sat around sharing stories, Johnny came over and cleared the table, removing empty liquor glasses and beer bottles that their friend had treated them to. As Jake was about to pour another glass of vodka, Queenie came down the steps, dressed in a smart burgundy suit. Jake put his glass down when he saw her. Nothing was as sexy as Queenie walking down those steps. She smiled at him, but he was not sure what it meant so he continued his usual jive with the boys.

From the opposite end of the room, Queenie observed Jake closely. He was a handsome man. In fact, he was much better looking than his best friend was, but he was a cripple. What Cameron had was good looks and a big strong healthy body to match. Jake had a perfectly muscular body until you looked down at his legs.

"You hear the one about the old bull and the young bull?"

"I don't remember that one, Jake," Moses said, laughing already.

"The young bull galloped over to the old bull all out of breath, seeing the pasture full of cows, and he got all excited about the fact that he would be allowed for the first time to service the cows. You know what service means, right?" Jake asked. When a few men looked confused.

He said bluntly, "Fuck them." The men all laughed. "The young bull said to the old bull, 'Wow, look at all those beautiful cows. Why don't we run down the hill and fuck one of them?' The old bull looked seriously at the young bull and laughed, shaking his head, he said, 'You got a lot to learn son. Why don't we just walk down there and fuck all of them?'"

The room full of men laughed hard, enjoying their camaraderie, giving Jake the response he needed. The old man gave Jake another vodka, which he drank quickly. He saw Queenie staring at him out of the corner of his eye and wondered if he was imagining things. Maybe she had listened to him when he spoke to her about giving him a chance to prove himself. Getting excited over Queenie became a full-time job that he wanted to get rid of so he ignored her.

Jake told a few more, old jokes then sat down to play cards with the rest of the men. They had taken care of the problem as they had promised Cameron because as they saw with their own eyes the detective was no more, thanks to Noitop Cigam. The police officers on the roof were asleep and according to Cameron, they would sleep until four or five o'clock in the morning, by then everyone would be home in bed.

As soon as Queenie saw Jake heading up the steps with Pearl, and Dellah, she said, "How about a light, Jake?"

"I don't smoke."

"I have matches on the bar. Why don't you get one for me?"

"I think somebody wants you, Jake," Pearl whispered knowingly.

Jake was not going to make it easy for her, so he said, "If you can't light them, you don't need to smoke them," he said, continuing up the steps with Pearl.

Queenie not wanting to be out done said, "Pearl, come here, baby. I have something I need you to do for me."

Hating to leave Jake's side, Pearl reluctantly went to see what Queenie wanted. "Yes, Miss Queenie?"

"Take Jake to my bedroom and turn down the covers. Will you do that for me?"

"Yes, ma'am, I sho will," Pearl said, grinning at Jake and took him by the arm to escort him upstairs. Jake looked back at Queenie unsmilingly. Queenie smiled broadly and said, "Jake, I'll be right up. Dellah, would you ask Cora Lee to prepare a late breakfast for us. I'll call down when we're ready to eat."

"Miss Cora went t' bed, but I'll tell her first thing in the morning." Dellah said, smiling and leaving Jake's side.

Johnny said, "Come on. Dellah, sit down and help us celebrate."

The men in the room looked at Queenie then looked at Jake.

"What d' fuck's goin' on 'round here," Moses asked.

"Don't ask me. I don't even wanta know," Johnny said.

Ignoring the men's comments, Queenie said, "I'll be up in a minute, Jake, as soon as I close up. Gentlemen, we're closed."

"You putting us out, Queenie?"

"I sure am. Good night, gentlemen."

As the men filed out of the building, Luther cleared the ashtrays and glasses from the bar angrily not hiding his feelings regarding Queenie's rudeness and for what she was about to do with Jake.

"Have you gone crazy, woman?" Luther asked.

"I don't know. I'll let you know in the morning."

"You gon sleep wit a cripple man?" the old man asked, not believing his eyes or ears.

"Yes sir. I wanna find out what all the fuss is about."

"You ain't got to sleep wit him to find out," he said.

"Look, old man, you go home to your wife every night except Fridays, Saturdays, and Sunday. I haven't had any sex for months, and I need what I need. You know you aren't going to give it to me. So, don't get high and mighty with me. I have to take care of my personal business."

"What about us, Queenie?"

"We're still cool. If you want me, you can have me. At least this time, I'm not in love. But right now, you know what I want so let me go get it before I go crazy around here."

"Queenie?" She paused on the stairway. "I still love you," Luther said.

"I love you, too," she said honestly, giving him a broad, beautiful smile.

"Queenie, when can I see you?"

"Tomorrow is fine. I'm available."

Dellah, Azalene, and Pearl overheard the conversation and remained quiet until Queenie was well out of ear range. Dellah said, "Looks like you need to go in the kitchen and git you some nutmeg and make you a love potion."

"That shit don't work," Luther said, disgusted.

"It worked for me," Azalene said. "And I know what I'm talkin' bout."

"That's what dat crazy ass Lucille said, but the shit don't work," Luther said, cleaning the bar.

"You must've done somethin' wrong," Azalene said.

"I put it in her shoe, but nuthin' happened," Luther said.

"That ain't all you's suppose to do, fool. You have t' put it in her shoe for one-week everyday at twelve noon, then you suppose to put it in her shoe every night at midnight. The shit works. . . 'Cause dat's how I got my last husband and kept him til I got tired of his broke ass."

"I ain't got time to put no nutmeg in her shoe every night at midnight. Hell, I'm a gambler. At midnight, I'm makin' money. I ain't leavin' no game to shake no nutmeg in nobody's damn shoe."

"Dat's why you ain't got Queenie. . . You loves gambling 'n money mo' than you loves Queenie."

Chapter 31

That night when Cameron arrived home, Jazmine was waiting by the window, watching him as he got out of the car. Before he could put his key in the lock, she had opened the door.

"Thank God, you're alright."

"Thank God, I have you to come home to," he said, pulling her into his arms.

"Come with me. I have your bath ready. You need to relax and forget about everything."

"Your mother saved my life tonight."

"She wants to make sure that you marry me and take me off her hands." He looked at her seriously with concern in his eyes. "She told you, didn't she? I'm fine," she said, smiling.

"Are you sure?"

"Yes, I'm pregnant, happy, and doing just fine now that I have you in my arms."

"We're having a child?"

"Well, darling, let's just say that we are expanding our little family," she said, realizing that her mother did not tell him everything.

"Thank you for loving me and giving me what I never knew I wanted. I can't tell you what this means to me."

"You just did. Now, take your clothes off and bathe before I rape you."

When Queenie walked into her quarters, she saw that the bed was ready with Jake in the middle of it, reclining against the many pillows with the lights turned low. The muscles of his body showed up vividly even in the subdued light. There was a bottle of wine on the table with two glasses. "Where did all of this come from?" she asked.

"From my heart," Jake said. "If I had known, there would have been flowers too."

"Well, if you can do what you say you can do. . . I like roses."

When she started to unbutton her jacket, Jake said, "Let me do that." Her eyes sparkled. "Come here. I'm crippled, remember?" She slid onto the bed and started to take off her shoes. "Leave them on," he said in a husky voice that surprised her. As soon as she was on the bed, Jake took over. He pulled her easily over to him and started unbuttoning her jacket slowly. He clinched his teeth as he revealed her breasts, appreciating the way they pushed their way out of the burgundy lace bra she was wearing. He had never seen such beautiful underwear on a woman. He lifted her up, unfastened her skirt, and slipped it down over her hips. Before taking her shoes off, he admired her legs, running his hands along her inner thigh, then in one swift move, he pulled her panties and stocking off along with her shoes. His strength shocked and surprised her. She was a healthy woman, but she felt as if she weighted ninety-nine pounds instead of two hundred and thirty.

When all her clothes were off, he laid her in his arms, as if she was a baby and started kissing her on her nose, cheeks, and eyelids. Then he did what no man had ever done to her, he put both his hands in her perfectly styled hair, massaging her scalp and stroking through it as if it were gold, noticing details, as if he was committing everything to memory. With his lips, he traced the shape of hers and kissed her briefly but gently.

Caressing her breasts, he was in heaven as he traced her body down to her hairy mound, which was soft and curly. Placing his finger inside her warm cavern, he began to kiss her copiously and intensely on the lips. The sensation made her body rise, aching for more attention. Jake used his tongue in a slow darting motion to entice her into needing closer contact. Loving the feel of his lips on hers, she elevated her head to kiss him harder, but he retreated. Looking in his eyes, she wondered if he was teasing her. Just as she was about to speak, he smothered her in a deep penetrating kiss, which seemed to last forever, yet not long enough.

She opened her eyes to see him staring pensively at her body. Sliding down in the bed, he cuddled both her breasts at one time, kissing and rubbing them until they hardened, setting off a blaze inside her that made her want him to rush. Enjoying the feel, size and taste of her breasts, he began to moan sweetly as he trashed his tongue in every conceivable

direction over their round shapeliness. Stopping abruptly, he used his
strong hands to massage her body and her back while kissing her sides
and navel. He kissed her thighs, giving both long sinuous strokes. Gently
spreading her legs apart, he used his finger to examine her clitoris and
the layers of fleshy tissue inside. Feeling, observing, and stroking every
part, as if he was in a science class, he placed his middle finger inside
her moist opening, he kissed the crown of her womanhood, eliciting a
deep cleaning sigh from her body. In a leisurely and expert manner, he
made love to the center of her universe, filling her with hunger, making
her want more of him until her body bolted out of control. She tried to
push him away so she could give him pleasure, but he was not finished.
Pushing her back down, he continued to kiss her sweetness until she had
to beg him to stop. When he rose up to mount her, she saw what he had
been bragging about, an oversized fully-erect penis that curved upward,
standing at attention.

"My God, Jake," she said not able to withhold her reaction. "You
have your own cork-screw down there."

"I told you I had what you needed," he said.

With that, he entered her while pulling her on top of him. After he was
fully inserted, he began pushing and trashing his hips until she moaned.
After several exquisite minutes, he pulled her down on her side, entered
her from the back, and proceeded, to give her the best 'treatment' she
ever had. He was deep inside her where she could feel all the muscles in
her aroused canal sing out in praise. Then using the top of the headboard
to balance himself, he pulled her body across the bed where her pillows
usually sat and made love to her hard and fast. It did not take much more
of his wonderful aerobics for her body to shiver and shake climaxing
for what seemed like hours. Feeling her give in to him, he joined her
in the most sexually physical and emotional climax in his life. They
both lay wet and exhausted on the mattress. The sheets, pillows and the
bedspread were on the floor. As she was relaxing, he reached on the side
of the bed, grabbed a washcloth, and gently began to clean her up. He
wrung the cloth out and cleaned her again. Then he took care of himself
with another cloth and lay back holding her in his arms.

"Jake. . . That was wonderful. How do you know so much about a
woman's body?"

"I read a lot."

"Please, don't ever stop reading," she said, kissing him on the
mouth.

"You'll be surprised what you can learn. It helps you understand how to have good sex with a woman like you."

"Like what?" she asked still breathing hard.

"Like this little thing here," he said, feeling her clitoris. "It has only one function, and that is to give you pleasure."

"It certainly does that," she said, enjoying the stimulation.

"It's small but it's just like a man penis. It gets hard and erect. It should get the same attention as a penis. That's why I spend so much time taking care of it. It's your center," he said, continuing to caress her.

"You need to teach this stuff, 'cause other men think that just putting their little dicks in and moving up and down will do it."

"That's because they don't know anything about the female body and its parts. Each part has a function, knowing that helps me. . . Help you come and come and come," he said, kissing her deeply. "I want to show you something," he said.

"What?" he placed her hands on his penis; it was hard as a rock.

"Jake," she said, looking at him in surprise.

He looked like he was in physical pain. "I always need to do it twice. I hope you don't mind as he placed a rubber fuzzy ring around his penis.

"What the hell is that thing?"

He looked at her and smiled naughtily, noticing the deep breaths she took, making her breasts rise and fall erotically. "It's called a pussy tickler," he whispered.

"A what?"

He placed his finger on her lips to silence her, "Don't worry. You'll love it," he said, sliding down under the covers.

As the sun rose in the sky, the police officers on the rooftops began to wake-up, each realizing that they fell asleep on the job, leaving them embarrassed and ashamed. No one admitted to their co-workers that they had fallen asleep. It was daybreak when they looked down and saw the detective sitting on the ground with several dead rats around him while he sat cursing and spitting out racial slurs. His language was so vile that everyone around him was embarrassed. The police surveillance officers came down from the rooftops to see what was wrong with the detective and were shocked to see him in such a filthy, putrid condition. The odor was so inhibiting that none of the officers would go near him. They called for emergency medical assistance and waited around to ponder what had happened to the once ruthless and highly ambitious detective.

Cora Lee and Addie Mae got up early that morning to start their kitchen chores and Johnny made it his business to get up, knowing he had some unfinished business to complete. Cora Lee was about to put the coffeepot on the stove when he arrived in the kitchen. While waiting for the coffee to perk, Johnny sat down at the kitchen table watching the ladies as they prepared breakfast.

"Fucking niggers." The offensive sound soared through the air and into their peaceful morning. "Hit dat black mutherfucker, hit 'em."

The women looked at each other then at Johnny, who looked as if he was just as baffled as they were. They all went to the window to look out and found uniformed police officers standing around the crazed detective as he ranted and raved on the ground, sitting in the midst of dead rodents.

"Catch dat black motherfucker," the detective said, thrashing about the ground like a mad man. "Shoot dat black son-of-a-bitch's ass," he shouted.

"What's going on out there?" Cora Lee opened the back door and asked the police officers.

"Looks like the detective had a nervous breakdown or something," one of the officers said, scratching his head.

"Kill dat black bitch," the detective yelled, pointing his finger at Cora Lee.

"What's he doin' in our yard?" she asked.

"He was on a special assignment. Nobody knows what happened t' em, looks like he's gone crazy or somethin'," the officer said.

"Whatever he did, you needs t' git him out here b'fore Miss Queenie wakes up."

"What's dat stankin' smell?" Addie Mae asked.

"Looks like Detective Lee had an accident," the officer said.

"Accident? That man's done shitted all ov'r hisself," Addie Mae said. "My Lord, hurry up 'n git him outta here."

"A wagon's coming t' pick him up. Here it comes now," the officer said, pointing at an ambulance backing towards the rear yard.

"D' sooner d' better," Cora Lee said, going back into the house and closing the door. Before she could close the door, an officer knocked.

"If it's not too much trouble, kin we have a cup o' your coffee, Cora Lee?"

"Did you put yo' hands on dat man?"

"No, Ma'am," he said too loudly. "No, I didn't."

"I'll give ya some coffee, but you ain't brangin' dat smell in my kitchen," she said, handing him a few cups. "Addie Mae, sit dat pot out on d' back porch."

"We gotta boil dat pot 'n clean it wit Clorox, 'fore we kin use it agin. It sho' stank out there," Addie Lee said before going outside.

The ambulance attendants loaded the detective into their vehicle as he continued his rantings. Johnny, Cora Lee, and Addie Mae were watching as the medical crew fought with Detective Bailey Lee to get him into the straight jacket then forced him into the ambulance to carry him out of Buttermilk Bottom for the last time. They could still hear him ranting, "Mutherfuckin' niggers, string 'em up. . . Now."

The rest of the morning passed quietly as Luther waited for Queenie to come downstairs, but she never appeared. It was almost five o'clock, and she still had not come out of her room. Dellah and Azalene were sitting on the bar polishing their nails a bold red, watching Luther watch the steps. They secretly laughed and teased Luther because they knew exactly what happened to Queenie.

"Where's Queenie?" Luther asked for the hundredth time.

"She ain't down here yet?" Azalene asked, winking at Dellah.

"Maybe, she went out shoppin' early dis mornin'," Luther said. "She must've went out t' buy some mo' clothes. Dat's all she ever care 'bout."

"Well, Cora Lee said she ain't seen her 'n she wuz up early dis mornin'," Dellah said, tapping Azalene on the shoulder. "She's usually up 'n 'round by now."

The two whores looked at each other, knowingly. "She wuz wit Jake last night, right?" Azalene asked, watching Luther's reaction.

"She sho' wuz," Pearl said.

"Den her ass is still is bed," Dellah said, as Pearl and Azalene broke out laughing hysterically.

"What you's talkin' 'bout?" Luther asked.

"Jake is layin' it on her ass, dat's what's happenin', old fool," Dellah said, as the three ladies laughed uncontrollably.

"I bet ya anythang, he done wore dat fat ass out," Azalene said, hitting her friend playfully on the shoulder while sharing a secret joke.

"A dollar bet?" Dellah said, reaching in her bra and placing her bill on the table in front of her.

"Not dis time o' day," Luther said.

"Put yo money on d' wood, and make d' bettin' good, fool," Dellah said, tapping her one dollar bill.

"I wants some o' dis, 'cause I know dat nigger," Azalene said, pulling her one-dollar bill out and placing it next to Dellah's. "They's still in bed."

"At dis hour?" Luther asked, showing his jealousy and placing his cash to match the bets placed in front of him. "It's nearly five o'clock."

"Shit, dat ain't nuthin'. Jake kept my ass in bed fo' three days one time. I told Queenie, I couldn't work 'cause I had a cold," Azalene said, mimicking her coughing dramatization.

"One time, I pretended I had a sore throat 'n couldn't talk 'cause dat fool jes wouldn't stop fucking me," Dellah said, laughing.

"Dat's d' dumbest thang I ev'r heard. Dat man's cripple, fo' God's sake," Luther declared.

"Yeah, we know. Ya'll keep sayin' dat shit if you wanna. . . But dat no leg man kin fuck all ya'll under d' bed 'n we know, don't we girls?" Dellah said

"Sho do," Azalene and Pearl said.

"Keep on takin' a mutherfucker fo' granted. He'll steal all ya'll's women 'n yo son's too if ya don't watch out. Jake knows what he's doin'. I'm tellin' you that man knows alotta stuff," Dellah said.

That evening Queenie slowly awakened to exquisite sensations that had her teeming with pleasure and excitement in her dreams. In her partially dreamlike state, she discovered the reality of her fantasy. Jake's head was lying between her legs, waking her with sweet murmurs and tender lashings on the tip of her pleasure zone.

"Jake?" He ignored her as he stepped up the pace of his liquid strokes. "Jake?"

"Yes, baby," he said dreamily.

"What time is it?"

"Time for an appetizer before. . . Breakfast," he said, taking long tender strokes between each phrase. She uttered a moan that sent shivers through his body as her body began to move in sync with his rhythm.

"Jake?"

"Relax, Queenie, I'll take good care of you," he said, kissing the inside of her thighs before suckling on her genital knob until she exploded with multiple spasms for several uncontrollable moments. Afterwards, she laid in satisfied exhaustion as he held her in his muscular arms so tightly that she could not have moved if she wanted to.

"That's a first for me," she said as he buried his head in her hair. "You just don't stop, do you?"

"I've wanted to love you since the day I first saw you. I have no intentions of ever stopping."

"I'm sorry it took me so long to realize what I've been missing."

"Don't worry, I'll make it up to you," he said in a husky voice. Taking her breasts into his mouth, he began to do what she could only describe as paradise. She tilted her body to him unable to stop herself from bending to his will. "Queenie, turn over."

"What?" she asked as he looked at her with a serious yet curious look on his face. At that moment, he was the sexiest man she had ever seen.

"What are you going to do now?"

"Make you happy."

"You did that already," she said, allowing him to roll her over on her stomach. She noticed a jar of Vaseline sitting on the table beside him.

"What's that for?"

"Relax, Queenie, just relax, and let me love you. I know what you need."

A few minute after eight the next day, Queenie appeared at the top of the steps as the women were predicting what Jake was doing to her to keep her locked in her room for hours.

"SShhhh," Dellah said. "Here she come."

"Good morning," Queenie said cheerfully, dressed in her bathrobe with her hair whirled about in no consistent style for the first time in anyone's memory.

"Good afternoon." The women smiled at each other, knowing the reason for Queenie's unusual appearance.

"It's evening. . . Almost nine o'clock," Luther barked too loudly.

Queenie was not concerned about their jokes or insinuations, she said, "Azalene, would you ask Cora Lee to send up two breakfasts, plenty of coffee and some extra orange juice to my room? She can leave it outside the door and knock. I'll get it." She started back up the steps and turned around just as the girls were about to resume their conversation about her and Jake. "Luther, I'm going to sleep late, don't expect me down this evening," she said, turning to walk back up the steps.

"Queenie, what about our date?" the old man asked quietly.

"I'm going to be tied up for a long time. I don't know when I can get back to you," she said dreamily.

"But ya said ya ain't "in love dis time," he continued to whisper.

"I don't know anything except that I. . . Have to get back upstairs as soon as I can. Please tell Cora Lee to hurry with that food. I'm starving."

When Pearl, Azalene and Dellah heard Queenie's door close, they all burst out laughing, saying "Dat girl gon 'n lost her mind," Pearl said.

"What I tell you? Jake fucked her brains out," Dellah said.

"Lucky, bitch. You think she'll ever let him out o' her room?" Azalene said.

"I wouldn't if I wuz her," Dellah said.

Chapter 32

The school year began with Grace at the helm and Horace working at her side; Grace as principal and Horace, as the student counselor. Every morning since Horace broke into Grace's house to rescue her from her deep depression; he picked her up at home, took her to school, and brought her back home again. The evenings, they spent together watching television, playing games, or just talking. Horace did not intend to leave Grace alone because he needed to be around her, and he did not want to risk her slipping back into the horrible void that he found her in months before.

On a Friday evening, around six o'clock, Horace arrived on time to take Grace out for dinner. They established a routine of meeting for dinner every night, which began the night of Grace's bout with depression. The moment Horace dropped her off from school Grace began preparation for a special dinner. She felt she owed it to him for helping her when she was in such a mess, which he cleaned up then restored her to her job, a job that meant the world to her. The door was unlocked because she was expecting him to arrive in minutes. Putting the last touches on her makeup and the meal, she rushed around to finish her preparations as soon as he called to say he was on the way. When he walked in, he placed his coat on the chair next to the door then he noticed the dimmed lights and the formal looking table setting with candles and wine.

"What's going on, Grace?" He took notice, appreciating the romantic seductive scene and the erotic scent of perfume, as soon as he hit the door. To his surprise, Grace appeared out of the kitchen in a sexy outfit.

"I thought we deserved something special. We've been through a lot together, and I wanted to show you how much I appreciate you being here for me."

"Couldn't you just tell me that?" he asked, admiring her in the sexy dress, fighting to keep from touching it.

"No. I wanted to show you. Come on, sit down. I've prepared a delicious meal for you."

"Why are you dressed like that?"

"Like what?"

"Like that," he said as he pointed to her beautiful shapely body in the unbelievably sexy dress.

"Don't you like it?"

"I like it fine but you didn't have to wear that for me."

"I wanted to," she said, putting her arms around his waist.

He laughed, pushed her away, and said, "Woman, go put on some clothes and turn the lights on. What are you trying to do? Seduce me?"

"Well, I thought it would make us closer. It's been a long time. . . And . . ."

"And. . . And what? You thought you could seduce me with the soft lights, a sexy outfit, and sweet smelling perfume?" He turned on the lights and blew out the candles.

"I thought you would want to. . . To be with me, but I guess I was wrong," she said, growing angry.

"You horny, little rascal, come here," he said, holding her close to him. "I love you. You don't have to play games with me or try to seduce me. I told you when I know that you love me and only me. . . I will make love to you."

"But I do love you, Horace."

"I know you do. . . But you are not 'in love' with me and what I need from you is your complete love, Grace. I don't want to just have sex with you. . . I want the real thing."

She held her head down. "How do you know what I'm feeling?"

"I know. And. . . I'll know when you love me from the look in your eyes. I need you to want me more than you've wanted anyone in your whole life. It will be like someone turning on a light in a dark room. . . That's how I'll know. When I see that, I'll make love to you and not a minute before. Just so, you'll know. . . When we make love, Grace, it will be in my bed. . . In my house, and I'm going to keep you there with me. . . Forever. I only know one way to love you and that's with all my heart. I want the same intensity from you. . . If we are to be together. I want everything you have to give and more," he said, looking at her lips, making her want to kiss him. When she tried, he pulled away and stood looking into her eyes and at her lips. She wanted desperately to kiss him, but he said, "Now. . . Go get dressed. I'm taking you bowling."

"Bowling?"

"Yes. You need something to keep your little nasty mind off sex. Bowling should do it," he said, laughing.

"I doubt it," she said under her breath as she slowly walked into her bedroom to change clothes. "What about the wonderful dinner I prepared?" she said from the other room.

"Don't worry, I'll put it in the refrigerator," he said, laughing at her antics. "You little short, horny devil. . . Setting a sex-trap for me."

"You don't have to keep rubbing it in," she said from her bedroom.

"Oh, yes I do, too. I can't get over you," Horace said, laughing as he covered the food and placed it in the refrigerator. He stopped and said softly, "When you are ready. . . I'm going to tear your little foxy ass up."

"Did you say something?" she yelled.

"Yeah. . . I said, hurry up."

Chapter 33

In a small Catholic Church on the West Side, Cameron and Jazmine married in the presence of their closest friends in the small chapel of Jazmine's family church. The twins, Cora Lee, Addie Mae, Betsy, Johnny, Moses, Pastor Freeman, Smoke, Noitop, and her son was present to witness their nuptials. Jake stood as best man while Kenny and his sister stood smiling right up front with the happy couple as they took their vows. One of Jazmine's co-workers served as the maid of honor and Blair proudly gave his sister's hand in marriage to Cameron. The ceremony was simple, but it honored the commitment and love between Cameron and Jazmine as well as their love for the two children whom they vowed to care for within the sanctity of their home and marriage. Dressed in their finery, the guests sat attentively and blessed the union of the newly formed family.

Following the ceremony, Cora Lee and Addie Mae along with the twins prepared a wonderful meal at the newlywed's new home. Everything was delicious and beautifully prepared. There was laughter and lots of storytelling at the party. The twins were delighted that they had finally met Noitop, Cora Lee, and Addie Mae. The five ladies sat around the kitchen table and talked for hours. It was amazing to see them interact in such an open, jovial, and animated way. The laughter of the five women often resonated throughout the house but everyone knew better than to complain. Cameron could see that they were getting along well, and he enjoyed knowing that he had something to do with the newly formed friendships.

While talking to the men in the basement office, Cameron decided how he wanted to establish himself in a business. While discussing his plans for the new house, it slowly dawned on him that he could start a construction business.

"I'm planning to install outdoor lighting and upgrade the electricity inside the house, if you know of a good electrician, let me know."

"If you want the best all you have to do is turn around. Moses over there is a licensed electrician," Jake said. "He started doing carpentry work when he couldn't find a job in the electrical field."

"I never knew that," Cameron said.

"He can't find a decent job paying anything. If he gets the job, he can't get the money. The same goes for Johnny; he learned plumbing in jail, but he can't find work anywhere. He's talking about going north. It's the same old story; if you're black you're always out-of-season," Jake said, taking a sip of his vodka.

"I experienced the same thing when I lost my teacher's license. I was qualified, willing, and able, but I had no place to go," Cameron responded.

"What is a black man supposed to do?" Jake said.

Cameron thought for a little while and said, "Make his own way. We need to create our own jobs, Jake," Cameron said thoughtfully. "And. . . That's just what we are going to do."

"It sounds good. But, how?"

"I could use some of the money that I saved to start a construction business. You could help. You are the fastest talker I know. You could get the licenses and contracts for us, and I could work with the men on the actual work site. What do you think?"

"I think you're crazy."

"That's okay, as long as you say yes. We could call some of the guys who need work and figure out what each one of them does best. Then we could sit down and decide what services we want to offer and divide them in work groups. It'll be a cinch."

"You're serious about this, aren't you?" Jake asked.

"You bet I am. We can get started right away. It will take a while, but we could get it all set up and running within a couple of months. I hope Queenie won't mind."

"Don't worry about her, she's coming around."

"We were hoping she would come today."

"I was too, but she said the last thing she wanted to see was you marry somebody else. I think she would really like Jazmine if it wasn't for you."

"Who knows maybe one day they will become friends."

"Don't bet on it," Jake said. "Some shit is best left alone."

"Tell me something, has she fallen in love with you yet?"

"I'm still working on that but right now she loves what daddy can do for her. Since that first night, we haven't spent a night apart. She won't let the girls come near me."

"She's jealous, huh?"

"Yep, she wants me all to herself."

"You deserve to be loved too, man. I know that better than anyone."

"I told you before, I'm a big boy. I can handle what I'm doing. Right now, I'm enjoying handling Miss Queenie. Wait until I tell her we're partners in a construction business. It'll blow her mind. Do you really think it'll work?"

"Sure I do. We can start out using our basement for office space, but when we get bigger, we can move to a commercial location."

"That means we'll be working together every day."

"We need to start our jobs early every morning, seven o'clock. It's a long way out here so I'll need to pick you up by six o'clock."

"When do you want to get started?"

"After my honeymoon, in a couple of weeks."

"You'll only have to pick me up for about a week because I ordered one of those cars with the hand control."

"Great man, I knew you could do it," Cameron said, slapping his friend on the back.

"I passed the driving test, now all I need is the car."

"Then it's settled. We'll be partners working with our friends in a business we all will love."

A few weeks later, Grace's girlfriend, Carrie, rushed into her office and told her about Cameron's marriage and surprisingly, Grace was not upset. "I hear that they are also pregnant."

Grace thought for a minute and smiled. "Good for them. I wish them the best."

"What? You're not upset?"

"No. I admit several months ago I would have been devastated; but now. . . I realized that he loves someone else and my future is pointing me in another direction."

"Well, I am shocked. I never thought you'd take it so easily."

"Neither did I," she said, smiling.

"Tell me, are you and Horace getting together? Is that why you are not bothered by Cameron's marriage?"

"I admit . . . Horace and I are getting closer but the reality is that Cameron never loved me. I know that now. . . That's the reason I lost him."

"Well, you have come of age, haven't you?"

"Yes, I guess I have."

At a staff meeting, Grace sat listening to her staff make suggestions about how they could improve the upcoming semester. They wanted more assistance in the classroom, more books, and more parental involvement. Although Grace was listening as she daydreamed, her fantasy life was in full swing because she had no sex life since her involvement with Cameron. She missed having sex, although she had to admit that she no longer missed Cameron, but she missed having sex because she loved the intimacy as well as the male body. She looked at Horace, who sat at the conference table across from her, next to Susan, the music teacher whom he dated in the past. The beautiful young music instructor was in awe of him, speaking to Horace quietly throughout the entire meeting, smiling and laughing, as she glared at Grace across the table. Everyone knew or suspected that Grace and Horace were dating, since they were always together and Grace was certain that he no longer saw the music teacher, although Susan tried to pretend otherwise. He spent too much time with her for her to doubt him, but there was no progress in their relationship.

As she sat watching them interact, Grace wondered if he still loved her because, for some reason, Horace no longer told her or expressed his passion or feelings for her, and it had been weeks, since he attempted to kiss her. *Maybe he lost interest because I took too long to make up my mind, or maybe he's ready to move on. Could he be dating her again?* After a few moments, she thought about it and decided that it could not be true because they were together all the time, and he actually did not have time to date anyone else. *But why has his attitude and demeanor toward me changed . . . He seems too cool and distant,* she thought. As she pondered their platonic relationship, she realized that he was staring back at her. She smiled at him, but he did not reciprocate. *What is he thinking? Maybe he was waiting for me to get stronger so that he can break the news to me that he wants someone else.'* She tried to convey her feelings to him because she could not continue being with him and not loving him. *He said he would be able to tell if I loved him, but he hadn't acknowledged any of my overtures over the last few weeks.* Her heart began to pound as she contemplated another rejection. She could not take another day of torture so she decided she would end it before he did. The meeting ended and she rushed to her office not wanting to see him with the music teacher or anyone else, for that matter.

"Are you ready to leave," Horace asked, sticking his head in Grace's office door.

"Yes. . . But if you have something else to do. . . You can go ahead. I still have work here to do," she said, determined not to cry.

"What are you talking about?" he said, stepping into her office, closing the door behind him.

"I just thought. . . That I may be monopolizing your time. You don't have to pick me up for school every morning and drive me home every afternoon. My car is working just fine. I'm sure you have something better to do," she said, fumbling with the papers on her desk, not looking at him.

"What is this about, Grace?" he asked cautiously.

"Nothing. I just thought. . . You may have something better to do. . . That's all."

"Something better than loving you," he said, leaning over her desk.

She closed her eyes as she let out her pent-up frustrations in one big breath of air. "Do you still love me?" she asked, slowly raising her head to look in his eyes.

"I still love you," he said, burning her with his urgent feelings. "I will always love you, Grace."

"You haven't said so for such a long time. . . I thought maybe you found someone else," she said, wiping the tears away that fell spontaneously from her eyes.

"Grace, I have been with you. . . Waiting for you to love me," he said, watching her closely. She took a deep cleansing breath as her tears clouded her vision. "Why are you crying? Have you forgotten what I told you?" She was so full of emotions that she could not speak. "Grace, I've been waiting to see love in your eyes. . . For me. I wanted you to want me."

"I do. I do. I have for a long time."

"Yes. . . I know, but today. . . Across the conference table was the first day that I saw that you actually needed me."

"Then you're not very observant. I have been needing you for a long time," she said, wiping the tears away, but he stopped her. Stepping behind her desk, he pulled her to her feet and into his arms, making her body quiver. Taking his handkerchief from his pocket, he wiped her tears away.

"I wanted you to be certain about your feelings because what I want with you will be permanent. Our future and our love is too important to me."

It's important to me, too."

"Good. Are you certain you are ready for me?"

"I'm certain that I can't see myself loving anyone but you ever again."

"And. . . That other guy?"

"He has disappeared. Horace, I only love you."

"Good. Then we need to go home. I'm taking you home with me. . . And Grace, it will be forever. There's no turning back for me because I can't love you and leave you or allow you to leave me. You will have to stay with me. . . Forever. That means marriage. . . Plenty of hot sizzling sex and a house full of children. . . The whole package. Grace, are you ready for that?"

"Yes, oh yes," she said, throwing her arms around his neck.

"Then let's go home. I'm going to show you what it feels like to be loved by a man who truly loves you," he said, looking into her eyes. "By the end of the day. . . I'm going to have you screaming my name."

"Horace," she said, surprised at his statement.

"Yeah, that's right, baby. . . Start practicing that because by the end of the day you will be screaming that name, I promise you. Today is Friday and I have the whole weekend to keep you in bed and show you that nobody. . . Anywhere. . . Can love you the way I can," he said, kissing her neck and lips while unbuttoning her jacket, pulling her breasts out and devouring them all in one smooth motion. After several sweet erotic minutes, he said, "Woman, I love you," he said, reaching under her skirt. "Take them off."

"What?"

When she did not move, he pushed her against the wall and bent down and raised her skirt, unfastened her stocking then pulled her panties off. Moved by his own need for fulfillment, he kissed the crown of her glory, taking what he craved, and loving her as his heart beat strongly in his chest. Taking her breath away, he caressed her beautiful legs and her wonderful shapely hips as he spent precious time making love to his future wife. With her leg resting on his shoulder, Grace was in heaven as her body responded sensuously to his amazing lips. She wanted to make love to him and spend time loving him with the same passion that he gave her, but he pushed her away and stood up, kissing her for several spectacular moments.

"Horace," she said, surprised at his aggressiveness.

"Keep saying my name, baby. I love it," he said, kissing her deeply. "You won't need any of these, ever again," he said, chunking her panties in the wastebasket. Grace laughed, loving him and wanting to join with him as quickly as possible. "I want to always be able to touch you and love you," he said, making Grace breathe deeply and filling her with an urgent need for him. "You need to always be ready for me. I have a healthy and insatiable appetite for loving you," he said, drowning himself in the splendor of her moist tender lips. "Come on. . . Let's go before I explode. I want to love you in my own bed, where I have dreamed of loving you since the first day that you walked into this school. First, you have some packing to do because I am never going to let you out of my sight."

Chapter 34

Jazmine's pregnancy was just beginning to show. She sat down thinking about the life growing inside her, thankful that their guests departed early, and the children were sleeping soundly in bed. Holding a glass of juice while Cameron opened a bottle of champagne to drink for both of them, she admired the handsome man as he acted with such authority over to her.

"I love you," he said, kissing her, toasting their union. "You have made me a very happy man."

"You have made me a happy woman... Completely full of happiness," she said, rubbing her stomach. He sat down next to her and touched his unborn child.

"I can't wait to see what he looks like."

"He? Does this mean you think it's a boy?"

"No, it means that your mother told me it's a boy. I am hoping that the next one will be a little girl, one that looks just like you."

"Well, you will get your wish, there is also a little girl growing inside here."

"What? Don't tell me your mother was wrong?" he said, looking baffled.

"No, there is also a little boy. I told her not to tell you."

"What?"

"Darling, we're having twins. I hope you don't mind," she asked cautiously.

"Mind? I think it's wonderful. Just wait until I tell Essie and Gussie. They are going to be thrilled."

"Are you sure you don't mind," Jazmine asked, touching her husband's cheek.

"I'm positive, besides that means, we only have two more to go, before the baby making is over then I can spend the rest of my life loving you," he said, placing his head on her stomach. He enjoyed listening to all the activity inside. Now that he knew there were two of them, he planned to listen more often. "Do you think I will make it as a good doting parent until everyone is out of college and married off?"

"Of course."

"How can you be so sure?"

"Remember when you were forcing me to pay attention to you, and Kenny ran to you, looking for you to help him. I could see then what a wonderful father you would be. That little kid loved you so much. I always knew that you would make a perfect father."

"Oh yes, Kenny interrupted us and almost drove me crazy. I was so angry. There I was trying to get next to you, and he pulled me in the opposite direction. I could have killed him that day."

"I remember. You looked as if you were going to bust."

"I was. I wanted you so badly . . . I would have been on my way to the insane asylum if I couldn't have you. I was half out-of-my-mind, and you tried to run away from me, woman."

"I knew you would follow me. I knew the first time I saw you that I wanted to marry you."

"Why were you giving me such a hard time?"

"Because I had been wrong before, this time I wanted to make sure."

"Are you sure now?"

"Do you see this," she said, rubbing her belly. "I am very sure."

"I love you, Jazmine."

"I know."

"Do you realize how deeply, and completely I love you?"

"Yes."

"You are the first person I have ever been in love with. . . I never knew what it felt like before I saw you. It felt like a bolt of lightning hit me, but I loved and needed every tortured minute of it. You gave me a real, hard time. You know that, don't you?"

"I had to be sure, but I knew I wanted to marry you the first time I saw you."

"The first time you saw me, you looked as if you wanted to strangle me."

"That was not the first time I saw you."

"I thought I saw you first."

"No, you didn't. I saw you months before when you whipped that man for beating his small child with a belt. You weren't angry when you did it, you were disgusted with the idea that a man would cause harm to his own child. You thought, *How can a man hurt someone he helped to create?* I knew then that I had to meet you. In addition to that, you were so good looking. I held the image of you holding that child in your arms for months, right here in my heart. I wanted you to father my children."

"I don't remember seeing you. If I had, you would have known it."

"I know. The second time I saw you, you scared me. When I looked into your eyes, I got the distinct feeling that you only used women, and I didn't want to be one of them."

"Used women? Where on earth did you get an idea like that?"

"Remember, the night it rained so hard? You had to wait on the porch of the juke joint for the rain to stop? Two people ran into you while they were trying to get out of the rain?"

"That was you?"

"And, Blair. You had just finished having. . . You know what . . . With you know who. And, you were thinking that the only thing a woman could do for you was. . . Sizzling hot sex."

"Oh, my God but that was before I knew you. Before I even knew what love was."

"I found that out later. Your strong feelings scared me at first. All I saw that morning at the top of the hill was lust, not love. Then I saw you standing on your porch. You called out to me."

"But I didn't talk to you."

"No, but your heart did."

"I thought Blair was your husband or boyfriend, and that I had to steal you away from him. I was plotting to kill him to get next to you."

"I heard your thoughts, pleading for me to love you. Your feelings were so sincere and overpowering that I couldn't help but respond."

"That's why you turned around so abruptly?"

"Yes, I heard you."

"Thank God you did. I have never been in love before; it took me by surprise. In fact, it scared me." He kissed her, trying to share all the love he felt for her. "It's time to go to bed, my darling wife. Just think, I get to make love to you, whenever I want. It just blows my mind whenever

I'm this close to you. It's like living in a dream," he said, looking into her eyes.

"Do you think you can spend the rest of your life loving me?" she asked.

"Our life will be excellent and filled with all the passion and ecstasy that God has blessed us with. Our love is my only reason for living," he said, losing his voice as he tried to express the depths of his feelings for her.

"You are my sweet dream . . . My dream that came true."

"You are reading my mind again," he said, smiling. "I want you to always know and understand how much I love you."

"I do, darling. I do."

"Tonight, I want to show you how much I love you," he said, picking her up in his arms, kissing her.

"Daddy?" Both Jazmine and Cameron looked surprised to see Missy and Kenny standing in the family room door, looking at them. "Can we have a glass of milk?" Kenny asked.

"I forgot . . . We are parents already," Cameron said, kissing her one last time before carefully putting her down.

"I'll get it," she said.

"No, I'll get it. You go to bed and wait for me," he said, kissing her deeply. "Okay, milk," he said, clapping his hand, turning toward the children, "Let's get a glass of milk for everyone then it's off to bed, okay?"

"Can you read us a story?" Missy asked.

"I'll go git the book," Kenny said, but Cameron stopped him.

"No, wait." Cameron cursed to himself, but then he became inspired. "I know, I'll tell you a story while you are drinking your milk. Then you can go straight to bed where Daddy can tuck you both in so that you can go fast asleep. Then Daddy can go tuck Mommy in bed. Is that okay?" he asked Missy, tickling her.

The child screamed, laughing as he sat her down at the kitchen table next to her brother. "Could we have one cookie?" Missy asked still laughing, holding up her little finger.

Jazmine laughed, "I knew you would be a great father . . . But I never envisioned how funny you would be."

"Go to bed, woman," he said seriously. "I have a non-verbal bedtime story to share with you."

The next morning, Jazmine had a list of telephone numbers on the table ready for Cameron when he woke up. It was almost noon before he crawled out of bed. He wandered into the kitchen for a late breakfast and saw the list on the table.

"What's this for?"

"The numbers you will need to start your construction business. The phone company will be out tomorrow to put extra lines in your office. I figured you would need it since Jake will be coming here to work. I ordered another desk for him. I hope that's okay."

"That and you are perfect, but I have no intentions of starting anything right away. Next month will be soon enough. This is our time to do with as we please."

"That means we will be in bed for thirty straight days," she said.

"Do you mind?"

"No, baby, not at all."

"Then come with me, I need my wife," he said, pulling her into the bedroom.

Chapter 35

Ten Years Later. . . .

"Hey, man."

"Hey, Jake," Cameron said.

"What are you doing?"

"Strolling down memory lane, I guess. I can't believe it's been almost ten years, since we lived here. There is a lot of history on these dirt roads, man."

"I know. Some of that history is best left alone," Jake said, looking out toward the healthiest part of Buttermilk Bottom, the kudzu vines.

"It seems strange not to have children running around playing, or the paper boy yelling."

"Don't forget the vegetable man. I loved to hear him yelling in the street for people to come out and buy his fresh produce."

"Yeah, me, too."

"The streets could use a few drunks stumbling around, remember the ragman?"

"Sure do."

"We have to have a few clansmen riding through the streets raising hell, and it wouldn't be complete without a witch doctor and a few bad-ass wives gunning for their cheating husbands," Jake said, laughing. Cameron joined him, throwing his arm around his friend's shoulder.

"Man, this place was unreal. No one would ever believe half the shit that went on down here," Cameron said.

"You're right. No one ever will. Johnny and Moses are waiting on top for you to give the signal," Jake said.

"Are you ready to knock this mother down?"

"Hell yeah, let's do it," Jake said.

Cameron waved to the men at the top of the hill and heard the engines purring. The engines of various construction vehicles and machines were starting up ready to demolish all the ragged, dilapidated buildings that had provided shelter to many of the city's most deprived and fascinating people, a community that lived long pass anyone's expectations.

"How's Queenie?" Cameron asked, walking up the hill.

"Fine as ever. She can't get use to being a mother again. Little Queenie is nine years old now and Jake Jr. will be six in a few days. I can't believe he's getting ready to go to school."

"Time flies, doesn't it? Are you and Queenie still hanging in there?"

"You bet. She's still the love of my life," Jake said.

"We both have been very lucky," Cameron said.

"How could we miss? We both are lucky, loveable, and lustful."

All the physical evidence of a people's struggle to survive and eke out a living against unbelievable odds. I spite of the hatred and prejudice that were forced on them was being torn down, erased from the face of the earth. It would be gone forever as the two, oddly-paired best friends walked up the hill on the dirt road for the last time.

"Jake, I've been meaning to ask you. . . Where did the name Buttermilk Bottom come from?"

"There are two stories. The first story states that there was an old horse-drawn milk wagon that came down here on a regular run. It was loaded down with buttermilk because the milkman sold out of everything, but the buttermilk before getting here. The milkman always sold the white milk before getting to The Bottom, saving the buttermilk to sell to the colored folks. It had rained that day, and you know how the roads were when it rained in this hole. When the wagon came down the irregular, muddy road, it frequently turned over and the milk from the wagons often spilled out turning everything white, and that happened several times a week. The other story says that the residents use to work for local white families around here, and that they were paid with quarts of buttermilk instead of money."

"Which story do you believe?"

"The first one because although black people love buttermilk. There is nothing they love more than money."

The End.

Epilog

"You are listening to WERD in Atlanta Georgia and here is the news for this morning, April 21, 1968. Today, workers on the new Civic Center project uncovered a mystery that plagued police investigators for the past ten years. Workmen clearing land for the new project discovered a patrol car belonging to two missing police officers today under mounds of kudzu vines. There was no sign of the missing police officers. Many believed that the officers might have met a tragic fate. With the discovery of the missing vehicle, investigators may uncover the evidence regarding the whereabouts of the missing officers.

April 21, 1968
"This is WAOK radio in Atlanta GA. Workers found a missing police vehicle in the mountain of kudzu vines behind the now defunct community of Buttermilk Bottom. The patrol car was missing for over ten years along with the two police officers assigned to the vehicle. The fate and whereabouts of the two police officers have not yet been determined.

April 21, 1968
Headline: "Missing Police Vehicle Found"—The Atlanta Constitution
Headline: "Policeman Still Missing—Patrol Car Found"—The Atlanta Daily World

Author's Notes

Buttermilk Bottom was a real place. It was a bona fide community that progress and urban renewal, swept into non-existence. Black people in the area dubbed the process 'urban removal' because they knew that their happenstancial location was too close to downtown Atlanta for the established and rapidly growing business community and political system to leave them alone. All the characters depicted in this body of work are fictitious except for four fascinating tales that I heard and included because they were too funny and unbelievable not to share, and they are: 1.) The story of the man who urinated in the policeman's mouth in back of the paddy wagon; 2.) The story about the man who came home and found his whole family standing on his bed because of the rats; 3.) The rat story about the man who opened the oven and saw eyes looking back at him; and 4.) Lastly, several people living in the area at the time told the story of the foot-stomper. He was a real person who was sought by the police.

While these incidents came from the tales told to me in my interviews of people who either lived or worked in Buttermilk Bottom, the personalities, behaviors, and events around these incidents have been fictionalized in order to place the incidents in the story. The two rat stories came from my family's folklore that was told to me on my husband's first trip to Atlanta by my storytelling brother-in-law, Frank Anthony while we were having dinner in the revolving restaurant (The Polaris) atop the Hyatt Regency. He actually did move away from The Fourth Ward because of the rats that chased his four sons and wife to the center of his bed. All other characters and events in this story never existed except in this author's imagination.

When I lived in Atlanta as a child, Buttermilk Bottom was the place my parents would not allow my siblings or me to visit. Although, it was completely off limits, it held for me, a sense of mystery, a forbidden place with secrets too intriguing to ignore. My mother and her friends sat on our front steps and whispered about incidents that happened on weekends in the forbidden neighborhood. Whenever children approached, they quickly changed the subject.

This story is the product of my assiduous fascination with the forbidden neighborhood that had an equally fascinating location and history. Its nickname, 'The Bottom', was recognized primarily by those who lived in or near the area. The story, like the characters enclosed in these pages, are sitting in the historically correct backdrop of the struggle for civil and human rights, which unfolded slowly in cities all over America. We must all keep in mind that the civil rights movements did not start in the fifties and sixties as most people now assert. It began the day the first enslaved African had shackles placed on his hands, feet, and neck, and with the first enslaved African, forced on a ship bound for the Americas. The struggle continued on the first day the enslaved arrived in this country and with the first black person who stepped on an auction block. The history of the civil rights struggle in Atlanta continued with the formation of organizations whose sole purpose was to liberate the African Americans living in deprived, neglected, and impoverished conditions. Civil rights groups organized long before the passing of the thirteenth amendment that outlawed slavery in the United States. In segregated communities like Buttermilk Bottom, blacks were forced to exist under separate and unequal conditions with inhumane and unreasonable restrictions that affected every aspect of their lives.

For your enjoyment and mine, I conjured up the characters in this book and events around them solely from what I imagined could have happened there, in hope that they may pay homage to the memory of the people who once lived, loved, and worked there. For me, the stories and characters in this book are the answer to questions I was afraid to ask as a child. Who lived there? Why were certain establishments called a bucket of blood? What were they like? Why was it off limits? What happened there? Why were people whispering every time they talked about Buttermilk Bottom?

The whole community of Buttermilk Bottom actually dwelled in a gigantic hole that recessed about fifty feet into the landscape. From the top of the hill at the entrance of Buttermilk Bottom, you could see the whole neighborhood. You could stand on the sidewalks of streets bordering the notorious neighborhood and find that your waistline was even with the rooftops of the buildings that sat in the sunken earth. All the streets in and around it were unpaved roads that always appeared wet or damp due to its inability to handle the run-off of water from streets that surrounded and drained into the sunken community.

The dwellings in Buttermilk Bottom were made of aged, unpainted wood that turned a dark ashy gray from many years of neglect. There were a few single dwellings made of brick but the majority of the dwellings were two family dwellings or four unit two-story wooden apartment buildings with large open porches that had external staircases leading to the second floor. There were two-family dwellings with porches extending the length of the property. Most of the apartments had no more than three rooms. Most units had a front room, a middle room, a kitchen, and bathroom. The concept of a living room had not been introduced to residents of Buttermilk Bottom, and the idea of anyone having their own bedroom did not exist no matter how many children, parents, and grandparents lived in the household.

In our three-room, Fourth Ward apartment on Hilliard Street, which was walking distance from Buttermilk Bottom, my parents were experts in the use of space. My mother always purported that, "If there is room in the heart, there is room in the house." With those unbelievable words, she proceeded to pile her nine children in the totally inadequate space along with a grandparent or two for yearly visits that ranged from a week to three months of our summer vacation. As she welcomed visitors from out of town, we learned to sleep in yet smaller spaces. Very few apartments had two 'middle rooms', but there were a few and no matter how many people were strategically placed inside the inadequate space. The kitchen was always filled with the sweet aromas of bread pudding, fried chicken, collard greens, black-eyed peas, and homemade biscuits, pies, and cakes.

Buttermilk Bottom was a small isolated community located in the Fourth Ward between Piedmont (North), Bucannon (South), Pine Street (East) and Forrest Avenue (West). The activities on Friday and Saturday nights made The Bottom legendary. There was always a fight, a shooting or a stabbing that occurred bringing in outsiders to cart away the dead bodies and guilty parties. Outsiders were anyone black or white that did not live within its boundaries. The most unwelcomed outsiders were the police, which had a very complex yet dependent relationship with the residents. They came when there was a need, and yet they were not welcomed because the residents very often fell victim to their persistent prejudice and abuse.

The insiders had their own private society, though depraved it was complete with dance halls, gambling houses, whorehouses, dilapidated churches, and stores. They had their own social events and celebrations, which were laced with the mellow sounds of the blues, the intoxication of alcohol, the sweet smell of pork chops sizzling on the stove, and the precious noise coming from children playing on its dirt roads.

For those of us who knew of Buttermilk Bottom, walked its dirt roads, shared stories, lived, and worked there, we will always remember the spirit of its people who survived against incredible odds and unreasonable circumstances. Their ability to live under deliberate and structured racism demonstrates man's innate ability to overcome hardships and degradation no matter how obtuse and severe. The lives they led are testaments to the amazing strength and determination of the African, living in America.

On the following pages, I have included few interviews from my upcoming book on Buttermilk Bottom with people who knew the area when it was in its zenith. It was my privilege to speak with each of them, and I will remain greatly appreciative to them for their colorful stories, and their amazing insight.

Memories of Buttermilk Bottom
Dorothy & Pete Weaver

Dottie: We lived near Buttermilk Bottom from March of 1961 to August of 1961. Our house was the third house from Piedmont Avenue with a screened in porch. There was a café and a store on the right, both made of clapboard. Our Address was 239 Pine Street. We rented the upstairs of a single-family house right behind Buttermilk Bottom. We had two bedrooms, living room, kitchen, and bath. Our land-lady, Miss Sally stayed in the basement, and her front door faced Buttermilk Bottom. She was always fussing with her daughter about going down there. The Civic Center sits there right now. We moved in March of 1961 and moved out in August of the same year because it was so bad. We had to stay with my cousin, Maynie, because we didn't have anywhere else to go. In December of 1961, we moved to Eza Church Drive.

The Bottom was quiet until five o'clock on Friday. People went to work all week then on Fridays corn liquor would be floating all through there. . . *Bathtub liquor* they called it. People let their hair down on Fridays. In 1961, I was making twenty-five dollars a week and Pete made seventy-five cents an hour at Wendell-Roberts Drug Store.

It was rough back in those days. I use to stand in my kitchen and look right down on Buttermilk Bottom. I never walked in Buttermilk Bottom because I was nineteen years old too scared to go out of the house. My mother visited me and asked me, "What is this place?" We could hear gunshots, noise from house parties, music blaring from the Forest Arms. On Mondays, you could hear people talking about who appeared at the Forest Arms, Henry's Grill and the Royal Peacock. All the big singers appeared at these places. Pete and I went to the Royal Peacock twice.

Once to see Chuck Jackson, he sang, "Any Day Now," and the other time, we saw Jackie Wilson, the man with the waves in his hair.

Buttermilk Bottom had a bunch of row houses, black dirt, unpaved streets, a bunch of shacks. . . Nothing was made of brick, and none of the buildings looked like they had ever been painted. The dirt down there always looked wet from my window. I didn't know anybody down there."

Pete: "It started shooting on Friday at five o'clock and the shooting lasted 'til mid night on Sunday. We had to stay in the house because we could have gotten shot. There was a big black bald policeman who shot the man next door to us. The police raided the house and shot the man dead. It was a liquor house. My uncle Dock stayed next door. That was the first time I saw anyone stretched out dead."

"Do you know how Buttermilk Bottom got its name?"

Dottie: "I hear that the white people use to pay the people down there with cornbread and buttermilk instead of money. Then I heard it was because the people down there loved buttermilk."

- Dorothy & Pete Weaver, Atlanta, Georgia

Mr. N. A. Davis, *A retired Atlanta police officer, who patrolled Buttermilk Bottom starting in 1958.*

"I was an Atlanta Police Officer and Buttermilk Bottom was on my beat. We reported to a white captain. Some of the white police officers placed themselves in charge of the illegal activities. Their behavior was unethical because they took payments from gangsters, number runners, liquor, and gambling houses.

"What kind of people lived in Buttermilk Bottom?"

"Poor black people. Some were racketeers and some were very good people.

"What were the houses like in Buttermilk Bottom?"

"All the houses were wood framed. . . Shotgun houses."

"Shotgun houses?"

"That means straight through. You could shoot a shotgun through the front door and have it go straight out the back with nothing stopping it. Most of the houses were unpainted and the wood had turned gray from the weather. The streets were unpaved alleys wide enough for two cars to barely pass each other. All the roads were dusty and sometimes appeared wet from the water that drained from Forest Avenue and Piedmont Avenue. The street was nothing but an alley that ran toward Bucannon Street. The main entrance was on Forest Avenue, which was the main drag. There were successful black businesses on Forest Avenue. Cooper's Drug store was black owned. Jews operated businesses there. Everybody in Buttermilk Bottom walked; there were no cars down there. I remember the first person who bought a car down there. It was a white Ford. That was the first time I ever saw a new car parked in Buttermilk Bottom. There were about ten apartment houses in The Bottom off Forest Avenue, I don't remember where it stopped."

"The Forest Arms Hotel was near Butler Street. The owner ran the place. He was really renting rooms, but he wanted the best clientele. He tried to upgrade the services there many times. Our call box was right in front of The Forest Arms Hotel. There were some good restaurants on Forest Avenue. . . Good soul food restaurants."

"When did they hire black police officers for Buttermilk Bottom?"

"In 1948; they hired eight men who were not allowed to wear their uniforms on the streets, unless they were working. The first police officers were stationed at the Butler Street Y M C A. The black police officers had to bring their uniforms to the Y and change into their uniforms in the basement."

"Why?"

"Because the feeling was that black men in police uniforms would be offensive to the white people. They were only allowed to patrol the black areas like Forest Avenue and Auburn Avenue. By 1958, when I joined the force, we were stationed at the police station at Butler St and Decatur, and we could wear our uniforms."

"What do you remember most about being a policeman in Buttermilk Bottom?"

"We were well received by the people who lived there. They gave us a lot of respect, but the white officers were not kind to black officers. When we called-in to say we had a prisoner, they would take their time getting there and when they arrived at the call box, they would never get out of the car to assist us with a perpetrator, even if we were having problems with them. We had two call boxes in the area, and we had to call in every hour. It was for our protection as well as a way to monitor our work in the neighborhood."

"One incident that always stuck in my mind was when I was called to a house in Buttermilk Bottom, a man had a shotgun wound to the stomach. When I arrived on the scene his intestines were hanging out, but he was so calm as he talked to me telling me everything that happened to him. I'll never forget how calm he was. When the ambulance arrived, the white attendants had to bring the stretcher for that man because there was no way he could have walked to the ambulance on his own. Normally, when we called for an ambulance from Grady Hospital, the driver and the helper would make the patient walk to the ambulance because they didn't want to carry a black person on the stretcher. No matter what was wrong with you if you were black, they made you walk to the vehicle."

"What was it like living back then?"

"The city was very segregated. When blacks moved onto a street normally occupied by whites, they would change the name of the street where the white folks lived so that blacks couldn't say they lived on the same street as whites. Jackson Street, for instance, had two other names. . . . Parkway Drive and Charles Allen Drive but it's all the same street. Forest Avenue changed when it crossed Boulevard to Forest Road where the white neighborhood started. At one time only white people lived on Boulevard but when blacks started moving into the buildings that faced Boulevard, they boarded up all the doors and windows facing Boulevard so that blacks couldn't look out on their street. Blacks had to enter the building from the side streets so that they would not to have a Boulevard address."

"What was a typical Friday night like in Buttermilk Bottom?"

"We had mostly domestic calls. Black people were closely policed. I never understood why, but they were. There were lots of fights, shooting and stabbing on the weekends. There were some people who lived in the alley had families and tried to live a decent life. The Bug Man was the big man around there, but he rarely lived in the area. Almost every Saturday night the liquor houses would have a fish-fry and sell 'white lightin', which was corn liquor . . . Sometimes they called it *mellow yellow*."

"What is a Bug Man?"

"The number writer always had a boy who went around and collected his money. The boy always got a cut of the winnings, and he also distributed the winnings, if someone won. People would always look in the evening paper, The Atlanta Journal, for the number; the first two numbers in the stocks and the third in the bonds. The Bug Man always had a banker. During that time, the Banker was a big business man on Auburn Avenue, and he always drove a big Cadillac. One man made so much money, he built a house for his wife and his girlfriend on the same street."

"What were some of the businesses in the area during that time?"

"The Forest Arms Hotel, Copper's Drug store, Scripto, Milton Bradley, The Forest Theater, The Savoy, Red's Taxicabs, and Raylock, a parts manufacturing plant. Grady Hospital was the only hospital that would take blacks, and Georgia Baptist and Crawford Long were for white people."

-    Mr. N. A. Davis, Atlanta, Georgia

Anonymous

The biggest number writer in the 4th Ward came from the country. He was so country when he first came to Atlanta that they had him blowing out light bulbs. When he started making money, he would keep all the change and give his landlord all the paper money. He died a very rich man and left his family with a lot of money. The street lottery was big business."

Bartlett H. Hargro, College Park, GA

The first thing that comes to my mind when I think about Buttermilk Bottom is that the main thoroughfare was Forrest Avenue. The street was named honoring Nathan Bedford Forrest, a confederate general and one of the founding fathers of the KKK.

In Atlanta and throughout the south, major thoroughfares were named honoring Civil War Generals and Hero's. Forrest Avenue is currently Ralph McGill Boulevard; Hunter Street is Now MLK Jr. Drive; Gordon Road is currently Ralph David Abernathy Blvd and Ashby Street is now Joseph E. Lowery Blvd. Now the streets honor local civil rights leaders.

Another Atlanta street naming genesis was in Red-Lining or separating the Races by street names. I remember one street, located east of Buttermilk Bottom (running north and south) from Piedmont Park to Edgewood Avenue. This street has three different names. The same street—its Jackson Street from Edgewood to Highland Avenue; it's Parkway Drive from Highland Avenue to Ponce de Leon Avenue and It's Charles Allen Drive from Ponce to Piedmont Park entrance. As Whites moved out and blacks moved in, the street name was changed. This is why driving in Atlanta can be a nightmare to new comers; the street layout is unplanned and totally illogical.

Back to Buttermilk Bottom. My family lived on the eastern fringe of Buttermilk Bottom in an area known as the Old Fourth Ward. Downtown Atlanta was on the west end of Buttermilk Bottom. We traveled through the Bottom walking to school, shopping at the 5 & 10 cent stores or to attend the Forrest Avenue Theater. I remember The Bottom as an area to avoid after dark. I witnessed my first robbery and mugging traveling through the Bottom as well as a lot of Saturday night general drunkenness and fist fights.

Anonymous

The thing I remember most about Buttermilk Bottom was my elementary schoolmates who lived in the heart of the Bottom. They had the best "Yo Momma" jokes repertoire in school. We called it "JONEING" and they were masters of talking about your mother. In the black community talking about ones mother was off limits. If you got on the bad side of a Bottom Kid, they were quick to retaliate with a verbal barrage of 'yo momma' insults or worse, a beat down.

Larry D Anthony, Sr., Decatur, GA.

I got a true story. I was helping my daddy, Frank Anthony, clean up floors at Walter Loan Company on Butler Street. I was nine years old. I saw my Dad get his due from a white man, who said to my daddy, "Hey Boy!! Hey you! Boy, you got a rest room in there I can use?" Frank looked at him and said, "You look here. I got all my sons with me and you must be talking to one of them. These are boys. I am not a boy. My name is Mr. Anthony to you. So, if you want to go to the bathroom, address me as Mr. Anthony and I will think about it." So, the man said, "Hey, Mr. Anthony, I'm sorry I called you that. Mr. Anthony, do you think it will be okay if you let me use the restroom." My father said, "Go ahead." My father turned and looked at us and said, "Don't never let anybody dismiss you and do nothing or say nothing to put you down. Stand up for yourself and I better not hear that you didn't stand up for yourself." So, when the white man came out, my daddy said, "I left a mop by the door. Just mop yourself out." The man took the mop and mopped the floor as he backed out of the restroom then said, "Thank you."

CPSIA information can be obtained at www.ICGtesting.com
Printed in the USA
LVOW08s1120100416

482961LV00002B/192/P